YOUNG CLAUS

YOUNG CLAUS

A NOVEL

JAMES MAGNUSON

FORT WORTH, TEXAS

LIBRARY OF CONGRESS CATALOGING-IN-PUBLICATION DATA

Names: Magnuson, James, author.

Title: Young Claus : a novel / James L. Magnuson.

Description: Fort Worth, Texas : TCU Press, [2023] | Summary: "Before Santa Claus was Santa Claus, he was a boy, and this is his story. Young Claus is both an origin story and a children's fable for adults, in the tradition of The Little Prince and The Last Unicorn. Young Lars Claus loses his father in a logging accident and, with his mother and grandmother, has to move to a strange land in the Far North, a land of exiles, outcasts, and survivors. Here he encounters a school where the children only laugh at the misfortunes of others, where small, bizarre creatures are imprisoned beneath a fish liver oil factory, and where his widowed mother is wooed by the malevolent Mayor Wolfpaw. This is a wild romp of a book that soars into the skies and plunges deep beneath the permafrost. It is a book filled with marvels and ghosts, a book where Lars, with the help of invisible helpers, will learn to carve, where he will discover sorrows as deep as his own and eventually the healing powers of gifts. Certainly no one has been the subject of more lies by parents than Santa Claus. This book attempts to find the simple human truths buried beneath those awkward lies. It charts the journey of a boy beset by grief who will, after many trials, fashion a vision of generosity that will encompass the entire world"— Provided by publisher.

Identifiers: LCCN 2023030124 (print) | LCCN 2023030125 (ebook) | ISBN 9780875658360 (paperback) | ISBN 9780875658421 (ebook)

Subjects: LCSH: Santa Claus (Fictitious character)—Childhood and youth—Fiction. | LCGFT: Novels. | Fantasy fiction. | Fables.

Classification: LCC PS3563.A352 Y68 2023 (print) | LCC PS3563.A352 (ebook) | DDC 813/.54—dc23/eng/20230718

LC record available at https://lccn.loc.gov/2023030124

LC ebook record available at https://lccn.loc.gov/2023030125

TCU Box 298300
Fort Worth, Texas 76129
817.257.7822

Design by Julie Rushing

DEDICATION

I would like to dedicate this book to my grandchildren,
Ferris and Cecile, Katherine and Emma

ACKNOWLEDGMENTS

I WOULD LIKE TO THANK Taya Kitaysky for the wonderful cover as well as for her keen eye for the smallest slipups. God bless the novelist Edward Carey for urging me onward, giving me crucial notes, making me read the biography of Hans Christian Andersen, and lending me a book about fires in the Arctic. Bless too my remarkable agent Emily Forland for sticking with me through this long journey and remaining as thoughtful and good humored as ever. Tony Giardina, Steve Harrigan, Hugh O'Neill, Peter Jovanovich, Maya Perez, S. Kirk Walsh, Susan Zeder, Sonja Rethy, and Fatima Kola all weighed in with major insights. Thanks also to my son, Billy, for all those great conversations about this book; to my daughter Martha to whom I first began telling bedtime stories that fired up my imagination so long ago; and to Hester, who has been the greatest support any writer could dream of for the past forty-plus years.

"Only Coleridge's phrase will do—Jim Magnuson's *Young Claus* is a miracle of rare device. This tale of how a boy became the legend has it all. It blends the power of myth with the pleasure of mirth, combines high adventure with delightful invention. This anthem of hopefulness is somehow charming and thrilling at the same time. I could go on and on about this book—a beautiful, beautiful act of imagination."

—**HUGH O'NEILL**
Author of *Daddy Cool*

ONE

Lars Claus was as skinny as a pike pole and his belt went twice around his waist. In the winter the cold winds swirled up the arms of his oversized coat like icy weasels chasing mice. His mother would slip gingersnaps in his pocket before he left for school and heap an extra serving of pickled herring on his plate at dinner. At bedtime when he went to kiss her goodnight, she would try to tempt him with a thick wedge of strudel or a steaming cup of cocoa topped with whipped cream.

But Lars had no time for food. There was schoolwork and there were chores—eggs to be collected, animals to be tended, ashes from the fireplace to be carried out, water to be lugged from the well. There was skating on the pond with his friends, sledding on Bergman's Hill, snowball fights in the meadow.

But what Lars loved most of all was being out in the forest with his father. His father was the chief woodsman for Lord Borland, and on days when there was no school, his father would wake him before dawn. Boots squeaking in the snow, they would trudge down to the barn, harness the horse, and make their way to the pine grove along the Hammerskjold River.

Anton and Emil, the old bachelor brothers who lived in Lutefisk Hollow, would nearly always be there, waiting to join them. The three men would set to work with their axes and crosscut saws. Lars's job was to bring them coffee when they asked for it, clear away chips and bark, and tend to the horses. Sometimes when the men didn't need him, he would follow the tracks of rabbits and foxes and deer in the snow, or make tiny fairy houses out of twigs and moss and icicles.

When it was time for one of the huge trees to fall, Lars's father would call out to him and Lars would come running. His father would put an arm across Lars's chest, holding him close as Anton and Emil delivered the final blows with their axes.

There would be a crack and then a groan and then another crack, louder than the first. Anton and Emil would back off, axes swinging at their sides. The giant pine would give way slowly at first, but then gain speed, finally thundering to the earth, shaking the ground all around them. After it fell, Lars's father would lift his arm, turning Lars free, and the whole forest would be silent for several seconds.

As the men set to work sawing off the branches, Lars's task was to haul away the smaller ones, trim them with his hatchet, and stack them in neat piles to be used as kindling in Lord Borland's giant fireplaces.

When the tree was stripped, they would chain it to the horse and drag it down to the frozen river. Lars would stand with his father on the sledge, and sometimes his father would let him hold the reins.

When the day's work was done, his father would lift Lars onto the horse and they would make their way home. They would unharness the horse and Lars would brush him down, then climb up into the loft to toss fresh hay bales into the stall.

His mother would have kettles boiling on the stove when they came into the house. She would pour steaming hot water into two blue metal bowls, and Lars and his father would wash off the dirt and the sawdust and the pine needles and dry themselves with huge towels.

After they got into clean, dry clothes, Lars and his father would come to the table. His mother and his grandmother would bring the food in from the kitchen. There was always more than one kind of meat. It might be chicken and rabbit, or venison and grilled trout from the river, or lamb and the pork sausage that Anton's sister made. But almost always there were stacks of potato pancakes and hot fluffy biscuits and a pitcher of cold milk and bowls of hot gravy. The dessert came out later—applesauce or pudding, or, on special occasions, lingonberry pie.

The Clauses had always been legendary eaters, but Lars's father was the greatest of them all. He could rip the meat off a joint of mutton with his teeth faster than a bear or pop a half dozen rolls in his mouth, one after the other, as if they were no more than peas. He could down a glass of milk in a single gulp and filet a trout with a single stroke of his knife. He was always a happy man, but nothing made him happier than eating, whether he was sucking his rabbit bones clean, wiping gravy from his beard, or chasing the last lonely lingonberry around his plate with a spoon.

Lars could only look on in awe. Sometimes he would try to keep up, but he was no match for his father. Two rolls and a chicken drumstick and he felt as if his stomach was about to burst. It was almost hard to believe he was his father's child.

After dinner his mother did dishes while his father sat by the fire and played his fiddle and sang. Nanu curled up with Lars on the bench, telling him all the old stories she'd been told when she was a child. Lars listened, mesmerized by the tales of elves and trolls, of the headless giant who rowed without oars and used only his enormous arms, of the girl with the pitcher of her dead mother's tears.

Lars's mother did not approve of these stories. She thought they were too frightening for a child, too filled with magic and sorcery and all the dark arts, but Lars loved them.

Some people in the village thought that Nanu was a witch. There were wild rumors of her being able to raise the dead and cure a sick child by rubbing a live toad across the infant's blistered lips. Many were terrified when they encountered her walking alone on a country road or sitting motionless in a forest glade, eyes closed, face raised to the sun.

Lars knew all the talk was preposterous. It was true that Nanu had a fearsome temper and that she had books under her bed, books that she consulted and never let anyone see. But even if they were books of magic, what did it matter? All that mattered was that she had tended, bathed, and fed him from the time he was a baby and taught him songs and riddles.

It was understandable that people might think her strange. She walked a little sideways, scuttling like a crab, and had a large mole on her chin with a twisty black hair growing out of it. She muttered to herself and sometimes burst into song for no reason. She wore a long black cloak, summer and winter, and shoes of cracked reindeer hide with the toes turned up like some old Laplander.

Boys at school would sometimes tease Lars about her, and a couple of times he had nearly gotten into fights defending her, but he had learned to pay them no mind. He knew who she was and they didn't; that was enough.

At some point during the evening storytelling, his father would fall asleep in his chair, his hands folded across his ample belly. Lars would kiss his mother and Nanu good night, pick up his boots that had been drying on the hearth, and tiptoe back to his room. His head still buzzed with Nanu's stories as he climbed into bed. On cold nights, he would pull his covers up to his nose and stare out at the woods. There were times when he swore he saw small creatures scurrying across the snow, flitting from tree trunk to tree trunk. But sooner or later, his eyes grew heavy and his mind drifted, the hooting of the owl in the pine tree that towered over their house lulling him to sleep.

This was the way it had been for all of his twelve years, and Lars assumed that this was the way it would be for years to come.

Of all the lords a person could work for, Lord Borland was not the worst. He was not cruel. He wasn't a drunkard. But he was a fool, and after several years of early frosts and bad harvests, he managed to make things infinitely worse by losing several thousand kroner at the backgammon tables in Stockholm.

He was forced to close his stables and sell most of his cattle and several of his smaller estates. One afternoon in December, Lord Borland came to inform Lars's father that they would need to sell twice as much timber as they had the year before.

Judging from his father's mood that night at the dinner table, the meeting had not gone well. After his father gave them the news, the four of them ate in silence until his mother got up to get more pancakes from the kitchen.

"Are there enough trees to do that?" his mother said.

"Of course there are enough trees!" his father said. "There are trees from here to Denmark!"

"But are they ready yet?"

"How ready does a tree need to be to go through a sawmill? They're ready enough."

Lars gave his father a glance. He had never heard his father speak this way. His father had always treated the forest the way you treat a fawn. For him it was a living thing that needed to be nursed, protected, and handled with care. He had always tried to cut trees only when it was time to make room for the younger ones growing up in their shadows.

When his mother returned to the table with pancakes, his father stabbed two of them, slid them onto his plate, and lathered them with butter. Watching him with narrowed eyes, Nanu tamped down the tobacco in her pipe.

"But what about the river?" Nanu said. "You think it can handle all that timber? Aren't you always telling me it's not wide enough and deep enough the way it is?"

His father gave Nanu a sidelong look, his cheek bulging with pancake. "Well, I guess we're going to see how much it can handle, aren't we?"

TWO

His father began going off to work an hour earlier in the morning and coming home an hour later at night. His mother, after making breakfast for Lars and Nanu, would hurry off to join him. Several of the neighbors pitched in, working with Anton and Emil for over a week, building a new flume that would slide the extra loads of timber from the high bluffs to the river. Nanu took over the cooking and carried lunches out to the forest, while Lars showed up after school, using the marking hammer to stamp all the freshly cut logs with Lord Borland's initials.

In the evenings there was less and less laughter in the house. His mother, who'd been taking turns on the crosscut saw with the men, would sit at the kitchen table, wrapping her raw and bleeding hands with bandages. His mother was a beautiful woman, tall and blonde with startling blue eyes and a braid that came down nearly to her waist. She was strong as well. In her youth she had been an athlete, a wonderful skier and swimmer who could outrace and outswim all the boys her age.

As capable as she was, she was not as relentlessly upbeat as her husband. She had her moods and kept things to herself. Lars was her son, and sons can see things in their mothers that other people can't see, and what Lars saw in those startling blue eyes as the winter months passed was fear.

The logs were piled on the ice higher than ever. For the first time, Lars noticed open sky above him as he walked through the thinning woods. Most of the animals seemed to have fled. Once in a while he would see a deer foraging among the stumps, but it would bound instantly away as soon as it spotted him. The skidways to the river had turned into a gash of mud and dirty snow.

When spring finally came for good, it came quickly. One day there was the drip of icicles outside their windows, and three days after that, snow was sliding off the roof of the chicken coop. It rained steadily for a week, which kept everyone in but his father, who went out each afternoon to check on the river.

Then, just before dawn on a Friday, Lars woke to the sound of someone rapping loudly on a window. He leapt out of bed and scrambled to find his shoes, but by the time he stumbled out of his room, his mother and father were already at the front door.

Emil stood on the stoop, rubbing his bald head with both hands, grinning as if it was someone's birthday. The ice had finally broken free.

His mother pulled on her coat while his father went to the closet to dig out the pike poles. He jiggled them up and down, testing their weight, and then tossed the lightest to his son. "Up and at 'em, Lars," he said. "We're going to need all the help we can get."

For two days Lars worked alongside Emil and his mother on the shore, pushing stranded logs off the bank and gravel bars with his pole while his father and Anton worked in the middle of the river, leaping from one slowly spinning log to the next, tugging and pulling at the big pile-ups, trying to keep everything moving downstream.

The ice may have been broken, but there were still huge slabs of it clogging everything. The great pyramids of timber they'd spent all winter building tilted, slid sideways, and collapsed into the churning water. Sometimes it seemed to Lars as if the river was angry at all the work it had been asked to do. It roared and groaned and bucked, sending five-hundred-pound logs sailing through the air like leaping salmon.

Twice Snell, Lord Borland's overseer, came by on his horse to check on their progress and rode away without speaking to anyone. In his black coat and battered black hat, he looked like a storm in scuffed boots.

It was the first time Lars had ever helped his father with the spring log drive. It was the most exhausting work he had ever done. He came home at the end of the first day with huge, squishy blisters on his hands, and his muscles were so achy he could barely go to sleep.

He had worked valiantly those first ten hours, determined to keep up with the men, but by the second day he was wearing down. Even though his father had given him the lightest of the pike poles, it was still taller than he was and had begun to feel as if it were made of lead. He was increasingly clumsy with it and kept getting in Emil's way.

Late in the afternoon, the hook of his pole snagged on a log. He slipped down into the icy water, all the way up to his waist, and had to be pulled back up the bank by Emil.

Lars sat shivering on a stump while his father unlaced his wet laces, and Anton went to get him dry socks and dry trousers. Lars could tell his father was upset from the way he yanked off Lars's sopping boots. His father asked Emil to go get Lars's mother to take him back to the house. Teeth chattering, Lars tried to argue, but his father wasn't listening. They'd lost enough time the way it was. In the river behind them, the logs sped by, thudding and slamming against one another.

〰〰

His mother tucked him into bed as soon as they got home. He kept shaking, even though she brought him bowl after bowl of hot soup and nearly buried him under heavy quilts. It wasn't until Nanu sat down with him to play cards that sleepiness finally overtook him and he was able to doze off.

He didn't wake until his father came into his room in the early evening.

"What time is it?" Lars said.

"Not late."

Lars rubbed his eyes with a knuckle. He was still feeling light-headed and weak. "So how did everything go?"

"Just fine," his father said. "If it keeps going this well we should be able to finish tomorrow."

The whole bed tilted when his father sat down next to him. "So how are you feeling?"

"Okay."

"Good."

He slapped Lars on the knee, rose from the bed, and went to the window. He knitted his fingers on the back of his head and stretched for a moment, making a soft groan. His hands seemed big as shovels. In the corner of the room was the trunk of toys with his father's carvings, a tiny bow and arrow, a toy cannon, a wooden cup with a ball attached by a string.

"I've got something for you," his father said. He dug down in his pocket, pulled out a pinecone, and tossed it on the bed.

Lars picked it up and examined it. It was two inches long, perfectly intact and a little sticky with resin. The scales were just beginning to spread.

"So what is it?' his father asked.

"A fir."

"There you go, Lars, exactly. It's a beauty, isn't it? Everything's been so wet, it's pretty much closed, but once it starts to dry out, it should open up just fine. Make your room smell good." His father went to the door and turned back. "You want us to bring you anything to eat?"

"No, I'm fine."

"Well, good night then, Lars."

"Good night."

After his father left, Lars turned on his side, the pinecone clasped tight in his fist, and was asleep within seconds.

Lars woke up the next morning with chills and a high fever. His father had already left for the river and Lars wanted to go join him, but both his mother and Nanu insisted that he stay and rest.

He was too weak to put up much of a fight. He napped off and on, tossed and turned. His mother, who'd stayed behind to tend him, brought him hot broth and crackers.

His fever broke just before noon. He emerged from his room swearing that he was as good as gold and ready to go back to join the men. His mother and Nanu weren't so sure. To their eyes, he still looked a little unsteady on his feet.

After some argument, a bargain was struck. His mother would let him go back to the river as long as he didn't work the banks. She would let him bring the men their lunch: a wicker basket loaded with cheese and sausage sandwiches, pickled herring, and potato salad.

It was a little humiliating being demoted to food-carrier, but in the end it didn't matter. What mattered was that he was going to be out there, standing next to his father when the last log went floating down the river.

He slipped into the forest with a high heart, the wicker basket swinging at his side. Leaping puddles, running and walking, he hurried as fast as he could. Deep in the woods, the brush piles they'd stacked during the winter were still snow-covered.

As he neared the river, he heard a rumble. At first he thought it was thunder, but then he realized it wasn't. It sounded like a hundred bowling balls rolling down a bowling alley all at once.

Lars scrambled through an aspen grove to a low bluff where he could see the river. It was filled with logs from bank to bank. They slammed and knocked against one another, rose up like panicked animals in a pen, trying to crawl over one another.

Emil sat slumped on the shore, looking dazed and sucking on his hand. Thirty yards further downstream, his father rode the rolling timbers halfway out in the river, tugging at a stuck log with his pike pole.

But his father was no match for the river. He stutter-stepped left and right, flailing with his free arm, trying to keep his balance. The logs rose and fell under his feet like a billowing carpet. Twenty yards beyond him was a small waterfall.

Lars tore down the slope, skidding and sliding. He didn't know what he was going to do, but he knew he needed to do something.

As he stumbled along the shore, Emil finally raised his head and shouted something. It was impossible to make out, but it was enough to stop Lars for a second. Emil had a terrible gash on his forearm. They gestured furiously back and forth, making no sense.

Lars turned back to the river just in time to see a huge log shoot up behind his father and slam him in the back. He was gone in an instant.

Lars stood on the muddy bank, motionless, unable to understand what he'd just seen. Somehow the jam had broken and the logs tumbled over the falls, one after the other, and disappeared into the churn and foam.

Lars ran along the shoreline. He spied a pike pole slicing between spinning logs. His father was too strong and smart—he must have found a way to shore, but Lars didn't see him anywhere.

Lars ran for as long as he could, slipping and sliding in the mud and slush. When he couldn't run any longer, he fell back against the bank. He gasped, closing his eyes, pinching at the corners of them to keep back the tears. He opened them again at the sound of honking overhead.

At first he couldn't see anything, but then he did. Far, far up, ten white dots struggled across the sky in a V formation.

THREE

His father was buried on a sunny, windy afternoon in a small graveyard just fifty yards behind their house. The ceremony was brief, attended by a dozen neighbors, plus Anton and Emil, Lars, his mother, and Nanu.

The sad-eyed parson said a few words that Lars had difficulty following. The casket sat at the edge of a freshly dug hole in the ground. Just beyond the casket was a small fir, rippling in the breeze. It was a young tree, no more than six or seven feet high, but flawless, with lustrous green needles and cones upright as candles.

When Lars's mother began to weep, he tried not to look at her. He knew that he should be weeping too, but he couldn't. All that he felt was a deep emptiness, a hole in his heart that went down and down and down. Nanu muttered to herself, carping about how boring the parson's sermon was, clenching and unclenching her fists as if she was ready to hit somebody.

As the parson asked them to bow their heads in prayer, a thrush swooped down and disappeared into the young fir tree. Lars watched the needles stir as the bird moved about and finally emerged, hopping to the very highest branch.

It began to sing for all it was worth, puffing out its chest. From time to time it stopped, tilted its head, and listened to the other birds answering it from the woods. After a minute it flitted away. It was spring after all. Life was beginning, and there was much to be done.

For the next week the neighbors came with food—roasts and casseroles and fresh-baked pies. If his father had been there, it all would have disappeared quickly enough, but with just the three of them, they were barely able to make a dent in any of it, and in a few days most of it had to be thrown to the chickens.

For the next week his mother slept on a quilt in Lars's room and never explained to him why. Nanu raged about the house, and Lars gave her a wide berth, spending as much time as he could out in the barn, tending to the animals. He was lonelier than he had ever been in his life. Without his father there was no one for Lars to arm-wrestle with in the evenings, and no carved animals for him to discover under his pillow in the morning.

For three nights in a row, a brilliantly red fox appeared at the edge of the woods right at sunset, and melted away as soon as Lars stepped out the door.

What was going to happen to them? That was the question that hung over everything, that followed them from room to room like a hungry cat.

His mother stopped eating, and sometimes when he spoke to her she looked at him as if she had never seen him before. It was as if she had gone somewhere deep down inside herself, as if there was some other small creature huddled in there, blind and angry, who knew no one and was beyond caring. One afternoon she went out to begin work on her garden. When she didn't come back Lars and Nanu looked for her for two hours until one of the local farmers pulled up in his wagon, with Lars's mother sitting next to him on the buckboard. He had found her, he said, two miles down the road, and she wasn't able to tell any of them why she was there.

Rumors had been going around for years that Nanu was a witch. Now, with her son's death, the rumors took on new life. One of the woodsmen swore he had seen her at dusk, hovering like a hummingbird above the small waterfall where Lars's father had died. Another claimed he'd seen strange lights speeding through the trees at night. Lord Borland's maid, a notorious gossip, said she had seen Lord Borland's mug begin to rattle and slide of its own accord before smashing on the floor.

The final confirmation of all that the people thought was when Nanu was spotted on the great lawn in front of the Borland's mansion, chanting in a language no one knew. One of the footmen came out to chase her away, but the damage was done.

The story spread like a fire in dry grass. A neighbor who'd come by to buy eggs from Lars's mother had already heard the news and gave her a full, if somewhat embellished, account.

An hour later Lars was in the barn, pitching fresh hay into the stalls, when he heard shouting. He tossed his pitchfork and raced outside.

Lars had never seen his mother shout, but she was shouting now. She stood over Nanu, who sat by the pump, peeling potatoes with the shame-faced look of a small child being chastised for biting a playmate.

"What could you possibly have been thinking? Are you really trying to make things impossible for us?" They had an audience. The animals in the barnyard—the horse, the two oxen drooling at the trough, the cow, the three pigs—were all staring, dumbfounded.

Nanu rose from her chair and pitched the bowlful of peels into the garden of dead stalks. All the chickens came running. "I don't think it was me who made it impossible," she said. "And I will ask you to never shout at me like that again." She limped to the house, cradling the glistening peeled potatoes in her apron.

The next morning, Snell rode into the yard. Lars and Nanu came out on the back porch to greet him.

Fearsome in his black coat and battered black hat, Snell was someone who enjoyed hitting people when they were down on their luck. He loved his job, whether it was galloping after fleeing poachers or riding stately through the straw-hatted workers sweating in the hay fields, swinging their scythes.

His horse was magnificent, at least sixteen hands high, and glowing with an inner fire. In its dark, wide-set eyes was a glint of wickedness. Together Snell and the stallion would have made a fine statue.

The overseer had come to inform them that they had forty-eight hours to vacate the premises.

Nanu spat over the porch rail. "Can you tell us why?"

"I'm sure you know why," Snell said. His musket rested in a scabbard lashed to the back of his saddle.

"I do," Nanu said. "I just want to hear you say it." She came down the steps into the muddy yard. Lars dug his nails into the palms of his hands, fearing what she might do next.

"I make Lord Borland uneasy. That's it, isn't it?" she said. "And you too. But really, you have no cause to worry. I'm just a poor country woman who has just buried her son."

She put her hand out to let the stallion smell her. The horse went still, its eyes liquid. It was as if Nanu had some power over it.

"This is a beautiful horse. But it needs some water."

"No, it's fine, thank you."

Nanu crowded the stallion. She only came up to Snell's knee. "It will only take a minute."

When she grabbed for the bridle, the stallion reared. Snell cursed, retrieved a short whip from under his saddle, and began to lash the horse's flanks.

Hooves flailed the air. Lars rushed down the steps to pull his grandmother to safely.

The horse pirouetted in the yard and there was nothing Snell could do to hold it. The stallion was possessed, a whirling dervish, an instrument of retribution. It bucked and reared so high on its rear legs Lars was sure it was about to topple on its back, crushing Snell under its weight.

Snell managed to kick free of his stirrups, slid out of his saddle, and thudded on the ground with a muddy splash. The stallion trotted off a few steps, then stopped to look back at what it had down, tranquil as a Buddha.

Wiping mud from his trousers and sleeves, Snell staggered after the horse. It offered no resistance. Snell wriggled and heaved his way back into the saddle and galloped off down the road.

When Lars's mother returned from the butcher's they told her the news. She listened calmly without saying a word. It was not hard to imagine what she was thinking. The way Nanu was behaving now, she needed to be tethered to Lars's mother's arm like a child.

But Lars's mother was an empty vessel now, emptied of anger, emptied of hope, emptied of every I-told-you-so. It all felt fated to be.

The conversation that needed to happen was put off until they were finishing their dinner. For an hour they went round and round, debating where they might go, what they might do. The last rays of sunlight shone through the window and lit up his father's empty chair.

"But couldn't we just go back to Lord Borland and apologize, ask him to give us another chance?" his mother said. "Maybe they'd let us stay. Isn't it worth a try?"

"Absolutely not," Nanu said.

"Well, what then?" said his mother.

"Just hold on. I'll be right back."

Nanu hobbled off to her bedroom and was gone for two or three minutes. Lars fiddled with the remains of his blood sausage. He felt the cat brush his leg under the table, prowling for scraps. Doves cooed in the woods outside.

Nanu returned holding a piece of paper between a thumb and forefinger. It was water-stained and yellow with age, so brittle it looked as if a single tap of a quill would cause it to crumble into dust.

She gently wafted it onto the table. It was a map, but of the most eccentric sort. It looked as if it had been drawn by a child. There was an ocean, indicated by a series of wavy lines, and a cluster of boxes to stand for a village. Three or more more isolated houses dotted the coastline. A series of dashes marked a road through a mountain range. Drawings of musk oxen and polar bears and walruses decorated the borders of the map.

"What is this?" Lars asked.

Nanu pointed to one of the houses along the coastline. "This is your new home."

They both stared at her. "What do you mean?"

"This is the one place in the world where you wouldn't be beholden to anyone."

"But why, Nanu?" Lars asked.

"Because I own it."

"You *own* it?" Lars said. "How could you own it?"

"My great-grandfather lived there. It was the grandest house, with balconies that looked over the sea and two fireplaces. When he was very old he moved south for his rheumatism, but he kept the house and gave the deed to my grandfather, who gave it to my father, who gave it to me. I still have the deed in my trunk."

Lars was amazed; his mother reached out to turn the map slightly, as if she was having trouble making it out.

"Have you ever been there, Nanu?" He stared at a tin of sugar cookies that one of their neighbors had brought, sitting in the middle of the table.

"No."

"How do you know that it's still there? What if someone's moved in?"

"I have the deed. If someone's moved in, we'll have them thrown out."

Lars scrutinized the map. "Where is this, Nanu?"

"On the Northern Sea."

"But, Nanu, wouldn't it take us weeks to get there?" Lars asked.

Nanu cuffed him on the arm. "Oh, come now, we could do it!"

"There's nothing up there but ice and snow," his mother said. "No one can live in a place like that."

"People have lived up there for centuries."

"I know, but it just seems so extreme. Surely we can come up with something better than that."

"All right then, you name one!"

Lars stared down at his hands. Nanu folded the old map with trembling fingers, stuffed it in one of her many pockets, rose, and stomped out of the room.

That night Lars tossed and turned, too wrought up to sleep. They were being thrown out of their home, and all over such stupidity. As much as he loved Nanu's stories, the truth was that he hated magic. He didn't believe in it, not for true, but he did believe in the trouble it could cause. His grandmother wasn't a witch. She was just very old and very eccentric and she had just lost her son, and now she was about to lose everything else as well.

They started packing first thing the next morning. His mother retrieved a dozen burlap bags from the root cellar and stuffed them with clothes and bedding. The cuckoo clock was wrenched off the wall and drawers of silver were pulled out and dumped into pillowcases. Lars climbed up on the counter, got the jar with all their gold coins down from the cupboard, and poured them into a satchel.

Farmer Thornberg, the kindest of all their neighbors, came to lend a hand, offering the use of his wagon and helping to carry the largest items out to his buckboard—the kitchen table, the sofa, and several chairs.

None of what they were doing felt real to Lars. The wagon was quickly filled. All of his father's tools were going to have to be left behind. When Lars dragged his toy chest out of his room, his mother said there wasn't going to be enough space. He had to settle for a handful of his father's carvings.

Farmer Thornberg insisted on driving them, and none of them were in any position to say no. Years later, all Lars would remember of that first day of their journey north was the creaking of the wagon, the clopping of hooves, and a half dozen birds circling over a small field where a peasant was beginning his spring planting.

Farmer Thornberg left them the following morning, and they continued on in a second wagon pulled by a fresh horse and driven by Lars. They spent three nights in small alehouses, and several times Lars woke in the hour before dawn to hear his mother and Nanu having terrible arguments outside the door.

As the days passed, the landscape became increasingly strange. They had a hand-drawn map Farmer Thornberg had made for them, but nothing was familiar, not the church spires in the distance, not the names of the small villages, not the abandoned domed castle. There were deep forests, but they were different from the forests of home: darker, more impenetrable, and full of whispers. Two old men with heads slimy as toads, baiting their hooks on a bridge, gaped at them as they passed, as if they had never seen anything as odd as a boy so young driving a wagon by himself.

Hours would pass without anyone speaking, all of them lost in their own thoughts. Lars's mind kept coming back to it: he had stood by the bank until they had retrieved his father's body from the river. He had walked alongside the sledge that carried his father back to the house, and he remembered the sight of his father's arm, outstretched, white and cold, swaying with each step of the oxen.

Over the second week the trees became scrawnier and wilder looking, the tea-colored rivers wider and shallower. The three of them began to wear their heavy coats, even during the day.

At the beginning of the third week they hit the tundra. Lars had never seen a place so empty. The land rose and fell, and there wasn't a tree anywhere. The sky was enormous. Snow began to fall. Nanu tried to cheer them up by pointing out lemmings scurrying in the tawny grass, a musk ox drinking at a pond, their first reindeer herd off in the distance, but the most she got out of Lars's mother was a grim nod. The horse plodded on, taking them over swell after snowy swell, as if they were turning the blank pages of a book yet to be written.

All the open space spooked the horse, and as snow began to accumulate, the horse struggled more and more. One night in a desolate one-room trading post, they sold the horse to a short, bustling man named Søren, who agreed to take them by dogsled the rest of the way to the sea. The man talked so fast and his accent was so harsh, Lars could barely make out what he was saying, but Nanu seemed to understand him perfectly. The two of them bickered back and forth for an hour, working out all the terms of their agreement.

At the other end of the trading post, three rough-looking trappers ate fish heads with their bare hands and downed flagon after flagon of ale being served up by a hunched old woman. Every once in a while they would stagger to their feet, dance, sing a song, jump up, bump chests, and fall down in a heap, laughing.

Lars slipped out to say goodbye to the horse. After two weeks of hauling a wagon across tundra and snow, it was scarcely the same animal that had pranced and tried to kick down its stall on their first day together. There were sores on its neck, rubbed raw by the harness, and when Lars stroked its coat, he could feel the ribs beneath, the quiver of nerves. When Lars fed it a handful of dried currents, it accepted meekly, nuzzling his hand.

The sound of approaching footsteps crunching in the snow made Lars turn. It was Nanu, bundled up like a great owl.

"So it looks as if you're going to have your first dogsled ride tomorrow."

"Guess so," Lars said. He tugged his fingers through a snarl in the horse's mane.

The singing from inside the inn grew more and more raucous. "I am so sorry," Nanu said.

"Sorry for what?"

"For causing all this."

The horse jerked its head up at the howling of wolves far out on the tundra. Lars grabbed the horse by the halter, but its ears were back, its eyes wide and glistening.

"What's going to happen to us, Nanu?"

She bent down, picked up a rusted horseshoe, and flung it away. The horse was being kept in a poor excuse for a corral with frozen piles of droppings from unknown animals making it necessary to be very careful where one stepped.

"I have no idea. The only thing I know is that your fate will not be like the fate of other boys. But when it comes to you, do not be afraid, but embrace it. Embrace it with your whole heart."

FOUR

n the morning Søren showed up with his two brothers, Henrik and August, whom he'd talked into driving the second and third sleds. But when they started to unpack the wagon, it quickly became apparent that even three sleds weren't going to be enough for all their possessions.

Lars, his mother, and Nanu huddled together under the frozen eaves of the trading post, trying to decide what to keep and what to leave. Only the essentials could be kept, they knew that, but what were the essentials? Clothes, certainly. Cooking utensils. But what about the rocking chair that Lars had been rocked to sleep in every night when he was a baby? Or the music box his father had given to his mother the night he asked her to marry him? They had already been asked to leave so much, and now they were being asked to leave more.

Søren, Henrik, and August sat on their haunches, chewing tobacco, waiting patiently, but the harnessed dogs barked and whined, ready to hit the trail.

Lars lugged several chairs, a bench, and a sackful of tools back into the trading post and left them on the counter. One of the trappers was still sound asleep on the floor, an arm thrown across his face. The hunched old woman looked up from washing flagons in the back, nodded to him, but didn't say anything.

Lars, his mother, and Nanu each had a sled and a driver, and once they were all strapped in they set off to a great chorus of barking. Lars glanced over his shoulder at the horse, standing next to the empty wagon, looking bewildered. Lars waved. The horse whinnied, shook its mane, and went back to nosing through the snow.

For three days they drove the dogs north, staying at night in abandoned huts and trappers' cabins. The world had turned an endless white. When the drivers stopped to cut pads of sealskin for the dogs' bleeding feet, Lars would get out of his sled to go back and check on his mother and Nanu. They would raise a bulky sleeve to greet him and exchange a few muffled words, but they were both bundled all the way to their eyebrows, so it was hard to say exactly how they were doing. All Lars could tell for sure was that they seemed a little stunned—like baby owls blinking in the hole of a tree.

The trip was turning out to be much longer and harder than anyone had bargained for. At night, Lars could hear Henrik and August grumbling to their brother, threatening to turn back.

Several times they had to get out to push the sleds across fields of broken ice, and on the fourth day, Lars's sled tipped over. He could hear things splintering and shattering as he was thrown out onto the snow. The dogs, harnesses tangled, scrambled to get back on their feet and keep going, even as Henrik tried to pull them to a stop.

It took all three of the drivers to get the dogs untangled and tip the sled back on its runners. There was no time to unpack and see what the damage had been. The wind was too fierce, and they had miles to go before they could rest. Søren, Henrik, and August shouted the dogs up, leapt onto the sleds, and they were off again.

On the morning of the fifth day, they entered the mountains. After numerous consultations with the drivers over the map Nanu's grandfather had given her, they began to climb through mists, skirting deep fjords and immense glaciers. Lars's mother, who had a terrible fear of heights, clung to the railings of the sled, refusing to look. The wind sent up great swirls of snow. The exhausted dogs slowed to a walk, and the drivers cracked their whips to get them moving.

At the top of the final pass, they were in the clouds, which made it impossible to see what lay below. Yet something had changed, something Lars couldn't put his finger on. Perhaps it had to do with the moaning of the wind, the roll of distant thunder, or the odd dimming of the light even though it was the middle of the day.

Lars wasn't the only one who sensed it. The drivers stood on the runners of their sleds, speaking to one another in a language foreign to Lars, but it was clear that Henrik and August were reluctant to go on. Søren had to speak sharply to them before they relented, sullenly cracking their whips and beginning their descent.

Coming down took them four hours. Once they were safely out of the mountains, they had another long discussion over the map and made their way along the half-frozen sea.

Søren finally pulled his sled to a stop at the top of a rise and pointed. The other sleds pulled up behind him as he pointed again, more emphatically this time. Lars understood before anyone else. He tossed his blankets aside and bounded through the snow to the edge of a sheer rocky overlook.

At the bottom of the bluff was a house. Or to put it more precisely, the remains of a house. Much of the roof was collapsed, the front door was gone, and a tattered curtain fluttered through a broken window. The side where the roof had caved in was covered with pillars of ice, as if the jaws of winter were about to swallow it.

Lars felt a hand on his shoulder. He glanced back at Nanu and his mother, who was biting at her lower lip, her eyes glistening with tears. A gust of wind buffeted them all.

"So this is it?" his mother said.

Nanu pulled out her map, looked at it, looked back at the house, and back at the map again.

A hundred yards beyond the shattered house was the skeleton of a ship. Beyond the ship was the ocean, and far out in the mist Lars could just make out the dim outlines of a couple of mammoth icebergs. To the north was a palisade of high cliffs, covered by drifting clouds.

"Nanu, is this it?" His mother repeated the question. Her voice had become more strident.

"I don't know," Nanu said.

"This can't be! We can't have come all this way for this . . . for this . . . " She gestured, unable to find a word equal to her disgust.

Nanu looked back at the drivers, as if they were all playing some practical joke on her. "There must be some mistake," she said.

Lars was dumbfounded. How could Nanu have been so wrong? Nanu was never wrong.

It looked as if the house had five or six rooms, and at least three of them seemed to be intact. There was a chimney, which was good news, particularly if that meant there was a stove. There were a few slats of a fence sticking up through the snow and a pile of what looked like driftwood and whale bones.

His mother turned on Søren. "We cannot stay here." He stared at her with huge uncomprehending eyes. "You are going to have to take us back!"

Søren raised his hands, shrugged, and shook his head sadly. "Our dogs are exhausted, madam. They will never be able to get a load like this back over the mountains. I am sorry."

"You're going to leave two women and a child to freeze to death out here, is that what you're telling me?"

Again he shrugged, looking even more sad and hopeless.

Out of the corner of his eye, Lars saw a flicker of motion. He turned to see Nanu heading down the slope as if she was in a trance. Henrik and August ran to catch her. Her whole life she had dreamed of her family's grand house, with its balconies and two fireplaces and views of the sea. For it to turn out to be nothing more than a pile of rotting timbers was more than she could bear.

When her boot broke through the crust of the snow she pitched forward, but the two drivers were quick enough to grab her by the back of her coat. She struggled to get free.

His mother and Søren were still arguing. Søren was a small man, and the angrier his mother got the more she towered over him. She looked as if she was ready to smack him.

Lars felt as if his head was about to explode. Had everybody lost their minds? He tugged at his mother's elbow. "Mom," he said. "Mom. Maybe it's not as bad as you think. Maybe we should go see."

"But I *can* see! I can see perfectly well!"

"I know. But we need to take care of Nanu. We need to get her out of this cold."

She pursed her lips, not pleased that Lars was speaking to her as if she was the child and he was somehow the parent. She flexed her fist inside her mitten. The dogs whined and bit at their traces, anxious to get going.

"We could at least take a look, shouldn't we?" he said.

"All right then," she said, still unconvinced. "Let's have a look."

~~~

They maneuvered the dogsleds down the steep slope and pulled to a stop alongside the broken fence. His mother led Lars and Nanu into the house, pushing a heavy beam out of the doorway.

The front hall was as slick as a skating rink. There was a pot-bellied stove and a table that seemed to be in good shape, but a third of what must have been the kitchen was buried in snow that had drifted in through the collapsed roof.

His mother stared up at the hole in the ceiling, disbelieving, murmuring over and over to herself the first curses Lars had ever heard her utter. Henrik and August peered around the corner of the doorway, too spooked to enter.

His mother began her inspection, running a hand across blood-stained countertops, yanking at drawers, lifting the massive metal top on the stove.

Thinking it might be wise to get out of the way, Lars took Nanu on a tour of the other rooms. They found frozen fishing nets draped over a sagging bed, the charred remains of a fire in the middle of the floor.

Nanu clung to Lars's elbow. She was unsure of everything now, even her balance. Her eyes darted, looking for some sign that she hadn't been a fool for bringing them here, and in the final room it seemed, for a moment, as if she'd found it.

On a low shelf she spied a massive book in a tattered leather binding, furred by frost. She lugged it to a collapsed bed, cracked it open, and began to flip through the frozen pages.

"Look, Lars, look!"

He peered over her shoulder at what seemed to be an ancient ledger of fish bought and sold, faded receipts, and a few scrawled notes. Through the frosted window he could see the three brothers having a heated conversation out by the sleds. No one seemed happy.

Nanu held Lars there for five or six minutes, going through the oversized book, determined to will some connection to her great-grandfather into existence, no matter how far-fetched.

But when Lars heard the voices of Søren and his mother rising from the far end of the house, he patted Nanu's shoulder, excusing himself, and slipped out of the room.

In the kitchen they were at it again. His mother dug down in her satchel and laid all the money they had down on the battered table, one coin at a time. Unmoved, Søren shook his head, arms folded across his chest.

"But this is hopeless," his mother said. "No one can live here. You wouldn't have your dogs live in such a place."

"My heart goes out to you, madam. But if you had only been honest with us from the start, if I'd known that this was where you wanted us to take you, I would have never agreed, not in a million years."

"But you did know. I did tell you."

"Not really. Not this place. You didn't say this place."

"And you have been here before?" Lars put his fingers to his eyes. The room was such an insane jumble, it made him dizzy. It was like having a ski slope go through your kitchen.

"No. But I have heard stories."

She was scornful now. "And what kind of stories were those?"

He had no intention of answering her question. "We will make sure your stove is working and we can give you some of our food. But I cannot ask my brothers to do more than I already have."

She began to scoop up the coins and drop them back in her satchel. "Lars, where is your grandmother?"

"She's in the back."

"Well, I'd appreciate it if you would go get her. We're going to need her to help unpack."

After the sleds were unloaded, the three brothers cleaned out the stove and got a fire started. August found the front door in one of the back rooms (someone had been using it as a fish-cleaning table) and set it back on its hinges.

Now that it was decided that they were going, the three of them couldn't have been more solicitous, even helping with a makeshift repair of the roof, angling a couple of fallen beams across the worst of the holes and covering them with blankets.

According to the map, Søren said, it looked as if there was some sort of village about a mile to the south. If they wanted, he and his brothers could stop on their way out and arrange for some of the villagers to look in on them.

"We are quite capable of taking care of ourselves, thank you," his mother said. Lars found his mother's response quite astonishing, but decided to keep his mouth shut.

Lars walked Søren, Henrik, and August out to the sleds. He stood watching as they cracked their whips and whistled and shouted. The dogs barked, scrambling for footholds in the snow. The sleds jerked forward and they were off, picking up speed quickly as the dogs realized they had only a fraction of their old burden to bear.

That night they huddled around the stove and ate a meal of mummified biscuits and scraps of fried scrod. Afterwards, in the flicker of firelight, the serious unpacking began. As Lars's mother set things out—her favorite blue tea kettle, the cookie jar with the plaster squirrel handle, the winter quilts—her mood began to improve. They lifted the cuckoo clock out of the bed of pillows they'd created to keep it safe. When they set it on the mantel and wound it up, it started ticking right away and everyone clapped.

When Lars swung the last bag onto the kitchen table, he could hear things shifting inside, but when he unzipped it, everything on top seemed fine. There was a mirror that had miraculously come through unscathed, a milk pail, some heavy woolen sweaters, and hats.

But when he turned the bag on end, he caught a glimpse of the shards of glass and splinters of wood that had settled to the bottom. Some of it was of no great importance—a painted dessert plate, a vase of blue glass, a wicker basket, battered and somewhat shredded. But mixed in with it all were the toys that Lars's father had carved for him, now all smashed to smithereens—the troll hiding under his umbrella, the dancing wolf with his tambourine, the goose pecking at a bowl of corn. But worst of all was the now-mangled music box.

He poured it all out on the table and his mother gasped, covering her mouth with her hands. Lars poked through the wreckage, but the only thing he found intact was the pinecone his father had given him the night before he died.

They slept that night curled up next to the stove. Every hour or so Lars's mother would get up to put more wood on the fire. Buried up to his eyes in quilts, Lars stared out the window at the frozen sea, at the mountains of ice glowing in the darkness. Noises kept waking him—the blankets they'd used to patch the roof fluttering in the wind and, every now and then, some far-off booming he couldn't identify.

He clutched the pinecone tightly in both hands. When he held it to his nose, he could almost imagine that he was in a pine forest, walking with his father, axe and hatchet swinging loose at their sides; that in a few minutes the sun would be coming up and they would be working again with a whole long day stretching out before them.

FIVE

or the next two days they labored hour after hour, shoveling snow out of the house, gathering driftwood and dead shrubs for the fire, shoring up the roof, sealing up the broken windows with towels. There was no end of unwelcome surprises. Sweeping under the bed, his mother let out a shriek. Lars looked up just in time to see a family of lemmings scamper across the floor and disappear into a hole behind the stove.

They debated off and on about the wisdom of walking into the village and introducing themselves. Whether they were going to stay or leave, they were going to need help. His mother was reluctant. Though she wouldn't admit it, part of the reason was pride. She hated the idea of anyone seeing them in such a humiliating state.

But even if they weren't interested in seeing people, they were being seen. Several times when Lars stepped out of the house, he saw dark figures silhouetted on top of the ridge, figures that quickly melted away as soon as Lars lifted a hand.

On the dawn of the fourth day, Nanu woke with chills and a fever. After vigorous protest, Lars and his mother were finally able to persuade her to rest, and got her settled on the sofa with a cup of hot tea and a pile of blankets. She fell soundly asleep within minutes.

It was perhaps an hour later that they heard the barking of dogs. Lars and his mother went to the window and stared out at a pair of sleds racing along the top of the ridge. The sleds skidded to a stop, sending up a great plume of snow.

A rotund man with a florid complexion and a ratty fur cap dismounted and clomped over to help his companion to his feet.

His companion was an elegant man in a magnificent coat with brass buttons, a stovepipe hat, and an expensive scarf that kept blowing across his face. The rotund man, who looked a bit like a coachman in his black satin knee breeches, rummaged about in the back of one of the sleds until he found a brown jug and a small packet wrapped in butcher paper.

The two of them hurried down the slope, heads down against the wind.

The knocks on the door were thunderous. Lars and his mother looked at one another. They could scarcely pretend they weren't there. His mother nodded to Lars to go ahead and open it.

Lars opened the door just a crack and the man with the florid complexion poked his head in and raised the brown jug in greeting. "Good morning, young fellow! And who might you be?"

"Lars," Lars said.

"And this is your mother?" The man in the magnificent coat stood behind him, still wrestling with the pesky scarf.

"Yes."

"My name is Bjorn Snortblossom. And this is Mayor Wolfpaw." He waggled the jug. "We've brought you some whale oil for your lamps. Would it be all right if we came in for a minute?"

Again Lars glanced at his mother. She nodded yes. It was not in her nature to be rude.

In they came, Snortblossom and Mayor Wolfpaw behind him. The mayor took a seat at the table, unwrapped his scarf, and folded it on his lap, revealing the ugliest face Lars had ever seen.

Lars's mother stifled a cry. The mayor acted as if he hadn't heard. Lars found it almost impossible to avert his gaze. The mayor's face was terribly scarred. One of his ears was mangled, and the torn pouch of skin below one eye had not properly healed, so it looked as if one eye was lower than the other; his lower lip appeared to have been snagged by an invisible hook, giving him the suggestion of a leering clown's smile.

Bjorn Snortblossom set the brown jug and the packet of butcher paper on the counter and surveyed the house. He seemed quite amazed by it all—the blue tea pot, the cookie jar with the plaster squirrel handle, the mirror in the hallway.

"My, my," he said. "You seem to have done wonders." He clapped his hands. "And look at this! A cuckoo clock! I haven't seen anything like that in years! Hurrah for you!"

Lars's mother put a finger to her lips, warning Snortblossom to keep his voice down. She pointed to Nanu napping, buried under a mound of blankets and pillows on the couch. "Lars's grandmother," she whispered.

Snortblossom gave an apologetic wince. "Ah," he whispered back. "So sorry."

The mayor didn't have the slightest interest in cuckoo clocks. He hadn't taken his eyes off Lars's mother. Color was rising in her cheeks.

"So have you been mayor for a long time?" she asked.

"Quite a long time," he said. He took off his stovepipe hat and set it on the table. "So is your husband with you?" he asked.

"No, I'm afraid not. He died just a month ago."

"Oh, my dear!" said Bjorn Snortblossom. "And where are you from?"

"Someplace I'm sure you've never heard of. We were living about fifty miles west of Stockholm."

"Good Lord, you've come a long way!" Snortblossom said. "But why would you come here? To a place like this?"

"WE CAME HERE BECAUSE WE OWN IT!" Nanu may have been buried under her blankets, but that didn't mean she hadn't been listening. Her voice, clear and strong, made them all jump.

A pillow tumbled to the floor as Nanu emerged from the pile of blankets, rubbing a rheumy eye. Snortblossom stared at her, incredulous.

"You own it?"

"It belonged to my great-grandfather." Nanu took a sidelong glance at the mayor sitting at the table. If she was shocked at his appearance, she did a very good job of not showing it. The mayor still had not taken his eyes off Lars's mother.

"Do you have any proof of that?" Snortblossom said.

"I have the deed."

"Really? We'd be very interested in having a look at that."

"And I'd be very happy to show it to you."

Nanu wrestled with her blankets and finally tossed them aside. She searched the pockets of her vest one by one, and smiled when she found what she was looking for.

She teetered to her feet to hand the deed to Snortblossom. He examined the yellowing piece of paper for nearly a minute without uttering a word and handed it on to the mayor.

"This is a hundred and fifty years old," Snortblossom said.

"Yes."

"Now let's get serious. No one in their right mind would say you still own a place you haven't lived in for a hundred and fifty years."

"Who does own it then?"

"Well, the mayor does, I suppose. He and his family before him have been using it as a fishing camp for as long as I remember."

Nanu made a small spitting sound. "They've been squatting on our property, is that what you're saying?"

The mayor stared down at his huge hands, listening, staying out of the fray. Lars tried to imagine what had happened to him. Had he been attacked by animals? How long had he been like this? Whatever Nanu might have been thinking, it was clear she didn't have an ounce of sympathy for him. As he bent forward, the lantern light shone off the lacework of scar tissue.

"It sounds as if we've made a terrible mistake. Perhaps we should try some other settlements," Lars's mother said.

"Alas, I'm afraid that's not really possible," Snortblossom said. "I spoke to one of our deputies this morning. He said there have been a whole series of avalanches over the last couple of days. All the passes are closed."

Nanu scowled, took out her pipe, and began stuffing it with tobacco. "And when will they be open again?" she said.

"No time soon, I'm afraid. It could be months. It could be longer."

"Are you telling me that we're trapped here?" Lars's mother said. Wolfpaw rose from the table and walked to the water barrel, clearly not happy with the way the conversation was going.

"Oh, please," Snortblossom said, "let's not get hysterical. There are some perfectly acceptable places in the village we could move you into. It's just that this place does belong to the mayor . . . "

Mayor Wolfpaw's swing came without warning. His fist caught Snortblossom flush on the jaw and sent him reeling across the floor where he collapsed against a wall. From the way Snortblossom cowered, it was clear that this was not the first time he'd been hit. No one knew what to do.

"Sir, what did I say . . . "

"These people are not going anywhere." The mayor's voice was velvety-calm, without a trace of anger. "They have come a long way and we are not going to make them move again."

"I understand that, sir, it's just that . . . " The mayor took a step forward and Snortblossom raised an elbow as if he was about to be hit again. The mayor retrieved his elegant scarf from the floor and swirled it around his neck.

"But how will we ever be able to live here?" Lars's mother asked.

The mayor turned back to her and in his strange, off-kilter eyes, there was a trace of kindness. "We will find a way."

SIX

hey were all unnerved. After the mayor and Snortblossom left, Lars and his mother and Nanu huddled around the table for three hours, trying to make sense of it all.

Lars's mother was hysterical and angry. She blamed Nanu for talking them into this fix and blamed herself for going along with it. "We've got to find a way out of here."

"But you heard them. There is no way out."

"I don't believe that. I refuse to simply take his word for it."

"Okay, then, fine," Nanu said.

"Perhaps I should just speak to the mayor again."

"I would not do that," Nanu said.

"And why is that?"

Nanu gave Lars a quick glance. "I don't think we need to speak of that in front of the boy."

"Nanu," Lars said, "what do you think happened to him? For him to look like that?"

"I don't know," Nanu said. "But I'm sure we can find someone to tell us."

Over the next several days there were a number of visitors—a dim-witted old man trying to sell his sled dogs, two dirty-faced young beggars in ragged parkas, shaking empty burlap sacks before them, pleading for food. She grilled each of them. Surely they must know someone who could help her and her family. Surely there was some alternate route that could take them safely back to the civilized world, if not through the mountains, then out across the sea ice. Surely there was someone she could pay.

Her visitors all shook their heads sadly. They all said the same thing: once you are here, you are here for good. And when she asked them about the mayor, they all turned shifty-eyed and uneasy, claiming to know nothing.

Each day that passed, they felt more in peril. One night Lars heard heavy footsteps tromping around the roof. One afternoon he glanced up to see faces peering in a frosted window, faces that vanished as soon as the snoopers realized they'd been spotted. At night Lars dreamed of Mayor Wolfpaw standing over his bed in his elegant coat, his scarred face glowing in the moonlight that streamed in the window.

Nanu and Lars's mother resolved not to open the door to any more visitors, but they were forced to go back on their word when one morning they were interrupted by loud banging at the front of the house. They tried to ignore it, but the banging continued, intermittently. Whoever was out there apparently did not have any intention of going away.

Lars went to the window and peered out. At first he saw nothing, but then as the knocker backed away from the door, he saw her quite clearly, a small sparrow of a woman, quite irate, with a satchel over her shoulder. It took her a second to realize that she was being watched. The woman raised her satchel and pointed at it with some indignation, as if to indicate that she'd brought food.

"Mom," Lars said. "I think maybe we should let this woman in."

Their visitor's name was Taya Kerensky, and though she was a bit huffy about being made to stand out in the cold for so long, when she calmed down she turned out to be quite charming, as well as big-hearted. She'd brought them a number of things, including a large bowl of batter consisting of pulverized fish bones and minced lichen.

She was their nearest neighbor, she said. She was not young. She had an air of faded grandeur, wore purple leggings, and had a long blue and white scarf wrapped fashionably around her neck. It was evident that she still took great pains with her appearance, but her face was alarming, covered with cakey-white makeup to cover some old smallpox scars. Her cheeks were rouged and brilliantly red. Lars couldn't have said for sure, but he would have bet money that she had false eyebrows of mouse-skin.

She was also bossy. They had no choice but to stand and watch as she commandeered the kitchen. She got all the utensils she needed from the kitchen, greased the skillet, and clanged it onto the stove. Once it was hot, she ladled out dollops of batter that hit the pan with a satisfying sizzle. Within minutes the house was filled with a distinctively odd odor.

She was more than willing to fill them in on her life history as she tended to the tiny pancakes. She claimed that her great-great-grand-father had once been the czar of Russia, but when he was murdered by treacherous counselors, his wife and small daughter had to flee into exile. Though she didn't expect anyone to refer to her as the czarina, she still had hopes that one day she would be restored to her rightful place on the throne. She had been a dancer in her youth, and had once tried to open a ballet school in the village, but it had not gone well.

When the pancakes were ready, Taya Kerensky insisted that the three of them sit down at the table while she served them. She'd not only brought batter, but a bowlful of glistening black fish eggs, and a container of reindeer milk that she quickly whisked up into something resembling whipped cream.

She slid four small pancakes onto each plate, poured some of the glistening fish eggs over each stack, and topped it off with thick white swirls.

When she set the plates in from of them, Lars's mother glanced up at her. "Aren't you having some?"

"No, please. This is all for you."

Lars raised his fork. The creation on his plate was so beautiful it seemed like a crime to cut into it. It was the kind of food that he'd only dreamed of, the kind of food that was meant to be eaten by a much finer caliber of person than himself.

But when he put the first forkful in his mouth he began to cough, like a cat trying to hack up a furball. The pancake tasted like sawdust. Or ashes. He tried to chew, but the mash of pancake clung to the roof of his mouth like wet plaster. He looked over at Nanu. Her lips were pursed like a person who'd just swallowed a mole. Lars's mother was at least trying to be discreet, cutting her pancakes into smaller and smaller pieces and scooting them about in the black goo and whipped cream. Taya Kerensky sat watching from the couch, eyes bright behind her chalk-white mask.

"This is so kind of you," Lars's mother said, wiping at the corner of her mouth with a napkin. "Could I ask you a question?"

"Of course."

"The mayor paid us a visit a couple of days ago."

"I imagine he did."

"And, if I may be frank, we found his appearance alarming."

"Yes."

"We thought there must be a story . . . "

"There always is, isn't there? I would be happy to tell you. But first I must tell you a bit about this place."

SEVEN

his is the story that Taya told them. Since the eruption of the volcano, the village had been ruled by three generations of the Ratvass family: first Torgny, then Hildegaard, and after her, Oskar, with his two pampered twin sons, Ragnold and Raynor, expected to ascend to power after their father's death.

The economy of the village was totally dependant on the skarn-liver-oil factory. The skarn was a blind white fish with fearsome fangs that grew in the waters beneath extinct volcanos, and its oil was reputed to have remarkable qualities, though many of the school children required to take it daily found that it had depressive and dizzying effects.

As odd as that may have been, even odder was the fact that all toys had been banned in the village since the time of the volcano. To be found with a toy was an unspeakable crime. What made this law particularly unnerving was that the definition of "toy" was a wide one. It did not include just painted tin soldiers and porcelain dolls. Since a child was capable of taking a stick and turning it into a horse or throwing a sheet over two chairs and turning it into a house, nearly any act of play or imagination was considered off-limits.

Though there was the usual amount of grumbling, the village ran well enough, and Oskar's major worry was whether his twin boys were ever going to amount to anything.

Then one day a pair of hunters flushed what they thought was a wolf cub out of its den. Their dogs chased it across the tundra, and when they corralled it in a fishing shack it put up a ferocious fight.

One of the dogs was killed and another maimed, but it wasn't until the hunters firmly collared the wolf pup that they saw that it wasn't a wolf pup at all, but a boy. The boy continued to snarl and and tried to fight them as they tied him down to their sled.

They brought him to Oskar, who had no idea what to make of this strange creature. The boy panted with his tongue out and bared his teeth. His hair was long and matted, his knees thickly callused from living on all fours. He seemed to be deaf and dumb. He had suffered terrible wounds in his battle with the dogs, and even when the wounds healed, he was left with a face so disfigured it made Oskar wince to look at him.

All the villagers had heard the story and were dying to have a look at the boy for themselves. After a month, Oskar finally bowed to pressure and once a week set the boy out on display in his cage in the village square.

The villagers all marveled at him. Some pointed and jeered, others gaped in amazement, others shielded the eyes of their screaming children. Those who were brave enough pelted the cage with snowballs or ran up to it to drop in scraps of raw meat.

In time the villagers lost interest and the weekly spectacles were halted.

What to call this creature was a problem. Some called him Pup. Others referred to him as Slobber-Puss. There were those who preferred Lobo. In the end he was given a name, Nikita, and his long, matted hair was cut short. A tutor was hired to teach him how to speak, how to sit at a table, use silverware, and wear clothes.

Oskar instructed his two sons to treat Nikita as their brother. This did not go well. The two boys were jealous of all the special attention Nikita was receiving, and insulted that this bizarre-looking little creature was supposed to be part of the family.

They would sneak into his room at night and rattle sticks along the bars of his cage to startle him out of his sleep, kick his shins under the table when he first began to join the rest of them for dinner, and mock his first attempts at speech. They would toss live lemmings and voles into the cage and roar with delight as Nikita cornered the tiny rodents, played with them, and ate them. Nikita grew to hate the twins with his whole heart.

The only ones to treat him with kindness were Bengstrom, his tutor, and Marius, a stooped old man who tended the tomten. Often, after the day's lessons were done, Nikita and Bengstrom would go over the story about how Nikita had been found. Nikita had so many questions: What had happened to his wolf-mother? Had she been killed by hunters or a rival pack of wolves? Had she been caught in a trap? Could her pelt be mounted on the wall of some villager's shack?

And what had happened to his human mother? Had he been her only child? Or maybe he had other brothers and sisters, and when he came along maybe he had been one too many to care for. Perhaps she had fallen ill or been banished from the village for being pregnant and had frozen to death.

Bengstrom responded the best he could, but he had no answers. All he knew for sure was that she had loved him and that when he had been born he had been a beautiful child. Nikita, six years old, his face deformed by welts, listened quietly, staring with huge soft eyes.

Sometimes in the evening Bengstrom took out his knife and whittled. Nikita would watch, fascinated by the shapes his tutor could discover within a simple chunk of wood. Over time Bengstrom's carvings became more and more distinctive and recognizable. His most elaborate creation was a three-masted schooner, perfect in every detail, with a cannon mounted on the prow and tiny wooden sailors hard at work on the deck.

It was the most miraculous thing Nikita had ever seen. Bengstrom was leery of letting the boy even touch it (Nikita was still an impulsive and clumsy child), but after weeks of begging, Bengstrom finally let him play with the schooner for a few minutes every night under his watchful eye. Bengstrom and Marius were the only two aware of the toy's existence.

But one evening Ragnold and Raynor burst into the room and found Nikita lying on his back in his cage, dreamily waving the schooner above his head as it was ploughing its way through a typhoon. Bengstrom, sitting in his easy chair, leapt to his feet to explain, but it was too late. The twins raced down the hallway to tell their father.

By the time Oskar and the twins returned with Marius in tow, Bengstrom had stashed the schooner in one of the cupboards. It was a sorry excuse for a hiding place, and the schooner was quickly found.

Oskar stomped on the carving, smashing it into a hundred pieces in front of Nikita, and the next day Bengstrom was hung in the village square.

Nikita howled for two days straight. For three weeks he refused to eat. He was chained to a wall in the basement and whipped daily.

The story of what had happened quickly made the rounds. The village was in shock. No one living had ever seen a toy, and for most of them, it didn't even seem possible that such a thing had happened.

Nikita's spirit was broken. When he was finally let out of the cellar and allowed to walk the streets, he was reviled and mocked. Shame hung over him like a cloud.

A massive change came over him. He became obedient and dutiful and barely spoke a word to anyone. He became an expert boxer and a crack shot. He began to show up at the factory to learn the business from stem to stern. The workers learned to fear him, and nothing ran as well in his absence.

When Oskar died the debate raged: who would become the next mayor of the village, Ragnold or Raynor? Fisticuffs broke out at the trading post. Bricks were thrown through windows. Lies and slander spread like wildfire, and family members ceased speaking to one another.

The truth was that neither of the twins was an ideal candidate for higher office. Ragnold was vain and lazy and spent his days lying on a sofa eating chocolates, while Raynor was crazy—prone to rages and laughing fits.

A council of elders was appointed to resolve the issue, but one week before they met, the two brothers were found murdered in their beds, throats slashed.

The village was paralyzed with fear. No one was brave enough to step forward, or even to leave their houses. Then one morning a messenger came round to every dwelling to say that Nikita wanted to address them all at noon on the following day in the village square.

The square had not been so packed since the day the five-year-old Nikita, snarling and wild, had been put on display in his cage.

Everyone was there, mothers with babies strapped to their backs, the infirm carried on chairs by their children and grandchildren, sullen deputies, seal-hunters with their harpoons. Whispers rippled through the crowd. Eyes flitted nervously. People murmured in low tones. At noon the sun hung just above the horizon, casting weak light.

Nikita kept the villagers waiting for nearly a half hour. When he strode through the crowd he took none of the hands extended to him, met no one's eyes.

He climbed the steps of the grandstand that had been hastily erected for the occasion. Though still in his early twenties, he was a powerfully built, fully grown man. The musk-ox robe wrapped tightly around his shoulders made him all the more imposing.

He looked out across the crowd, and his eyes were without mercy. He was not a practiced speaker, and his accent was strange.

He told them them they had nothing to fear, that whoever had committed these atrocities would be brought to justice. This announcement was greeted by a hundred blank stares. There was no one in the crowd that didn't believe that Nikita was the one who had murdered the twins. But it didn't matter whether they believed him or not. All that mattered was that there was no one brave enough to stand up to him.

"We are all still in shock. I have lost my two beloved brothers. And I know how close each of them was to many of you. We will all grieve for them, each in our own way. But the truth is that we have brought this on ourselves. Some of the things that have gone on have been appalling. We have feuded and fought and said unforgiveable things to one another. It hurts me to say this, but the council of elders has been no help.

"We allow this kind of behavior to continue at our peril. Because of the extraordinary circumstances we find ourselves in, I would like to propose that I step in as your acting mayor, for the time being at least."

Silence fell over the crowd. One of the elders at the back of the throng spit in the snow. A dog barked down one of the alleyways. A mother clutched a feeding child to her breast. Finally one of the seal-hunters raised his harpoon in the air.

"All for Nikita say aye!"

"Aye!" came an answering cry from the far side of the square. Several seconds later came a third cry and then a fourth. People looked around to see what their neighbors were doing before joining in. The cries of acclamation spread and turned into a chant, calling out his name. "Nikita! Nikita! Nikita!"

Nikita gave a thin smile. He pointed, acknowledging one person in the crowd, and then another. He finally raised both fists in the air. Beaming now, he turned so all could see him. The rays of the falling sun glowed on his face after bathing his mangled ear, the imperfectly healed scar at the corner of his mouth, the drooping eye, transforming it all into a mask of triumph.

When Taya finished her story, no one said anything for more than a minute. Lars shifted the last wad of pancake from one side of his mouth to the other, swallowing as best he could.

"It must have been terrible to go through all he went through," Lars's mother said.

Taya and Nanu both gave her an odd look. "You're not feeling sorry for him, are you?" Nanu said. "The man is a killer."

"No. I'm not feeling sorry for him. I'm just saying . . ."

As Taya leaned over the lantern to adjust the flame, it brightened her white mask of a face from below, made it seem to float free of the rest of her. "Think whatever you want. Just so you understand that he is not a man to be taken lightly." The cuckoo clock on the wall chimed ten. "My goodness! It looks as if I've taken up your whole morning. Now can't I leave some of this with you? There must be enough for at least another meal or two."

"No, please," said Lars's mother. "You've been more than generous. Here, let me help you." She got to her feet and held the satchel while Taya Kerensky re-packed everything—the bowl of batter, the fish eggs, the container of reindeer milk.

After Taya was gone, the house was quiet. Lars went out to fetch more driftwood for the fire while his mother and Nanu tended to the dishes. When he came back in, Nanu was hanging the wet towels above the stove to dry.

"What do you think, Nanu?"

"I think she didn't tell us the half of it."

There turned out to be a school. This bit of unpleasant news came from one of their neighbors, along with the fact that attendance was mandatory. Lars argued that this was probaby nothing but a rumor, and even if it wasn't, it was still a terrible idea, having to troop off to some place he'd never seen, that he knew nothing about, to be with a bunch of children he'd never even met before. Besides, what would his mother and Nanu do without him? He didn't like the idea of leaving the two of them alone and unprotected in a place like this. And didn't they really need him to help get the house in shape?

His mother wouldn't hear of it. The last thing they needed right now was to get off on the wrong foot with everybody. And besides, after all they'd gone through, it would be good for him to be with children his own age, to get back to something like a normal life. There was no telling: he might even make some friends. Lars was dubious.

He appealed to Nanu. It was clear that the whole business troubled her, but she was reluctant to buck Lars's mother. In the end, it was the same old story, grown-ups versus kids, and Lars was outvoted two to one.

The next morning he was up early. His mother already had a steaming bowl of porridge for him, but he was in no mood to eat more than a couple of mouthfuls. She and Nanu fussed over him, running a comb though his hair, straightening his belt, and making sure he was bundled up as warmly as possible. His mother offered to walk him to school, but he said no. If he was going to do this, he wanted to do it alone.

The neighbor had made a map for him that he stuffed into his pocket. He kissed his mother and Nanu goodbye and waddled to the door. Under his coat he had two extra sweaters, and on his head a huge fur hat with ear flaps that had once belonged to his father and came down to his eyes.

A sharp, bone-chilling wind whistled off the sea as he labored to the top of the ridge. It was still dark. He could just barely make out a few of the landmarks penciled in on Taya Kerensky's map—the Walrus Cliffs, with the forty-foot-high icicles hanging down like giant tusks; the stone towers; and Woolly Mammoth Glacier, slanting to the sea.

For the first ten minutes or so, it felt as if he was the only person in the universe, the only sounds the moaning of the wind and the squeak of his boots in the snow. Then at some point he was quite sure he thought he saw several ghostlike figures, heads down, trudging far out in the gloom, but after a moment they disappeared.

He fished the map out of his pocket. It had gotten wet, and some of the details had washed away. He was furious at his mother and Nanu for making him do this, but he wasn't going to turn back, not now. He stuffed the wet map back in his pocket. He began to sing an old logging song Emil had taught him as he set off again.

The sea was directly below Lars now. Along the shore were hundreds of spires of blue ice, glittering in the darkness and all slammed up against one another. It reminded Lars of the pictures his father had shown him of the big cathedrals in Stockholm.

He passed the sagging ruins of a couple of huts and a stone tower. A light sleet began to fall. The school had to be close. But where? He was skirting the edge of a frozen pond when, once again, he heard the howling of dogs. He stopped, bewildered, and lifted the brim of his oversized hat so he could see. Were the howls coming from behind him? Ahead of him? He wasn't quite sure. Could the three dogsled drivers possibly have taken pity and come back to get him?

It was five or six seconds before he was able to spot a dot on the horizon, coming from the direction of the collapsed huts. It grew larger and larger. It was just one sled this time, and it was being pulled by a pair of blonde dogs the size of ponies. An enormous driver loomed over the sled. He looked as if he could have crushed the sled between his hands like a walnut. He wore a shaggy black fur coat and a carved tusk around his neck. A red scarf covered his face up to his eyeballs.

The sled veered away at an angle, almost as if trying to steer clear of Lars. Lars waved and shouted and then waved some more. At first it didn't seem to have any effect. The sled sped directly across the pond, but when it reached the far bank, the driver leaned back and stabbed a metal hook into the snow. The dogs struggled to maintain their speed, but the hook was too powerful a brake. The sled slowed and finally came to a stop.

Lars's heart leapt. Maybe all the terrible things Lars had been thinking about people up here weren't true at all. He ran across the pond, slipping and sliding. The two blonde dogs rested in the snow, blinking at him. One of them licked at a massive paw. The metal hook dangled at the driver's side. Lars could see eyes twinkling under the hood of black fur.

"Thank you, thank you so much," Lars said. He was just ten yards away when the driver shouted "Mush!" and rattled the handles of the sled. The two dogs bolted, nearly lifting the sled off the ground. The driver swung to the left and then to the right before regaining his balance. Lars could hear him cackling as the sled disappeared behind a curtain of sleet.

Just when he was convinced that he'd gone too far, Lars found the school nestled at the back of a frozen cove. There was a ramshackle barn, a corral, several small sheds, and one long domed structure, at least forty feet high, that looked like a beached whale.

Alongside the building was a wide snowfield where a couple of dozen sleds were parked. A cluster of students gathered around their dogs laughed and pelted one another with snowballs. A bowlegged boy danced about, flicking his scarf at one of the dogs, making it leap and snap. Another boy huddled with his girlfriend, rubbing noses.

Lars crossed the snowfield, his heart pounding like a muffled drum. At the entrance of the school, two fearsome-looking men with red armbands stood guard, wearing narrow wooden goggles to protect them from snow blindness.

Lars yanked the heavy door open with both hands. The hallway teemed with students jamming their belongings into what looked like giant walrus skins hanging from hooks in the ceiling.

A bird flew up and down the corridor, squawking, as kids bombardeded it with chalk. Farther down the hall, a crowd had gathered. People were shouting, some of them hopping up and down to get a better look. As Lars approached, he saw that a fight was going on.

One of the combatants was the boy who had tricked Lars into thinking that he was giving him a ride. He was still in his shaggy black coat, but his hood was pushed back, and Lars could see the sneer on his lips, the meaty red cheeks, the tangle of blonde hair he had to keep blowing out of his eyes. His jaw looked as sturdy as an anvil, and he was at least a head taller than any of the other students, his shoulders as muscled as the shoulders of Lars's father's oxen. He had his left arm out, ramrod stiff, his hand planted in the middle of the forehead of a small, bucktoothed boy, keeping him at bay. The smaller boy flailed away, but all his punches fell a foot short. The face of his tormentor shone with malice and delight.

The smaller boy had taken his lumps. His shirt was torn, one eye was puffy and red, and blood trickled down an elbow. "Squash him like a bug, Arkady!" A girl with carrot-colored braids shouted, bounding up and down. "Let the pipsqueak have it!" A boy with a face like a wedge of moldy cheese hollered, "Come on, Arkady, show him what's what!"

Lars looked up and down the hallway for someone to restore order, but there was no one. Arkady was just toying with his opponent now, but the bucktoothed boy showed no signs of giving up. Though none of his punches ever landed, they became wilder and more determined. When Arkady yanked his arm away, the smaller boy stumbled forward and Arkady grabbed him around the waist.

"Whoopee!" Arkady shouted as he swung his adversary around, quite pleased with himself until the smaller boy bit him on the hand. Arkady bellowed and threw his opponent aside. Holding his wounded fingers, Arkady shouted terrible things in a language Lars had never heard before. The bucktoothed boy dove at Arkady's ankles, and Arkady toppled like a felled pine.

For several seconds the bucktoothed boy disappeared under the enormous black coat. Thumps were followed by squeals followed by more thumps. The shaggy coat rippled like a sack of furious tomcats. Arkady grimaced and growled and gritted his teeth, his red cheeks growing even redder.

When Arkady finally rose to his feet, he held the bucktoothed boy upside down by his legs. Everyone cheered and threw their caps in the air. A couple of Arkady's friends leapt forward and grabbed the bucktoothed boy by the arm, helping to march him to a wastebasket.

Lars raised a hand to protest. Part of him wanted to say something, and part of him knew better, knew that nothing anyone could say would make a difference.

When they tried to stuff the bucktoothed boy into the basket, he twisted and turned, fighting back with such spirit they finally had no choice but to step away, leaving him perched on the metal ring like a furious frog sitting on a lilypad.

A bell rang. The students fled, running off down the hall, leaving Lars and the bucktoothed boy all to themselves. If the boy was aware of Lars's presence, he didn't show it. He checked the blood on his elbow, sinking slowly down into the trash basket. When he finally raised his head and saw Lars staring at him, he scowled.

"Think you're tough?"

"No," Lars said.

"Think you can take me?"

"No."

"Then what are you looking at?"

"Nothing," Lars said.

"And where do you think you're going?"

"I don't know."

The bucktoothed boy squinted at him curiously out of his good eye. "You don't know anything, do you?"

"I guess not." Lars ducked as the bird winged its way down the corridor.

"You must be the new boy everyone's been talking about."

"I guess I am."

"Well, lots of luck with that." He pushed himself out of the trash can. "My name's Pytor."

"And I'm Lars."

Pytor plucked at his torn shirt. "Well, let me take you down to the schoolmaster's office before you get yourself into a lot more trouble."

Lars slumped in a chair, dazed, his chin nesting in his palms, while Mr. Smorgas, the schoolmaster, consulted the charts on the walls of his office. He was round as a rum ball, smelled like one as well, and sported a polka dot vest.

"Classes, classes . . . now what exactly are we teaching this year? Ahh, here we've got two ice fishing sections. Jigs and Lures. Do you have a harpoon?"

Lars could only stare. As affable as the schoolmaster had initially seemed, it was clear now that he was a lunatic. "No, I'm sorry, but I don't," Lars said.

"All right, then," he said. "What about Reindeer Husbandry?"

"Well, I suppose . . ."

"Superb choice!" Mr. Smorgas scribbled on a small white card. "And math . . . why not? It never hurts to learn how to add. Now here's a nice one. Birds of the Arctic. You look like a boy in need of some ornithological wisdom. And the History of Snow. That's always a crowd-pleaser. One more now, one more. Ah, I see we have a spot in Ancient Civilizations, which should round out your schedule rather nicely." He pressed the card against the wall, wet the tip of his pencil with his tongue, and wrote furiously for a minute. He handed the card to Lars. "There you go, my boy. Anything else?"

"Not really."

"Hold on a second, I have something for you."

The schoolmaster rummaged through the drawers of his desk and pulled out a tall glass bottle filled with what looked like eyeballs. He removed the cork and slid one of the slippery white ovals into his palm.

"Want to try one?"

"What are they?"

"Pickled skua eggs. They're delicious."

"No, thank you, I'm fine."

"Suit yourself." He popped the egg into his mouth and glanced at the clock on the wall. "They should be about done with the anthem by now. So off with you. You don't want to be late for your first class." Then, as Lars turned for the door, he called after him. "Young man?"

Lars pivoted on his heel. "Yes?"

"We don't get many new students. It's been several years. And I fear that our ways may take a little getting used to. But it will all work out, I promise you. It always does. Just do what you're told and be patient. It should be an adventure. Just try not to cry in front of the others."

EIGHT

n math class, the teacher, Miss Sunvold, an old woman with disordered eyes, went around the room asking the simplest of multiplication problems: two times four, three times five, six times eight. To Lars's amazement, only half the students were able to even come close to the right solutions. They twitched in their seats, knitted their brows, stared at Miss Sunvold with open mouths as if staring into a dense mist. Pytor, his swollen eye half-closed now, sat next to the window, trying to count out the answers on his fingers.

But if it was discouraging to be in a class where the students knew nothing, it was even worse when the teacher's command of his subject was zero. In Ancient Civilizations, the teacher, Mr. Ostertag, a giraffe of a man with an enormous Adam's apple, lectured nonstop until the bell sounded. The problem was that he seemed to think that the medieval crusaders were able to leap their steeds across the Straits of Gilbralter, that the Tigris and the Euphrates were not rivers, but twin orphans who had been suckled by a she-wolf and founded Rome, and that Africa was overrun by kangaroos.

There were no books in the class, and apparently there had been no books in the village for a hundred years, so perhaps Mr. Ostertag could be forgiven for the garbling of the facts. Since it had been passed down from generation to generation without reference to any reliable texts, his information suffered from both the failings of memory and the fancies of the imagination.

Lars's third class of the morning, Reindeer Husbandry, was blessedly down-to-earth. He was assigned to shovel manure out of the barn while the other students herded the reindeer from a corral into stalls where they could be brushed down and fed.

The best thing about the class was a small, dark-haired girl with verve who acted as if she owned the place and gave him a quick smile as they turned the reindeer out of their stalls. He was too shy to speak to her, but she wasn't shy at all. Twice he caught her looking his way with a bold curiosity. He also learned her name when the teacher asked her to gather up the milking pails. Miko, he called her. Miko. Lars didn't have any idea what kind of name that was, but it didn't sound as if she was from here. Any more than he was.

On the way out to recess, one of Mr. Smorgas's assistants grabbed Lars and brought him back to the office to assign him one of the walrus skins and fill out a sheaf of forms. When they were done, they spent twenty minutes rummaging in a storeroom for a fresh supply of dunce caps and boxes of chalk. By the time they finished it was time for lunch.

There turned out to be two lunch rooms, one for the younger students, and one for everyone over thirteen. It being Lars's first day, he, of course, picked the wrong one. He followed a slow-moving boy through the door into a massive room and was presented with one of the most bizzare sights of his life.

A pair of cooks with puffy white cooks' hats stood behind a table, looking solemn as priests. One of the cooks held a large platter piled high with glistening white cubes. A long line of students edged forward, each of them taking a cube of fat (it looked like blubber) and dipping it in into a shallow bowl of golden liquid held by the second cook. They held the rectangle of blubber aloft for several seconds to let some of the oil drip off and then popped the fatty morsels into their mouths. They reminded Lars of the slimy slugs he and his mother picked from their tomato plants each summer.

Some of the students gulped them down in a single gulp. Others chewed patiently, like cows at work on their cuds. One of the older students went down on one knee and let the cook put the dollop of fat on his tongue.

One girl made a face. One puckered her lips as if she'd just swallowed a lemon. It was clearly a struggle for all of them. Some shuddered; some started to gag and then stifled the impulse; but nearly all had oddly vacant faces of sleepwalkers, the meekness of sheep being led to slaughter.

"What are you doing in here?" Lars turned to face a boy in a crinkly shirt, behind him in line.

"I'm sorry?"

"How old are you?"

"Twelve."

"You eat across the hall. You've got to be thirteen to be in here."

Once Lars found the proper lunch room, it seemed grim, but pretty much what he would have expected. A number of his fellow students were making their way to an open fireplace where they fished hunks of black bread out of a bin and ladled soup out of an enormous cast-iron kettle.

By the time Lars got to the bin it was empty of all but a few scraps. The soup wasn't much more encouraging, a pale-yellow broth with what looked like silvery gills occasionally bowling to the surface.

Nearly all the tables were full, and everyone seemed absorbed in bolting down their food. No one looked up to smile and invite him over. No one moved to the side to make a place for him.

There was one empty seat, however, next to Pytor on the far side of the room. Lars made his way through the tables and tapped him on the shoulder.

Pytor squinted up at him with his good eye. The other one that had been walloped in his fight with Arkady was totally swollen shut.

"Anyone sitting here?" Lars asked.

"Suit yourself."

Lars sat down. Pytor paid him no mind, slurping up his soup. Lars picked up a scrap of bread and tried to gnaw on it. It was hard enough to break a tooth. He set it back down again.

"Pretty bad, huh?" Pytor said.

"Pretty bad. But I guess it's better than having to eat across the hall."

Pytor gave him a swift look. "Somebody tell you about that?"

"I saw. What is going on over there?"

"Oh, I don't think you want to know. Not on your first day here."

Lars had an entire afternoon still to deal with. The hours passed relatively uneventfully, though in his Birds of the Arctic class, the teacher made him get up and introduce himself to everyone, and she wasn't about to let him get away with just giving his name. She asked about his family and what his father did. When Lars said he was a woodsman, she asked what a woodsman did.

"He tends to the forest." The teacher's name was Miss Bord, a prim, long-necked woman with the quick, darting movements of a bittern.

"And what is a forest?"

"Just a bunch of trees, really."

Miss Bord turned to the class. "So how many of you have seen a tree?" she asked. Miko, sitting by the window, put a knuckle to her lips, looking quite scornful. Only the boy with the wild, unwashed hair raised his hand. The rest sat motionless, eyes glazed. "Oh, come on, now! Surely you must know what a tree is! Haven't you seen them in books?" It was not clear that any of them had ever seen a book. "Lars, could you explain?"

"Well, a tree, let's see. It's got a trunk and branches and leaves. Or needles sometimes. Some of them grow to be a hundred feet high."

There was a guffaw from the back of the room, but when Miss Bord whirled around everyone flinched, and the room fell silent.

"And your father's job was what exactly?"

Lars struggled not to cry. "Once a year he would chop some of the trees down. With axes and these really big saws."

"And would you help him?" Miss Bord paced along the side of the room, rubbing the back of her long, undulating neck.

"Not really. Sometimes he would let me drive the oxen."

"So what would you do then?"

Lars pressed his fingers to his eyes. Was Miss Bord ever going to stop? Lars could almost see them now, his father at one end of the crosscut saw, Anton and Emil at the other. Back and forth they went, chips flying. The sunlight filtered down through the treetops as if they were in a massive church, and when Nanu would show up with everyone's lunch, Lars would shout and go running to her and bury his face in her skirts.

"I'm sorry, Lars, what did you say you would be doing?"

"Some times I would make fairy houses." The entire class burst into laughter, not just the handful of Arkady's rough friends, but the woebegotten and half-starved as well.

"Fairy houses? How do you do that?" Now even Miss Bord seemed amused.

"Out of twigs and moss." Miko covered her face with her hands; this was hopeless.

"And do you believe in fairies, Lars?"

"When I was a kid, I guess I did. But not anymore."

By the time classes let out, there was just the thinnest band of pale light in the afternoon sky. Lars trudged past the yipping dogs and the tangled sleds, speaking to no one, but he knew that behind his back they were all talking about him. Several of the older students were back at their stations on the slope, staring out toward the sea.

He saw Arkady help one of the girls onto his sled and snap the reins over the backs of his giant blonde dogs. As the sled came wheeling around, Lars saw that the girl was Miko. His heart filled with dismay. Miko was Arkady's girlfriend? Well, so much for her.

Lots of people have bad first days at school, but no one could possibly match this. He labored up the hill, head down. He'd made a total fool of himself. How could he possibly have said anything about the fairy houses? How was he ever going to show his face in this place again?

When he reached the top of the bluff, a gust of wind buffeted him, turned him sideways. Somewhere off to his left was the frozen sea, wrapped in mist and deepening darkness.

He plodded on for ten minutes and then fifteen. He'd somehow lost Taya Kerensky's map that had been his guide that morning and was totally on his own now, searching the horizon for markers. From time to time he could hear the distant barking of sled dogs. He could barely believe it, how stupid the whole day had been. The Tigris and the Euphrates suckled by a she-wolf? It was ridiculous. And how could those kids not know what a tree was?

If he hadn't been so angry, he might have almost felt sorry for them. They were starving, they were pathetic, and didn't you have to feel sorry for people who'd never walked through the forest early in the morning, with all the birds just waking up and the smell of pine in the air?

But, really, it wasn't them he needed to feel sorry for, it was himself. Because as he trudged on alone, step after step, it became clear to him in a way that it never had before, that he would never walk through that forest with his father again, never hear his father sing to him as he hefted his axe onto his shoulder. All there was ahead of him now was an endless white expanse and a wind so cold it froze the tears on his cheek to ice the instant they formed.

NINE

I f Lars's first day of school had been strange, his second day was perhaps even stranger. He arrived early enough the next morning for the singing of the anthem, hurrying down the hall with a throng of other students as the sound of singing grew steadily louder.

Lars came to a set of double doors, flung them open, and stepped into a packed auditorium. Everyone was singing, belting out the verses, full-throated as robins at dawn.

Up on the stage, an elderly woman in blocky black shoes pounded away on a piano. One of the teachers, a horse-faced man with a shock of white hair, handed Lars a piece of sheet music and pointed out where he could join in.

> Arise, arise, mighty children of the North
> The time has come to cast off your baby ways
> No more the cup and ball, the Jacob's ladder, the gaily painted ball
> The time has come for every boy and girl
> To spurn the loathsome toy
> And stride forth in strength and joy
> We trample these baubles in the mire
> We burn them in the raging pyre.

Lars found all of this astonishing. Was it a joke? A song about going to war against toys? It was preposterous. The pianist rocked back and forth on her bench, eyes closed, fingers flying up and down the keyboard.

Brow furrowed, Lars stared down at the words, making no attempt to sing. More than anything he wanted to escape, to go running home, but the auditorium was too closely packed for him to even move.

A girl on the far side of the room was watching him. She was small, with dark hair and dark, bold eyes, and it was clear that she was amused by him.

Embarrassed, he stared down again at the sheet music.

He saved us from the fire and he saved us from the ice
He saved us from the howling storm and spewing lava
Our foolish trinkets are finally banished
We march with him against the foe
We root out those who would betray him
And run them through with spear and harpoon
Every enemy we gladly slay
Until this frozen land
Will be truly his again.

The pianist ended the anthem with a flourish, throwing both arms in the air, and all the students broke out in a cheer. "Wolfpaw! Wolfpaw! Wolfpaw!"

Was there no end to strangeness? Lars was deeply rattled by what he'd seen and needed someone to explain it all to him. The problem was that he didn't know anyone unless he counted Pytor, who didn't seem like a brilliant choice.

But in the end he couldn't come up with anyone better. After school let out, he hung around the flagpole for a good half hour, watching his classmates zoom off on their sleds before Pytor finally came sauntering out of Beluga Hall.

Pytor saw Lars standing there but did his best to ignore him, bending down to strap on his snowshoes. Lars was in no mood to be brushed off. He raised a hand in greeting, called out, and when there was no response, ambled down the slope.

"Which way you headed?" Lars asked.

Pytor, without enthusiasm, pointed to the bluff. The last thing anyone wanted was to get stuck with some needy new kid.

"I'm going that way too," Lars said. "Mind if I go with you?"

Pytor's swollen eye looked worse than it had the day before. It had taken on color, purples and reds and yellows. "Sure," Pytor said. "Why not?"

They set off together, neither of the boys speaking for the first five minutes. Lars did his best to keep up, but he was on foot and Pytor had snowshoes, which made it difficult. Pytor finally took pity on him, stopping to fiddle with the straps of his backpack near Woolly Mammoth Glacier, giving Lars a chance to catch up.

"I turn off here," Pytor said.

"Well, thanks. I'll see you tomorrow then, I guess."

"How's it all going?"

"What's that?"

"School."

"All right, I suppose. It's a little confusing."

"How do you mean?"

A fog bank rolled in off the ocean, obliterating everything. Seals barked far below.

"Well, you know . . . like that song?"

"What about it?"

"You sing that every day?"

"Not every day. Once a week, usually."

"You don't think it's weird?"

"Not particularly."

"But the whole point of it seems to be that toys are banned here."

"You got it."

"But why would that be?"

"Oh, come on. Think about it for a minute. Toys are dangerous."

"Who told you that?"

For a second Lars thought Pytor was about to hit him. "Everybody knows it. You can poke your eye out. You can swallow one of those things and die. There was this girl? Somebody gave her a toy guillotine and she cut off both her thumbs."

Lars decided it would be prudent not to argue. "And what happens if they catch you with one?"

"They'll kidnap you, and you'll never see your family again."

"Oh my gosh."

Pytor spit between his buck teeth. This new boy was odd indeed. "Did you ever have toys?"

"Sure, lots of them. Every kid I knew did."

"Like what?"

"Little metal soldiers. Hoops and sticks. I got a bull-roarer once."

"And nothing bad ever happened?"

"Losing them. That was bad."

It took Pytor some time to digest all this. A dog had been following them for a half-mile, drifting in and out of the fog. Pytor called out and it came loping up. Pytor got down on one knee, took a piece of jerky from his pocket, and held it out in his palm. The dog wagged its tail, came crawling up on its belly, and snapped up the scrap of meat in two quick bites.

"Can I ask you one other thing?" Lars said. The enveloping fog was like an icy sponge pressed against his cheek.

"Of course?"

"Yesterday I went into the other lunch room by mistake and there were all these older kids, down on their knees, taking this stuff."

"Skarn-liver oil."

"What?"

"Skarn-liver oil." Pytor was getting exasperated, having to explain everything. "The village wouldn't even exist without it."

"But it looks as if it tastes terrible."

"And it tastes even worse than it looks." Pytor rose to his feet and shoved the dog away. "But it's all about getting them in shape."

"In shape for what?"

"Going to work in old Mayor Wolfpaw's factory."

"It looked as if it was making them sick."

"It does that. People get the shakes, some have fits. A lot of them walk around like zombies for a while. But that's the price you have to pay for getting hired around here."

Lars gave him a long look. He wasn't sure how much of what Pytor was telling him he should believe. This was, after all, a kid who didn't know how to multiply.

"But, hey," Pytor said, "you don't have to worry. You're twelve, right? They don't start you on that stuff until you're thirteen."

Lars was haunted by what was going on in the other lunch room. Nearly every day he would try to sneak down the hallway and peek in the window to see what he could see. He was too far away to make out much more that a row of bowed heads: the platter of rich, golden oil held by a teacher; a girl staggering to her feet, shuddering like a beheaded chicken in its last throes; a heavy-lidded boy, drifting off, his head bobbing from time to time into his soup.

Walking between classes, Lars would scrutinize the older students. Perhaps it was just his imagination, but it seemed to him that they were all deeply sad, as if they were carrying a terrible weight, as if the light had gone out in them.

One day he walked into the bathroom after lunch to find an older boy named Eric bent over a sink. Eric wiped his upper lip and every few seconds he would shudder.

"Are you all right?" Lars asked.

"No." Eric's voice was mournful. He was enormous and looked like a nauseated walrus. "I'm not all right. I'll never be all right." A tear rolled down a fat cheek. "But thanks for asking."

For nearly a week Lars resisted telling his mother and Nanu anything about what was happening at school. But after a long and particularly dispiriting day, it all came spilling out.

Lars and his mother were washing dishes and Nanu was lying down on the sofa, taking her customary after-dinner nap (because of her problems with gas, twenty minutes of rest and quiet belching was necessary for her to have a reasonably tranquil evening).

Lars's conversation with his mother had started innocently enough. She'd been asking about his class schedule, but when she asked him about how they usually started the day, he let something slip about having to sing this ridiculous song.

Of course she wanted to know what ridiculous song that was and when he got evasive, she pressed all the harder. Lars had never been a good liar, and he ended up telling her everything.

Before he was halfway done, Nanu was sitting upright on the sofa. Both women were outraged. Toys being banned? Children being forced to drink some foul oil that gave them fits?

"This is too bizarre," Nanu said. "We've got to get out of this place."

Lars's mother snapped back like a shot. "There is no way out of this place, remember?"

His mother was not in a good mood. For over a week she'd been out every day looking for work, offering her services as a seamstress, a shoveler of snow, a tender of small children, and found no takers.

"But he does need to stop going to that school," she said.

Nanu stumbled out of a tangle of quilts. "He's not going to stop going to that school!" Nanu said. She let loose an enormous belch.

"But I'll tell you what does need to happen. I'm going to that school tomorrow and give that schoolmaster a piece of my mind!"

"No-o-o!" Lars moaned.

The two women ignored him. "I'm sorry," his mother said. "If anyone's going in to see that schoolmaster tomorrow, it's going to be me."

Lars slapped his wet towel down on the counter to get their attention. "Please!" he shouted. "I don't need anyone doing anything! You're only going to make things worse."

"Worse?" Nanu said. "I don't see how it could be any worse than it already is. We are living in a land of buffoons."

Back and forth they went, for more than an hour. Things got so heated that two lemmings, frightened out of their nest by all the noise, scampered along the rafters. Nanu threw a pillow, but a truce was finally agreed upon. Both Nanu and Lars's mother promised that they wouldn't go in to see Mr. Smorgas for at least a week. In return, Lars promised to be honest with them and they would all see how it went.

That night when he went to bed, Lars wondered if he was going to be able to take either of them at their word.

Just as Lars feared, the truce did not hold. The next morning as he passed between classes, he heard angry voices coming from Mr. Smorgas's office. One of those voices was his mother's.

Making it all the worse was that everyone in the small crowd gathered outside the door seemed to know it was her as well.

Some looked back at him, smirking. Lars felt his face turn beet red. Arkady's girlfriend pressed a finger to her lips, her eyes dancing with delight.

What greater humiliation could there be for a twelve-year-old than to be seen as a mama's boy? Within twenty-four hours the whole school was talking.

The teasing, once it began, was ruthless. He was called a crybaby, a delicate flower, a goody-goody two-shoes, a snotface taking refuge behind his mother's skirts. One of his classmates had overheard his mother saying they were all a bunch of barbarians, whatever that was, and no one was going to let that pass. "We're not good enough for you, is that it? Well, isn't that just your tough luck."

The only ones to offer Lars anything like relief were the older students. They were too befogged to understand what had happened or to feel insulted, and they didn't tease him, though on occasion he would catch them looking over at him with soft, puzzled eyes.

Lars's mother had heard a rumor that some of the fishermen needed their nets mended. But when she trekked down to the village pier to investigate, there turned out to be nothing to it, unless she was willing to mend nets for free.

Just getting to the village had taken an hour-long slog through bitter cold. This was followed by an hour of fruitless bickering, standing on the pier with a cutting wind picking up off the ocean. By the time she and the fishermen parted company, she was chilled to the bone.

The docks were deathly still. After the demise of whaling more than a century before, the docks had become a ghost town. The remnants of three sunken ships tilted out of the ice, and most of the piers had been ransacked for firewood. The nearby streets were filled with abandoned warehouses, slaughterhouses, taverns, and boarded-up hotels.

She used her ski poles to propel her up one of the alleyways. Stopping to catch her breath, she looked up and saw Mayor Wolfpaw on his sled at the intersection of the next street, thirty yards beyond her. The sight of him gave her a start. It was as if he had appeared out of nowhere, materialized out of the frigid air. A lantern hung from one of the handlebars of his sled. Lit from below, his scarred face might have been mistaken for the face of a fiend.

He pulled the team of dogs around, guided them down the alleyway, and yanked them to a shuddering stop.

"You look awfully cold," he said.

"I am."

"Can I give you a ride home?"

"No, I'm fine, really."

He scrutinized her. The tips of his mustache were frosted with ice. "I'm not so sure about that. I think we need to get you warm. I've got the keys to some of these warehouses. Let me open one of them, and we'll see if we can get a fire going."

"No, please, that's not necessary."

He put a hand up; he wasn't about to hear any more arguments. He hopped off his sled, grabbed his lantern, and took a moment to unlock the nearest of the buildings. He put his shoulder to the door. It groaned open. He gestured for her to enter.

The wind battered the back of her parka. How could she possibly say no? She slipped out of her skis.

The warehouse was enormous. It was empty, except for a pile of rusted traps in the corner and a half dozen racks of furs, fox and wolf, musk ox and bear. The heads of some of them lolled over the edges of their shelves, with teeth bared and ragged holes where eyes should have been.

Hundred-foot-tall shadows swayed above them as the mayor swung his lantern, searching for firewood in the far reaches of the building. He expertly arranged a dozen sticks into a small cast-iron stove and added a handful of dried lichen he'd found in a crate. She stood watching, still as a rabbit.

"So what in Heaven's name could have brought you down here?" he said.

"I heard there might be a job mending nets."

"And was there?"

"No." She folded her arms across her chest. The chills had gotten worse. It felt as if mice were racing up and down inside her skin. Leaning over the stove, Wolfpaw struck two pieces of flint together, again and again. A spark finally caught. The lichen flared and flames rose quickly.

"Here," he said. He took her hand and pulled her closer to the stove. "I must say, I admire your spunk. It sounds as if you must have tried everybody."

She clenched and unclenched her stiff fingers over the fire. They had begun to thaw. As wary as she was of him, she had to admit there was something comforting in being taken care of by a competent man. It had been a long time. He brushed her shoulder as he moved to poke two more slabs of wood into the stove.

"But it's hard for me not to feel a little humiliated."

She gave him a quick look, caught off-guard. "What do you mean?"

"Oh, come on, now. Everyone knows I'm the one you need to see if you want work. The fact that you seem to be boycotting me has the whole village talking. Some might find that insulting."

She felt the color rush to her face. "That was not my intention."

High up in the rafters, the wind moaned. For the first time she was afraid. The thought came to her that he could lock her up in here forever if he chose.

The fire was roaring now. Wolfpaw slid the metal lid over the flames. "I hear you've been to see the schoolmaster."

"And that is why you are here?"

"In part."

"Is there some problem with that?"

"No, not really. You just don't want to get the reputation as a malcontent. If I may, let me tell you something for your own good. Do not spit in people's faces. Mine or anyone else's. The schoolmaster is terribly sensitive. If you and your son are going to survive here, you're going to have to deal with things that are not altogether to your liking. I'd hate for you to get off to a bad start." The threat behind his words was unmistakeable. "Let me see those fingers."

She held out her hands and he examined them. He turned them over and ran his thumbs over her palms. She saw, for the first time, how things were here. "It looks as if you're going to be all right."

"Thank you," she said. "So do you still have openings?"

"One or two," he said.

"I would be honored if you would find a place for me."

His eyes widened in surprise and then he broke out in a grin. "Well, good," he said, "good. I am so pleased. It will be nice to have a person with a little backbone working for me. Most of the people I employ are such grovelers. And if it's all right to say, I find you very beautiful. I'm sorry, I'm embarrassing you."

He went to the rack and, after a moment, yanked a pair of ragged fox pelts from one of the piles. He draped them around her shoulders and then pulled them tightly under her chin with certain solemnity, as if it was some sort of coronation.

"Now this should keep you warm. Let's get you home."

Before she entered the house, Lars's mother removed the two fox pelts, balled them up, and tucked them under her arm.

Opening the door, the rush of warm air felt like a blessing. It was mid-afternoon, and Lars was home from school early. He was helping Nanu fix dinner.

Nanu peeked over her shoulder. "Oh, good. We were starting to get worried. Did those fishermen have any work for you?"

"Nothing I would want," Lars's mother said. As she moved across the room, she let the balled-up fox pelts slip out from under her arm and fall to the sofa. But if she'd hoped this would go undetected, she was sadly mistaken.

"What's this?" Nanu said.

"Oh, these? I ran into Mayor Wolfpaw and he gave me these to keep me warm."

Nanu went to investigate. She picked up the two pelts and shook them out to have a better look. "To keep you warm? I'll bet *he* wanted to keep you warm."

It was not the best way to start a conversation. Lars, sawing away at a stale loaf of bread on the counter, chose not to raise his head.

"So you must have spoken to him?" Nanu said.

"I did."

"About what?"

"He offered me a job." The stew that Nanu had made for supper cooled in the sink. Lars's mother dipped a finger in and had a taste.

"And what did you say?"

Lars's mother made no attempt to soften the blow. "I accepted."

Nanu was incredulous. "Good Lord!" She threw the fox pelts back on the sofa. "Have you lost your mind? He murdered his two step-brothers and who knows what else. The man is a monster."

"So they say."

"And you know better?"

Lars's mother was still for a second. She had seen at least a glimmer of kindness in the mayor. But how could she ever explain? "There is more to him that you think."

Nanu's nostrils flared with indignation. "No doubt there is. But you know what they say about dancing with the devil . . . "

Lar's mother's jaw tightened with anger. "If you're so all-knowing, how did we end up here? The mayor's factory is the only place to work, and I'm not going to let us starve. End of discussion."

She went to the closet and hung up her parka and hat. Nanu picked up the two pelts from the sofa. Lars set down his bread knife, poised to intervene.

His mother's back was turned as she bent to pull off her mukluks.

What happened next happened so fast there was no time for Lars to do anything. Nanu scuttled to the stove, quick as a rat running off with a piece of cheese. She used the metal prong to pry the metal top loose, sent it clattering to the floor, then stuffed the pelts into the flames.

Lars and his mother both pounced on her, but the damage was done. Smoke began to fill the room. Throwing her arms around Nanu, Lars's mother steered her out of harm's way. Lars pulled the fox pelts out of the stove, threw them on the floor and began to stamp on them.

"Nanu, Nanu, what is wrong with you?" Lars's mother said.

"Filth!" Nanu cried, "filth!" Nanu writhed in her daughter-in-law's arms. "This will not end well. I know these things." She finally wriggled free and hurried out of the room, weeping.

Lars and his mother glanced at one another, shaken and ashamed. He went back to doing his little dance on the smoldering pelts. They weren't the easiest things to put out. Every time he thought he'd done it, he would spot another spark glowing deep in the fur.

"Lars, I had no choice," his mother said.

"I know," he said. "But you know how Nanu can be. Do you want me to throw these outside?"

"I think so. I can't imagine that they'd be of any use to anyone."

Lars's mother going to work for the mayor was a breach that was not going to be easily mended. But after that terrible night, they didn't argue about it again. Nanu didn't have the heart for it.

She was failing. As the weeks passed, she ate less and less, slipping her meager portions onto Lars's plate when he wasn't looking. Whether she admitted it or not, she blamed herself for the fix they were in. She was physically worn down, and the trek north had been brutal.

As much as she tried to help with the repairs on the house, she quickly found herself exhausted and in need of a nap. All of her life she had needed to feel she was useful. When she lived in the forest, it had been her job to feed the chickens, milk the cow, weed the garden, make breakfast for Lars's father before the rest of them were awake. But in the north, there were no chickens, no cow, no gardens, and Lars's father had been dead for three months. On top of all that, her daughter-in-law was barely speaking to her.

The teasing at school continued on relentlessly, with only Pytor to defend him. Making it even worse, Arkady had taken it into his head to make Lars as miserable as possible. He would accidentally-on-purpose ram into Lars in the hallway. He would fix him with murderous stares in math class. Once, in the lunch room, he stuck out his foot as Lars passed and sent Lars cartwheeling through the air and spraying the closest three tables with soup.

Worst of all was recess. Arkady had shamed Lars into joining the whale ball games, which presented Arkady with the opportunity to give Lars a daily drubbing.

Lars tried to say no. He tried a million excuses—that he'd never played before, that he had a sprained ankle, that surely they could find somebody better. He tried to weasel out of it by saying he didn't know the rules, but there were no rules. People were playing with broken noses and dislocated elbows.

Arkady was merciless. He would knock Lars down a half dozen times in an hour and jab him in the kidneys when everyone was thrashing about in a dog-pile. He would hunt him down no matter how cunningly Lars tried to hide himself on the edge of skirmishes.

Sometimes when Arkady intercepted a pass he would come thundering across the field, setting his sights on Lars. He would bellow like a moose and raise the inflated whale bladder over his head. Lars would run for his life with Arkady in hot pursuit. When Lars swerved to the right, Arkady swerved to the right. When Lars swerved to the left, Arkady did not miss a step.

When Arkady finally threw the whale ball, Lars was sometimes able to dodge out of the way, but about half the time the ball caught him in the back of the knees and toppled him to the ground, or hit him on the shoulder and sent him reeling.

But no matter the outcome, everyone burst out laughing—the players on the field and the girls in the bleachers. They seemed to find Arkady's bullying of Lars the most hilarious thing they'd ever seen, comedy of the highest order.

To his great surprise, the one person who ever came over to check on him after he'd been flattened by one of Arkady's most brutal throws was Miko. It happened on a Wednesday, on Lars's third week of school.

All the other players had run down to the far end of the field. She had come down from the bleachers and was peering at him, her hands on her knees. "Are you all right?" she said.

"I guess."

"Why did you move here?"

"Because my father died. We had to go somewhere."

"That was pretty stupid," she said. "Do you think I'm cute?"

"Kinda."

"Most people think I'm cute. But they're afraid to tell me. Because Arkady is my boyfriend and they're scared of getting beaten up. Bye."

Several nights later a blizzard moved in for several hours, and the next day the ceiling in Mr. Smorgas's office collapsed, burying the schoolmaster, deep in his mid-morning nap, in an avalanche of fresh snow. If it hadn't been for the heroic actions of the cooks, who quickly found shovels and set frantically to work, Mr. Smorgas would have been entombed forever, frozen in repose on his couch, like the pharaohs in their pyramids.

It took no more than three or four minutes to dig him out, sputtering and confused, but the school was in such an uproar of excitement there was no choice but to cancel classes for the rest of the day to make repairs and tend to the hysterical schoolmaster. This announcement, coming just before lunch, was greeted by universal cheering.

Lars trudged home through the new drifts as the pink glow of midday light first appeared on the horizon. He was looking forward to telling Nanu the news, but when he got home, there was no sign of her.

He went from room to room, calling out her name, then went to the front door and stared at the welter of tracks in the fresh snow. There were his mother's tracks, made as she set off to work, and there were his own, made as he went to school and came back. But there was a third set as well, circling back behind the house and heading out toward the sea.

This was not the first time she'd gone wandering off on her own. Just the week before he'd found her up on the ridge with no idea how she'd gotten up there.

Lars strode quickly, and then began to run, leaping from bootheel to bootheel, fearing disaster. But as he came over a gentle rise he saw her sitting primly in a chair at the edge of the cliff. Her hands were in her lap, palms up, and she was singing a song in a language he'd never heard before.

He approached carefully, wary of frightening her. She was in her best clothes—black dress, black shawl, boxy fur hat, and deerskin boots. She looked a little like an old country woman waiting for a wagon to take her to church.

"Nanu?"

She stopped singing. It was several more seconds before she turned to see him.

"Lars, what are you doing here?"

"They let us out early. But what are you doing?"

"Just taking a little air."

"I don't think so, Nanu."

She rubbed at the corners of her mouth. For the first time he saw the rune stones planted in a circle around her, fifteen feet out. "I am of no use to anyone."

"That's not true." Far out there were breaks in the sea ice, patches of open water.

"It is true. And you know it. People get old. There comes a time for everyone." Lars chose not to argue. Neither had forgotten that it had only been two days since she'd forgotten to put the lid on the stove and nearly burned the house down. "I know I have much to answer for. If it hadn't been for me, you would still be living in Sweden, going to school with your friends . . . I know that I have brought ruin to this family."

"It's really cold out here, Nanu. Let's go back inside. I'll make you a cup of tea."

She wasn't about to let him interrupt her. "But I swear to you, every story that was passed down from my great-grandfather to my grandfather to my father to me, was about how grand this place was, about how glorious the summers were, how they put the summers in Sweden to shame, how the sun would be up nearly twenty-four hours straight and the boats would come in with full nets and the children would search for bird eggs in the cliffs and sometimes you could see as many as a dozen spouting whales. My father told me stories about how the fires would crackle and pop in the giant fireplaces, about the spoons carved of ivory walrus tusks and the soft furs they would sleep under at night. . . ."

Lars stared down the cliffside. Four or five beggars moved slowly along the shore.

"You don't think they were just making it all up?" Lars said.

"They were not the kind of men who lied. Something terrible happened here. I know what they say. I know they say it was the volcano, but no volcano could have done this. And no one will talk about it."

"Okay, Nanu, that's enough. Here."

He stepped in front of her with his hands extended, insisting, and she finally took them and let him pull her up. They made their way back to the house, Lars lugging the chair with one arm and steadying his grandmother with the other. She made no reference to the circle of rune stones.

When they stopped at the front gate she peered at him intently for a long time.

"What?" Lars said.

"I remember when you were three," she said. "You had a pony and you didn't want anyone else to ride it."

"I remember, Nanu."

"And when you were six, you told the teacher it was your birthday when it wasn't, just so everyone would sing to you and you would get candy."

"I know."

For the first time it occurred to him that she'd been on the verge of doing something unthinkable.

Her gaze broke. She turned away, pulling down the flaps on her fur hat. "Look, Lars."

He pivoted. Where he had been quite sure there had been nothing, there was now something, far out at sea: an iceberg glowing in the failing light, large as a cathedral.

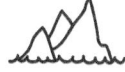

Sometimes he would see things on his way home. One day he spied a boy throwing a snowball up in the air and running to catch it, over and over. Another day he saw a boy spinning an axe on a rock pile as if he was trying to make it balance. On a third day he watched two girls on a porch, rocking pieces of firewood in their arms, cooing and talking baby talk.

But the most bizarre thing he saw was on the afternoon of the great wind, when he spotted a boy standing alone on a promontory above the sea. The boy had a cord tied around what looked like a ratty foxpelt. Lars couldn't figure our what he was doing at first. The boy would run directly into the wind, dragging the pelt behind him. Every now and then he would tug at it, as if he hoped the wind would catch it, and every now and then it did, lifting the madly flapping fox pelt a few feet into the air before sending it nosediving back into the snow.

One morning after Reindeer Husbandry class, Lars was shoveling manure out of the stalls when Miko appeared out of nowhere.

"You ever have a girlfriend?" she asked

"Not really."

"You want one?"

"I don't know."

"Do you like to flirt?"

"I guess so."

"I like to flirt, but nobody's going to flirt with me as long as I'm with the big bozo."

TEN

ne afternoon Lars got home early from school to find the front door ajar. His heart dropped. He gave the icy doorknob a shove. The only light on in the house was an oil lamp on the kitchen table, and at first all he could make out was a shadowy figure rummaging at the counter.

"Nanu?" he said.

She whirled around, as if she'd been caught doing something she shouldn't. She was bundled up in coat and scarves, her fur hat pulled down to her eyebrows.

"Where do you think you're going?" he said. She started at him dumbly for several seconds as if she hadn't heard the question.

"I'm going to feed the birds."

"Birds? But there are no birds. They've all gone south for the winter."

"Not all of them. I heard them when I got up. They were making a terrible racket. If I don't do something, they'll all be dead by morning." She tightened the drawstrings of a small leather bag and tucked it inside her coat. Wind sighed in the chimney.

"Well, let me go with you then," he said.

She frowned, retrieving her crutch from its hook on the wall. "You don't need to go with me," she said. "I won't be gone long. You should just stay and warm yourself by the stove."

"I'm not going to let you go by yourself," he said. Nanu raised a skeptical eyebrow. "I'm not, Nanu."

"All right then. Suit yourself."

Walking with Nanu was a major operation. She clung to his arm as they made their way outside, then inched their way past the snow wall and down the slope. The cliffs were barely visible in the fog.

The iceberg that had been drifting closer and closer for the past several days was now so near to shore it almost seemed as if he could reach out and touch it. Until now, the biggest thing Lars had ever seen was Lord Borland's mansion, but this was a hundred times as big as that. It looked like a giant's castle, with towers of blue ice and curving archways.

When they stopped to rest, Nanu stared at it intently, as if searching for some sign. It was making grinding sounds on the shore. The grip on Lars's arm tightened.

"Are you okay?" Lars asked.

"I'm fine."

"Nanu, I haven't heard anything. I'll bet those birds have gone to bed for the night. I think we should probably go back." On the hill behind them, the stone cairns kept appearing and disappearing in the fog like ghosts.

"But we can't just leave them. They'll all starve."

A hoarse cry pierced the air. Nanu spun around, her eyes suddenly bright. She pointed up at the high cliffs. "Did you hear that? What did I tell you? You hold this."

She handed him her crutch and fumbled around inside her coat. "Ahh! Here we go!" She tugged out her bag, undid the drawstrings, and began to strew handfuls of seeds onto the snow around her. Her balance wasn't the best, but when Lars reached out to steady her, she slapped his hand away. She hobbled about, chuckling, throwing with an easy, practiced motion, as if she was feeding her chickens back in the forest.

Lars didn't have the heart to interfere. She made two complete circles before she ran out of seeds. Digging down in the bottom of her bag, she screwed up her face.

"Oof-dah!" she said. "This old mind of mine . . . Lars, I need you to do something for me. I cut up all these apple slices. I must have left them sitting out on the counter. Could you run back and get them for me?"

"But Nanu, don't you think . . . "

"The birds just love them. And don't worry about me. I'll sit right here. I won't budge."

Lars could hear boulders clicking under the dark stretches of open water. "You promise?"

She clutched his sleeve and lowered herself cross-legged in the snow. "I promise." She took the crutch from him and set it across her lap.

"I'll be quick," he said.

She reached up to squeeze his finger and then pulled him down until their faces were no more than six inches apart. He could see the trouble in her eyes.

"Lars . . . " she said.

"What?"

"I have two things I want to say to you." Spires of ice floated in the mist above them "First of all, I'm sorry about making things so hard for your mother."

"You haven't made it hard."

"No, I have, I have. But the other thing . . . " She adjusted her fur hat with her free hand. "The world is so much bigger than you think. You can't even imagine. And it's going to be there for you. All of it."

The situation was awkward, his stooping down, her holding him there. He wanted to straighten up, but she wouldn't let him. She gave his face another quick pat.

"You go on now."

He ran back up the slope, and when he got to the house he looked back, just to be sure she hadn't moved. She was still there, sitting in a ragged circle of seeds, still poking around in her leather bag. She waved, and he waved back.

When he went inside he couldn't find the apple slices. They weren't on the counter and they weren't in any of the cupboards or the bushel baskets in the hallway. The only thing he found was the paring knife, sitting on the cutting board. All he could do was shake his head. It was so much like her these days, thinking she'd done something when she hadn't.

He went to the door and pulled his earflaps down tight before he stepped outside, but as soon as he did, an arctic gust caught him full in the face. He put an arm up to protect himself from the wind and plodded blindly down the slope, not looking up until he heard a series of sharp caws.

Bewildered, he stared at the circle of seeds fifty yards ahead of him. The crutch lay in the snow and there were three huge black birds waddling about pecking at the black specks, but there was no Nanu.

Lars ran down the hill, calling out. The birds ran and then took flight. When he came to the spot where he had left Nanu, he found her footprints. He followed them down to the edge of the sea. He stared at the iceberg towering over him and floating slowly away. The black birds cried out above him, soaring in and out of the fog.

ELEVEN

or two days Lars, his mother, and Pytor searched the coast-line for Nanu. On the second day they were joined by a handful of Mayor Wolfpaw's deputies, but no trace of Nanu was found. Had she fallen into the narrow stretch of freezing water and drowned? Had she become disoriented, wandered off, and been attacked by a polar bear?

Taya Kerensky was convinced that Nanu had done what all the old ones did. "She put herself out on that iceberg and floated away. She hated being a burden to the two of you. Give her credit. There aren't many people who have the backbone to do what she did. I know it sounds harsh, but with one less mouth to feed, it will make things easier. Mark my words."

But it didn't make things easier. For Lars's mother, it was fiercely hard. They had not ended on good terms.

They shut up Nanu's bedroom to save on heat, but one afternoon when Lars came home from school, he found the door ajar. He peeked in and found his mother standing by the window, holding Nanu's baggy blue sweater to her mouth, weeping.

Clothes were piled high on the bed. She'd been emptying the closet, folding Nanu's things and setting them in one of the large cedar chests. The room was icy cold, the air still rich with the smell of pipe smoke.

"Mom?" Lars said.

She turned, came to him, and held him tight. "I'm just so sorry, Lars. I know how much she loved you and how much you loved her. And though it scarcely ended well between the two of us, I loved her too. In my way."

The Reindeer Husbandry teacher had been called unexpectedly to the office, leaving his class unattended, which was never a good idea.

The reindeer were out on the playing field, pawing their way through the snow for lichen, and the students were supposed to be tending them, though not much tending was going on.

A snowball fight had broken out, with kids running and ducking in every direction. Some of the girls were making snow angels, and some of the boys had started a snowman. Lars stood alone, watching a frisky pair of calves chase one another. Twenty feet off, Miko sat on the bottom step of the bleachers, shaking ice crystals out of a mitten, paying Lars no mind.

The day was warm, warmer than it had been for months, only ten degrees or so below freezing, and it had started to snow, huge wet flakes. It felt like a holiday.

Lars was whistling for the two calves when a snowball splattered on the back of his neck. It had been thrown hard and momentarily buckled his knees.

Stunned, Lars turned and saw a gleeful Roope being congratulated by his friends.

"Hey, crybaby," Roope shouted. "Better watch your head!"

"Hey, bully boy, why don't you go pick on somebody your own size!"

For a second Lars was bewildered, unsure where the second voice had come from. He glanced over his shoulder and spied Miko bending low to pack a snowball. It took her no time at all. She charged at Roope, her snowball held high, and Roope and his friends ran off, laughing. Her throw landed ten feet short of its mark.

Lars rubbed at the back of his neck. He had to give Roope credit. He had quite an arm; the spot Roope had hit still smarted.

Spanking her hands together, Miko approached. "Thank you," Lars said.

"Don't mention it," she said. "But one day you're going to have to learn how to stick up for yourself."

"I guess so."

"No, seriously."

When she swept some of the snow out of the hood of his parka, her fingertips brushed his cheek. "I'm sorry about your grandmother," she said.

"Mmm," he said.

"You've had a lot of bad luck."

"Yes." Lars saw that the teacher had just emerged from the school. The reindeer were scattered all across the playing field.

"Some people just do. It's not really fair."

She was the most beautiful girl at school and wasn't afraid of saying so. She was the leader of a small army of girls and always said what she thought. She had once accused her best friend Annuchka of having the brains of a sandwich, and yet was capable of moments of kindness. There was a rumor that her father had been a harpoonist in the South Seas. She claimed to speak Japanese, though no one had ever heard her. Every day she wore a wide orange belt with a design of chrysanthemums and bamboo.

Lars had never seen so many beards. Most of the male cooks and teachers had them, and all of the fishermen and trappers Lars would run across in the village. No doubt these beards were a great protection from the cold, but it also seemed that they were a matter of some pride.

Some came all the way up to the top of the cheekbones so that little was visible of the face except for the eyes. Some flared out like whisk brooms. Some were combed out till they glistened. Others were wild and untamed and glittered with bits of ice.

Some of the older boys at school were starting to grow them as well—a bit of peach fuzz on the upper lip or a few hairs sprouting at the tip of the chin. Lars's face, however, was as soft and smooth as a baby's bottom. All these men in beards were not, by and large, enviable men, but Lars did envy them their facial hair. Would he ever, he wondered, have a beard to match theirs? He couldn't imagine it.

It wasn't long before Mayor Wolfpaw was giving Lars's mother a ride home every afternoon after work, and not much longer after that she began to invite him in for tea.

If Nanu had been there, this bit of flirtation would not have been possible. But Nanu was not there. The only other person there, on most days, was Lars, back from school. This created some awkwardness, but the mayor had never been deterred by awkwardness.

Lars knew perfectly well what the mayor's intentions were and watched him like a hawk. The mayor, in turn, behaved impeccably, and in time persuaded Lars to have a game of checkers with him. The mayor played well, making furtive goo-goo eyes with Lars's mother behind the boy's back.

The mayor explained what Lars's mother's job was (she was keeping his books up to date), the history of the factory, and its importance to the village.

It was a business, plain and simple, despite all the rumors, he said, and a prosperous one as well. Once a year he and his deputies loaded a thousand jugs of skarn-liver oil onto fifty sleds and made the hair-raising trip through the mountains to the capitals of northern Europe. The oil would be sold at increasingly extraordinary prices before being distributed to schoolchildren far and wide.

Wolfpaw was eloquent. Wolfpaw was persuasive. In the end, Lars knew there was much he wasn't being told. He had to trust his eyes. He'd seen the effect the skarn-liver oil was having on his schoolmates, and no one was going to be able to convince him that it only had to do with business.

One afternoon, after winning three games of checkers in a row, Mayor Wolfpaw said, "You know what I think needs to happen, Lars? I think you need to come to the factory and let me show you around."

Lars looked up, astonished. "No, that's all right," he said. "I don't want to put you to any trouble."

"It wouldn't be any trouble at all," the mayor said. Leaning over the table, he stacked the checkers into a wooden box. "And if you could just see for yourself how it works, it might make a lot more sense to you." Lantern light gleamed on the squiggly scars up his neck, slick as the slimy trails of snails.

"Oh, I don't think he needs to do that," his mother said. She stood over them with a fresh plate of gingersnaps. "It's not the most pleasant of places."

"Maybe not," the mayor said. "But he should find it interesting. How about tomorrow afternoon?"

As Lars glided over the top of the ridge, he could see the factory perched on towering cliffs. At first it seemed like nothing more than a long dark bruise set against a moonlit sky, but after a dozen slow, cautious strides forward, he could see that it was a series of buildings wreathed in low-hanging, foul-smelling smoke.

Most of the buildings were squat, ramshackle affairs, but one nearly three stories high stood out from the others. In front of this main building was a gathering of men and dogsleds.

Mayor Wolfpaw was the man in charge, reaching down into the toolbox on the back of his sled to retrieve and distribute a pair of axes, some planks, a coil of rope, a mallet, a saw, and what looked like a sack of nails.

Once the equipment was handed out, the workers leapt on the runners of their sleds and took off in the direction of the cliffs. The mayor watched them speed away, and then, turning, spied Lars standing on top of the ridge.

"Lars!" he shouted. "I'm so happy you came!" A great clatter rose from inside the main building, nearly drowning out his voice. "Get down here, young man! Nothing to be afraid of!"

As Lars glided down the slope, the stench from inside the factory grew so strong he had to cover his nose. The mayor strode to greet him, slapped an arm around his shoulders, and gave him a shake.

"Come on, son, let's go have a look."

Wolfpaw waited while Lars took off his skis, then slammed the door of the factory open, took the boy by the arm, and led him in.

Lars wasn't sure what hit him first: the wall of noise or the rolling cloud of stinging mist. His smarting eyes flooded with tears.

For a moment it was impossible to tell what he was looking at, but once he wiped his tears away, he could make out several conveyor belts snaking across the floor, all powered by masked men madly pedaling bicycles. The most repulsive fish Lars had ever seen—pure white, slimy as eels, and equipped with lethal-looking fangs—tumbled out of a chute only to be snatched by a team of masked women who slit them neatly with knives. The skarn were then flipped onto a conveyor belt where a second team of masked women plucked out their livers.

The livers were tossed onto a second conveyor belt that delivered them to Team Number Three. The job of Team Number Three was to squeeze the livers and dribble the oil into small vials without spilling a drop. Once the vials were corked they were whisked away so they could first be tucked into small, box-like containers, twelve vials per container, and then stacked into larger crates.

Lars scanned the building, looking for his mother, and finally spotted her on a second-floor balcony. She bent over a desk, entering figures in an enormous, frayed ledger; the figures were being recited to her by a jittery, high-waisted man sifting through a sheaf of papers.

Lars raised a hand in greeting. His mother finally looked up, saw him, and returned the gesture. She didn't look at all happy to see him. She rose, traipsed down the stairs, and disappeared in a rabbit warren of snuggeries at the back of the first floor.

The floor was slick with oil and fish guts. Scarcely older than Lars, several dull-eyed boys in blood-stained coats roamed up and down with brooms, sweeping the offal down rusted drains. Large men with tin badges pinned to bulky coats patrolled a series of ramps, keeping their eyes on the workers like jailers keeping tabs on prisoners. Stout billy clubs swung at their sides.

The din was three times as loud as it had been when Lars was outside. To Lars's left, knives flashed. To his right, women plucked the bloody livers out of the skarn as if they were plucking the heads off flowers. Beyond the conveyor belts was a towering metal door secured by enormous locks. The door looked as if it must weigh a ton or more and was stamped with an emblem of twining antlers.

The speed and intensity of all the activity was daunting. The only lulls came when the cyclists began to tire and the conveyor belts slowed. This was remedied by a horn that would sound, riling up two cages of puffins attached to the ceiling, setting off a frenzied beating of wings and peals of parrot-like laughter. The birds' laughter would snap the cyclists to attention and they would pick up the pace, putting their heads down and pedaling like maniacs.

Wolfpaw was trying to explain things, but Lars could only catch snatches of what he was saying. What was clear, however, was how proud he was of what he'd created.

"I know it's not pretty, Lars. It can be an assault on the senses. It can seem brutal. But it works. It's fast and it's efficient and these people are so much better for it, you have no idea."

There was some evidence, as they moved across the slick, bloody floor, that what he said might be true. They were stopped by one worker after another, waiting to shake the mayor's hand or have a word with him.

One of the men, smelling of alcohol and packing containers of oil into crates, poked Lars in the chest and fixed him with a mad stare. "Young fellow, you don't know how lucky we are. We all would have been dog meat if it hadn't been for this man."

Was this what the mayor had invited him for? To see everyone fawn over him? Did he think Lars would be impressed?

Lars was impressed in a way. He had never seen anything so grand and ingenious as the factory in his whole life. But what these people were engaged in was a horror, and no one seemed to notice. Were they all deaf and blind? What they had made themselves party to was the obliteration of childhood. What the village's prosperity rested upon was the shameless peddling of a poison that had the capacity to turn all the youth of northern Europe into the same sorrowful creatures as Lars's older schoolmates.

The mayor led Lars to the conveyor belts and lifted one of the skarn out of the slow-moving procession of fish. He held it up, close enough for Lars to see that it was blind, with pink membranes where its eyes should have been.

"Pretty ugly, right? You want to hold him?"

"No thanks." The fish opened its mouth to hiss and Lars could see the double rows of jagged fangs. "I don't believe that I've ever seen anything like it."

"I'm sure you haven't. The only place you'll find them is in the waters under extinct volcanoes."

Mayor Wolfpaw tossed the skarn back and crouched to examine a row of containers rattling along one of the other conveyor belts. He plucked a vial out of a quaking container as it passed. He held it up, scrutinized it, shook it twice, and examined it again. Just the sight of the syrupy golden liquid flowing slowly back and forth in the slender glass tube nearly made Lars ill.

An enormous crash made them all stop and stare. One of the stacks of crates against the far wall had toppled. Broken glass was everywhere, and a shallow lake of skarn-liver oil spread slowly across the floor.

All work ceased. A hundred set of eyes went wide with alarm above a hundred white masks.

"Who's responsible for this?" The mayor's voice echoed in the huge silent space.

There wasn't much doubt who was responsible. A jug-eared boy, no more than two years older than Lars, was down on his knees, his hands pressed to his cheeks.

"I'm so sorry, sir. It just slipped."

"Slipped? How could it slip?"

"It was heavier than I thought, sir. I'll pay you back, I promise."

This promise seemed unlikely ever to be kept. It looked as if all the jugs in one of the crates had been shattered, and that was just the start of it. Skarn-liver oil still pulsed from several other crates like blood from a deep wound. Lars had no knowledge of these things, but he guessed that Wolfpaw's losses could run into tens of thousands of kroner.

Picking his way carefully to avoid stepping into the spreading pool of oil, the mayor went to explore the damage. Whether or not it was all for Lars's benefit or not, the mayor was preternaturally calm. The jug-eared boy was white with panic.

"I would like you to meet me in my office." Wolfpaw's voice was smooth as velvet.

"No, no, please," the boy pleaded. Two of his fellow crate-stackers moved closer, each putting a hand on the boy's shoulder, offering what comfort they could.

"It will be fine," the mayor said. "We just need a bit of an explanation." He turned to Lars. "I'm sorry," he said, "but I'm going to need to tend to this. I hope you're not offended.

"No, no," Lars said. The truth was, he was more than happy to get out of there.

Wolfpaw clapped his hands. "Back to work, everybody! And let's get some mops over here."

Lars's exit was scarcely noticed. Once he was outside, he was finally able to breathe again. Retrieving his skis, he saw that the toolbox on the back of the mayor's sled was still open.

He peered in at a tangle of dog collars and ganglines. In the great tangle Lars spotted a snow hook, a hatchet, a flintlock pistol, a rusty gutting knife, a flask of whiskey, and a bristling key ring.

He had never seen so many keys. There were fat ones and thin ones, short ones and long ones, but most extraordinary of all was a bronze key, twice the size of the others, thick as a piece of teacher's chalk. The bow was decorated with a delicate ivory carving that seemed to throb with its own inner light in the dark afternoon.

Lars picked up the key ring. The carving on the bronze key was of branching antlers, a perfect replica of the antlers stamped on the massive door behind the conveyor belts. Several of the dogs resting in the snow tilted their heads, trying to puzzle out what he was up to.

Lars turned his back so the dogs couldn't see what he was doing, twisted the bronze key off the metal ring, and dropped it in his pocket.

Every week they gathered in the auditorium to sing the anthem. It had gotten to the point where Lars knew it by heart. After the anthem an array of speakers lectured them on the dangers of toys.

These speakers were a grotesque lot. There was a man with an eye patch who'd poked out his eye with a tin soldier when he was four. There was a woman who'd become so mesmerized by her dolls she didn't notice when her house caught fire and her entire family burned to death. There was the doddering grandmother on a cane who was still distraught sixty years later when she recalled how her little sister had expired when she swallowed the broken wing of a whirligig. There was a man with a terrible tremor whose brother had become so absorbed in his toy horse with wheels he'd wandered away from home, fallen off a cliff, and been eaten by a bear. A man who'd had a spike driven through his skull somehow survived and was left without a fear of animals.

As far as Lars could tell, these speakers were all liars, frauds, and charlatans, and he had no idea where Mr. Smorgas had managed to dredge them up. Lars did his best to shut them all out.

What he couldn't shut out were his older classmates, wandering through the hallways, sitting silent and alone in otherwise empty classrooms. Lars had become friends of a sort with a number of them, but it wasn't always easy.

For one thing, they were losing the ability to play, if they hadn't lost it already. When Lars tried to have a game of catch with the boy called Gunnar, he would lob a snowball underhand as gently as he could. If Gunnar managed to catch it, which wasn't often, Gunnar never seemed able to toss it back.

That wasn't the worst of it. In Lars's Ancient Civilization class, Mr. Ostertag asked Inuksuk, one of the older boys who'd been held back for a year, to imagine what he might do if he'd been one of the first Romans to spy Hannibal crossing the Alps on elephants. Inuksuk thought and thought, his face growing redder and redder, until he finally burst into tears. "But I can't imagine. I don't know how."

Lars found himself drawn to all of them: to Abigal, whom he would always lead by the hand back to the school when he found her wandering lost on the playing field; to Finn, the boy who always quivered and shook; to Maja, who would always stare blankly when she was told a joke.

In exchange for all the joy drained from them, they were becoming Wolfpaw's ideal employees—subdued, obedient, and unlikely to cause trouble.

Lars knew he had to do something. But what? All he had was the key he'd taken from the mayor's toolbox. He thought he knew the door it would open. Where that door might lead, he did not know. But he was going to try to find out.

TWELVE

n the way home from school, Lars and Pytor trailed behind a half dozen boys throwing snowballs. One by one they peeled off, and then there was only a girl pulling her little sister on a sled and singing a sweet song. But after several minutes the girl and her sister disappeared into the darkness, and all that was left was cold and silence.

"Remember when I told you a couple of weeks ago about the mayor giving me this tour?"

"Yeah," Pytor said.

"There was one thing I didn't tell you." Pytor had shorter legs than Lars and had to work to keep up, stabbing the snow furiously with his ski poles like a man trying to kill moles.

"What was that?"

"I took something."

"Really?"

Lars glided to a stop, pulled the key from his pocket, and held it out for Pytor to see.

"And where did it come from?"

"Mayor Wolfpaw's toolbox."

"Are you telling me that you stole it?"

"I suppose you could say that." Pytor stared at him with newfound respect. Hundreds of spires of blue ice glittered on the shore far below them. "I'll bet it goes to this big door inside the factory. I was thinking maybe I'd like to see where it goes."

"Huh."

"You probably wouldn't want to go with me."

"I don't know . . . "

"It's probably really dangerous."

"Yeah. Really a stupid thing to do." The voices of the two boys rattled in the vastness like two coins in a beggar's cup.

"And I'll bet they have guards," Pytor added.

"And if you got caught . . . Oh, my God."

"Right. When were you thinking of going?"

"Tomorrow night maybe." They had come to the pile of stones at the top of Rasmussen Ridge, where they usually parted company.

"Sounds good."

The next day his mother put in long hours at work and went to bed early, which made it easy for Lars to slip out of the house. Lars got to the cairn on top of Rasmussen Ridge a little early and squatted by the jagged stack of stones, scanning the horizon. Heavy low clouds rolled in off the sea, and it felt as if a storm was coming.

Lars kept checking to be sure the key was still in his pocket. Five minutes passed and then ten. He got to his feet and put a mitten to the side of his face, trying to peer into the thickening mist. Could he somehow have gotten the time wrong?

A snowball plopped a few feet behind him. When he pivoted, he saw Pytor trudging out of the murk, his hands in his pockets.

"Hey," Lars said. "I was getting worried."

"Well, that was pretty dumb," Pytor said. "It just took me a little while to get out of the house."

"You still up for this?"

"I'm here, aren't I? Come on, let's go."

As they began their trek, the sky began to spit snow. A few houses appeared in the distance, lights twinkling. But once they turned left onto the dogsled trails that led out to the peninsula and the skarn-liver-oil factory, it was as if all the lights were snuffed out. They plunged into a velvety darkness.

It was a half hour before Lars caught the first foul smell. He grabbed Pytor's sleeve. "I think we should probably get off the trail now."

They shuffled down the slope into deep, untouched drifts, which made the going tougher, but where they would be less likely to be spotted. It was only a couple of minutes before they saw the glow of lights through the falling snow.

They scrambled back up the embankment, crouching low, and threw themselves down on their bellies. The skarn-liver-oil factory looked twice as large as Lars remembered it. It was surrounded by blazing torches, set twenty yards apart, and the two high windows flickered with reflected light like two massive, glowering eyes.

Sharing a bottle, two guards, bundled under furs on their dogsleds, sang off-key ditties. A third dogsled sat unoccupied, a few feet off.

"Lars, I'm not so sure about this," Pytor whispered.

"Just wait," Lars whispered back.

They did wait, and after a minute the huge front door creaked open and a third guard emerged. He hollered to his two friends, gave the door a shove behind him, and lumbered across the lot to join them.

Lars squinted through the slow swirl of snow. The guard may have given the door a shove, but he hadn't shoved it hard enough. It was still ajar by an inch.

The three guards passed the bottle around and talked for a couple of minutes. They finally roused their dogs and set off, one to the left, one to the right, and one that came straight back down the trail toward the two boys. Lars and Pytor wriggled a foot or two down the embankment.

Lars could hear the barking of dogs and the cracking of a whip as the sled approached, but then, without warning, there was the rasping of a snow hook and shouts of "Whoa! Whoa!"

The sled came to a dead stop directly above them. Lars wormed himself deep into the snow. The guard got off his sled and began tramping about.

"What's that?" he shouted. "What? I can't hear you. No, I thought we said an hour. Back here. And watch yourselves. This storm is going to be something."

The guard got back on his sled and with a whoop and a double crack of the whip he was off again. It was only seconds before the barking of dogs faded into nothing.

Lars pushed up on his elbows and wiped the ice crystals from his numb cheeks. Pytor had rolled over on his back and was shaking snow out of his mittens.

"Well, so much for that," Pytor said.

"What do you mean?"

"What do you mean what do I mean? We need to get out of here."

"No way. You heard them. They're not going to be back for an hour."

"And what if they come back early?"

"They're not going to."

"You know that?"

"You scared?"

"No, I'm not scared. But I'm not an idiot."

"Fine. But I'm going in there with you or without you. I'll tell you all about it tomorrow at school."

Pytor fluttered his lips, disgusted. "Oh, listen to you. Give me a hand up, would you?" Lars yanked him to his feet. "Okay, I'll race you. Last one there's a monkey's uncle."

Together they raced across the hard-packed snow. Though the door was ajar, it took both of them pulling together to budge it enough for them to slip through. Once they were inside, the only light came from the beams of gritty muted haze angling down from the high-up windows, and it took a minute for their eyes to adjust to the darkness.

The other time Lars had been inside the factory it had been a dizzying whirl of clatter and rush, but now it was so still it felt like a museum. The puffins slept in their cages, and the white coats and masks of the workers glowed faintly from pegs on the wall, looking like sorrowful pirates hung for their crimes.

The two boys took baby steps as they moved across the slick floor. Lars's eyes watered from the stink. When Pytor banged into one of the conveyor belts, a puffin muttered in its sleep.

Lars had remembered correctly. As they neared the massive metal door beneath the catwalk, he spotted the emblem of twining antlers, pulsing with light. The lock was a foot above Lars's head. Standing on tiptoes, he tried to slip the key in the lock without success. He jiggled it and wiggled it, angled it up and angled it down, turned it over and tried again. No luck.

"Come on, Lars," Pytor said. "What are you doing? We don't have all night."

"I know. Just give me a second." His hand trembled. Could they have come all this way only to have the wrong key?

Pytor had lost patience. He found a stool and hauled it across the floor. "Here, let me try."

Lars didn't fight him. Pytor stepped up on the stool and took off his gloves. He did no better than Lars, not at first. But then he wiped the key on the sleeve of his parka and held it up to his nose for a thorough inspection.

When he tried again, he was delicate as someone trying to feed a day-old puppy with an eyedropper. The key made a tinkle and then slid all the way in. Pytor gave the key one vigorous twist and the massive metal door swung open.

Quite pleased with himself, Pytor stepped down from the stool and handed the key back to Lars. Together they stared down a staircase that led into inky blackness. Neither of them spoke. After several seconds Lars thought he could hear the sound of the sea, but it was so faint and faraway he couldn't be sure. Then, more distinctly, there was a splash, followed by a low snuffling and a squeak.

"I'm not so sure we should be going down there," Lars said.

"Hold on a minute," Pytor said.

Without a word of explanation, he turned and made his way across the slick floor, vanishing behind the conveyor belts and the stationary bicycles. Lars could hear him tinkering in the darkness, and when Pytor returned he had a lantern with him.

Pytor removed the glass and set it carefully on the floor. "Hold this for me, would you?" He handed the lantern to Lars and retrieved a match from his pocket. He lit it and brushed the guttering flame back and forth across the wick until it took.

Light rose in the huge room, casting fresh shadows. A drowsy puffin croaked, ruffled its feathers, and settled back into sleep. Pytor adjusted the wick, cutting the light by half, and reset the glass.

"You really think . . . " Lars said.

"I thought this was your idea," Pytor said. "Am I right?" Now that there was some light, Lars could see the old wicked gleam in Pytor's eyes.

Pytor led the way. The metal staircase was rickety and echoed with each step. All sounds below them had ceased. Lantern light glistened off wet rock walls. When Pytor brushed against the railing, one of his gloves tumbled from his pocket and fell into the darkness.

"Pytor!"

"Shh!"

Lars tugged at the back of Pytor's parka, but Pytor reached back and pushed Lars's arm away. It was still again, the only sound the slow drip of water from the walls.

Pytor moved down one step and then another, but Lars didn't move. Something hissed from the darkness. The banging started again. Pytor raised the lantern above his head and swung it slowly around.

They had entered a vast cavern that rose fifty feet above them and fell fifty feet below them to the sea. The metal staircase followed the edge of an enormous wire mesh enclosure. Inside the enclosure several conveyor belts snaked their way from the underside of the factory to a rock ledge just above the water. There was a very distinct smell of rotting fish.

Two wooden troughs sat on the ledge and were tended by eight tiny men in soiled green jackets. Pytor and Lars were too far away to tell exactly what these tiny men were doing. But as the two boys descended step by step, it became clearer.

The two troughs were filled with thrashing, glistening skarn. Six of the tiny men were feeding them, tossing handfuls of what looked like bloody entrails into the snapping jaws. Another of the tiny men moved from conveyor belt to conveyor belt with hammer and screwdriver, making repairs. Another made random inspections of the skarn like a veterinarian. He snatched them out of the water, held them at arm's length to avoid the fangs, and examined the gills before throwing them back into the thrashing mass of its mates.

Lars was reluctant to move any closer, but Pytor was fearless. As he took another step down, he brushed against the railing. One of his gloves tumbled from his pocket and bounced down the metal stairs.

Below the two boys, all activity stopped. The little men were as alert as deer. Two of them picked up clubs. The one coward in the lot abandoned his work on the conveyor belts and scrambled up the far wall and took cover in a small cave.

The seven little men surrounding the troughs began to jump up and down, jabbering in high-pitched voices and baring tiny sharp teeth. Lars's first thought was that he had to run back and tell Nanu.

But then he remembered it was too late for that. These were the tomten, there was no doubt in his mind, just as bloodcurdling as she had
described them.

Several of the tomten began to hiss, but Pytor was not about to be
deterred. "Here," he said, "hold this." He handed the lantern to Lars
and moved down several more steps, putting his palms up to show he
meant no harm.

He addressed the tomten in the most soothing of voices. "It's okay.
We're not going to cause trouble. Me and my friend, we wouldn't hurt
a fly."

Lars followed Pytor down the stairs, but only to a point. With each
step, the smell of rotting fish grew stronger. Lars was finally close
enough to make out what the skarn were being fed. Two heavy-laden
wheelbarrows were filled with the factory's refuse, the gutted corpses
of the skarn's brothers and sisters, aunts and uncles. Lars put a fist to
his mouth, afraid he was about to throw up.

Pytor was doing a remarkable job of quieting the tomten. He had
made it all the way down to the ledge and all the hissing and jabbering had stopped. He talked to the tiny men through the wire mesh as
if they were old neighbors. On his side of the enclosure and behind
him, a stone arch flared into a narrow tunnel.

Lars closed his eyes for several seconds to settle his stomach. When
he opened them, a glimmer just beyond his right shoulder caught his
attention. Set in the wire mesh was a gate, and bolted to the gate was a
bronze plate engraved with the image of the twining antlers.

It was exquisitely done. As Lars ran his fingers over the embossed
metal, a small squeak immediately behind him made him jump. He
turned. The faint-hearted tomte who had fled into the small cave had
re-emerged and now stood on the opposite side of the fencing from
Lars, no more than five feet away.

"My goodness," Lars said. "This is quite a place you've got here."

The tomte tilted his head sideways, as if he didn't understand what Lars had said. Seen up close, the tomte didn't seem particularly fearsome. He barely came up to Lars's waist. He had fur on his ears, bluish lips, the tiniest wisp of a beard and large, owl-like eyes. His tattered green jacket was in sorry shape.

"So you guys feed the fish, huh?" Lars mimed shoveling something into his mouth.

The tomte made a couple of high-pitched chirps and put his hand to the wire mesh. It was so small, not much bigger than the paw of a squirrel or a rabbit. After a moment, Lars put his palm up against it. His hand must have been twice the size of the tomte's hand, but Lars could feel the warmth of it through the cross-hatched wire.

The tomte took a step back and pointed to the gate. "What's that?" Lars said. "Oh, no, I couldn't do that."

The tomte's owl-like eyes glistened with tears. He looked as pitiful as a drenched dog. Lars glanced down at Pytor. He and the other tomten waggled their fingers back and forth famously.

"Listen, I understand how you feel," Lars said, "but I should probably go down and check on my friend here." Lars patted his pocket, hoping to find some morsel, some forgotten treat to give the tomte, but all he felt was the bronze key. The tomte fell to his knees and put his tiny hands together under his chin.

"No!" Lars said. "Begging is not going to help! When I say no, I mean no!"

A huge tear rolled down the tomte's cheek.

"Oh, boy, oh, boy." If Lars had a weakness, it was that he was a real pushover. It had gotten him into trouble before, and it was about to get him in trouble again. "I know I shouldn't be doing this, but what if I let you out on the sly here? No one else needs to know. This is just between us, all right?"

The tomte nodded eagerly. Lars stared at him for several seconds, just to be sure, then set the lantern down and slid the key from his pocket. He took one last glance over his shoulder. On the ledge below, one of the other tomten was showing off for Pytor, dangling a handful of bloody entrails over the trough and making the skarn leap and snap for it.

Lars took a deep breath and rattled the key in the lock. He eased the door open an inch at a time, trying not to make a sound, but the tomte on the other side of the mesh was in no mood to be patient. He finally threw himself against the door, knocking Lars off-balance just long enough for him to squeeze through. The tomte ran up the steps and punched the air, delirious with freedom.

Lars righted himself and tried to shush the tomte, putting a finger to his lips, but it was hopeless. The tomte gave a series of high-pitched, exuberant chirps.

On the ledge below, all of the other tomten stared up at them.

Pytor's voice echoed in the vast space. "Lars, what are you doing?"

The seven tomten were no fools. They saw immediately what Lars had done. They charged up the incline, leaping along the inside of the enclosure on all fours like a band of incensed chimpanzees.

Lars could see perfectly well what was about to happen. He tried to bang the door shut, but the latch didn't catch, and the door swung open again.

In too much of a panic to think clearly, he patted his pockets for the key, but of course the key wasn't there—he had just used it. But where was it? It must have been knocked out of his hand when the tomte had thrown himself against the door.

Frantic, Lars scanned the stairway below him and spied the key two steps down. He stretched out as far as he could with one hand to retrieve it while still trying to keep the door shut with the other.

One hand wasn't enough. The seven tomten flew at the door full-speed and sent Lars sprawling. A blur of green jackets streamed out onto the stairway.

The seven tomten wasted no time joining their companion. One at a time they hopped onto the railing and then onto the rock wall.

They climbed, hand over tiny hand. They were astonishingly strong, scurrying like lizards darting up a wall. Because they were heading into the darkness, it was hard to see exactly what happened to them, but they seemed to be disappearing into cracks between the rock and the underside of the factory.

"Boy, you've really done it now, haven't you?"

Lars twisted around. Pytor stood in the open door, breathing hard from his sprint up the incline.

"I guess I have," Lars said. "I'm sorry." He scrambled to his feet. "We better get out of here."

"Not quite yet," Pytor said.

"What do you mean, not quite yet?"

Pytor raised a finger as if he was about to explain, but then decided against it. He ducked back into the enclosure and vaulted down the incline.

"Pytor? Pytor, what are you doing?"

Pytor put his shoulder to one of the troughs and strained with all his might, but wasn't able to budge it.

"Pytor, stop! Don't be ridiculous!"

Pytor paid him no mind. He straightened up and stretched out his back. He spit in his hands and gave the trough a second try. It tilted up one foot and two and then, with a final heave, over it went. Water and a hundred glistening fish sloshed out. Skarn slid across the wet floor, slippery as wet bars of soap. A few toppled into the ocean.

"Pytor!"

Pytor might as well have been deaf. He swaggered over to the second trough like a little Samson. The second trough was easier to deal with than the first. Pytor groaned, gave a mighty yank, and it was upended. The ledge was suddenly awash with fish. The skarn flopped and writhed, gasped, and sank their fangs into one another. Some bit at Pytor's trousers, and he had to kick again and again to be free of them.

The far-off sound of mocking laughter made both Lars and Pytor pivot. It was impossible to tell at first, in the vast echoing space, where the sound had come from. But the diabolical chuckling grew, coming not from one source, but a dozen. It was the puffins back in the skarn-liver-oil factory, awake now and sending up the alarm. From even farther away came the faint sound of men shouting.

The two boys looked at one another in the dim lantern light. They were cut off. There would be no going back the way they had come. There were a series of shallow caves dotting the far rock wall, but none of them were deep enough to hide a twelve-year-old boy.

Pytor pointed past the overturned troughs, past the wire enclosure. Lars stared, bewildered. Pytor kept pointing insistently until Lars finally understood. Pytor was pointing to the stone archway and the narrow tunnel behind it.

Pytor retrieved a small hatchet leaning against one of the wheelbarrows and slashed at the wire mesh of the enclosure. He had opened a sizeable gash when the blade caught in the wire and he lost his grasp on the handle. The hatchet clattered at his feet.

Pytor bent down to retrieve it, and a skarn leapt up and sank its fangs in his face. Pytor cried out, grabbed at the glistening white fish, but the skarn's jaws were strong as a blacksmith's vise.

Lars raced down the stairs, taking them three at a time. The skarn's jaws were firmly clasping over Pytor's nose and mouth and Pytor swung around like an elephant swinging a gleaming white trunk. Revived by the scent of blood, the other skarn began to leap and snap, two or three of them clinging to his trousers, another attaching itself to his parka. Deprived of water, they were in their death throes, but it only made them more vicious. It was as if he'd been attacked by wolves.

Lars ducked through the gash in the wire. He swung the lantern as if he was swinging a scythe and most of the fish shrank back. Lars set the lantern down and grabbed Pytor by the shoulders, trying to quiet him.

He worked furiously, yanking off the skarn attached to Pytor's parka, the three clinging to his trousers.

The skarn that had dug its fangs into Pytor's face was another matter. At Lars's lightest touch the skarn dug his fangs even more deeply, making Pytor cry out. Up close now, Lars could smell the skarn's foul breath.

"Pytor, you've got to be still!"

Pytor did his best, but he was in too much pain to be still, twisting away every time Lars reached for him. The sound of men moving through the factory above them was more distinct now.

Lars fumbled in his pocket and found the key. What he intended to do he knew he needed to do quickly. He grabbed the slimy fish firmly around the gills and jabbed the key into the eye socket and twisted it as if he was undoing a lock. The skarn shuddered, made an unearthly hiss, released its grip and fell to the ledge.

Pytor bent over double and cupped his palms to his face without ever touching it. Lars put a hand around Pytor's shoulders and retrieved the lantern. "Let me see," he said.

Pytor straightened up. His face was already swollen and the skarn had left behind a circle of puncture wounds, all oozing blood. It looked as if he had been adorned with war paint, and his eyes had a far-away look to them.

A musket boomed somewhere within the factory. The first thing that sprang to Lars's mind was that the tomten had been spotted.

"Come on, let's get you out of here."

Lars took Pytor by the elbow and helped him through the gash in the wire mesh. Inside the rock archway was a small tool shed, a loading dock, and a scarred, waist-high door. Lars wrestled the door open and, holding the lantern out in front of him, stared in at a series of stone steps leading up into the darkness.

He glanced at Pytor, who was wiping a trickle of blood from his cheek.

"This has got to be a way out, don't you think?" Lars said. "What else could it be?"

Pytor didn't seem to have an opinion one way or the other. Lars took him by the hand and led him up the stone steps. It was a struggle. Whoever had built this staircase had not been a master craftsman. In a half dozen places there were gaps of a foot or more between granite blocks, and they had to leap across like mountain goats. Twice Pytor stumbled and nearly fell, but as they moved higher they could once again feel the bite of Arctic winter.

When they finally emerged into open air, they were buffeted by swirling winds. It wasn't just snowing outside anymore. It had developed into a blinding storm. They were on a steep slope and to their right and high up was bleary light, which Lars guessed must be the torches surrounding the factory. Below them was the frozen sea.

Pytor was breathing hard. Lars waited a moment for him to recover and then pointed. They made their way around to the left, zigzagging silently up the slope. When they reached the top they were two hundred yards from the factory yard and the glow of the torches.

The new-fallen snow and the whipping winds made for slow going. Every minute or so there was a flash of lightning or a distant roll of thunder, as if the whole universe was trying to punish them for what they'd done.

To a degree, the cold seemed to revive Pytor. From time to time he would fall back, but whenever Lars stopped and looked over his shoulder, Pytor was still coming, hunched in his torn parka, tough as a nut and refusing to quit.

Heads down, they just kept putting one foot in front of the other. Lars was too exhausted to think two coherent thoughts in a row, but he knew that he and Pytor were in terrible trouble. Letting the tomten go had been bad enough, but what would Mayor Wolfpaw do when he found the overturned troughs and the hundreds of dead fish? Someone was going to have to pay for this. Lars was furious at Pytor and at the same time, more than anything, he wanted him to be all right. Lars took the bronze key out of his pocket and pitched it into the drifts.

When they came to Rasmussen Ridge, Lars stopped and waited for Pytor, who limped along a good twenty yards behind.

"You okay?" Lars asked.

Pytor nodded that he was, but Lars wasn't so sure.

"Does it still hurt?"

"Oh, God, yeah. How do I look?"

Like you've just run into a hornet's nest, he wanted to say, but he didn't. "Kind of weird. But it will be better in the morning. If you want, I can walk you home," Lars said.

"I'm not a four-year-old. I can take care of myself."

"I know, but seriously, it wouldn't take me far out of my way."

"I'll be fine. But what am I going to tell people?"

"Tell them you've just been attacked by a wolf."

He punched Lars softly in the chest. "I'll see you at school."

He watched as Pytor teetered off into the snowstorm. "Hey!" he shouted finally, but Pytor had already been swallowed by the darkness and the wind.

Lars turned, wiped the ice from his eyelashes, and headed for home. It took nearly twice as long to get to his house as it should have. The driving snow obliterated all the familiar landmarks, and several times he was sure he was lost.

Lars wasn't quite sure what saved him. Maybe it was just his imagination, maybe it was just that he was deliriously tired, but at least twice he was convinced that what set him back on the right track was a glimpse of a tiny arm in a soiled green sleeve, waving him through the blinding curtains of snow.

THIRTEEN

His mother had gone off to work by the time Lars woke the next morning. Still groggy from a shortened night of sleep, he bolted down a few spoonfuls of cold porridge for breakfast, pulled on his parka, and stumbled outside to strap on his skis.

Everything was buried in fresh snow for as far as Lars could see. The abandoned whaling ship down by the shore had been transformed into a gently sloping island of white. The stone cairns on the ridge had vanished.

Lars labored his way to the top of the hill, wet snow clinging to his skis, and set out across the tundra. Except for a few slender grooves left by dogsleds that he guessed marked the passage of his schoolmates an hour or two before, there were no signs of life.

But he kept looking. Somewhere out there too were the tomten. He couldn't imagine how they could ever survive in this cold, wearing their thin green jackets.

It seemed impossible that he and Pytor had done what they'd done. Had they lost their minds? He tried to imagine Wolfpaw's fury when the guards told him what had happened.

Panic came in gusts. Lars had always been a good boy. He'd always followed the rules. The only trouble he'd ever been in was when he was throwing rocks at the cat and accidentally broke a window in the shed. But this went way beyond trouble. This was a total catastrophe. This was like Samson pulling down the walls of the temple (except that he and Pytor were no Samsons, and the skarn-liver-oil factory was a long way from a temple).

He needed to find Pytor. They needed to get their stories straight, needed to come up with foolproof alibis, protection from the uproar that was sure to come. For the moment, he didn't have a single idea.

One good bit of news was that there were no deputies waiting to cart him off when he arrived at school, and the hallways were silent as he hung up his coat and hurried off to class. Math was nearly over by the time he slipped quietly into the back row. Miss Bord paid him no mind as she returned everyone's homework. It looked as if Lars wasn't the only one who'd had trouble getting to school. There were six empty seats, and Pytor's was one of them.

It was not much better in Lars's next class, though a couple more stragglers showed up late. There was still no sign of Pytor. Lars tried to convince himself that Pytor must have overslept, just as he had, but he was beginning to get nervous. He just hoped that nothing had gone wrong.

Pytor was nowhere to be seen at recess. Or in animal husbandry class, either. Lars's worry turned to irritation. Could Pytor have lost his nerve? It was a mean-spirited thought, but Lars couldn't help but think it: what if Pytor had spilled the beans, confessed everything to his father? If he had, there would have been no way Pytor's father would have ever let him go off to school.

The teacher had everyone put halters on the reindeer and trot them around the playing field to get some exercise, while Lars was left behind to clean out the stalls.

It was not the most pleasant work, but Lars didn't mind. It gave him time to go over everything and calm himself. His only company was a sickly yearling with a hacking cough. Lars moved from stall to stall, shoveling out the dirty straw and wheeling it in a wheelbarrow to the pit behind the school.

He was working on the last stall when a knock made him look up. Mr. Smorgas peered at him from around the barn door.

"May I come in?" Mr. Smorgas said.

"Of course."

Mr. Smorgas was not the sort of person who enjoyed a barn. He was a fastidious man who always kept his shoes polished to a high sheen, and he picked his way across the floor, careful not to step in any fresh dung.

He waggled his finger at the wheelbarrow. "I see they're leaving all the dirty work to you."

"I don't mind."

Mr. Smorgas scrutinized Lars for several seconds, then took off his fur hat and rubbed his hand across his shiny bald head. "You're a good friend of Pytor's, aren't you?"

"I guess."

"I've seen the two of you together a lot. Quite a lot." One of the barn cats crept across the floor and tried to rub itself against the schoolmaster's pantleg, but Mr. Smorgas gave it a swift kick and sent it scampering off. "Lars, someone was in my office."

"And what did they say?"

"This is very hard for me, Lars. I'm sorry."

Lars banged the shovel against the wheelbarrow and scraped off the last bits of dirty straw. Pytor has told him. That's all it can be. It felt as if a great pit had opened under Lars's feet. The friend he trusted more than anyone in the world had betrayed him and there was nowhere to stand.

"So the person you spoke to in your office . . . "

"Pytor's dead."

A sound came out of Lars as if he had been punched. He swayed and reached for the nearest stall. His shovel clattered to the floor. The schoolmaster crumpled his fur hat in his hands, looking miserable.

"But what happened?"

"No one knows. But when his father got up this morning, Pytor wasn't in his bed. It looked as if he'd never slept in it." The yearling gave a soft cough. "Somehow his father managed to get hold of one of the neighbors and they organized a search party. They found him about a hundred yards from his house, frozen to death. Someone said it looked as if he'd been attacked by wolves."

Lars stared through the open barn door. Out on the playing field a few of his classmates were still leading their reindeer dutifully through the deep snow, but several of the reindeer had escaped and were being chased down.

The teacher barked orders, but no one paid him a bit of attention. Everyone seemed to be having a grand time. One of the runaway animals stood in front of the bleachers, braying like a donkey. At the far end of the field a snowball fight had broken out.

Mr. Smorgas extended a single finger, touching the wet nose of the yearling through the slats of the adjoining stall. "There was such a storm last night. All anyone can figure is that he must have gone out looking for fuel for the fire and gotten turned around. You know how easy it is to get confused once it starts to snow. It can be hard to tell up from down."

"Oh, yes," Lars said. "I know."

"That's the thing about the Far North. Sooner or later it strips you of everything."

When Mr. Smorgas announced at lunch that Pytor had died, there was a long, stunned silence, followed by a giddy laugh as if someone thought it was a joke. Mr. Smorgas explained what he knew, as best he could, but Lars found it impossible to listen.

Lars was wrapped in a cloud. Everything felt miles and miles away. Nelly Chinchilla had started to weep. Arkady leaned over Roope's shoulder, whispering into Roope's ear. Afterwards, in the hallway, Maja, from the other lunch room, came up and took his hand for just a second.

On the way home from school, he could see, here and there, the signs of people digging out after the storm. Mountains of freshly shoveled snow surrounded a number of the houses. He spotted two or three dogsleds crawling across the horizon and feeble scrawls of smoke spiraling from distant chimneys.

His thoughts spiraled too. Furiously. Out of control. But there was one thought that was still too painful to go near, that lurked like a scorpion in a boot. It was all his fault. If he hadn't talked Pytor into going to the skarn-liver-oil factory with him, or if he had simply insisted on walking Pytor all the way home, Pytor would still be alive.

How had it been for him, Lars wondered. Had he gotten lost? Or had he lain down in the snow, thinking he would rest for just a minute, and then not been able to get up? Had he been afraid? Had he called out Lars's name as the snow kept falling, slowly burying him?

When he got home his mother was there and had heard the news.

"Oh, Lars," she said. "Oh, Lars." She held out her arms as if she wanted to hold him, but he didn't want to be held.

"I'm fine," he said. His voice was cool. "I'll be back in a second."

He went back back to his room, closed the door, and threw his satchel of books against the wall. He sat down on the bed and ground his fists into his eyes, then hurled himself backwards onto his pillow.

He wanted to blame her for everything—for bringing him to this godforsaken place, for always asking Wolfpaw in for tea, for being too nice, for being blind.

When he was small he thought she was the most perfect, most beautiful person in the world. Whatever she told him, he believed. She was the one who taught him not to be tempted by the brilliant red of the poisonous toadstools, not to run behind a horse that's being saddled, not to pick up a baby bird that's fallen from its nest. But now she just seemed ridiculous to him, and the thought made him ashamed.

Pytor's funeral took place three days later. Because it was the dead of winter and the ground was frozen solid, the men of the village had erected a temporary tomb of stones.

Lars and five of his classmates were pallbearers and carried the casket past the tilted crosses and through the small gathering of mourners. The sky was gray and depleted, with torches blazing all around. The boys set the casket down at the entrance of the crudely constructed tomb and lined in a row for the ceremony. Pytor's father sat in front, wearing a fur hat. He had on wooden goggles with narrow slits, the kind people wore to protect against snow blindness. It was impossible to see his eyes, but his hands kept working, clutching the arms of his chair as if he was afraid of being swept away in a great wind.

Several of the workers from the factory were there, looking gaunt as scarecrows, and many of the kids from school were as well, shivering in the cold. Lars spotted three or four of them whispering to one another.

Mayor Wolfpaw was on one side of the gathering. Lars's mother was on the other. Lars kept an eye on both of them. Every now and then the mayor would shoot her a glance, but she made a point of paying him no mind.

The mayor looked as if he hadn't slept in days. Either everyone was giving him a wide berth, or he had chosen to stand apart from the others. He wore a long black cape, and with his grim white face and the rings under his eyes, he looked like an enormous vulture.

Several of the women rose to sing an ancient chant that was traditionally sung for whalers lost at sea. Mr. Smorgas said a few words, and then a doddering priest in shaggy fur robes muttered a blessing.

Two of the workers lifted Pytor's father to his feet and ducked their shoulders under his arms. They carried him forward and he touched the casket, saying farewell to his son.

A horn sounded. A gust of wind guttered the flames of the torches, billowed Mayor Wolfpaw's cape, made him look as if he was flapping his wings, about to take flight. When the priest gave them a nod, Lars and the other pallbearers slid the coffin into the tomb.

A waist-high pile of stones had been set out. Lars and the other boys took the stones and lay them in the entrance of the tomb, building a wall, sealing the coffin in. The rocks were glazed with ice and of all shapes and sizes. They did the best they could, but the rocks kept slipping loose and had to be reset and packed with snow.

Lars thought, if only Pytor were here, he would make fun of all this. He would have done something ridiculous, dropped a snowball down Arkady's back, something to create a stir.

The wall rose to Lars's waist and then to his chest. Inside the tomb, the coffin was being swallowed up by shadows. In my whole life, Lars thought, I will never have a friend like Pytor again.

Mayor Wolfpaw knew that big trouble had arrived. Holed up in his house, he refused all visitors except Bjorn Snortblossom and fired the four guards who'd been on duty the night the tomten had disappeared.

One night when he was unable to sleep, he snuck out of his house and skied silently back to the skarn-liver-oil factory. He let himself in through the secret passageway at the base of the cliffs and crept down the stone steps by lantern light.

The troughs had been righted and were once again filled with skarn, but the gashes in the wire mesh had yet to be mended. He trudged up and down, examining every nook and cranny of the enclosure, the conveyor belts snaking all the way up to the underside of the factory, the shallow caves in the rock walls. Now and then he would hear the puffins in the factory, muttering in uneasy sleep.

He was stymied. He didn't believe that the tomten could have escaped on their own, or had the strength to overturn the massive troughs. But who could have helped them? Or gotten past his guards?

There was no sign of forced entry. Part of the mystery was that the towering door at the far end of the factory floor had been open and the key to open it was missing from his key ring.

Whoever had done this must have planned it all. How many of them had been in on it, he wondered. Eight? Ten? It had been so well executed, they must have been planning it for years. But who were they? There had aways been those who scorned him, who were repelled by him, talked about him behind his back, considered him less that human. He was going to have to root them out. His very existence depended on it.

Having found nothing of any use, he climbed back up the stone steps and out into the Arctic cold. The aurora borealis licked across the sky, blue and green. He was far enough away from the factory there was little chance of his being spotted by his newly hired guards.

He scanned the cliffs and the endless sea beyond. Where could the tomten possibly have gone? It was impossible to imagine that they could have gotten far. There wasn't one of them that had a brain in his head. Mostly likely they'd all frozen to death and were buried beneath a week's worth of new snow.

It was hard for him not to feel wounded, not to take it all personally. He knew they had their resentments, and while some might say that he'd kept them caged up inside the wire enclosure like slaves their entire lives, it was also true that the mayor had treated them royally, clothed and fed them, treated their ailments and tolerated their eccentricities.

They could be as ill-tempered as rabbits and unruly as children. They may have dreamed of freedom, but it was delusional to think that freedom could do much for such spoiled and unpredictable creatures.

Mayor Wolfpaw wandered along the cliff edge looking for some sign of them, then angled back across the tundra, moving farther and farther from the factory. Two or three times he found himself calling out the names of the tomten and received only silence in return.

Then, as he passed a small frozen pond, he caught a glimpse of a shadow gliding across the moonlit snow behind him. When he turned, it had vanished.

"Hugo? Berthold? Is that you?"

Again, silence. Perhaps it had been nothing. Perhaps it was only in his mind. The moon was nearly full and a low mist was gathering slowly. He began to walk in the direction where he'd last seen the gliding shadow.

He hadn't gone ten yards before he heard a patter of feet, somewhere out in the mist. He stopped dead in his tracks.

"Okay, now, I know you're out there! Let's just stop with the fooling! It's going to be better for all of us if you come forward and we'll hash this all out."

He raised his lantern. After a moment he could make out three or four shapes drifting in the mist, none of them more than waist high.

"Did you hear what I said? Is this your idea of a joke? I've about had it with you guys! You get over here, the whole bunch of you, and if you don't, I'm going to just leave you out here to starve!"

There were now six of the shapes circling him, floating ever closer. Then, as if acting on command, they all froze. Huge yellow eyes glowed in the low mist.

Mayor Wolfpaw retreated a step as six wolves emerged from the mist. Two of them, ears flattened, snarled and bared their fangs.

The mayor considered yelling for the guards, but he feared they were too far away to hear him. He fumbled for his knife under his parka and yanked it out of its sheath, even though he knew it wouldn't be much protection if they decided to rush him. But there weren't many options; to run now would have been suicide.

The hair bristled on the backs of the wolves as they edged nearer, strutting stiff-legged. The largest of the wolves, a massive gray, made a bluff charge and pulled up short when Wolfpaw slashed the air with his knife. But even before the mayor could straighten up, one of the younger wolves flew at him from behind.

Mayor Wolfpaw swung the lantern and caught the young wolf solidly in the chest. Everything happened at once. There was a yelp, the sound of glass shattering, a sudden burst of flame as the whale oil ignited. The young wolf sailed through the air and landed hard on its side. It beat a quick retreat, tail between its legs, whining and pawing at its singed muzzle with its paws.

All of the other wolves were still. None of them knew how the mayor had done what he had done or if he might do it again, but they knew to fear fire.

The mayor advanced on them, knife in one hand, extinguished lantern in the other. He snarled and showed his teeth. The wolves were confused. They had never seen anything like this mad, disfigured creature who somehow could speak their wordless language.

An old she-wolf crouched and crawled forward on her belly, whimpering and wagging her tail. The mayor lowered his knife. He knew his wolf-mother was long dead, but every move, every signal of the old she-wolf was familiar to him. He felt a pang of regret.

There had been a time when he had believed that he belonged here, in a pack much like this one, but the truth was that he had never belonged anywhere, not in the world of beasts or the world of men.

He put his knife back in its sheath and knelt down next to the she-wolf. He ran his fingers through her thinning fur. He was weeping. He leaned back and emitted a long, mournful howl. In a second, all the others joined him.

FOURTEEN

Mayor Wolfpaw knew that sooner or later he would be obligated to give a full account of the catastrophe that had befallen him. He had put the day of reckoning off for as long as he was able, hoping that he would somehow be able to pull the fat out of the fire, to fix the situation, or at least come up with a shred of explanation.

But one night he was awakened by a strange flickering of lightning at his window that went on for several minutes and was followed by a trembling that shook the entire house. He knew that he had been summoned.

The following morning he ordered his servants to harness the dogs. He put on his fur coat with trembling hands and set his stovepipe hat firmly on his head. When he checked his appearance in the mirror, he was startled by how pale he was, how the terror shone in his eyes.

The huskies were in top form charging across the snow. After a half hour they plunged into a long narrow inlet and bounced past frozen hummocks and haycocks, over ice rinds and ridges. When they reached the far side of the bay, they climbed out of a steep fjord and made their way across a windswept plain to the strangest of landscapes surrounding the rim of an extinct volcano.

It had been a century since the volcano had erupted, but it was still surrounded by fumaroles, bizarre ice towers ten to fifteen feet high, created by escaping gases in the vents of the earth. Some looked like faceless snowmen, others like misshapen igloos, giant sentries wrapped in white blankets, or the upturned prows of sinking ships.

The mayor got off his sled, got the dogs nestled down in the snow, and lit a lantern. He slogged down the slope to a fumarole that resembled a slightly tilted Chippewa tipi. On the far side of it was a narrow opening. Mayor Wolfpaw crab-walked through the cranny into a cave filled with blue light. The air was warm, no more than a degree or two below freezing, and had a sulphurous smell. Water dripped from icicles on the low ceiling.

He continued on down a steep passageway where he had to squeeze between ice boulders and piles of rubble, entering one room of shimmering blue ice after the other.

The further he descended, the stronger the smell of gases became. Every few seconds there was a sighing sound, coming from deep below, that at moments sounded like the whispering of voices.

The passageway narrowed and flared, narrowed and flared again. He finally came to the largest of all the rooms. Icicles vaulted from the floor of the chamber to the ceiling, some as big around as the columns that held up the cathedrals in Stockholm. But there were smaller icicles as well, thousands of them, lining the roof, delicate and glittery as hung jewelry. Shafts of light shone through three or four vents.

A dozen two-foot-long skarns glided back and forth in a steaming emerald pool, sliding over and under one another like monstrous white worms. Now and then a head would break the surface and Mayor Wolfpaw could catch a glimpse of glistening fangs, the thin pale pink membranes where eyes should have been.

Mayor Wolfpaw went to his knees and put his stovepipe hat and the lantern down next to him. "Oh, mighty one, your servant awaits!" His voice echoed back from the depths of the endless shaft. On a bench of blue ice on the far side of the chamber sat a long-handled net, a bucket of fish intestines, and a stout six-foot-long pole.

Mayor Wolfpaw leaned back on his haunches, listening. The only sounds were the periodic sighing of gases and the drip of water from the icicles above. With all his heart he yearned to get up and leave, but he knew he couldn't do that. The fish may have been blind, but they were aware of his presence—perhaps they smelled him?—roiling the water, lifting their heads to hiss like snakes.

Mayor Wolfpaw called out again. Again the only answer was silence. But then, as he was about to push to his feet, the walls of the chamber began to tremble. The icicles on the ceiling began to tinkle and several broke free, shattering around him.

The shaking stopped. After several seconds it started again, but this time it was even more violent. Icicles showered down on him. Mayor Wolfpaw put his forehead to the stone floor. All he could do now was pray, pray that he wouldn't be shut up in here forever.

His heart thudded in his chest. It was another minute before he heard the clattering of hooves, far off at first, but then growing louder. He shut his eyes tight. There was the smell of ashes, and a sound of rustling, like wind blowing through leaves.

The smell grew stronger and more rancid. Mayor Wolfpaw could feel the presence directly above him, and then a hot foul breathing in his ear, sniffing like a huge curious beast.

"Why have you come to bother me?" The voice was low and guttural.

Mayor Wolfpaw opened one eye and peered up at Nacht Ruprecht, the immense straw body towering above him. The eight deer legs, sinewy and oddly delicate, were close enough for Mayor Wolfpaw to reach out and touch, but the tangle of antlers was so high up they could nearly scrape the icicled ceiling. Nacht Ruprecht's fists, protruding from wrists of flax, were gloved in gray leather.

"I am so sorry, sir, but I'm afraid that I bring unfortunate news." As Nacht Ruprecht turned, Mayor Wolfpaw could see where a face should have been, a single glowing coal behind a curtain of straw. "Someone has broken into the factory and freed all the tomten."

Nacht Ruprecht retrieved the long pole from the bench of blue ice. He held it out in front of him, working his gray-gloved fists back and forth on the handle. His limbs were bound together with twine at the elbows and the knees. In the flickering lantern light the coarse woven straw of his torso shone like gold, flecked with burrs and hulls and dried thistles.

He whirled around, the slender pole whistling through the air. Mayor Wolfpaw raised an elbow to fend off the blow, but he wasn't quick enough. The pole slashed him across the shoulders and knocked him flat.

He lay stunned for a moment. The stinging across his back was so intense it was all he could do not to cry out. Far above him the six twining antlers swayed in the pale light fron the vents.

"Do you know how many centuries those tomten have served me?"

"Well, I don't know exactly, sir, but I'm sure it's been a long time." Mayor Wolfpaw felt a trickle inside his shirt as if the blow had drawn blood. "The thing is, sir, we don't want to overreact. It may be nothing. In a way, it may be good riddance. You know how difficult they could be. I'm sure we'll be able to get along just fine without them."

Nacht Ruprecht bent down, grabbed him by the throat, yanked him off his feet, shook him like a rag doll. Gasping for air, Mayor Wolfpaw kicked and flailed, clawed at the gray-gloved fists, but it was all to no avail. Nacht Ruprecht's featureless face was just inches from Mayor Wolfpaw's, and the mayor could feel the heat from the single smoldering coal behind the curtain of straw. He was about to black out when Nacht Ruprecht swung him around and tossed him away like you might fling away something repulsive, something of no use to anyone.

Mayor Wolfpaw landed in a heap and banged his head against a wall of ice. Coughing and spitting, it took him more than a minute to recover his breath. He tried to push himself even further up into the corner, but Nacht Ruprecht was standing over him. He placed the tip of the long pole firmly on the mayor's temple and pressed two of his hooves on the mayor's shoulders. It was as if he had been pinned down by an enormous, hairy spider. Afraid to move, the mayor watched Nacht Ruprecht out of the corner of his eye.

"Do not tell me this is nothing. This is just as it was prophesied."

The mayor did not know what it meant to say that it had been prophesied, or who might have issued the prophesy, but he knew better than to ask.

"You've got to find out who is behind this," Nacht Ruprecht said.

"Yes."

"You were nothing once, a mere beast. It is time for you to be a beast again. I want you to hunt this person down. And when you find him, you will show no mercy."

The tip of the pole pressed even harder into the mayor's temple. It felt as if his skull was about to explode. He shut his eyes, trying to block out the pain.

"No mercy, do you understand?"

"No mercy," the mayor murmured through clenched teeth.

The pain vanished. The tip of the pole, the two hooves cutting into his shoulders, all gone. Mayor Wolfpaw opened his eyes. Nacht Ruprecht was nowhere to be seen. A huge bird winged its way between vaulting icicles and disappeared into a farther chamber, heading even farther down.

As he had done every day since the funeral, Lars went to visit Pytor's tomb after school let out. Several of the rocks had come loose and he spent a half hour wedging them back in place. A curious ptarmigan watched from a few feet away, tilting its head this way and that, before finally waddling away. Lars continued on, the only sound the chink of stone against stone and the moaning of the wind.

When he was finished, he turned to go and saw Miko shivering atop one of the frost heaves, her arms folded across her chest. Could she possibly have followed him, he wondered? And how long had she been standing there? He retrieved his satchel, strapped on his skis, and made his way up the slope.

"What are you doing here?" he said. He hadn't meant for it to come out as rude as it sounded.

"I was walking home."

"I thought Arkady usually gave you a ride."

"Usually he does. But I don't know where he went. Somebody said he went to help Snic find his dogs." She stamped one of her snowshoes, trying to shake loose the clinging snow.

Lars frowned, scrunched up his nose, and wiped a mitten across his mouth.

"Would you like to walk me home?" she asked.

"Walk you home?" Lars was astonished. "I don't know. Maybe. Well, what's it hurt, right? Sure, why not?"

They set off in silence, Miko on her snowshoes with her satchel swinging at her side, Lars on his skis. He had never walked a girl home before and wasn't sure how he was supposed to do it. A hunting party passed on a high ridge with an enormous seal strapped to the lead sled.

"Have you been going there every day?" she said.

"Going where?"

"To Pytor's tomb."

"Pretty much."

"That's what I thought."

"But what made you think that?"

"Because I've watched you. Headed that way."

"Ahh," he said. They were crossing a wide valley where the frost heaves rose and fell like sand dunes in the Sahara. At a distance he spied three men clambering around an abandoned cabin, and though he was too far off to be sure, they looked like three of Mayor Wolfpaw's deputies.

"You must miss him," she said.

"I do."

"What was he like?"

"He always made me laugh. He was always showing me things. Watching out for me."

"Really? He always seemed like a troublemaker to me."

"I never thought he was. But I know he and Arkady didn't get along."

"I know," she said. Up and down her snowshoes went in the soft snow, plot, plop, plop. "I never understood why that was."

"Probably because Arkady's such a bully."

"Probably."

They wove their way between a series of small ponds.

"You know a lot of people at school think you're weird," she said.

"Weird? Why would they think that?"

"Remember all that crazy stuff you told everybody about the forest? Everybody was sure you had to be making it up. About the fairy houses? Trees a hundred feet tall? You must have thought we were all a bunch of dodos."

"It was all true."

"Oh, come on now." A flock of tundra swans rose and flapped off and settled again at a great distance. "So where do they come from, these trees?"

"From pine cones."

"And what's a pine cone?"

He gave her a look. Did she not have a brain in her head? "They're about this long." He held a thumb and a forefinger an inch apart. "They're usually hard and scratchy, but they've got these scales that can open and shut and they've got seeds inside. Once they fall to the ground and it rains, they take root. And then they grow and grow and grow. For a hundred years, if no one cuts them down."

She held up her thumb and forefinger. "You're saying they're this big?"

"Yeah."

As they neared the end of the valley, Lars spied a tumble-down shack in the distance surrounded by columns of carved ice. In the middle of the afternoon the moon was just coming up, and in the silvery light it looked as if there were beaked figures with huge staring eyes set on top of one another on the columns.

"You've actually seen one of these things?"

"Millions," he said. "I even have one at home. That my father gave me."

Her eyes sparkled with delight. "You're quite a liar, aren't you, Lars?"

"I'm not lying."

"That's the most ridiculous thing I've ever heard." She held up her thumb and forefinger a second time. "This big?"

"That big."

She started to giggle, and once she started he couldn't help but join her. She bent down and scooped a big handful of snow. "If you don't tell me the truth, I'm going to wash your mouth out."

"I am telling you the truth. And even if I wasn't, you could never catch me."

Lars kicked off his skis and started to run. A second later a snowball whizzed over his head. He knelt and packed a snowball of his own. She was running now and let out a yelp when his throw caught her on her ankle.

She stumbled free of her snowshoes, and back and forth they went, throwing, laughing, chasing one another, carefree as five-year-olds. In the flurry of snowballs, everything else was obliterated—the cold, the dark, his grieving heart.

She was fearless, with a rifle for an arm. When he was out of snowballs he crouched down behind one of the frost heaves to pack a fresh arsenal. He looked up just in time to see her charge at him with a great white clump the size of a hunched rabbit raised in one hand, and he knew from the maniacal look in her eye that she intended to stuff it down the back of his parka.

Lars twisted away just as she grabbed his hood and they both fell back in the snow and erupted into gales of laughter.

Lars pushed up to his elbows. "I like you a lot," he said.

"I thought so," she said. "I like you too."

"But what about Arkady? You like him too, right?"

"Oh, what a bore. But I guess I like him well enough."

"Have you ever kissed him?"

She stared at him for a moment as if offended. "I have. How about you, Lars? Have you ever kissed anybody?"

"No."

"Do you want to?"

"Well . . . "

"Just so you know what it feels like?"

"Yes, I guess so."

She reached across and took his hand. Her eyes searched his and she smiled. He leaned toward her. He somehow thought it would be a shy kiss, but it wasn't. He was shocked by how soft and warm it was and by how long it lasted. Lars felt as if he was about to pass out.

"Just don't get any big ideas," she said. She leapt up, went back to put on her snowshoes, and strode off furiously toward the beaked columns of ice.

The next morning Lars took the pine cone from the window sill where it had sat since their first night in the house, stuffed it in his pocket, and set off for school in the most wonderful mood.

He got to Beluga Hall nearly an hour early and loitered in the corridor until he was sure the coast was clear, then slipped the pine cone into Miko's walrus skin and scurried away.

When Lars came out of school at the end of the day, there was a grand snowball fight raging between the lower grades. Lars tried to skirt the battle, but as he skied toward the playing field, Roope, squatting next to the bleachers, rose to his feet as if he'd been lying in wait.

"Hey, Lars!" he shouted.

Lars coasted to a stop. "Hey."

Roope trudged toward him, hands plunged deep in his pockets. "Listen, you got a minute?" he said. "Arkady needs to see you."

"This isn't the best time," Lars said. "Maybe I'll just try to catch up with him tomorrow."

Roope seemed amused. "If I were you, I'd go see him now. Seriously."

"Okay," Lars said, as if was no big deal to him, one way or the other.

Snowballs thudded harmlessly around them as Lars followed Roope back into a jungle of dogs and snarled harnesses. Arkady sprawled on his sled in his shaggy fur coat like a king on his throne, one of his boots planted in the snow. He was surrounded by his usual underlings, including Snic and Snee.

"Roope said you wanted to see me," Lars said.

"I did," Arkady said. "I wanted to show you something."

He leaned to one side, pulled the pine cone out of his shaggy jacket and held it aloft as if it was one of the crown jewels of Sweden.

"Where'd you get that?" Lars said.

"Where do you think?" Over Arkady's shoulder, Lars could see one of the younger boys doing a dance as he retreated toward the school, cradling his head with his arms as he was pelted by a half-dozen snowballs. "You got a little crush on her or what?" Arkady said. Snee began to titter.

Lars held out his hand. "Could I have it back, please?"

"What do you use this thing for? Cleaning out the old earwax?" Again Snee giggled, as if he thought Arkady was the wittiest person in the world. "Or scrubbing your teeth in the morning?"

Arkady lunged forward and swiped the rough pinecone across Lars's face. Lars jerked back, covering his stinging cheek with his palm.

"She told me you said it had a nice smell to it, but I swear I couldn't smell anything. How about you, Roope?" He handed the pinecone to Roope who gave it a couple of solemn sniffs before shaking his head no. "How about you guys?"

The pinecone passed from hand to hand. Sniff followed sniff, all with the same disappointing results. A number of curious students had begun to drift over. Lars spotted a couple of Miko's friends, Annuchka and Nelly Chinchilla, standing on tiptoes at the back of the crowd, trying to make out what was going on.

"Where's Miko?" Lars asked.

"I have no idea."

"She just gave it to you?"

"Of course she gave it to me. You surprised? She told me all about it. About how it had all these little seeds in it, and how your father had given it to you, how it was supposed to be a good luck charm or some goofy thing like that. We had quite a laugh about that."

It was all Lars could do not to take a swing at him. "If you don't mind, I'd like it back."

"You would, would you? I don't know why. As far as I can tell, it's not really good for anything."

Arkady held the pine cone out at arm's length and when Lars reached for it, he lifted it over his head. Lars heard the pine cone crunch and crackle as Arkady closed his fist tight. Lars lunged for it, but Arkady was too quick. He lobbed the pine cone to his dogs, who pounced on it the way they would have pounced on a lemming.

"No!" Lars shouted. He sprang forward and grabbed the collar of one of the dogs to pull it back, but Arkady was on Lars in a second, wrestling him to the ground. Lars struggled to get free, but Arkady had him pinned. All Lars could do was watch as the dogs tore the pine cone to shreds. They shook it in their teeth, tossed in the air only to leap on it again, snarling and chomping.

Lars heard Miko shout something, but he couldn't make out exactly what it was. Arkady finally stumbled to his feet, wiping his mittens on the front of his parka. Lars spat out a bit of dirty snow. He lay on his stomach, eyes closed, listening as the others climbed onto their sled, shouted and whistled to their dogs.

Only after they'd pulled away did he raise his head. It seemed impossible that they could have all vanished so quickly. A sharp pain shot through the middle of his back. The snow around him was speckled with tiny scales. The frozen rope clanged against the flagpole. The wind chased curtains of snow across the top of the hill, like the fleeing ghosts of everyone and everything he'd once cared for.

FIFTEEN

When Lars got home that afternoon, the fire in the stove had burned down to embers. He went back outside to fetch more wood, and as he stacked the icy lengths of planking in his arms, he heard a series of piercing cries coming from the base of the cliffs.

Turning back, he saw a dozen black birds making a great ruckus along the shoreline. It looked as if they were fighting over the body of a dead animal, but they were battling with such ferocity it felt as if there must be more than that.

Lars let his armful of wood tumble to the snow and tromped down the slope to investigate. The birds flapped off at his approach, shrieking and wheeling in a wide circle before disappearing into the mist.

The object of their attention was the mangled carcass of a young puppy. It was too painful to look at. How the puppy had gotten there, Lars could only guess. It might have gotten lost in a snowstorm, or just wandered away from its mother and been set upon by predators.

It was the saddest thing Lars had ever seen. He knew that he needed to go back and put more wood on the fire, but a huge wave of sorrow caught him unawares.

He sat down and pulled his knees to his chest. Protected by the towering cliffs, he was out of the wind, and the moon glinted off a train of icebergs, far out at sea.

Waves lapped on the frozen shore. A wolf howled on the ridge. He began to sing one of the sea chanteys the music teacher was always singing as she ambled down the hallway. He couldn't remember all the words, but he did the best he could. He began to shiver. Using a mitten as a cushion, he put his head down on the snow. Everything slid sideways. The prow of the ruined ship pointed up at the moon; the dark sea, the cliffs, and the pack ice were a jumble.

"So it's cheer up my lad, let your hearts never fail,
while the bonny ship, the Diamond, goes a-fishing for the whale . . . "

He was asleep before he got to the second verse.

A terrible grinding woke him. Lars lifted his head and stared up at the largest iceberg he had ever seen, just a few feet from running totally aground. He pushed to his feet, heart racing, and stumbled along the shore, trying to take it all in. Frozen rocks scraped and clanked at the bottom of the sea.

At the foot of the mountain of ice was a sheer cliff. Further back were two jagged pinnacles separated by steep glistening slopes. The two pinnacles looked like fangs, or a giant witch's teeth if the giant witch had already had a few of her canines pulled. It was all very strange, and what made it all the stranger was that there was a light flickering in the valley between the two peaks.

Lars stared at the flickering for a long time. He tried to tell himself that it was some sort of trick of the light, the moon reflecting off the ice maybe, but moonlight wouldn't have been that yellow or that uncertain, flaring, dying away, and then flaring again. Lars was anything but a daredevil, but he was still a boy, and sometimes boys need to do foolish things.

The way out to the iceberg looked deceptively easy. It wasn't very far and there were three boulders out in the frigid water, close enough together they were almost like stepping stones. From there it looked as if it would take a good-sized leap to reach the shelf of ice at the base of the white cliff.

Lars's hops to the first two boulders went fine, as did his hop to the third, even though he skidded a bit on the landing and had to flail his arms to regain his balance. The iceberg towered over him. The nearer he got, the taller it got. Lars couldn't even imagine how many tons it must have weighed. As much as some countries, he guessed.

He shook out his arms, flexed his knees, and blew into his mittens. Now that he had a better look at it, he saw that the gap between the third boulder and the ice shelf was greater than he had thought.

He crouched low and swung his arms back and forth like a baby eagle trying to get its courage up to dive out of its nest. He jumped as far as he could, landing heels first on the frozen shelf, water splattering all around him.

The ice was mushy as porridge and he had to move nimbly to keep from sinking altogether. He bounded from sludgy floe to sludgy floe and finally flung himself onto a solid ledge at the base of the looming wall.

Lars stared up at the cliff, spiderwebbed with cracks and stretching fifty feet above him. This was getting to be more than he'd bargained for. He patted his pockets, looking for something he could use, and, to his surprise, he found it: the baling hook from Reindeer Husbandry class.

Lars had always loved to climb trees, but an iceberg is no tree. It took him nearly fifteen minutes to scale the wall, jockeying his way up chimneys of ice, stabbing the baling hook deep into fissures and praying they wouldn't give way. He groped for handholds and footholds, refusing ever to look down.

By the time he reached the rim, he was exhausted and trembling. The flickering he'd seen from shore was nowhere in sight. There was a shallow coulee meandering up the side of the first peak, and his guess was that if he could make it to the top of that, he'd be able to get a better view of things.

Lars picked his way along the coulee, bending low, the cold radiating through the soles of his mukluks. Far off he heard what sounded like thunder, which didn't make any sense, because the sky was clear, and then he realized it had to be part of the iceberg, sloughing off and plunging into the sea.

When the coulee gave out, he straightened up and surveyed the whole new world spread out before him. Below, in the saddle between the two peaks, a small fire flickered in a hollow that was no more than ten feet across. A figure bent over the fire, unmoving. But then it did move, leaning even further over to warm its hands at the fire.

All of a sudden Lars wasn't so sure he wanted to be here. He didn't want this to be what he thought it was. Or maybe he did. Like a boy in a spell, he planted his feet sideways on the slope and made a slow, crunching descent.

A small stack of driftwood sat on the rim of the hollow. As Lars moved closer, the figure pulled its gray cloak tight, poking at the fire with a stick. Two steaming cups cooled on a low metal rack.

Lars stopped short, not wanting to take whatever creature this was by surprise. A tiny puff of smoke rose from the hood of the figure's cloak, followed, a few seconds later, by another. The smell was as familiar to him as the smell of his own kitchen.

"Nanu?" he said. "Nanu, is that you?"

The figure went on jabbing at the fire, never looking up. Lars took a step closer. Moonlight shone off the sides of the hollow. He took a second step. The figure tossed the stick into the fire, sending sparks floating in the freezing air. Taking a deep breath, Lars willed himself to move closer.

Hand shaking, he pulled back a corner of the bent figure's hood. Wreathed in pipe smoke, Nanu grinned up at him as if she'd been waiting for him, as if they'd just been playing a game of hide and seek.

Lars fell to his knees. "Oh, Nanu! I can't believe it! You've come back! Oh, my, oh, my! Here, take my hand. I can show you the way down."

When he reached out for her, she waved her pipe at him as if warning him to keep his distance. "I think it would be best if you just sat for awhile." Her tone was stern enough that he just did as he was told. She eyed him silently for several seconds. Maybe it was just Lars's imagination, but he was quite sure he felt tons of ice shift beneath them, like a beast stirring in its sleep.

"Have you been out here all this time, Nanu?" he asked. "What have you been living on? And how did you make your way back here? Can you really steer an iceberg?" She rubbed her nose, not answering. The tips of her fingers were black with frost-bite.

"I'm sorry," he said, "I don't mean to pester you, but just think of it. This is so great. We'll be able to play cards again every night. And you can make me porridge in the morning, just like old times. No one makes porridge as good as you, Nanu. And my mother is going to be so happy to see you."

Nanu took the pipe out of her mouth and whacked it with the side of her hand, knocking ashes onto the snow. "That won't be possible."

"Not possible? But why not?"

"Because I am not one of you any more."

"Not one of us? Then what are you? Are you dead? Are you a ghost?" She leaned over to spit in the snow. "Does this mean that you can't stay with us?"

"No, Lars, I can't stay with you."

"Then why did you come back at all?"

"I needed to see how you were."

"I'm terrible."

She kicked a stray ember back in the fire. "Is it as bad as that?"

"It's just this stupid girl."

"Ahh," Nanu said.

"I just don't understand . . ."

"That may take you a few years, Lars. But tell me."

Once Lars began, it all came tumbling out—Mayor Wolfpaw's courtship of his mother, the freeing of the tomten, Pytor's death, Miko's betraying him, Arkady's washing his face in snow. Nanu listened gravely, her gnarled hands pressed to her lips. Lars could see the distress in her eyes.

"I have no one on my side, Nanu. If I could just float off with you on the iceberg, I would."

"But you can't, Lars."

"Why not?"

The iceberg trembled and groaned as if it was about to split. "Because you were meant for better things."

"You keep saying that, Nanu, but I don't know what you're talking about. I don't care what I was meant for. I just want what I had. I want my father back."

"Maybe it's time for you to be your father." She reached inside her cloak. She rummaged a bit and finally pulled out his father's carving knife. She offered it to him.

He took it from her, turning it over, running his fingers over the ivory handle, testing the blade with his thumb. "Where did you get this?" he said.

She wiped a bit of tobacco from her tongue. "I remember when his father and I gave it to him for his birthday. He was so excited. He took it with him everywhere. I think he even slept with it. He was always throwing it at trees to see if he could get it to stick, and once we even caught him throwing it at the cat. But once he started to carve, my goodness, he had such a knack."

Lars offered the knife back to her, but she put her hand up. "No, no, it's yours." She leaned forward and lifted one of the steaming mugs from the metal rack. "Here you go," she said. "This should warm you up."

Lars dropped the knife in his lap and took the mug from her. He took a wary sip. It almost tasted like hot chocolate, rich and foamy. He thought of all the nights his mother had made hot chocolate for him before he went to bed and how it seemed like the most delicious thing he'd ever tasted—but here in the Far North there was no chocolate.

Nanu took her mug from the metal rack, raised it, and the two of them clinked.

They sat there for five minutes, sipping at their drinks, not saying a word. When the embers began to die down, Nanu tossed another piece of wood on the fire. Lars leaned back, resting his elbows on the snow. The northern lights pulsed, red and blue and green. Every now and then something streaked across the sky like a fiery arrow.

Lars opened his parka to wedge his father's knife under his belt. All the warm milk was starting to make him sleepy. From a great distance, he could still hear the ten-ton slabs of ice roaring like lions as they cascaded into the sea, but somehow it didn't worry him anymore.

As he began to nod off, he saw Nanu peering over at him, puffing on her pipe. She finally patted her legs and he put his head in her lap. She covered him with a corner of her cloak—it felt as if he was being engulfed by a giant bat's wing—and the last thing he remembered before he fell asleep was her singing one of her old songs in her flat, off-key voice.

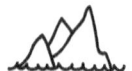

SIXTEEN

is cheek was numb. It was the first thing he noticed, even though the cloak was still over him, and a corner of it now bunched under his head like a pillow. He threw off the cloak, sitting bolt-upright. Moonlight glinted off of blue ice. The fire was out, bits of charred wood studded with furry white crystals.

Nanu was nowhere to be seen. Lars pushed to his feet and scrambled to the rim of the hollow. "Nanu?" He called. His voice echoed off the twin peaks. "Nanu, where are you?"

He surveyed the barren slopes. How could she possibly have done this to him? And it wasn't the first time she'd abandoned him, it was the second. It wasn't fair. He wanted to be furious at her, but he was worried too. For a person to leave their cloak like that and go wandering off into the Arctic night—there was no way anyone could survive.

Nothing made sense. Could she possibly have been living on the iceberg all this time? It didn't seem very likely, but maybe she had a boat stashed somewhere. Or maybe, since the mountain of ice was riddled with fissures and crevasses, she might have found a small cave.

How long had he been asleep? The moon slid slowly over his right shoulder. Hadn't it been over his left before? The northern lights had died away, flickering like insects. The only sound was the soft lapping of water. It seemed strange, it being that still, but he didn't understand why it should be so strange. Then it came to him. The terrible grinding had stopped.

He ran to the edge of the iceberg and stared out across the ocean. The lights on the shore were now at least a mile off, and the enormous cliffs where the birds made their nests seemed no bigger than anthills.

He was floating out to sea. How terrible this was going to be for his mother! She'd already lost her husband and Nanu, and now she was losing him.

Tiny lights moved up and down the distant coastline, and all he could imagine was that it must be people out searching for him. He was instantly sorry for every grumpy thing he'd ever said to his mother, for every time he hadn't carried his dishes to the sink, for every time he'd worried her. Who was going to gather driftwood for the fire? Who was going to shovel the snow off her roof?

As he reached up to wipe a frozen tear from his cheek, he heard a soft snort. At first he thought he must have just made it up, but then he heard it again. Nanu was a snorter, but she didn't snort like that. He spun around and looked up. On a shadowed ridge above him, a set of bright eyes was watching. After a second, the eyes melted away into the darkness.

His heart thumped. He felt for the handle of his father's knife. He was new to the Far North, but he knew enough to know that only one thing could live on an iceberg. A polar bear.

As terrified as he was, he knew that he had to keep his wits about him. His life depended on it. Lars backed away from the edge and made his way around the base of the pinnacle. He took his time about it, putting his hands in his pockets and whistling as if he didn't have a care in the world. Show no fear; that was the key. He knew that he couldn't outrun a bear, but someone had told him once that they weren't good climbers, so maybe if he could somehow get above him, he might have a chance.

He patted the pocket of his parka, making sure he still had the baling hook. With the hook in one hand and the knife in the other, he should at least be able to put up a good fight.

When the slope steepened, he used the hook and the knife to pull himself up, looking over his shoulder every now and then to be sure he wasn't being stalked. After twenty minutes of huffing and puffing, he found a tiny cave just twenty feet below the frozen peak.

It wasn't much of a cave. If you raised your head too quickly, you were sure to bump your head, and lying flat felt like lying on a bed of frozen nails. The best thing about it was that the entrance was way too small to admit a bear.

He tried to tamp down some of the icy spikes with the handle of his knife and then curled up, knees to his chest. He was shivering, but now that he was out of the wind and in a narrow, confined space, his hope was that he would be able to gradually warm up.

He shifted from side to side, trying to get comfortable. He tried to imagine he was under the warm quilts on his bed, that in a few hours he would wake up to the smell of porridge cooking in the other room. He wondered which direction the iceberg was headed. Nanu had told him once that icebergs had minds of their own, but if they had minds, Lars thought, they must have been like Arkady's, slow and mean. If the mountain of ice was headed south, it would only be a few days before it disintegrated altogether.

He was half asleep when he heard another snort. He jerked up so fast he whacked his forehead on the roof of the cave. Had the bear been following him? All this time? The sound hadn't seemed that close, but it hadn't been that far off either.

Rubbing at his sore head, he tried to figure out what to do. If he stayed where he was, he would at least be able to defend himself. But the thought of being trapped in here suddenly horrified him. He needed to know what he was up against.

He took a deep breath and grabbed the knife in one hand and the baling hook in the other. He crept slowly out of the cave, balancing himself on his two weapons like a beast with mismatched claws. He peered over the side. On a ledge thirty feet below him was a sleigh and eight harnessed reindeer. They stared back at him, heads raised.

Lars covered his eyes and counted to ten, but when he took his hand away, the reindeer were still there.

One of his teachers, maybe it was Mr. Bakunin, had told Lars that one of the signs that you're freezing to death was that you start seeing things, but the reindeer all seemed real enough. One of them nipped at his neighbor and got a kick in return. One of them shook his sleigh bells, belching softly. Another pawed through the snow with his broad, cloven feet.

How could they possibly have gotten up on this narrow ledge? There was no way Nanu could have driven them up here. He tucked his knife in his belt and dropped the baling hook back in his pocket. The slope from the cave where he stood to the ledge below was steep, but it wasn't far.

Lars took the most direct route, sliding down on his bottom, landing with a thud and a puff of snow. The lead reindeer was impressive, with huge antlers the size of shovels that put Mr. Smorgas's chair to shame. He lowered his head, eyeing Lars dubiously, as if Lars was no more than some addled seagull that had veered radically off course.

Lars got to his feet and brushed himself off. He approached the reindeer slowly, a step at a time, extending a hand in front of him, speaking in low tones.

"Hey, girl. How you doing there, boy?"

The animals all seemed restless, some of them shaking their harnesses and shying away as he approached. There was no room, really, for anyone to go anywhere. The ledge was no more that five or six feet across, maybe thirty feet long, with the dark ocean directly below.

He eased his way around the reindeer, pausing to let one of them sniff at his pockets, giving a pat to another. The sleigh was a beauty. Made of lacquered black and red wood, with padded leather cushions and gleaming metal runners, the sleigh was decorated with a series of silver medallions, one of a dove, one of a grinning walrus, one of a pine tree. The reins lay coiled on the cushions, and under the front seat was a thick woolen blanket.

When he tried to pick up the blanket, something rattled to the floor of the sleigh. The startled reindeer skittered forward.

"Whoa!" Lars shouted. He grabbed for the reins and gave a hard yank. "Whoa!" The reindeer obeyed, but judging from their looks as they turned to glare at him, they were becoming seriously annoyed.

Nanu's crutch lay on the floor of the sleigh. He'd always known that his grandmother was different from everyone else's grandmother, but this was really something. He squinted up at the dozen tiny ice caves dotting the pinnacle above him.

"Nanu?" he shouted.

The reindeer shook their sleigh bells, moving back and forth in their traces. Lars reached for the crutch, but it was wedged under the seat at an odd angle. It slipped from his numb fingers and clattered to the floor all over again.

This time there was no stopping the reindeer. They were off and running, and Lars had no choice but to run with them. He lunged for the reins, caught one, but not the other. It was no more than thirty feet to the end of the ledge. Lars knew that if he didn't get them stopped, they were all goners.

He scrambled into the sleigh, flailing for the second rein. He caught it and pulled back as hard as he could.

"Whoa! Whoa!"

The first two reindeer disappeared over the ledge, followed by the second two, and the third. Lars tried to untangle the reins, now wrapped tight around his fist, hoping to make a last-second dive for safety, but he wasn't quick enough. The sleigh plunged, jerked down like a bobber being yanked underwater by a hungry trout.

Lars yelped. The sleigh fell end over end, and all he could do was hold on for dear life, clinging to the rails, pitching back and forth, feet braced.

The blanket flew up and wrapped around his face, blinding him. He ripped it away just in time to see the eight reindeer sail past him and a second later he sailed past them. Ocean, ice, and sky tumbled and blurred. Lars steeled himself for the splash, but the splash never came.

Instead there was a jolt, a creak and a shudder. The sleigh somehow righted itself. He was still falling, but not like before, not end over end. The sleigh rushed toward the sea like a toboggan on a steep slope, and out in front were all eight reindeer, antlers bobbing, hooves striding through the air in perfect unison.

The sleigh leveled out and the metal runners skipped along the tops of the waves. Lars put a hand up to shield his face from the spray. He was being tossed this way and that, and then all of a sudden he wasn't. The sleigh rose off the water like a glistening black swan.

Lars was too flabbergasted to do anything but hold on. The antlers of the reindeer ticked back and forth like the pendulums of clocks. They were rising so fast now it made his ears pop. They circled the iceberg and passed through a thin layer of fog. The reindeer took three perfectly synchronized strides, then tucked their legs under them to coast for several beats, like a flock of migrating birds.

They were heading toward the open ocean. Lars could hear their low grunts, see the rising and falling of their shoulders and haunches. Just because they could fly didn't mean they were all that smart. What Lars was afraid of now was that if he didn't find a way to stop them, they would go until they dropped of exhaustion.

One hand on the rail, Lars leaned out to corral the reins that were now streaming past the sleigh. He looped them tight around his fists and gave a sharp tug. Nothing happened. He gave another tug.

The reindeer surged forward harder than ever, heads down. Lars pounded on the side of the sleigh. "Stop it! Come on! I really mean it!"

The sleigh was being tossed around like a kite in a strong gale. His teacher in Reindeer Husbandry had told him stories about reindeer stampedes and how hard they were to stop. But that was on the ground. What were you supposed to do when they were in the air?

All he really knew about animals was what his father had taught him about driving the sledge through the forest, and these were not plodding oxen or worn-out draft horses. Still, anything was worth a try.

He shook the reins. "Gee!" he shouted. To his astonishment, the reindeer began to turn to the right. They all disappeared into a cloud bank, and when they emerged on the other side, Lars shouted, "Haw!" and they turned to the left.

He couldn't imagine how they knew all this, unless Nanu had somehow trained them. For the next ten minutes they did nothing but practice. Through trial and error he discovered that if he said "Antlers up!" they would shoot into the sky and that if he shouted "Tundra!" they would head down. Two clicks of his tongue would make them go faster and one click would slow them to an airy glide.

They were remarkably fast learners. It wasn't long before they were swooping and soaring, making long tilted loops through the night sky. Lars could have gone on like this for hours. He felt freer and more powerful than he'd ever felt in his life. "Antlers up" and they were heading up into the heavens, "Tundra" and they were zooming down to the iceberg-dotted sea. Arkady thought he was hot stuff because he was an expert in knocking people into snowdrifts, but what was that in comparison to this?

The problem was that the reindeer were tiring. He could see the sweat on their flanks, the foam at their mouths. Plus he could never quite forget how his mother must be suffering, not knowing where he was. It was time to be heading home.

Lars turned the eight reindeer toward the east. After five or six minutes they flitted in and out of a series of low clouds. As they approached the shore, a gust of wind buffeted the sleigh and knocked it sideways. The knife tumbled out of his belt. Lars lunged for it, but wasn't quick enough, and it was swallowed by the darkness.

They sailed over the roof of his house and coasted to a smooth stop just a stone's throw from the whaling ship. Lars leapt out of the sleigh and gave each of the reindeer a hug, patting them and warning them with a finger to his lips that they needed to be silent. Back up the hill, lights flickered in the kitchen window.

He fumbled with the harnesses, unhooking them one by one, and led the reindeer into the pitch-dark of the whaling ship. After their exhausting workout in the sky, they seemed as docile as old dogs.

Lars went back for the sleigh and tossed the harnesses and the rest of the gear into the front seat. Without eight reindeer pulling it, the sleigh was nearly unbudgeable. Lars huffed and puffed, pushed and tugged. Inch by inch, he was able to slowly work the sleigh down the slope into the belly of the whaler. The reindeer all watched, a bit bewildered by him, as he shoved the sleigh as far back under the quarterdeck as he could.

He hated to leave the reindeer, but he didn't see that he had any choice. He wasn't going to be able to stay here all night. He could sense their unhappiness as they explored their new surroundings, nosing the frozen coils of rope, the rusted windlass, the empty wooden tubs.

He knew they had to be hungry, but all he had was a few broken ginger snaps in the pockets of his parka. He went from reindeer to reindeer, parceling out what he had, letting each of them nibble a few cookie slivers from the flat of his hand.

"I'm sorry," he said, "I wish there was more. And there will be more, if you can all be patient with me. I don't know how I can thank you enough. I would have died out on that iceberg if it hadn't been for you. And what a ride! Oh, my gosh! You really had me scared for a minute, I'll admit it, but it was amazing, the most amazing thing that ever happened to me. I'm afraid I've got to go up to my house in a minute and check on my mom. I know she's probably worried sick about me. But I'll be back. I promise."

It felt strange, listening to himself give a speech to a bunch of reindeer, but if they could fly, who knew what else they were capable of? He gave them a little wave, as if he was running for mayor, and ducked out into the cold.

He walked up to the house, but when he got to the door he stopped short of opening it. He could hear voices inside. He stood silently for several seconds, just listening. One of the voices was his mother, one sounded like Mr. Smorgas, but there was a third he didn't recognize at all.

Taking a deep breath, he pushed open the door. His mother, Mr. Smorgas, and a huge, gray-faced fellow from the skarn-liver-oil factory stood shivering at the stove, warming their hands. They all turned.

His mother gave a tiny cry, rushed at him, and smothered him in her arms. It was bad. Lars tried to be patient, letting her sob and carry on for a bit, but he finally had to tap her on the back to let him up for air. It was embarrassing enough to be hugged by your mother, but you really don't want it to happen in front of the schoolmaster.

He tried to politely wriggle free, but his mother wasn't about to let him go. She clamped him by both shoulders and glared at him.

"So where were you?"

"Out, I guess." He tried to step back and stumbled over a pile of gear in the hallway—a pair of whale oil lanterns, some coils of frozen rope, and an ice axe.

"Out? We know you were out. What sort of answer is that? Do you have any idea how late it is? We've all been frightened to death. We've been out all night looking for you!"

"I probably should have left a note."

"A note? Do you hear that? He probably should have left a note!" She put a hand to her forehead. She looked a little crazy. The fellow from the skarn-liver-oil factory frowned, picking bits of ice from his eyelids. "Oh, my word. . . . "

Mr. Smorgas put a hand out, clearing his throat. "Mrs. Claus? Reynold and I, we best be pushing along home," he said.

Lars tugged the strings to his hood loose as his mother saw the two men out. She and Mr. Smorgas had a somber, whispered conversation in the hallway. Lars strained hard to listen in, but couldn't hear anything. When Mr. Smorgas clapped a hand on her shoulder and cracked one of his terrible jokes, they all laughed, way more than they should have. It made Lars think that this wasn't going to be so bad after all, that maybe he was going to get off easy. But as soon as the door closed and she turned to face him, he saw from the look on her face that things weren't going to be easy at all.

For twenty minutes she scolded and wept, demanding an explanation. When he tried to fib his way out of it, it only made it worse.

"I went over to Sniffles's house to help him with his homework," he said. It was nothing to be that proud of, but Lars had gotten quite good at lying to his mother. He sat in a chair, unlacing his mukluks. They were frozen and hard as stones. "We have this big assignment due. I guess I sort of lost track of the time."

"Lars, we talked to Sniffles."

"Oh." He set the mukluks by the stove, unable to look at her.

"How can you lie to me like that? If you were little, I'd spank you, I swear. We found your tracks in the snow, going down to the water. I thought I'd lost you forever. I couldn't bear it. . . ." He reached out to comfort her, but she put a hand up to stop him.

"I'm sorry I worried you," he said. "I should have left you a note. It's just that sometimes a person just needs to go be by himself."

It came out sounding a little too grown up for a boy to say, a little too made up, and she got a sour look on her face. "So you're not going to tell me where you went?"

He scratched his head. He tried to imagine what would happen if he told her the truth—that he had seen Nanu on an iceberg, that he had eight reindeer waiting to be fed down in the whaling ship, and if he and his mother chose they could go flying away from this dismal place.

"Mom, it's really too boring to go into."

"Well," she said. "I guess there's nothing for us to do but go to bed then, is there?"

"I guess not."

"When you're ready to tell me the truth, let me know."

Lars watched her walk off to her bedroom and close the door softly behind her. After a moment he could hear her muffled sobs. This was not what he'd meant to have happen. Things were no easier for her than they were for him. But what was he supposed to do?

He heated up a bowl of potato soup and ate it at the kitchen table. When he was finished he rinsed out his bowl. His mother had stopped sobbing and the house was still. Lars gathered together some crowberry rolls, a few scraps of stale bread, and a handful of peppermint sticks and tossed them into a satchel.

He pulled on his parka and his mittens. His mukluks were warm again after their hour drying by the stove. As he moved to the front door, he heard his mother cry out in her sleep. He waited, but she didn't cry out again, the only sound the shifting of the embers in the stove.

He ducked out of the house and eased the door shut behind him. A heavy fog had rolled in, blotting out the cliffs. The only way he would have even known there was an ocean there was the sloshing of the waves on the shore. The whaling ship glistened, black and damp.

When he stepped through the ragged gash in the hull, he was greeted by total silence and the pitch-black. Could the reindeer have vanished into thin air just the way Nanu had vanished? He had no clue what to expect anymore. He strained to see.

"Anybody here? I've got something for you. I think you'll like it."

Again, nothing. He fumbled for his satchel, pulled out one of the crowberry rolls, and waved it slowly in front of him.

Snap! The crowberry roll was gone. Hoofs clattered, were still, then clattered again. He felt a gentle nudge in the small of his back. One by one the reindeer emerged from the recesses of the ship. Some had been bedded down next to the windlass, others curled up behind the giant tubs, but they all crowded around Lars, some eating the crowberry rolls and peppermint sticks directly out of his hand, while others sniffed the floorboards for whatever dropped. Some, impatient, tried to climb over the backs of their neighbors.

They all seemed to be starving, and the food was quickly gone. Lars made the rounds, scratching them behind the ears, rubbing their warm flanks, promising that he would find them more by morning.

He listened to them chewing in the darkness. It amazed him, how those eight large animal bodies had warmed the place up. He would have been happy to have spent the whole night out here, but he couldn't risk raising another ruckus.

It was going to take a while for it all to sink in, everything that had happened to him. It was hard to know what was more astonishing, that reindeer could fly, or that his grandmother could set off on an iceberg and then appear before him a month later. It had been a terrible, terrible thing he'd put his mother through, but how terrible could it be, when the world was filled such marvels?

One of the reindeer swung his head around, and Lars had to put a hand up to fend off the mammoth antlers. This had been the greatest adventure of his life, he thought, but then he thought that wasn't quite right. The greatest adventure of his life had just begun.

The next morning, after his mother left for work, Lars gave the pantry a thorough search, much more thorough than his search the night before. It paid off. He came up with some dried apples, a few sprouty potatoes, and a large jug of slightly fermented pea soup.

He bundled up quickly and hurried down to the whaling ship, the jug banging against his side. The reindeer were all waiting for him at the ragged hole in the hull, jostling, grunting, and eager as puppies.

He pushed his way through the throng of animals. He pulled the apples and the potatoes out of his pocket and lobbed them into the four corners of the hold. It was a simple enough trick, but it worked. The reindeer clattered after their breakfast, and it gave Lars time to rummage through the sea chest in the old captain's quarters and find a couple of rusted metal bowls. He filled them with pea soup and set them out on the rotting floorboards for the reindeer's second course.

The pea soup turned out to be a big hit. Lars took a seat on one of the barrels and watched the animals eat. They didn't have the best manners—crunching and slurping and swinging their antlers around to scare off anyone they thought might be horning in on their sprouty potatoes—but they ate with gusto.

Was he ever going to be able to tell his mother about all this? His mother was the least fanciful person he'd ever known. She didn't believe in unicorns or tooth fairies, trolls or pots of gold at the end of rainbows. For her, things were what they were, and nothing more. Cabbages did not speak and kings did not sprout leaves.

If he told her that he'd been having hot chocolate with Nanu on an iceberg, it would send her round the bend. And if he told her about zipping through the clouds behind a bunch of flying reindeer? She'd probably put him in bed and start calling doctors.

He could, of course, bring her down here to see for herself, but he could only imagine how that would set her off. He could just hear her. Where did they come from? Whose are they? Someone's bound to be missing them, and the first thing we need to do is find out who that is.

And if she actually witnessed them fly? She would be convinced it was witchcraft. No, the reindeer needed to stay his secret. For now, and maybe forever.

SEVENTEEN

Somewhere in the village Mayor Wolfpaw had an enemy. He was willing to spare no expense to discover who that was. His very survival depended on it.

What made it difficult was that he had to proceed with discretion. Only a select few were even aware that there had been tomten working for him for decades. If it ever came to light that not only had these creatures smacking of the dark arts been there beneath the factory, but that someone had now freed them—had challenged the mayor's aura of invincibility—serious trouble was sure to follow.

The most obvious suspects were taken in for questioning—the lunatics, the scavengers who loitered around the factory night and day hoping to pick up a few scraps, the aggrieved whose mothers, fathers, sisters, and brothers had been fired or mistreated by the mayor over the years.

Some were questioned for hours. Some were threatened. Others were whipped to within an inch of their lives. None of them confessed. None of them could tell the deputies anything that might have been of use. All were vowed to silence about their interrogations when they were released. Several of the other villagers were put under survellience. A handful had their houses broken into while they were away at work.

No matter how many times the mayor's efforts came up empty-handed, he could not be deterred (he'd become so agitated, some were sure he'd gone insane). A number of the deputies were dispatched to scour the countryside. Too much snow had fallen for tracks to remain, and after two weeks of searching all they could come up with was a single, small, soiled jacket found under a rock.

It made the mayor shudder to think of how enraged Nacht Ruprecht was going to be when he had to report that he'd come up with nothing. For the past week, Wolfpaw had not been able to eat or sleep. Night after night Wolfpaw tried to imagine what it would be like to be shut up in a prison of rock and steam and roiling lava.

What he feared most was the never-ending darkness. The world he lived in now was a dark world, dark twenty-one hours a day, but at least there was sky, moonlight and starlight, and three hours of precious, feeble sunlight, glistening on the snow.

Whenever he asked Nacht Ruprecht questions about what the darkness was like, the answers were never satisfactory. Are there others there? Certainly. You would not want for company.

This thought haunted Mayor Wolfpaw. He couldn't help but conjure up these putrifying, soul-stripped ghouls, bumping into one another in the darkness, shuffling from one chamber to the next, crying and moaning. Some he imagined perched like crows in tiny crannies. Others he imagined trying to climb the vaulting walls like spiders, trying to make their way to freedom, only to inevitably fall back, screaming.

Mayor Wolfpaw had never had the benefit of a religious education, and there were questions he was afraid of asking. Should he fail Nacht Ruprecht and be punished, would he and all his fellow lost souls eventually go blind from being shut up in darkness for so long? What if, over time, limbs fell away from lack of use? What if they were all destined to be transformed into skarn, sightless, fanged, albino fish, swimming in thermal pools?

This line of thought, once launched, was unstoppable. What if he was finally netted, slit open, his liver plucked and squeezed, the oil doled out to schoolchildren, one tablespoon at a time, until all that was glorious in him, the cunning and all-powerful ruler of the north, would fade into nothing?

When Lars hid the reindeer in the old ship, he had not really thought about how hard it was going to be to keep them fed. Ordinarily in winter they would have been out digging through the snow for the frozen lichen and grass and crowberries that made up their usual diet. But now that they were cooped up, the task of keeping them from starving to death was all his.

Lars was forced to become more and more cunning. Standing in line for lunch, he would sneak as many dumplings in his pockets as he could before anyone noticed. Every time he passed Mr. Smorgas's office, he would duck in to scoop up a handful of candy canes from the jar at the front desk. Every couple of days he would raid his mother's pantry, careful not to take so much she might notice.

It didn't take long to realize that there was no way he was going to be able to go on feeding the reindeer by himself. On a cold Tuesday night, after he was certain that his mother was asleep, he crept down to the whaling ship. The reindeer milled around him huffing and clattering as he hauled the sleigh out onto the snow.

They'd been cooped up for too long, and they were raring to go. They kept grunting and tossing their heads as he got them into harness. He shushed them as best he could, rubbing a hand on their necks as he adjusted their bridles. The last thing he could afford to do now was wake his mother.

He clambered into the sleigh and pulled a blanket over his lap. He could see the reindeer breaths in the cold night air, eight little white puffs. What if the reindeer had forgotten how to fly? What if they ran into a big storm? Or broke a harness?

But one shake of the reins and all the what-ifs were forgotten. Four long strides through the snow and they were airborne, lifting into the sky as if they were being carried on the crest of an invisible wave.

The reindeer hadn't forgotten anything. Gee and Haw, Antlers Up and Tundra, it was like ABC to them. They curved above the cliffs and left the scattered lights of the coastline behind, heading inland.

If Lars had thought they were going fast before, they were going at least twice as fast now. Heads down, hooves flashing, they couldn't have been going any faster if lions had been chasing them. It was like going down the world's steepest slope on one ski with your hat pulled down over your eyes. He would have laughed, but he didn't even know what the joke was. He would have whooped, but the wind would have taken his whoop away. He would have beaten his fists against his chest, but he would have lost the reins. All he could do was to lean forward, clinging to the rails, and hope for the best.

They crossed two mountain ranges, three meandering rivers, four fjords, and a glacier before Lars spotted what he was looking for—a high, secluded valley where it looked like the drifts weren't too tall.

He circled the valley twice, tugging on the reins to get the reindeer to slow down. He scanned the ground below, and when he didn't see any sign of wolves, he brought the team down next to a frozen pond shaped like a horseshoe. The landing was flawless, the sleigh skipping lightly once or twice before coasting to a long, gradual stop, the runners sizzling in the snow like bacon in a skillet.

Lars hopped down and unbuckled the reindeer one by one. They seemed bewildered. One lowered his head and shook his antlers. The others stared at Lars, still as statues, as if awaiting instructions. Were they being abandoned? Was Lars punishing them?

One of the younger ones scampered off thirty yards or so, crow-hopping, then stopped and looked back over his shoulder to see if anyone was following him.

"Go on!" Lars shouted. He grabbed a handful of harness and waved it at them. "Eat! Eat!"

Reluctantly the reindeer began to edge their way out into the valley, all the while keeping one eye on the sleigh, not quite sure what Lars was up to. Lars pulled the blanket down from the front seat and wrapped it around his shoulders. Squatting on his haunches, he kept watch as the reindeer pawed through the snow, searching for lichen and frozen grasses. There was something almost painful about their hunger, but watching them feed, Lars was finally able to relax.

How long were they there? Lars wasn't sure, but it was a good long time. As the reindeer became more trusting they ranged farther and farther out in the valley. Heads down, they munched and crunched, nuzzled and ripped and tore. It was hard for Lars to imagine how anyone could love frozen lichen, but they did love it, more than his mother's crowberry rolls, more than Mr. Smorgas's peppermint sticks. For them a nice chuck of moss was better than chocolate cake, a clump of icy lichen better than baba au rum.

It was well past Lars's bedtime and he was struggling to keep his eyes open. He knew he couldn't afford to doze off, even for one instant. If he lost one of the reindeer, they would all be lost. There would be no way back with a seven-deer sleigh.

The night was filled with dangers. Getting up to shake out his legs, Lars spotted a low shadow creeping up from the far bank of the frozen pond. Lars took a step forward, thinking for a second that it was a wolf, but it turned out to be nothing more than an arctic lynx, picking its way daintily through the drifts.

The reindeer took no notice as the lynx trotted among them, sniffing the air, curious, and finally took a perch on a jagged rock outcropping fifty yards or so directly across from Lars.

The northern lights rippled across the sky. A white owl glided a few feet above the ground, looking for voles. A couple of the younger reindeer started to play, chasing and kicking and spinning like tops, but the rest of them still had their noses in the snow, rooting like pigs after truffles.

Lars squinted up at the stars. If you looked at them long enough, it almost felt as if a giant hand was lifting the entire valley up into the sky.

When Lars glanced across at the rock outcropping, it looked as if the lynx was gone, but after his eyes had a chance to adjust, Lars did see him, still keeping watch, white fur nearly invisible against the white snow.

The reindeer would have stayed and feasted all night, but Lars couldn't chance that. The last thing he wanted to happen was for his mother to wake up and not find him in his bed.

He was worried about how to get the reindeer back to the sleigh, but when he whistled once, they all raised their heads. When he whistled twice and waved his arms, they stared for a couple of seconds and then began the long trek back to the sled. Lars clapped his hands, shouting words of encouragement. The arctic lynx cocked his head, not moving from his perch.

The reindeer took their places in front of the sleigh, lining up as meekly as butlers. A few were still chewing, bits of icy moss dangling from the corners of their mouths.

Lars moved among them, scratching them behind the ears, telling them what good reindeer they were. As he bent under their necks to buckle them up, he could hear their stomachs rumbling, and one of the reindeer belched in Lars's ear.

He climbed into the sleigh. He was pretty sure they needed to fly west, wherever west was. The tangled reins had frozen together and Lars had to pry them apart. When he gave them a shake, the reindeer were off, but they ran longer and rose more slowly than before—maybe it was just the added weight from all those full bellies, or maybe they were just tired. They narrowly missed decapitating the stunned-looking lynx. When Lars looked back, he saw the lynx tearing through the snow, streaking for the safety of his den.

Lars became an expert at sneaking out of the house. Every night after his mother was asleep, he would slip out of bed, tiptoe across the kitchen, mukluks in hand, and ease open the door, lifting up so carefully on the latch it didn't make a click. Once he was outside he would quickly pull on his boots and dash down to the whaling ship.

He'd trained the reindeer to be silent as ghosts, and most nights he was able to harness them without tinkling a single sleigh bell. Off they would fly to their feeding grounds, where he would let them graze for a couple of hours.

Huddled under several blankets in the sleigh, Lars would stew for a time, going over all his troubles. What boy of twelve had ever been in such a fix? He didn't have a single friend, everyone in school laughed at him, his mother didn't understand him, and it was only a matter of time before Mayor Wolfpaw figured out that Lars was the one who'd set free all the tomten. And when he did figure it out, what next? All Lars could imagine was that he would end up chained to the wall in some dungeon for the rest of his days.

Round and round he went, one insoluble worry following the other as he shivered beneath his blankets. But no matter how dark his thoughts, he couldn't help but be affected by the calm and beauty of the stars overhead, by the silence, by the sight of the reindeer drifting up and down the Arctic valley, digging though the crust of the snow to the lichen and moss beneath.

Sometimes it would take an hour for all his fretting to burn itself out, sometimes longer, but eventually it would come to him that perhaps he was not as miserable as he thought, that perhaps he was lucky, even the luckiest of all. Who else had a team of flying reindeer? Who else had seen the world as he had seen it, from hundreds of feet up, mountains and frozen oceans and twinkling lights of the most remote trappers' shacks, miles from the nearest habitation?

Lars was ranging further and further out each night. There were adventures: a twenty-minute detour to chase a spooked polar bear and a half hour joyride through the peaks of a chain of icebergs.

One night on the ride home, Lars looked down and saw a young musk ox surrounded by a pack of wolves. Lars circled the team of reindeer, shouted, "Tundra," and down they went, Lars hollering and pounding on the side of the sleigh.

The wolves looked up, terrified. They'd never been attacked by reindeer before, and certainly had never been attacked by reindeer that swooped out of the sky. Most of them took off instantly. A couple tried to stand their ground, jumping up to bite at the runners of the sleigh, but after Lars gave them a couple of good lashes with his whip they tucked their tails between their legs and went yelping off to join their jibbering pack.

Every adventure made Lars a little bolder. One night he flew all the way to Heggenhougen and stole a dozen bales of straw from a barn to use for bedding for his reindeer. Other nights he would glide over the scattered houses of the village. Most of the houses were dark, but now and then he'd sail over a couple where there were lanterns still burning.

Once he'd worked up his nerve, he'd arc around and swoop in low so he could get a look in the frosted windows. As hard as he tried to slow the reindeer down, he was still going so fast he never got more than a glimpse, but one night he saw Nita Nystrom sitting in her kitchen with her head in her hands, weeping. Another night he saw Bjorn Snortblossom pacing back and forth, shouting and shaking his fist at the ceiling. The night after that he got a fleeting glance of Roope's mother chasing her son around the stove, swatting him with a broom.

It was a revelation to him. It didn't seem to matter whether people were good or bad, kind or cruel, they all had their private sorrows. Because he was a sweet-natured boy, he couldn't help but wonder what he could do to make them feel better. But he was also smart enough to know that this was a question only someone much older and wiser than he would ever be able to answer, one of those very old men with the long white beards.

But to say that Lars was simply a sweet-natured boy was not totally accurate. If he had simply been a sweet-natured boy, this story would've been so much easier to tell. And so much less interesting.

He was wounded. And nothing had wounded him more than the fact that he had given Miko a pine cone and been humiliated in front of the entire school for it.

The day after Arkady had washed his face in snow, Miko had tried to say something to Lars before Reindeer Husbandry class—she was almost pleading with him—but he had refused to speak to her. The next day she tried again, and Lars put his hands up, trying to get her to stop. "I don't think we have anything to say to one another. Seriously," he said.

After that, she was as wounded as he was, and it wasn't long before Arkady was giving her a ride home and she was joking back and forth with Arkady and his friends between classes, having what looked like a great old time. When she passed Lars in the hallways, the most he ever got out of her was a furious look.

One day Snic tripped Lars in the lunchroom and sent him sprawling. Snee came along behind and accidentally-on-purpose stepped on Lars's hand, and every table had roared with glee. Lars lay on the floor, clutching his wounded hand. Snic and Snee skipped around of puddle of green lichen soup from Lars's overturned bowl and sauntered away, congratulating one another with claps on the back. Watching them, Lars felt something seize tight in his chest.

That night, after his mother fell asleep, he set out with revenge on his mind. Snic and Snee lived with their parents in sod huts right next to one another on Beluga Bay. Four or five racks where their fathers had hung their nets were lined up between the huts and the shoreline. They were not in the best shape, tattered and glazed with ice.

When Lars and his reindeer came zooming out of the sky, the results were spectacular. They exploded through the racks, shredding the rotting nets, spraying ice everywhere, sending the poles cartwheeling across the snow. Dogs broke loose from their chains and raced off terrorized in the darkness.

"Antlers up!" Lars shouted and the reindeer tilted toward the sky, missing the top of the sod hut by inches. As they rose, Lars could see the lanterns going on in the hut, hear the faraway shouts of confusion and dismay.

As the days passed, Lars got to know the reindeer better and better. He began to see what distinctive personalities they all had, and he gave them each a name.

There was the overly friendly Alfred, who was always trying to lick Lars's face when Lars was trying to buckle him up. There was the vain Canute, who constantly strutted around the hold showing off his magnificent antlers, and the excitable Liv with the white blaze on her chest. There was the melancholy Hedwig and aged Boris who could not be rushed. Siegfried the troublemaker, Ulrike who drooled when she chewed, and Jonas the Shy.

They were not perfectly behaved. They bickered among themselves, butted and bit one another's flanks when arguing over who was going to sleep where. But when they were in the air, they moved as one, rowing on the wind.

EIGHTEEN

wo deputies who, following the mayor's instructions, had been scouring the farthest regions of the kingdom, showed up one afternoon at the factory, lugging a large sack. Breathless with excitement, they demanded to see the mayor, and, after a heated argument, were finally shown up to Wolfpaw's office by Bjorn Snortblossom.

Once the door was closed behind them, the deputies opened the sack, and slid out on the mayor's desk what they were convinced was the skeleton of one of the tomten.

The faces of Snortblossom and Wolfpaw fell simultaneously. It was obvious to them that what they were looking at was nothing more than the gnawed over (though not completely decomposed) remains of a large Arctic hare.

The tongue-lashing the deputies received was a terrible thing. The mayor called them fools. He called them imbeciles. He called them things that made Snortblossom blush. He threatened to have them whipped in front of the entire village or thrown into jail for a year.

After the deputies made their escape, Wolfpaw collapsed at his desk and covered his face with his hands. The ropy scars on his neck shone in the lantern light. The dull clanging of the conveyor belts sounded from the floor below like a death knell. It took Snortblossom several minutes to work up enough nerve to speak.

"Sir?"

The mayor raised his head. "Yes?"

"I'm worried about you. Losing the tomten was a terrible blow, but if I may say so, you can't let it destroy you."

Wolfpaw pushed up from his chair, eyes glistening like the eyes of a poisonous toad. "Destroy me? What do you mean destroy me?"

"All I mean, sir, is that you shouldn't let something like this take over your life. We all rely on you to be strong. To be fearless. We villagers are like children, unfortunately, but you can't let these people sense weakness . . . "

"Who said I was weak?" He was thundering now.

"No one, sir, no one." The already florid face of Snortblossom turned scarlet. The bones of the Arctic hare, which Wolfpaw had swept off his desk in the middle of his tirade, littered the floor. "All I am saying is that you're bigger than this. It was a dreadful business, losing the little fellows, but you have to remember that it was a once-in-a-lifetime thing. Nothing like it is ever going to happen again."

"You can promise me that?"

"Yes, sir, I believe I can."

Snortblossom had taken more abuse from the hands of the mayor over the years than anyone. He was an easy person to make fun of, portly as he was, strutting around in his black satin knee breeches. But he could talk to the mayor in a way no one else could.

In the weeks since the disappearance of the tomten, Snortblossom had seen the mayor become more and more obsessed. He had grown haggard, lost at least ten pounds, and would arrive at the factory in the morning with bloodshot eyes. He'd developed a tremor and would stare blankly at the walls of his office for an entire afternoon. If he was out for an hour or two, all he wanted to know upon his return was whether they'd heard anything from the far-flung deputies.

"Things are not nearly as bad as they seem. You've had a banner year here at the factory, and the Winter Festival is coming up in just a couple of weeks. You know how much you enjoy that."

"I do," the mayor said. "More than anything."

"What do you say we make this the grandest Winter Festival of all? Just to show them."

"Yes. Yes, that would be good."

The mayor took a deep breath, then rubbed his face vigorously as if waking from a bad dream. He came around from behind his desk and picked up the skull of the Arctic hare. He scrutinized it for a moment and then tossed it in the trash barrel.

"Thank you," he said.

"You're welcome," Snortblossom said.

"We've been together for a long time, haven't we?"

"Yes, sir. A long time."

"Do you think I was too hard on them?"

"You mean those deputies? Not really. Not after getting your hopes up so cruelly. Besides, they're pretty used to this kind of thing."

For as long as anyone could remember there had been a winter festival to reward the workers for meeting their yearly quota—one thousand jars of skarn-liver oil—crystal clear, golden, and uncontaminated. One week after the festival the mayor and his deputies would head south with a hundred sleds loaded with their treasure. They sold the jugs to eager buyers in Norway, Sweden, Finland, and most of the major capitals in northern Europe, ensuring that the mayor's coffers would be filled and survival of the village secured for at least another year.

And now, after being straightened out by Snortblossom's little talking-to, the mayor was determined to put all his worries and darkest fears behind him. This was going to be the grandest winter festival of all. A dozen musk ox would be roasted, and the villagers would be stuffed with enough seal and walrus to make them pop. There would be vodka sufficient for every grown-up to stay drunk for a week, games for the young, gambling tents for the old, music, and dogsled races.

A site was selected far out on the sea ice. Dozens of men were put to work erecting tents, building booths, and collecting fuel for the bonfire—discarded kayaks, driftwood, decaying timbers, anything that would burn. The finest ice sculptors were summoned and musicians hired.

At school, the lunch table conversation was now all about what girls had been invited to the festival by what boys, about who hadn't been invited yet, and who had had their feelings crushed after being turned down. Emotions ran high. Like the animals marching into Noah's ark, the entire school was being paired up, two by two—everybody but Lars.

There had been a time when Lars would have braved the wrath of Arkady and all his friends to invite Miko, but that time had passed. Not a word had been exchanged between them for weeks.

Skiing along the edge of the cliffs one afternoon, Lars spied, far out on the sea ice, a line of torches, sleds of workmen headed out to the site of the Winter Festival. Overhead, a great white bird faltered on the wind.

When he came to the top of the ridge above his house, he saw Mayor Wolfpaw's sled parked out front. It gave Lars pause. There had been a time when the mayor was giving Lars's mother a ride home from work nearly every afternoon, but that had stopped, for whatever reasons. Now here he was again.

The front door opened and the mayor came out, pulling his stovepipe hat down firmly on his head. Lars's mother appeared behind him, silhouetted by the lantern in the kitchen, her arms folded against the freezing cold.

They spoke briefly, and though Lars couldn't make out what either of them was saying, it was clear from the way the mayor's booming and wind-garbled voice carried in the cold air that he was in the grandest of moods.

The door closed. Wolfpaw strode quickly to his sled and ruffled the ears of his lead dog. Lars did not move as the mayor sped away. As he disappeared from view, Lars could have sworn the mayor was singing.

A minute passed. Lars knocked his skis together, ridding them of snow. He was filled with dread.

His mother re-emerged in her parka and fur hat, carrying a shovel, and began swinging it at the icicles hanging from the eaves.

Lars pushed off with his poles. Intent on her task, his mother was not aware of him until he came to a sliding stop by the front gate.

"Lars! Goodness me! You frightened me to death!"

"Are you all right?"

"Me? I'm fine." She took a whack at an icicle thick as a prize carrot and smashed it to smithereens. Lars put an elbow up to avoid being speared.

"I saw Mayor Wolfpaw," he said.

"Really? Did you speak to him?"

"No. He was just leaving."

She took a break from her work, letting the shovel rest at her knees. Broken bits of ice glittered on the snow. She did not look at all happy.

"What were you talking about?" Lars asked.

It took her a moment to answer. "Mayor Wolfpaw asked me to go to the Winter Festival with him."

"And what did you say?"

"It would have been hard to say no."

"So you said yes."

"I did."

NINETEEN

When his mother emerged from her bedroom the night of the Winter Festival, Lars was astonished. She had on her necklace with the tiny brass bells and her best dress, the one he'd only seen her wear once before, at the wedding of her cousin. The dress was long and white with a ring of red berries stitched on the sleeves.

"Oh, my," he said. "You look beautiful, Mom."

It was a compliment she hadn't expected, and she was moved by it. "Thank you," she said.

In the week since she'd told Lars she was going to the Winter Festival escorted by the mayor, it had been unbearably tense in their tiny house. They had talked about it, more than once. If she'd simply said that she'd agreed to Wolfpaw's invitation because she was afraid of losing her job if she didn't, he might have been fine with it.

But when she suggested that she felt a little sorry for the mayor, it outraged him. No one needed to feel sorry for the mayor. This was the man everyone lived in fear of. Who had murdered his two brothers, torn out their throats with his teeth, who was no more than half human, who was so grotesque in appearance it was painful to look at him.

"I know how much you loathe him, Lars. And there are many reasons to. But there is more to him than you think."

"How do you mean?"

"Oh, I don't know exactly. But there is something gnawing at him. Over the last couple of weeks he's just changed. He speaks to no one and has been in the worst of moods."

It was not the most charitable sentiment to have, but Lars couldn't help himself. The man has lost his eight tomten and doesn't know which way to turn. I am so glad to have been the cause of that, he thought.

His mother sometimes mystified him. She had grown up the daughter of prosperous farmers; she'd married beneath her when she married Lars's father. She'd always liked a party. His father hated them. She'd always enjoyed a chance to dress up, and the Winter Festival was certainly a chance to dress up. Lars knew she was not without vanity and that her life now was grindingly dull and oppressive. It hurt Lars to think that his mother might be so much more superficial than he'd ever thought.

There was a melee of shouting as sleds pulled up to the house. A chorus of voices called out his mother's name. Always sensitive to Lars's feelings, his mother had arranged for friends to pick her up and take her to the festival. It was a concession, but not much of one. Wolfpaw would still be there, waiting for her.

The voices called out again. It sounded as if everyone had already started drinking.

"Say hi to everybody for me," Lars said.

"I will. Do you want me to wake you when I get home?"

"No, I'll be fine."

As soon as his mother left, Lars pulled on his parka and boots, stumbled out into the cold, and reeled down the slope to the whaling ship. There was no way he was going to sit around the house feeling bad while his mother and the rest of the villagers partied the night away, making fools of themselves.

He ducked into the ragged hole in the hull and strained to see in the darkness. At first there was just silence and the familiar musky barn smell. But then, after a few seconds, there was a soft grunt followed by a rustling. Slowly the reindeer emerged from the shadows, looking a bit spooked.

"Everybody all right in here? I hope all that hullaballoo didn't scare you too much. But they're all gone now, and I say good riddance!" He got the brush and the curry comb out of the drawer under the stairs and held them aloft. "All right, who wants to go first?"

One by one he brushed them down, brushed them until their coats shone. He brushed with vigor, such vigor, in fact, that they could all sense the anger in his strokes.

"I hope they all have the time of their lives out there on the ice, dancing around like a bunch of idiots in their mukluks. You don't have to be feeling sorry for me. I'd rather be hanging around with you guys any day. And as far as that girl goes, I am totally over it."

The reindeer stared at him, disbelieving. The truth was, Lars wasn't over Miko at all. He almost wished she hadn't kissed him, as great as it had been. It just made everything confusing. He hadn't been able to sleep for two weeks, tossing and turning, unable to get her out of his mind.

He moved on to the last of the reindeer and knelt down, taking hold of the antlers so he could sweep his brush over the length of the quivering back. A drifting cloud of dander made him sneeze. Lars took up the curry comb, ran it through the soft white beard under the reindeer's jaw, and rose to his feet. "O.K., everybody, what do you say we find you something to eat?"

Once they were aloft, there was a wind at their backs, which made the flight to the valley quicker than usual. Their landing was smooth. Lars quickly unbuckled the reindeer and watched as they fanned out across the plain, heading for the prime grazing spots like anglers heading for their favorite fishing holes.

He tried to imagine what was going on at the Winter Festival. He hoped they were all having a terrible time, but he guessed that they weren't. None of the villagers had ever been treated to anything like this in their lives. The rumors were that Wolfpaw's chef and a team of cooks had been preparing food for weeks. There would be music and all the vodka they could drink, and games of every sort, dogsled races and blanket toss and seal-skinning contests.

He thought of Pytor overturning the troughs, struggling to free himself from the skarn that had dug its fangs into his face, slogging bravely through the storm, insisting that he was fine.

He thought of Pytor's father, who was no doubt alone tonight as well, huddled under his blankets in the abandoned church, drinking himself slowly into a stupor.

Lars thought once again of running away. How terrible his mother would feel to come home and find him gone. But it would serve her right.

He got down from the sleigh and whistled, waving the reindeer back in. They ignored him at first—as hungry as they were, they would have stayed and gorged themselves till morning if he'd let them—but when Lars whistled a second time and banged the lacquered black and white door of the sleigh, they reluctantly began to return.

On the way home, Lars made a quick raid on the remote barn outside of Heggenhougen to pick up a couple of bales of fresh straw. Once they got back in the air they began to buck a headwind that grew steadily stronger. Lars detoured to the south, hoping to preserve the reindeer's strength.

The night had turned strange. The moon seemed twice its normal size, and a herd of musk ox stampeded back and forth across the tundra far below, though there wasn't a predator in sight. A white bird flew alongside the sleigh for a time, making piteous cries before being torn away by the wind.

Lars was more than halfway home when a glow appeared far out on the ocean, flickered, and disappeared. At first he thought it was just his eyes playing tricks on him, or an odd flaring of the northern lights.

But then there it was again, winking faintly, like a distant lighthouse flashing a warning. This time, though, it did not go away, but slowly began to brighten and grow more insistent, licking into the frigid night sky.

It came to him in a flash, what it was. It was the bonfire, the high point of the Winter Festival. "Gee!" Lars shouted, pulling the reins hard to the right. All the reindeer glanced over their shoulders, giving him the fish-eye.

"Gee!" Lars shouted again. The reindeer might as well have been deaf. He grabbed the whip from the whipstand and cracked it over their heads. Slowly the sleigh began to angle toward the flames.

Lars just needed to go home. Don't be a dummy, he told himself, stay away. It can only make you unhappy. But there was another voice in him now too, a voice that grew louder the higher the flames rose in the sky.

Come on, the second voice jeered, what are you afraid of? Don't be such a shake-in-the-boots. Don't you want to see what your mother's up to? Of course you do.

Lars's heart thudded in his chest. As they drew closer to the festival, he could finally see just how enormous the bonfire was, lighting up the ice for a hundred yards in every direction. It must have been sixty feet tall, a colossus, tilting a bit like an old windmill. Flames roared through it, devouring a hodgepodge of junk—fishing poles, planks, driftwood, butter churns, kayaks. A half dozen gambling and drinking tents surrounded the blaze, and beyond them, Lars spotted a skating rink and a number of hulking ice sculptures.

As Lars pulled the recalcitrant reindeer in a wide circle high above all this, sparks and unidentifiable flaming scraps floated past.

The spooked animals shied and snorted, but Lars kept them in check.

"Steady now, steady."

Most of the village had turned out, and they seemed to be arranging themselves in two long columns, slow-moving and mysterious as ants. Lars strained to recognize faces, but he was too far up.

"Tundra! Tundra!" he hissed. The last thing the reindeer wanted was to get any closer to the fire, but Lars gave them no choice, whistling the whip past their noses.

Once the sleigh had dropped down another fifteen feet, Lars was able to see a few people he knew—Nelly Chinchilla in her gown of organza and wolf pelts, Donald Donkey-Ears in his sealskin tuxedo, old Mr. Schnuttgaarten downing a tankard of ale.

The two parallel lines, once they were assembled, stretched from the base of the bonfire to a carved ice throne, set well back in the shadows. Everyone's focus, however, was on the fire. They all shielded their eyes, peering intently, whispering to their neighbors.

A smoldering curl of fabric danced by, brushing the flank of one of the lead reindeer. He kicked and the animals behind him bucked in protest, the sleigh lurching left and then right.

"Easy now, easy!" Lars shouted. The fire raged beneath them, shifting and buckling. If anyone had thought to look up from below, there was a good chance they would have seen the sleigh and the reindeer flashing through the billows of smoke, but no one was looking. They were all spellbound by the crackling fire.

Lars was mystified. As far as he could see, there didn't seem to be anything going on at all. Three times he circled above them. Then, on his fourth turn, he spotted Arkady and Miko emerging slowly from opposite sides of the blaze. They threaded their way between the two lines of villagers. Because her head was bowed, Lars couldn't see Miko's face, but he didn't need to see her face to see how lovely she was, with her long dark hair spilling over the shoulders of her white gown.

Arkady swaggered alongside her, reaching back to exchange fist-bumps with one of his pals in the crowd.

At the sound of a horn, two other figures came out of the shadows of the ice throne. As they came into the flickering light, Lars saw it was his mother and Mayor Wolfpaw. She carried a small tiara and Mayor Wolfpaw carried a crown. The mayor put his hand on her shoulder and whispered something in her ear. The smoke brought tears to Lars's eyes.

Miko and Arkady went down on bended knee in front of the throne. Wolfpaw lifted the crown for all to see. Lars's mother lifted the tiara. She and Miko were a mixed set, both in white dresses, one with blonde hair, one with dark. Arkady grinned to the crowd, flexing a bicep and then kissing it.

It was more than Lars could take. He put the reins between his teeth, leaned across and scooped up a handful of wet snow from the running board. He packed it with a vengeance. Tossing his blankets aside, he rose to his feet and teetered a bit before regaining his balance. He wound up and threw so hard he had to grab a rail to keep from going overboard himself.

Who was he throwing at? Arkady? Mayor Wolfpaw? It was hard to know. In either case, it was a trillion to one shot. He was throwing from a speeding sleigh, there was a stiff wind, and the distance was daunting.

But for a moment it looked as if Lars was about to achieve the impossible. The snowball curved, grew smaller and smaller, miraculously on target. The crown was set firmly on Arkady's head, the tiara's on Miko's, as the snowball streaked through the air like a homing pigeon on its way to its coop.

Lars touched his lip with a knuckle, his heart filling with a wicked and delicious joy. But then Arkady rose, taking Miko's hand, and lifted her as well. He bowed, clowning for his audience, and swung her around.

The snowball missed him by an inch. There was a great splattering. It wasn't clear what the snowball hit, but it was as if a bomb had gone off. The tiara went sailing and Miko fell on her side. The mayor staggered backwards, arms flailing, and finally plopped down on his behind.

A huge gasp rose from the crowd. People rushed forward to help. They crowded too tightly around Miko for Lars to see anything of her at first, but then she broke free. She stumbled, wiping the mask of snow and slush from her eyes and hair, weeping. Her gown was a soggy mess.

Lars's mother ran to catch her. She took Miko in her arms and tried to comfort her. Everyone was in an uproar. Arkady shook his fist at someone in the crowd, and two or three fights broke out. Mayor Wolfpaw flopped about on the snow, trying to get up.

Lars crouched in the sleigh, looking down in horror. He hadn't meant for any of this to happen, but what did it matter now, what he'd meant? He collapsed on the seat of the sleigh, spat the reins from his mouth, and buried his face in his hands. How was Miko ever going to forgive him for this?

He pulled his blankets back across his lap. They had slipped all cattywampus and when he tried to straighten them, he saw that one of the corners was smoldering and spitting tiny red sparks.

Lars grabbed the corner of the blanket and beat it against the side of the sleigh, but the results were disastrous. Sparks showered everywhere. Some caught on the bales of straw and exploded into flame.

Lars yanked one of the cushions off the front seat and tried to beat the fire out with it, but there were at least a half dozen blazes going now, whipped higher by the wind.

Lars had no choice. He threw the two flaming bales overboard, followed quickly by the blankets and the smoldering cushion. The bales tumbled through the air, breaking apart as they fell. Three or four of the fiery sections landed on the tents, setting them ablaze like fresh tinder. The burning blankets floated like magic carpets.

Lars tried to regain control over the reindeer, but he might as well have been trying to gain control over a herd of stampeding buffalo. They'd been driven mad by the fire. Some had been singed, some had been stung, and it looked as if one of them had live ember winking under its tail.

Lars wrestled with the reins while the reindeer swooped and soared. When they did a complete loop in the air he braced himself with his feet, holding on for dear life. When they did a figure eight, he clung to the rails while the world spun, righted itself, and spun again. They shot straight up and dropped like a wounded bird.

Lars was too intent on just staying in the sleigh to make out much of what was happening on the ground. But out of the corner of his eye he caught glimpses of people dashing about, others down on their knees, crossing themselves. For a second he thought he saw his mother, but she quickly disappeared in a fleeing mob.

Everything that could catch fire was on fire. Flames reflected off the massive ice sculptures of wall-eyed walrus and snarly polar bears. Terrorized dogs raced across the frozen sea, rattling empty sleds behind them. Lars thought he heard someone shout, "Great balls of fire!"

After one final death-defying figure eight, the reindeer somehow managed to regain a smidgen of sanity and sped off into the darkness. Lars slumped in his seat, his fists still clutching the railings. What had he done? What if someone had spotted him?

Lars did not spare the whip going home. He lashed out again and again, trying to make the reindeer go faster, trying to put everything behind him. This can't have happened, he kept telling himself, but it had happened, it was still happening. There they had sat, all four of them cozy as peas in a pod, having a great old time. What could anyone have expected him to do, other than what he had done?

When they got back to the whaling ship, Lars unbuckled the reindeer in silence. They watched him with the sullen look of seamen who realize that their captain has gone stark raving mad. At least half of them had burns visible on their flanks.

"Come on, you guys. I didn't mean for that to happen," he said. "It was an accident, all right? If it would make you feel better, I can go get some butter to put on all that. What do you say?"

The reindeer were in no mood to be placated. One by one they lowered themselves onto their straw beds and rested their heads on their front legs, staring morosely at him. A long scorch mark glistened on the side of the sleigh.

"Well, suit yourself," Lars said. He slammed the whip back in the whip stand. "I'll see you tomorrow."

When he went back to the house he fell immediately into bed, but it was impossible to go to sleep. He tossed and turned, listening to every sound, imagining the most terrible things.

Was Miko all right? What if he'd really injured her? And what if his mother had somehow gotten tangled up in those collapsing tents and burned to death? He would be left with no one. As angry as he had been with her, he loved her. She was all he had.

He heard the cuckoo clock announce one o'clock and then two. Every half hour he would get out of bed and peer out the window, hoping to see a sled coming across the sea ice or the tiny dot of a skier, but there was never anything but moonlight glowing off the distant outlines of icebergs.

Though he was scarcely aware of it when it happened, he must have dozed off, because he woke with a start and sat bolt upright in bed. Dogs panted just outside the house. There was a slam of the front door followed by the sound of someone stumbling in the darkness.

"Careful, now, careful. Don't hurt yourself." It was his mother's voice. "Here, let me get us some light."

She must have lit an oil lamp, because all of a sudden Lars could see, through his partially opened bedroom door, the billowy sheet tacked up over the hallway window, glowing like a sail at sunset.

The sheet had been put up to seal leaks; now the shadows of Mayor Wolfpaw and his mother played across it, stretching long as taffy and then shrinking.

From the way Wolfpaw was weaving to and fro it looked as if he was about to swoon. He finally sat on the sofa, put his stovepipe hat down next to him, and covered his face with his hands.

"Are you all right?"

"I'll be fine. Just give me a minute."

"Look at you. You're shaking all over. Can I make you some tea?"

"A glass of water would be good."

"A glass of water? Is that all?"

"Yes, please."

The shadow of Lars's mother slid off the edge of the glowing sheet and disappeared. The cuckoo clock struck three. His mother's shadow reappeared with the shadow of a glass and the mayor took his hands away from his face to accept it.

"Thank you," he murmured.

"It was lovely of you to give me a ride. That wasn't necessary you know. I would have been fine. I just hated to pull you away in the middle of everything."

"Don't be absurd. There was no way I was going to let you go home by yourself. Not after all this." The mayor took a long drink of water, handed the glass back to her, and rose to his feet. "That was just what I needed. Now if you'll excuse me, I need to be getting back out there."

"Oh, no, don't do that! You need to go home and get some rest. You're in no shape to be going anywhere."

"Don't you understand?" His shadow disappeared from the glowing sheet and when he spoke again, his voice was faint and far away. "There is someone out there who is determined to destroy me. Someone or something. There can't be any more doubt about it. I have known for a long time that this was coming."

"Please don't talk like that. You're scaring me."

"I don't want you to be scared. But we have to face facts. I am doomed." Wolfpaw's silhouette appeared on the sheet again. His shadow rocked, grew and shrank like a reflection on the water.

Lars clutched his pillow to his stomach. None of this felt real. It was as if he was dreaming, or watching a nightmarish puppet show at the fair.

"There is so much . . . so much I haven't told you. Haven't told anyone. I am lost. No matter which way I turn. And when I am gone? No one will mourn me. They will rejoice. They will go through my house, they will pick through my things like vultures."

"Please stop," she said. "Please tell me what I can do."

For several seconds neither of them spoke. There was the sound of an animal scrambling on the roof. Lars knew he needed to do something to end this. He needed to cough or clap his hands, make a noise to let them know he was awake. Or go out to the hallway and tear down the glowing sheet. But he could do nothing.

"You could marry me," Wolfpaw said.

Her laugh was incredulous. "That's ridiculous. You're tired. It's been a long night. You don't know what you're saying."

"I do know what I'm saying. I have thought about this for a long time and haven't said anything for fear of frightening you. You are the one ray of sunshine in my life. Some days the thought of seeing you is the only thing that gives me the courage to go on. . . ."

As cruel as her question was, she put it gently. "But why would I marry a doomed man?"

"Because I could help you and your son. Because for a time, at least, I have resources. . . . You would be a very wealthy widow."

"Shame on you, Mayor Wolfpaw, shame on you. This is not worthy of you."

"I'm sorry, but I don't understand why you resist me so. Is it because of the way I look? Does this face disgust you?"

"Please . . ."

"You are frightened of me, aren't you?"

"I have heard stories, yes, of some of the things you have done."

There was a long silence. "It is true that I was raised by wolves. But in the beginning I had a human mother. I have no memory of her, but I imagine that she was a lot like you. I imagine that she was kind. And beautiful."

"Please go."

"I will go. I will do whatever you want." Mayor Wolfpaw retrieved his stovepipe hat. When he put it on, his shadow on the glowing sheet turned into an enormous bulbous-headed insect. "I don't expect an answer tonight. Or even tomorrow. But I will expect an answer."

After Mayor Wolfpaw left, Lars's mother snuffed out the lamp and the house went dark. Lars listened to her put something away in the kitchen, then feel her way down the hall and stop in front of his open doorway. Lars kept his eyes shut, pretending to be asleep. She must have been staring at him. She didn't move for a long time, but finally she came over to his bed and kissed him on the cheek. Lars was barely breathing. It wasn't until she had gone to her bedroom that he began to sob silently, his chest rising and falling as he clutched his quilts to his mouth to stifle any sound.

TWENTY

When Lars woke the house was dark, yet something in his bones told him it was morning. When he looked out the window, the moon had sunk to the horizon, and most of the stars were fading from the sky.

"Mom?' he called out. There was no answer.

He tossed his blankets aside and swung his feet to the cold floor. Toes curled, he pattered to his mother's room and peered in. Her bed was empty. He felt his way down the hallway and stopped just short of the living room; a figure huddled under a quilt on the sofa.

Panic came in a rush. Was it his mother? Could it be someone else? The fire in the stove was on the verge of burning out, the last embers winking through the iron grating.

He crept to the kitchen drawers, retrieved the matches, and lit the lantern.

A tiny flame guttered along the wick, caught and rose, illuminating the two rooms. As the figure rolled away from the from the light, a blonde braid flopped out of a corner of the quilt.

"Mom?"

His mother sat up and put her elbow over her eyes, squinting in the glare. She was still in her beautiful dress from the night before, but it was rumpled now and one of the sleeves was streaked with soot.

"Are you all right?" Lars asked.

"I'm fine. What time is it?" She glanced back over her shoulder at the cuckoo clock. It was nearly eight. "Oh, dear, look how late it is!" She stood and hobbled barefoot to the counter. "We need to get you something to eat."

She got a bowl down from the cupboard and began to ladle porridge the consistency of spring mud into it with a trembling hand. The house felt as dismal and dank as an otter's den.

"Mom, what happened?"

She slid the bowl onto the table. "I'd rather not talk about it."

"Please, Mom, please."

The story came in torrents and in almost lurid detail. About the balls of fire falling from the sky and the tents bursting into flame. People fainting. Screaming. The sled dogs howling and running off, leaving everyone stranded out in the middle of the frozen ocean. A dozen men with muskets rushing off into the dark to find their attacker. Minutes later all the shooting began out in the blackness, men firing blindly at one another at the slightest hint of movement.

Sitting at the table over his bowl of cold porridge, Lar covered his face with his hands, overcome with shame. He finally peeked between his fingers. "Was anyone hurt?"

"I'm sure. I don't know how many."

"But what do you think it was, Mom?"

"I don't know. It was beyond anything I've ever known. If someone had tried to tell me they'd gone through something like that I would have thought they were mad. People were down on their knees, screaming that it was the end of the world. One old man was wandering about, shaking his fist and shouting that it was the work of the devil. Some girl, not much older than you, was sure she'd caught a glimpse of an enormous, flaming serpent."

Lars stabbed at his porridge with a spoon. The thought of eating anything made him sick. If only he had the courage to confess that it hadn't been anything diabolical, just the actions of a boy who'd gotten his feelings hurt.

"I don't know, Mom. It seems to me that maybe people kind of went off the deep end. It could have been something perfectly normal. A meteor shower, maybe."

His mother frowned. She did not appreciate his skepticism. She went to the box of driftwood and began to sift through, looking for kindling. "It was not a meteor shower," she said.

"Or it could have been something else. Maybe Mayor Wolfpaw was behind it. You don't know. I wouldn't put it past him."

"He would have never done something like that. He had gone to so much trouble. I was standing next to him when everything broke loose. He just froze. I don't think I've ever seen a look of such fear in anyone's eyes. It was almost as if he was having some sort of a fit."

She pried the lid off the stove with the metal prong and jammed the kindling down into the remaining embers.

"What do you think was going on with him, Mom?"

"I don't know. It only lasted for a minute. Everyone was at him, grabbing, pulling at him, pleading for him to do something. And he was magnificent, really. Taking charge, giving orders, seeing that those who were hurt were tended to. I know how you feel about him, Lars. But there is another side to him. He's not all bad."

"But he's not all good either. He has done terrible things, Mom." Cold whispered up the legs of Lars's pajamas.

"I know."

"He is not good enough for you."

"What do you mean by that?"

"Are you going to marry him?" The house had begun to whistle like a diseased lung the way it always did when the wind came up out of the north. "I was awake, Mom. I heard the whole thing."

Her face turned scarlet. She was furious, yet when she finally answered him, her voice was low and emotionless. "I am not going to marry him."

"Are you sure?"

"No, Lars, I'm not. I'm not sure of anything. I am not sure how we will ever survive this place."

"I just don't want to lose you, Mom. You're all I have left."

As she crossed the room, a vole scampered out from under the sofa and disappeared down the hallway. She picked up the quilt, folded it, and folded it again. "I loved your father, Lars. But sometimes I get so angry at him. For leaving us like this. I am so lost."

Half the students didn't show up for school that morning, but those who did were in a state of high excitement. Any thought of getting any work done went quickly out the window. In class after class, all anyone could do was tell their stories to anyone who would listen.

Roope and Arkady both had burns up and down their arms from battling the fires, and Mr. Smorgas had one of his eyebrows singed off when a blazing plank had shot past his head like a spear. Everything had been burned to the ground. There was nothing left at the festival site now but charred ice.

Miraculously, no one had been seriously hurt, though a keg of gunpowder, tucked away in the corner of one of the tents for the blunderbuss competition, had exploded, causing the Reindeer Husbandry instructor to lose his hearing for several hours and Snic's grandmother, who'd fainted at the sound of the blast, woke up the next morning speaking Old Norse.

But for the students it had been a great adventure. They boasted about what heroes they'd been, shoving snow onto the inferno and chasing dogs down in the darkness. They argued about who'd been most frightened, and who had peed in their pants, told stories about nearly being crushed by the collapse of a thirty-foot ice sculpture and being showered with shards of glass when a dozen crates of vodka had exploded in the intense heat.

For Lars it was much more complicated.

When Miko didn't show up for their math test, he assumed she must have stayed home, but as he passed between classes he glanced in the dispensary and saw her sitting on a bench, holding an ice pack to her eye.

"Miko?"

When she looked up, she let the balled-up towel drop just enough for him to see the ugly purple bruise under her eye.

"Are you O.K.?" Lars asked.

"What do you think?" These were the first words she'd spoken to him in weeks.

Lars glanced up and down the hallway. "Can I come in?" She shook her head no as if she didn't think that was a good idea, but he came in anyway, and closed the door.

The dispensary was a small room administered by an ancient nun named Agnes who was rumored to be at least a century old. There was a stove and a barrel of ice chips, and on the wall was an apothecary's cabinet filled with cork-stoppered bottles of mercury, opium, and various herbal remedies.

Lars sat down at the far end of the bench. Neither of them spoke for several seconds. "What happened?" he said.

"I got hit by a snowball."

"But when?"

"Last night." The room smelled of camphor.

"You mean . . . "

"Yes." She seemed so forlorn and defeated. Lars could hear the laughter of other students, passing outside the door.

"I don't understand," Lars said.

"I don't either. It just came out of the blue. This was just a minute before all the big flames started falling."

"I'm so sorry," Lars said.

"Why should you be sorry? You didn't have anything to do with it."

"I know," he said.

She lowered the wadded-up towel. Nesting at its center was a watery blot of red. "Oh, gosh, it looks as if it's started to bleed again. Could you get me more ice?"

"Of course."

He took the towel from her, shook the remaining ice into the sink, and replaced it with new ice from the barrel. The bell rang in the hallway. He was now late for class, but he couldn't have cared less.

The wet lump of cloth in hand, he approached her cautiously. He could see a bit of dark blood welling from a small scar on her lower eyelid.

"Do you want me to call someone?" he said.

"No, I'll be fine. If you could just . . . you know . . . " she motioned with her hand.

He moved the ice pack to her eye with the care of someone trying to capture a butterfly. She winced when the towel touched the bruised flesh.

"Oops," he said.

"It's okay."

They stayed that way for a good long while, neither of them moving. Lars knew he didn't deserve to be this lucky after what he'd done, to be standing this close to her, his hand at her cheek, the two of them alone. She was still in her parka, her long dark hair resting on her pushed-back hood, trimmed in wolverine fur.

"Can I tell you something?"

"Sure."

"I didn't give Arkady your pine cone. Roope saw me playing with it and he told Arkady and then they just came and started quizzing me about it and I denied everything. But then they twisted my arm behind my back and yanked it out of my pocket . . . "

"Oh," Lars said.

"I thought it was a beautiful thing. One of the most amazing things I'd ever seen."

His hand was starting to get numb from the ice, but he had no intention of moving it. He wasn't moving anything until his arm fell off. It was just a smelly room full of apothecary bottles, but it felt as if they were marooned on their own little island.

"It made me so angry that you would think I would do something like that."

"I'm sorry," Lars said. "I heard they made you the queen or something."

"Not exactly. And what did you do last night?"

"Me? Oh, I just stayed home. It was pretty boring."

"I thought about you," she said.

The melted ice had started to drip down his wrist. "And I thought about you, too."

That night when Lars went down to the whaling ship, the reindeer and the sleigh were gone. A thorough search turned up nothing—not a fallen sleigh bell, a scrap of harness, a tuft of hair. He went back outside to check for hoofprints, but the hard-crusted snow was clean and unbroken.

At first he was angry. Who ever heard of giving somebody a team of flying reindeer and then just taking it back without a word of explanation?

But deep down Lars knew he had no one to blame but himself. What could he have been thinking, flying them over a raging bonfire like that? What reason did they have for ever trusting him again?

Without the reindeer, he knew he was one big nobody. There would be no more soaring over mountains and fjords, terrorizing wolf packs, no more secretly lording it over his classmates. He shielded his eyes and stared mournfully out to sea. Where could they be—Alfred, the overly friendly one; the melancholy Hedwig; Seigfried, who would always butt him when he had a chance? How would they survive without him? Canute would do fine, but Boris was too old to do much traveling, and poor, shy little Jonas needed such constant reassurance . . . The nearest iceberg was at least a half mile out, silvery and still, and it didn't look as if it would be drifting his way any time soon.

For three nights he dreamed of the brilliant red fox he had seen after his father's funeral.

Snortblossom had promised the mayor that it would never happen again, and he'd been wrong. For that, Wolfpaw was going to make him pay and pay and pay.

When the fire poured out of the sky, it was as if no time had passed. For Wolfpaw it was as if he was still six years old, naked, filthy, and cowering in a den, and the hunters were somewhere above him, laughing and pitching flaming torches in at him, trying to flush him out. He had been a wolf then, or thought he was, and he was a man now, but the terror he felt was the same, and the certain knowledge that to survive he was going to have to do battle with everything at his disposal.

For years the Ratvass family had done their best to rid their kingdom of superstition and religious zeal. They had sent their deputies out to burn the settlements of the Ecstatics, a small sect that sang hymns over the airholes of seals. All prophets, missionaries, and seers were banned.

In the end, it was all for naught. Many of the older villagers had ancestors who'd intermarried with the Inuit, and still believed in a spirit world, a world of shadow people and shape-shifters that could change into any animal of the Arctic they chose, yet could always be identified by their red eyes. There were spirits who called out in the dead of night, looking for shelter, and spirits who came in dreams.

All of this was stirred up now. Rumors were passed and passed again. Some believed that setting such a massive bonfire had been prideful. They had just been asking for trouble and bound to offend the gods of ice and cold. The wife of one of the trappers said it just went to prove that theater was the devil's handmaiden.

Mayor Wolfpaw scoffed at the childishness of the villagers' superstitions. He was the one who'd had direct experience of the supernatural. He was in league with a demon and had trembled in fear of it for years. But he had an even greater fear now, which was that somehow there was a demon out there even more powerful than his demon, one that he was obliged to search out and destroy. This fact was making him quietly hysterical.

He brought in four shamans from the eastern mountains to rid the village of witchcraft. They roamed the crooked alleyways, beat their drums, and chanted in their feathered headdresses, necklaces of bells, and long leather fringes, setting the dogs howling and generally unnerving the populace.

Wolfpaw also met with a dozen of his most hardened and battle-tested deputies. Half of them were assigned the task of building six lookout towers far out on the tundra. When the construction was completed, they were to man the towers, scanning the skies for signs of trouble. Six more would be sent to patrol the northern perimeter and three posted at the mountain passes.

Everyone would be equipped with enough provisions to last a month and a half. They would be issued spyglasses and muskets. Should they find themselves face-to-face with Wolfpaw's adversary, they should feel free to shoot to kill, no questions asked.

The meeting was held in a large, candle-lit and foul-smelling slaughterhouse on the dock. The dozen men slumped on barrels and crates were a rough lot, rounded up over the years from the fringes of society—a couple of reformed sled dog thieves, a trapper who was rumored to have killed his wife, a wall-eyed sailor with a long history of brawling.

But as thuggish and as intimidating as they were, their new assignment had them uneasy. Most of them had been at the Winter

Festival. Most of them had witnessed the fire plummeting out of the darkness and seen the destruction. The thought that they were being sent out to engage his unseen enemy had several of them shaken and white-faced.

"Will you be going with us?" the wall-eyed sailor asked.

"I'm afraid I won't be able to," Mayor Wolfpaw said. "I've got three thousand jugs of skarn-liver oil loaded on sleds at the factory and I'm scheduled to be heading south with them two days from now."

"Any chance of your postponing your trip?" All heads turned. The question had come from Ivan the Boneless, squatting on a crate, an insolent smile on his face. He'd acquired his name when, for a period of his misspent youth, he had achieved notoriety because of his extraordinary skill at squeezing through windows when the owners were away.

"I wish that I could. The problem is that we have a lot of Danes, Swedes, and Norwegians waiting for us. These are people who restock our coffers every year, who make it possible for our village's continued existence. We are not in the position of being able to put them off."

Mayor Wolfpaw fixed Ivan the Boneless with a long, baleful stare, and Ivan's insolent smile slowly faded away.

Everything the mayor had told them was a lie. The real reason he couldn't postpone his trip had nothing to do with replenishing the village coffers. It was because Nacht Ruprecht would have never allowed it. Aside from the crates full of kroners and sterling and guilders, the mayor was also bringing back twenty sacks whose contents were too gruesome to speak of, contents that were as essential to Nacht Ruprecht as the acrid volcanic air he breathed.

The sailor nursed a small fire in the iron barrel in the center of the slaughterhouse, breaking slates into manageable pieces and lobbing them into the guttering flames.

"Who will we be reporting to then?" asked one of the dog thieves.

The mayor gave a cool glance at Bjorn Snortblossom, who had been sitting in the back, not saying a word. Snortblossom was in the mayor's doghouse. He'd promised Wolfpaw that nothing as disastrous as the disappearance of the tomten would ever happen again, and he'd been wrong.

"I'm putting everything in the capable hands here of our friend, Bjorn Snortblossom." His tone was a bit chilly, certainly less than a ringing endorsement. All the same, Snortblossom bowed his head and closed his eyes as if he'd been blessed. He'd been given a second chance.

The trapper finally raised his hand. "I was just wondering, sir, if there's going to be enough of us."

"Enough of you? What do you mean?" He was on the verge of getting very irritated.

"Well, sir, it seems to me that we don't know what we're dealing with here. We don't know if it's human . . . or something more." The dog thieves worked their arthritic knuckles.

Mayor Wolfpaw took a moment to survey the twelve deputies. The building creaked. The slaughterhouse had not been used for more than a century, but many of the tools still hung on the walls—the monkey belts, a massive head strap, the rusting blubber hooks. Several thousand whales had been butchered here, and it sometimes felt as if their ghosts still haunted the place, moaning in the wind.

Mayor Wolfpaw pushed to his feet and shook off the front of his parka. "Do you think if I added a half dozen more men that would make a difference? Let me just say that if any of you don't have the stomach for this, feel free to go. We will wish you well. No hard feelings. All that means is that there will be that much more glory for the rest of us.

"If I may speak frankly, I know that none of you have the most sterling reputations. I am well aware of your various failings and moral lapses. But I also know that you are not cowards and that you are capable of boldness. So I am a little surprised to see the reluctance in your faces. Perhaps I have not made myself clear enough. What I am offering you is a chance to redeem your ill-spent lives. Should you succeed in discovering and destroying this unseen force that threatens us, you will be heroes." Wolfpaw made his way around the circle of men, putting a hand on one man's shoulder and then the next. "From generation to generation your names will be spoken of in awe . . . Anders and Leif and Rolf and Ivan the Boneless . . . " Snortblossom was the only one he ignored.

Slowly small changes came over the group. A head rose. The suggestion of a smile appeared on a grizzled face. Arms folded across chests in resistance began to unfold.

"I will not lie to you. This may not be easy. I am sending you out into the darkness. Blood may be shed. But those who shed it will have died with honor."

Mayor Wolfpaw went to the door and opened it. A gust of wind swirled in, ruffling the trapper's fur hat, sending sparks flying up from the iron barrel. "Anyone who would like to leave should leave now."

No one moved. The twelve deputies exchanged sidelong glances. The trapper rumored to have murdered his wife rubbed his knees furiously.

It was a full minute before Ivan the Boneless rose to his feet. Two of his fellow deputies murmured in surprise. Ivan moved slowly across the vast floor, swinging his bad leg behind him. Wolfpaw's face was devoid of any emotion.

As Ivan the Boneless drew near, the mayor pulled the door open a bit wider and gestured for Ivan to pass through, but Ivan had no intention of passing through. He clapped a hand on the mayor's hand resting on the doorknob. Not knowing what his lame deputy had in mind, Wolfpaw resisted and there was a brief tug-of-war.

Ivan prevailed. He finally yanked the mayor's hand free and kicked the door shut. Pivoting, Ivan raised Wolfpaw's arm into the air as if declaring the mayor the winner of a boxing match.

"Let's hear it for Mayor Wolfpaw! The greatest mayor in the Arctic!"

The others shot to their feet. "Mayor Wolfpaw!" they chanted, "Mayor Wolfpaw!"

The mayor was at a loss for what to do. Flushed with embarrassment, he grimaced, put his fingers to the corners of his eyes, and finally put his arm around the shoulders of Ivan the Boneless.

The roaring of the deputies had startled a half-dozen gulls from the perch in the rafters. They swooped down and circled, looking for a way out, and finally found it, flapping their way through a gash in the room and disappearing into the starry sky.

As the deputies filed out of the slaughterhouse, the disgraced Snortblossom stayed behind to have a word with the mayor.

"Sir?"

"Yes?"

"I just want to say that I deeply appreciate the fact that you still have enough faith in me to leave me in charge like this. I will not fail you again."

"For your sake, I hope not."

Every night Lars dreamed of the sleigh and the eight reindeer, of soaring through clouds and over high cliffs. He dreamed of the distant valley and the arctic lynx that used to watch the reindeer feed.

Several nights in a row, after his mother fell asleep, he would go down to the whaling ship, hoping that the reindeer might have magically reappeared. He put crowberry rolls out on the deck, hoping to lure them back.

One night, just before dawn, there was a moment when he thought he'd succeeded. He heard a far-off clattering in the sky. At first he tried to tell himself it was just his mind playing tricks on him, but the sound grew slowly louder and more distinct. He cupped his hands to his eyes, scanning the heavens, and finally a flock of honking snow geese burst out of the clouds, winging their way out to sea.

The day before Mayor Wolfpaw took off for the capitals of northern Europe was a backbreaking day for all his employees. A long column of workers heaved crates from hand to hand until they were all loaded onto fifty sleds. The line began inside the factory, made its way through the front doors, and snaked its way well down the road.

In the midst of it all Mayor Wolfpaw reigned supreme. He strode up and down like an admiral aboard his ship, bellowing instructions, clapping his hands, whistling and pointing sternly to those who were flagging.

Lars's mother was stationed just outside the factory door. She was stalwart and uncomplaining. The mayor was very aware of her and she was very aware of him, though not a word was exchanged between the two. Every now and then he would stare at her for a moment, and each time she managed not to meet his eye, deft as a swordsman.

The work was hard and dull. The only excitement was when a puffin broke free and flapped about, chattering, orange feet paddling in the wind as one of the sweepers pursued it with a broom.

The crates were loaded by dinnertime and the workers were let go, with just a handful of deputies staying behind to watch over the sleds during the night.

Down on one knee, Lars's mother was strapping on her skis when she looked up and was startled to see Mayor Wolfpaw standing over her.

"Let me give you a ride home," he said.

"Oh, that's not necessary," she said. "I'll be fine."

"It's been a long day." From the tone in his voice it was clear that he wasn't going to take no for an answer. "You've got to be exhausted. And it will give us a chance to talk."

She dreaded the thought. The deputies were at work throwing animal hides over the crates and lighting fires in a long line of barrels.

"Of course," she said. "I would like that."

She unstrapped her skis, rose, and slung them over her shoulders. Head held high, she ignored the curious glances of her fellow workers as she and the mayor made their way to his sled. The fires in the barrels glowed like candles in a royal procession.

Wolfpaw had given her a ride home dozens of times, but this felt different. There was a wildness in him, a barely suppressed anger. He lashed the dogs, shouted at them to go faster and faster. It crossed her mind that he might be kidnapping her. He fell silent for a long stretch, the only sound the rattle of the skis strapped to the frame of the sled and the panting of the dogs.

Just before Woolly Mammoth Glacier, he pulled the dogs off the hard-packed trail and sent them plunging through a series of unbroken swells.

They had gone perhaps a half-mile before they spotted the first of the markers, a stake angling out of the snow and bearing a tattered red flag. The second marker was another half mile on. The third, just a stone's throw from the second, jutted from the bank of a frozen river. How strange this was, she thought, like a trail of bread crumbs through a forest.

The mayor pulled the dogs to a stop at the third marker, dismounted, and rummaged in his toolbox until he found a short-handled shovel.

"I don't understand," Lars's mother said. She was still seated in the cargo bed with the fur blanket pulled up to her chin.

"It's nothing to worry about, my dear," he said. Shovel in one hand and lantern in the other, he strode to the overhang and slipped down.

For a moment she wondered if he intended to murder her and bury her here. Beneath the overhang was a steep depression in the snow and Mayor Wolfpaw began to kick at the snow in the hollow with the heel of his boot.

"What are you doing?" she called out to him.

"This was my home," he said. He set the lantern down in the snow and began to shovel out the loose snow. She got down from the sled and approached. The tundra stretched out endlessly in every direction. There was no sign of human habitation anywhere.

The mayor chipped away at the ice with the edge of the shovel and got down on his knees to scoop away the softer snow with his hands. She retrieved the lantern and held it over the mayor's shoulder.

He was not as mad as he seemed. There was a den and it looked as if it had been dug out many times before. The snow on the bank went down at least three feet and the snow inside the den went down another three feet. By the time he finished digging it looked as if the mayor was about to be swallowed by the earth.

"Could you do something for me?" he asked.

"Of course."

"There is a leather bag inside my tool box. Could you get it for me?"

"Certainly."

She set down the lantern, went to the sled and retrieved a bulky rucksack. She returned to the mayor and swung the bag down to him. Numb-fingered, he fumbled with the drawstrings and pried the bag open.

He pulled out several dead snowshoe hares and laid them on the icy floor of the den. Next came three gulls and a ptarmigan, all of which he arranged in a circle around the mouth of the den. She watched him work, her arms closed tightly around her chest, a clenched mitten to her mouth.

"This was my whole world," he said. He pointed to the farthest reaches of the den. "We fought battles here, my brothers and sisters and I, nipping and tumbling and charging at one another." He crumpled the rucksack and tossed it out on the lip of the overhang. "Every year I come back here, the day before I head south. I suppose it's my way of remembering. "

"And why did you bring me here?"

"Because I wanted you to see where I came from. Because I know how hard it has been for you, to have everything you knew ripped away from you. And it was that way for me too." The feathers of the dead birds fluttered in a sudden gust of wind. "When I first saw you, I thought I had never seen a person so sad. And yet, you didn't give in to it. You were too proud. You smiled at people, even the most wretched of beggars . . . There was no meanness in you, no bitterness. I think of you every night, Helga."

"Please . . . " she said.

"I don't know if you remember, but I asked you to marry me."

"Yes, I remember."

"I've been waiting to hear your decision."

Higher up on the river bank, the frayed banner danced at the top of the tilted stake. The harnessed dogs lay flat, eyes closed against the blowing snow.

"I'm sorry," she said. "I just . . . "

He climbed out of the den and took her hands. "It occurred to me while I was waiting that perhaps you were terrified of me. No doubt you have heard plenty of rumors."

She pulled free of him. She wondered if Lars was home yet, if he was worried about her. High above them a falcon hung motionless on the wind.

"Can I ask you something?" she said.

"Of course."

"When my son and I arrived here, we were told that there was no way out, that all the mountain passes were closed and would remain closed until God knows when. Yet you and your fifty sleds will be making your way south."

"Yes."

"How can that be?"

"Because I have the finest dog team in the world. And for years I have had an old man working for me who knows the mountains like no one else."

A second falcon had joined the first, circling a hundred feet above them. The sled dogs lifted their heads, ears up. They had heard something moving out in the darkness.

"I will make you a promise," he said, nudging the bloody ptarmigan with his foot.

"What is that?"

"If you will marry me, the next time I take the trip south, I will take you and your son with me. You will see light again, long afternoons of it. And trees, whole forests of them. We will live wherever you choose."

It was an insane promise, but from the fervent look in his eye, she was convinced he meant it. "Do you mean we would never have to return to this place?"

"It would all be up to you."

"Do you really think you would be able to give up your entire kingdom?"

"I do."

Far out on the tundra a wolf howled, and a second wolf answered, closer in. The scent of blood had carried farther and faster than she could have ever imagined.

TWENTY-ONE

acht Ruprecht had lived peacefully for centuries beneath a volcano in the Arctic, surrounded by lakes of boiling lava and the endless hiss of steam. He was content cultivating the blind white fish called skarn in the thermal pools.

But Nacht Ruprecht's idyllic life ended when war broke out to the south. Refugees began to show up. Not in massive numbers, but as many as forty or fifty at a time, and then the whalers and trappers began to arrive. After that came the prison ships, unloading their cargo of petty thieves, paupers, and even an occasional murderer. They were followed by other exiles—revolutionaries fleeing the czars, runaway slaves, religious dissenters with long, unkempt beards and blue eyes that never blinked.

For a time Nacht Ruprecht tried to tell himself that all this was a minor annoyance, that these people were nothing more than gnats to be waved away with a hand. Surely they wouldn't last for long. Surely they would either die off or stagger back to the south minus a few fingers and toes and noses lost to frostbite, and lugging a sackful of paltry belongings.

Many did die. Many gave up and left. But those that survived eventually began to do well, and the village grew in numbers.

As brutal as the winters were, they did have a few simple pleasures. There were always the brief Arctic summers to look forward to. They were just long enough for some people to plant gardens and for a few scraggly trees to grow out on the tundra. The children would make a game of it, standing on the headlands and seeing how many whales they could spot, blowing their spouts and rolling in the water like small mountains. Sometimes they would throw rocks at the seabirds making a racket in the high cliffs.

The problem was that these people didn't know when to let well enough alone. Real difficulties began when they started to assign someone each winter to cut down the biggest tree they could find out on the tundra (which was never a true tree at all, but usually a gnarly bit of thicket, seldom more than four feet high) and set it up in the village square.

The so-called tree would be decorated with candles and, on the shortest day of the year, all the children would rise early and race down to the square where, magically, there were now a pile of presents, all a-jumble, sitting under the green boughs.

The children all scrambled to find the present with their name on it. There were great squeals of delight as they tore off the wrapping to discover the toy inside. The toys were always modest—the children's parents were, after all, the poorest of the poor—but they created such a frenzy of excitement, such joy and wonder, not just for the children, but for their parents and grandparents as well. Ignoring the cold, they all oohed and ahhed over the simplest gee-gaws. And oh, the noise! It was more than Nacht Ruptrecht could stand.

The children would beg to know where these wonderful gifts came from, and every parent would have a different explanation. One claimed that all the toys had been found in the belly of a great white whale that had washed up on shore. Others told their sons and daughters that the toys had come sailing in on the wind or delivered by a blind musk ox pulling an enormous cart made of gold. Most persistant of all was the rumor of a band of half-dozen strange, dwarf-like creatures who lived somewhere out on the tundra and spent all their waking hours carving toys.

The children believed all these stories, no matter how ludicrous. And it was their innocent belief that gave the grown-ups the greatest pleasure.

It was this that sent Nacht Ruprect over the edge. Why did people need to make up all this tripe they didn't believe for a minute and then drill it into their children? Life was not filled with wonders and the miraculous. Life was short, brutish, and in the end they would all die.

Nacht Ruprecht was a demon of high seriousness, a demon of reason, equipped with a steel-trap mind, but he had no imagination. He didn't understand. He believed in the truth, unvarnished. Whimsy baffled him. The fanciful drove him mad. He didn't understand the hold these toys had on people, and what he didn't understand terrified him.

As the years passed, Nacht Ruprecht grew convinced that the toys were the cornerstone upon which the villagers' remarkable fortitude rested.

The tiny village continued to prosper. During the brief summer months the docks were lined with whaling ships from all over the world. The kingdom of silence and cold that had once been Nacht Ruprecht's alone was in danger of being overrun.

Nacht Ruprecht began to send storms at sea, blizzards, howling winds, and illness. Nearly half the village died in one epidemic, but in some way that Nacht Ruprecht didn't understand, all this adversity only made the people stronger. Every year, a tree was put up in the village square, gifts were given, and those damnable stories were told.

Nacht Ruprecht was in need of an ally.

The ally he found was a small, testy man by the name of Torgny Ratvass who operated a small, failing hotel down by the docks. After some negotiation a bargain was struck. Ratvass would run everything as long as two conditions were met. Toys would be banned, and on their thirteenth birthday, all youth would be required to have a daily dose of the potent skarn-liver oil, destroying the last traces of their childhoods forever. Nacht Ruprecht's blessed silence would be restored.

Two weeks after an agreement was signed, Nacht Ruprect unleashed the volcano. Early one morning, the earth began to tremble. Pans fell from cupboards. Grandmothers were thrown from their beds. Fire shot hundreds of feet into the sky above the volcano and spewed ash and burning lava down on the houses of the village, setting them aflame.

Everyone fled, leaving all they had behind. The village was buried in ash and the sky blotted out by smoke for several years. Temperatures dropped and no more trees grew. The oceans froze and became virtually impassable. All that remained of their whaling was a few abandoned ships.

After a decade a few of the old villagers began to straggle back, but the place they came back to was not the place they remembered. Not only were most of the houses gone and the cliffs that had once rung with the cries of birds silent, but there were no trees anywhere, not even the scraggly ones that the village used to gather around every year.

What they did find was Torgny, who had mysteriously survived the fires and the devouring rivers of lava, the years beneath the acrid dark clouds.

He was now a wealthy man, wealthy enough to build himself a virtual palace and erect labor camps for those who were homeless and penniless. He quickly put this new army of laborers to work constructing the world's first skarn-liver-oil factory. The tiny band of tomten carvers (who, as it turned out, did exist) were rounded up, and as punishment, put in charge of the care and feeding of the blind, fanged fish. It seemed only right that these creatures who spent all their time promoting childishness should make amends by helping destroy it.

It was not long before Torgny was going south each winter with dogsleds piled high with jugs of the precious oil, and year after year sales grew.

No toys had been seen in the village since before the eruption of the volcano. Dire warnings were posted around the village. Schoolchildren began their day by singing a song (composed by Torgny) condemning the evils of the toy. Rewards were offered for information leading to the arrest of anyone suspected of gift-giving. Rallies were held to denounce this taboo of taboos. There were parades and re-education classes for the elderly.

After Torgny's death, the Ratvass dynasty was ruled by his daughter Hildegaard, and then by her son Oskar. Oskar was the father of two worthless twins, Ragnold and Reynor. From an early age it was obvious to all that neither boy was a likely candidate to replace their father.

But everything changed when three hunters flushed a filthy feral child out of a wolf's den, captured him, and brought him to Oskar. The boy was just a curiosity at first, caged and put on display for all to mock and spit upon. But as the years passed, he slowly became half-civilized. By the time of Oskar's death, the old man had grown quite fond of the young man.

The brutal murders of the twins left the village in a state of shock. Chaos and uncertainty reigned. No one could say exactly who the murderer was, but the most likely suspect was the one to swiftly step forward and declare himself the new mayor.

The sheer gall of it astounded many. It was appalling, but no one could deny the boldness of it or that he possessed an instinct for command. But the one-time wild child had no intention of taking the Ratvass name, or of ever being referred to again as Nikita; he would be known henceforth as Mayor Wolfpaw.

TWENTY-TWO

With the mayor gone, a hush fell over the village. It almost felt as if there had been a mass exodus. One afternoon a dozen sleds driven by the fiercest deputies sped past Lars, a small army on its way to hunt down the mysterious assailant who'd attacked the Winter Festival from the skies. The next day the actors departed as well, and the day after that the shamans disappeared, a relief to those who'd been driven half-mad by all the chanting and drumming. The bleak hamlet was reduced even further to a dot of insignificance somewhere beyond the edge of all maps.

One bit of good news was that Miko's black eye had disappeared after a few days. What remained was Lars's memory of that moment in the dispensary, of his pressing the ice-pack to her bruised cheek, of standing so close he would have only had to lean forward another inch to touch her hair. What a fool he had been to have made such a mess, to think that she would have betrayed him to Arkady.

It was all different now. The few words they exchanged in Reindeer Husbandry class were awkward ones, the two of them as still and bewildered as ambassadors from opposite ends of the globe. She was still Arkady's girlfriend, after all. Neither of them knew quite what to do next. But they were at least talking.

But if they were emerging from silence, Lars's mother was retreating into it. More than once, at dinner, Lars would be in the middle of a story and then realize she hadn't heard a word he'd said. More than once he'd come into the living room to find her staring out the window at the gusting snow.

One evening they were playing a game of checkers before Lars went to bed. He was winning so handily it made him wonder if she wasn't letting him win. It was either that or she just wasn't paying attention.

She was down to her last two men and Lars had four, all kings. He was chasing her all over the board.

She put a hand on one of her men, then took it away, considering another move. "Lars, do you remember what it was like in summer? When the sun wouldn't go down until after midnight? And your father and you and I would go out in the boat to watch the fireworks?"

"Yes," he said.

She slid her man into the far corner. Lars slid one of his kings directly opposite her so he could jump her, no matter which way she moved.

"What if I came up with a way for us to go back home? How much would it be worth?"

He'd been staring hard at the board; now he jerked his head up to see if she was serious. "How much would it be worth? It would be worth everything."

"It would, wouldn't it?" Her voice sounded almost downcast.

The pile of black checkers at his elbow, already taken, shone in the lantern light. "Mom, do you really think there's a way?"

"I don't know, Lars." She put her long fingers on her last man. "I was just asking."

He missed the reindeer. He missed having his face licked by the overly friendly Alfred. He missed Canute and all his strutting around as if he thought he was the king. He even missed being butted by the truculent Siegfried.

They had become like family to him. They were the ones he was most comfortable with, the only ones he could confide in (even though they probably didn't understand a word he said). Without them he was earth-bound, Samson without his hair, a bird with its wings clipped.

So which one of them had convinced the others to desert him like this? Siegfried was the likely culprit, though it could have been Canute, having delusions of grandeur. But if Lars was being honest, he had to admit that he had no one to blame but himself for putting them through everything he'd put them through.

In his heart of hearts, he truly believed that he would never see them again, but one foggy afternoon, after returning home from school, he did. They were grazing along the shore, just below the house, digging through the snow with their hooves. In the heavy mist it was impossible to identify any of them with certainty, but there did seem to be just the right number of them—six, seven. . . . He wasn't sure but he thought he spotted the eighth as well.

His heart leapt. He set his skis against the side of the house. He moved slowly, afraid of frightening them. He took two steps and stopped, took another two steps and stopped again. He had gone twenty yards down the slope before the first of the reindeer raised its head. The first was quickly followed by a second and a third.

"Jonas, is that you? It's me, Lars. I'm so glad you've come back. Hedwig? Ulrike? I've been thinking about you guys every day."

They were all watching him now. The mist thickened, and they all began disappearing and re-appearing again, floating like ghosts.

"I'm just so sorry for the way I treated you. I'll be better, I promise . . ."

Lars skidded on his next step. He reeled forward, arms flailing to catch his balance. Spooked, the reindeer were off like a shot, vanishing into the mist.

Lars plunged head-long down the incline in pursuit. "Ulrike! Liv! Alfred! Stop! It's going to be okay!"

But there is no stopping a herd of panicked reindeer. Lars stumbled out onto the sea ice. All around him he could hear the clicking of reindeer hooves, the sloshing of big bellies, the snorting and grunting of thundering animals, but he could see nothing until for a moment the mist thinned, parting like a gauzy curtain, and he could make out not eight reindeer, but fifty, or even a hundred of them, all wild, an enormous herd that had been hidden in the fog. But as many of them as there were, they were all ordinary, all rooted to the ice and snow, and no friends of his.

They disappeared again into the murk, and the sounds of their running quickly faded. Lars fell to his knees. Silence folded around him like a blanket. How idiotic it had been of him to get his hopes up, to believe for a second they would have ever forgiven him.

He looked back over his shoulder. A lantern had just been lit in the house. His mother must have gotten home. He rose to his feet and made his way back to the shore. Every third step he kicked at the snow, furious at himself for being such a dope. On his tenth kick, his toe stubbed against something hard just below the crusted surface.

What it was wasn't immediately clear. When he bent down and fumbled to retrieve it, the slightly curved shape made him guess it must be a fragment of a reindeer antler. But when it tugged it free of the ice, he saw that it was a knife.

Could one of the seal hunters have dropped it? Or someone snooping around their house? It wasn't until he cleaned it of snow that he saw the familiar markings. It was his father's knife. He hadn't thought of it for weeks. But how had it ended up out here? All he could figure out was that it must have fallen out of the sleigh the first time he'd flown over the house.

Compared to a team of flying reindeer, a knife is understandably forgettable. But what had Nanu said when she gave it to him? "Maybe it's time for you to be your father."

When she'd said it, he'd had no idea what she meant. But he did now. What a terrible thing it was for a grandmother to tell a grandson. She might as well have told him to go stick his hand into the fire. She wanted him to carve toys in a place where toys were banned. What was she trying to do, get him into even more trouble? And what was he going to carve? There were no trees for hundreds of miles. And if he did carve something, who was he going to give it to?

Nanu had given him two gifts. He'd lost both. Now he'd managed to stumble across one of them and wished he hadn't.

For days he fretted over what to do. He hid the knife in one place and then another. He hid it under his pillow, in the back of the closet, under his bed. More than once he thought of just burying it in the snow and forgetting about it.

But the knife had taken hold of him. Sometimes at night he would remove it from its hiding place, lie on his bed, hold it up to the window and turn it slowly, letting the moonlight glint off the blade.

What a furor he could create! The idea scared and excited him all at once. Imagine that he, Lars, could restore justice to the land!

No, he was getting far, far ahead of himself. He was just twelve years old, he didn't know how to carve, and he had no one to teach him. His father had been taught by his father, who'd been taught by his father before him. His father had also been carving for all his life and had such strong arms and wrists. Lars knew from watching him how difficult the different kinds of wood could be.

The truth was that Lars most likely wouldn't be any good at it. On the other hand, what harm would it do to give it a whack? With no reindeer to tend to, he certainly had the time for it.

Finding wood in a land with no trees was no mean trick. Lars explored the farthest reaches of the whaling ship, the lantern swinging before him. He scrutinized the gangways, the wheelhouse, the walls of the cabins and the forecastle, the planks of the deck, stained black by the blood of whales.

He was willing to have a go at anything that looked halfway useable—spars, barrel staves, a broken rudder, chairs from the captain's quarters, but most of the wood was too old and brittle.

He stole a few shingles from their neighbor's roof, but they were no better. The best he was able to come up with were the seats in the whale boats that he was able to rip out and break into workable lengths.

His first attempts at carving were a disaster. Twice he nearly cut off his thumb. His hands and forearms were not strong enough, and the knife kept slipping. Worst of all, nothing turned out the way he intended. His bulls came out looking like beavers, his goose like a giraffe. His gorilla could easily have been mistaken for an angry chicken, his cow for a sofa. He ended up giving them all the toss. His half-finished efforts littered the floor of the whaling ship like malformed potatoes.

His skills as a carver progressed slowly. Nine out of ten attempts ended up as rejects, and he would just toss them over his shoulder. It wasn't long before they dappled the floor like toadstools after a rain.

One afternoon as he ducked into the ragged hole in the hull, his left foot skidded out from under him. There was a sharp, splintery crack and he went sprawling, hitting the floor hard.

It took Lars a minute to collect his senses. He finally pushed himself up to a sitting position and rubbed his sore knee. He patted the floor around him, searching for whatever had tripped him. He couldn't find anything at first, but he spied the shattered carving in a patch of moonlight, just a foot beyond his outstretched hand.

Lars retrieved the two broken pieces and held them up in the silvery light. The carving was one of his first attempts. It was supposed to have been a polar bear, rearing up on its hind legs, but one of the legs was missing now. Lars tried to gently poke the leg back on, but it wouldn't stick.

It was a woeful excuse for a bear. Its nose was too thick, the ears weren't the same size, and the eyes seemed to be going in opposite directions. It was genuinely horrible looking. He should have just pitched it, but he was feeling so wounded and betrayed, he needed to do something to calm down.

He lit the lantern under the stairs, took out his father's knife and began to whittle.

For at least an hour Lars shaved and chiseled and scraped. As Lars lost himself in his work, his imagination gradually took over. Maybe it was just the moonlight reflecting off the strange eyes of the bear, but weren't they beginning to seem almost alive? And didn't the outstretched arms resemble the outstretched arms of a man on a desert island?

Somehow the bear became a ballerina, standing on one foot with the other foot lifted straight up behind her. She wasn't the most beautiful ballerina, not with one ear so much bigger than the other, but she did look more like a ballerina than she had ever looked like a bear, and the way she held her leg up behind her would have put all the cheerleaders at school to shame. For the first time Lars had created something half good.

Lars had no idea how he'd done this. It was a miracle. All he could think of was how proud his father would have been of him. But what was he supposed to do with it? The only thing he could imagine doing was what his father would have done, which was to give it away. It was Pytor who'd told him that anyone caught with a toy would be snatched from his family and never seen again, but when his mother had asked the mayor about it, he said that was preposterous. And that was what Lars thought, too.

It was two nights later, sometime around 1 a.m. if the single stran-gled cry of the cuckoo clock was to be trusted, that Lars set out for Miko's house. There wasn't a sound from his mother's bedroom as he slipped out the front door. The wooden ballerina in his pocket, he skied through the fresh drifts.

Things scurried in the darkness, and at least once he heard the far-off howling of wolves. He sang a bit and whistled a bit, trying to keep his courage up. He missed the company of his reindeer. Occasionally he would see a light in the distance, but then blackness would swallow it and he would be alone again, his mukluks squeaking in the snow.

He knew there was something foolish in what he was doing, and he knew perfectly well how foolishness could lead to trouble. What if he ran into the deputies on their nightly patrols? If he wanted to give Miko a present it would have been a lot simpler to just give it to her in person. But the truth was that as bold as he had become in many ways, there was still part of him that was painfully shy, particularly around girls.

And what if she hated it? What if she laughed? The carving, even with all the work he'd put in on it, was still a pretty amateurish effort. But it didn't matter. She would never know who'd given it to her. He'd grown comfortable being out in the dark, when the rest of the world was sleeping. In the dark he could be daring. In the dark he could get away with nearly everything.

Lars turned at the old lighthouse and began the slog up the wide valley. It was another twenty minutes before Miko's shack came into view. Lars unstrapped his skis, stuck them in a snowbank, and proceeded warily on foot, passing two carved poles that listed like drunken sentries. A sickly Malamute, chained up, raised his head, gave a muffled woof, and went back to sleep.

Lars ducked under an archway of reindeer antlers. A knocker fashioned of ivory, feathers, and leather straps was nailed to the front door, but it looked as if it would fall at the slightest touch. Lars's heart pounded. He pressed down gently on the latch a couple of times before he heard it click. He edged the door open, slid inside, and closed it quickly behind him.

It took several seconds for his eyes to adjust to the dark. Embers glowed through the cracks of a cast-iron stove, giving off just enough light for him to see what a mess the place was. A thin layer of smoke drifted in the air, stacks of unwashed dishes filled the sink, and a man's boot lay sideways on a chair like a drowsing cat.

A kayak hung from the ceiling. A half dozen clotheslines, festooned with rags and towels and an enormous pair of men's long underwear, crisscrossed the small room. Rusted harpoons lined one wall, and on top of a battered cupboard, an altar of shells perched precariously.

There was a small mountain of blankets on the floor, and it wasn't until Lars heard it snore that he realized it was Miko's father. Further back, under the eaves, was a hammock. Just below the hammock dangled a foot (Miko's foot, it had to be), and on the foot was a blue sock with a hole in the toe. How embarrassed she would have been to know he'd seen it, that hole in her sock! But, when you thought about it, it really wasn't Miko's fault that she didn't have a mother to sew it up for her.

The smoke stung Lars's eyes. Her father coughed, threw a tattooed arm over his head and began whistling. Inches beyond his elbow a half-empty bottle glittered in the dim light. The shack was very warm. Lars felt his forehead prickling under his wool hat.

He was quite amazed to find himself here. If either Miko or her father woke, there would be a terrible row. What could they possibly think, except that he was a thief? He would be lucky not to be run through with one of those rusty harpoons.

He ran his tongue over chapped lips and fingered the wooden ballerina in his pocket. Something rustled behind him, but when he glanced over his shoulder, he saw nothing.

He scanned the room. Where exactly were you supposed to leave a present? He wanted to make sure that Miko saw it first thing when she woke up. The top of the stove was the most obvious place, but if a spark caught, it could burn the whole house down.

He heard the rustling again, but it was fainter this time and Lars ignored it, figuring it was just the shifting of embers or the wind in the chimney. He spotted a low bench with Miko's homework fanned across it. As he edged toward it, he felt something tickle his ankle.

But, no, it wasn't just his ankle. Something scurried up his shin, light as a feather, and leapt onto his knee. How he managed not to scream, he had no idea. He kicked wildly and swatted at his trousers. A tiny blur of white sped across the floor as Lars teetered on one leg.

Everything seemed to happen at once. Lars skidded on the half-empty bottle and sent it spinning. He flailed his arms, trying to keep his balance, accidentally snagged two fingers on one of the clothes-lines, and nearly pulled it down. He grabbed for a second clothesline, missed it, and lurched into a heavy-laden coatrack.

Only a desperate last-second dive kept the coatrack from slamming to the floor. Breathing hard, Lars set the coatrack back on its feet. The enormous suit of long underwear bobbed up and down like a ghost doing jumping jacks.

It was a miracle, but Miko and her father were sleeping as soundly as ever.

Nothing had been dislodged except for a trio of mittens and a red scarf. Lars gathered them up and, as he stuffed them in the pockets of one of the parkas, he spied a piece of sailcloth tacked to the wall above the altar of shells.

Something was painted on it. It was the crudest of pictures, and he had to tilt his head to make it out. It was the kind of thing a child of six or seven might do. There was a blue ocean and a yellow sun, palm trees, a mother and a father and a little girl. A whale with a big grin and huge eyes (with long eyelashes) sat on the horizon.

The father and the little girl held hands. The mother stood a bit apart from them, with her arms outstretched as if welcoming someone. As childlike as the painting was, there was no doubt in Lars's mind that the woman was Miko's mother.

Lars tiptoed across the room, ducking through the jungle of clotheslines. The remorseful lemming watched from under a chair, nose twitching. Lars set the ballerina on the altar of shells. The two women made a perfect match, one of wood, one of paint, both with raised arms and facing one another as if about to begin a dance.

Once Lars was outside, he broke into a run, jogging past the dozing Malamute and the tilting carved poles. After coming out of the overheated room, the cold felt twice as cold as before. He strapped on his skis, shivering uncontrollably.

All he'd done was give someone a present, a small thing. But somehow it didn't feel small. It felt as if something huge had shifted, as if he had finally done something he was always meant to do.

The way back was long, it was late, and he was tired. As he skied through the dark valley, he kept thinking about his father, sneaking into Lars's bedroom at night to slip toys under his pillow. His father was so good at it Lars never woke up once.

Lars, in comparison, had been a total bumbler. If Pytor could have seen him tonight, he would have roared. To be scared out of your wits by a lemming? Ridiculous. To go reeling around the room, grabbing at clotheslines, stumbling into things? He'd nearly brought the whole house down around them. What if he'd landed on her father's head? Or crashed into the stove?

At the top of a rise, he stopped to rest. He unstrapped his skis, lay back in the snow, and stared up at the moon and the stars that looked as if someone had taken a bucket and thrown a million bits of ice across the sky.

How had he gotten away with this? It seemed like the world's grandest joke. He thought of the suit of long underwear, bounding around like a man with St. Vitus dance. The more he thought about it, the funnier it got. He started to chuckle and the chuckles turned to cackles, and the cackles to guffaws. He couldn't help himself. He slapped at the snow with his mittens and stomped his boots as tears filled his eyes.

"Ho-ho-ho! Ho-ho-ho!" His laughter was not a boy's laughter, and not quite a man's. He was just twelve, after all, and his voice had started to crack, but the cliffs on either side of the valley echoed the sound back to him as if they were all in it together, the cliffs, the brilliant stars, the arctic night.

"Ho-ho-ho!"

The echoes faded into stillness. There was a trickle of snow inside one of his mittens. He shook it out before he got up. He strapped on his skis. There was still a long way to go before he got home.

Lars may have thought he'd done something stupendous, but at school the next morning it was business as usual. Snee got yelled at in geography for falling asleep; two girls were sent to the office for passing notes, and one of the younger boys burst into tears after getting his lunch money stolen.

Lars kept glancing over at Miko in class and, later, in the hallways, for some sign—a sparkle in the eye, a new bounce in the step, some trace of happiness—but there was nothing. If anything, she seemed perturbed and a little distracted.

Lars had no idea what to think. Could she not have seen the ballerina somehow? Or maybe she had seen it and didn't think it was much. Or maybe her father had snatched it before she awoke and tossed it in the stove. He'd given her something before, and that had not gone well. He prayed she hadn't shown it to Arkady.

Afternoon classes passed without incident. Lars couldn't deny that he was disappointed. He tried to console himself. There were a million things that could have happened. Maybe the carving had fallen under a couch. He almost had to laugh at himself, thinking about all the trouble he'd gone to.

At the end of the day, he passed the schoolmaster's office where Mr. Smorgas and a couple of the teachers were having a hushed conversation. The hall was empty except for a few stragglers. Lars pulled his hat down over his ears and buttoned the top button of his parka. As he strode by the science room, a low murmuring made him turn. He glanced in at Miko and Annuchka bent over a long oak table.

They seemed to be having a great time, giggling and whispering, but when they saw him, they fell silent. Lars meekly raised a hand in greeting and kept walking. It was clear that they did not want to be disturbed. But when he got to the gym, he pivoted and silently retraced his steps.

He peered around the corner of the door. Miko sat sideways on the bench with the wooden ballerina in her right hand, Annuchka standing at her shoulder. Miko skipped the tiny dancer back and forth across the table, making her leap and twirl to the kind of music only wooden ballerinas can hear.

It was quite silly, really, and Miko had the relaxed air of a piano player plinking idly away with one hand, but Annuchka was mesmerized. Miko had the ballerina finish her performance with a triple-spin and a deep, graceful bow. Annuchka burst into wild applause and then bent down to give Miko a tight squeeze.

A slow, slyly proud smile spread across Miko's face. Lars ducked away before either of them could see him. He hurried down the hall, the laughter trailing behind him different from any laughter he'd ever heard in the school before—giddy, delighted, and free of malice.

TWENTY-THREE

f Lars had stopped after giving one toy, he might have gotten away with it. But he didn't stop. Sneaking off to the whaling ship whenever he could, he began to rework his old carvings—turning a sorry attempt at a sea lion into a stalwart soldier, whittling a malformed wolf into a glowering musk ox. Realizing there was only so much he could accomplish with a knife as his only tool, he snuck a mallet and a gouge out of the shop at school. He found a holystone rummaging in the forecastle that he could use for sanding.

He began to create new carvings—a lynx, a cheetah, a giraffe, a roaring lion, an archer with a drawn bow, a wagon with wheels that could actually spin. It was intense, exhausting work. He got blisters, and the blisters hardened into calluses.

When he ran out of new ideas, he started to carve things he remembered from his old life—a sway-backed horse, a trio of woodsmen who looked a little like his father, Anton, and Emil, and an old woman smoking a pipe. The eyes didn't come out the way he would have wanted (he tried to give them a bit of a squint, and they ended up looking like snow goggles), but he did get Nanu's jutting chin right, right down to the corkscrew hair on her mole. When he finished, he carved a flock of chickens to keep her company.

At school Miko was carrying her wooden ballerina everywhere with her, tucked in the pocket of her sweater. It was as if he was watching the sun come up in someone. Every time he saw her, she was chatting and laughing with people, chasing Annuchka down the hallway, and one day in the lunchroom Lars spied her pulling one of the younger girls aside to let her have a peek at the tiny dancer.

Over a single week, Lars gave away three presents. For Present One, he had to sneak into the house of the bucktoothed girl called Masha and leave a giraffe on her pile of schoolbooks. For Present Number Two, he climbed into a window in Sniffles's house and put a tiny wagon in his boot. Delivering Present Number Three was more difficult. He had to quiet a pair of enormous, slobbering huskies with chunks of blubber and jimmy a lock in order to stuff the roaring lion inside the mitten of a boy nicknamed Wormy.

The day after Masha got her giraffe she went around beaming as if she'd lost her wits. The day after Sniffles got his red wagon, he caught Lars at recess and motioned him under the bleachers. Once they were safely out of sight of the others, Sniffles, his eyes shining, wrestled the red wagon from under his coat and ran his hands over the wheels to make them spin.

Wormy was another matter. The morning after Lars gave him the roaring lion, Wormy was late getting to school. Lars spied him creeping into the back of the auditorium halfway through the singing of the anthem. Lars could tell immediately that something was wrong. Not once during the singing of the final four verses did Wormy lift his bowed head or meet anyone's eyes.

When Lars saw him again at lunch, it was no better. Wormy sat by himself at a table in the very back of the room, hunched over his soup as if he was afraid someone might snatch it from him, and taking furtive glances at his neighbors. When one of the teachers came up behind him and put a hand on his shoulder to make sure he was all right, Wormy jumped as if he'd been shot.

What could Lars have been thinking? Certainly he'd been warned. Taya Kerensky had told them that the giving of toys would bring severe punishment. Every other week, they were forced to sing that dreadful anthem and listen to woe-begotten speakers lecture them on the evils of toys. It was true that Wolfpaw as well as his fiercest deputies were absent, so perhaps no one was quite as vigilant.

But it was the height of foolishness to trust a bunch of kids with a secret. What Lars was doing could spell doom for all of them. With evey toy that Lars gave away, the ice they were skating on grew thinner.

The truth was that Lars didn't know what he was thinking. Perhaps he wasn't thinking at all. Maybe it was just dumb. Maybe it was like playing with fire when you know you shouldn't. Or maybe it was like sneaking candies when you're going to keep on sneaking them until someone catches you.

But why did he even need to question it? All he knew was that his old moodiness had disappeared. The fact was, what he was doing just felt natural. You might as well ask a bird why it flies south in the winter, or ask a tree when it sheds its leaves in the fall.

Lars grew bolder. The next week Lars snuck into six houses. He left the musk ox for Mule Face, the lynx for Ludmilla, a girl in his math class, the cheetah for the cross-eyed boy named Wink, and the archer with his bow drawn to Donald Donkey-Ears.

All those who'd been given carvings knew how important it was to keep mum about it, but as hard as they might have tried not to give anything away, the changes in them were unmistakable. During the singing of the anthem Ludmilla blushed madly when they came to the verse about the loathsome toy, and Donald Donkey-Ears, who had been the butt of every joke for years, was strutting down the hallway with a smirk on his face as if he ruled the place.

The school was filled to bursting with secrets. Lars was getting seriously worried, but all the teachers—Mr. Smorgas flirting with Miss Bord in the hallway, Mr. Ostertag sneaking out between classes for a smoke, Miss Sunvold trying to puzzle out her gradebook with her disordered eyes—seemed perfectly oblivious.

The trouble began when Arkady broke his tooth on the tail of a lion. He was slurping down the last of his soup when he crunched down on a fragment of wood, not more than an inch long, bearing the marks of a carver's knife. It had ended up in the soup when Wormy leaned over the kettle of cod chowder a bit too enthusiastically, and his toy lion slipped out of his shirt pocket and, unbeknownst to him, glided silently to the bottom of the pot.

All of Arkady's friends had finished lunch and drifted off to terrorize some of the younger students. Arkady sat alone at his table, running his tongue over his chipped incisor and scrutinizing the sliver of lion's tail. He had never seen a toy before, but he was nobody's fool. Something very strange had to be going on.

But what? The thing was with someone as alert as Arkady, once they're on the lookout, it's only a matter of time before they spot something. Two days later Arkady's eye was caught by Muleface and Wink making animal sounds as they stealthily jousted with their musk ox and cheetah under their lunch room table.

Arkady waited outside of school for close to an hour before Wink finally came dawdling out. The hillside was devoid of sleds, except for Arkady's, his two huge blond dogs half-buried in the snow next to it.

"Hey, Wink, you got a minute?"

Wink was startled. He was so far down on the social ladder, he wasn't aware that Arkady even knew his name. "Sure, why not?"

"What do you say we go for a little walk? Maybe down by the barn?" Wink was now thoroughly confused, but he wasn't going to say no. "Fine with me," he said.

What Arkady didn't realize was that he and Wink weren't the only ones still around. When the reindeer husbandry teacher had asked for volunteers to come back at the end of the day to roll a dozen of the old grain barrels up to the custodian's shed, Lars had been the only one to raise his hand. At the time it had seemed like a simple enough task—now, not so much. The barrels had been retrieved from the whaling ships and been used for years to store feed. They were all as heavy as lead.

Lars was taking a breather before tackling the last of the barrels (soon to be reduced to firewood) when he spied Arkady and Wink ambling toward the open door of the barn. They made a strange sight together, Arkady, in a convivial mood, with his massive arm draped around Wink's shoulders, and Wink, a head shorter, looking concerned. Lars knew it was wrong to spy on people, but sometimes it's just too hard to resist. He stepped back into the shadows.

Ten feet short of the barn door, Arkady and Wink came to a stop. Arkady was no longer looking so convivial. "Oh, come on, Wink. You don't have to lie to me. You and Muleface were fooling around with something under the table, I saw you . . . "

"I don't remember, honest . . . "

"Well, if that's the way you're going to be." He gave Wink a shove in the chest, sent him stumbling back toward the door, and then shoved him again.

Lars glanced over his shoulder, looking for an escape, but there was none. The equipment room was locked; there wasn't enough time to climb the the ladder into the loft, and if he tried to squeeze into a stall with one of the reindeer he was only going to cause a rumpus.

Desperate circumstances call for desperate measures. Lars swung one leg over the edge of the one remaining barrel. He was hung up for just a moment, but then, bracing himself with both arms, swung his second leg over as well and dropped silently to the bottom of the cask. He squatted in darkness, elbows tight to his ribs.

"Okay, show me your pockets," Arkady said.

"No-o-o . . . " There were sounds of a scuffle and a thump as someone (Wink, most likely), banged against one of the stalls.

"Aha!"

"No-o-o," Wink moaned.

There was a long silence. Lars quivered like a woodchuck in its burrow. "Do you know what this is?"

"No," Wink said.

"I think it's a toy. Oh, Wink, I think you're in big trouble. I think this is what they've been warning us about all these years. Who gave it to you?"

It sounded as if they were standing next to the ladder to the loft. "Nobody gave it to me. I just found it."

"Found it where?"

"In my shoe."

Arkady's laugh was short and harsh. "In your shoe?"

Lars's nose began to tickle with the smell of grain dust and mold. He put a finger to his nose to keep from sneezing.

"It was there one morning when I woke up. I have no idea where it came from. But I'm not the only one. There are lots of others who've gotten them too."

Wink had just made a terrible mistake. "Lots of others? How many?"

"I don't know."

A great clatter nearly made Lars leap out of the barrel. It sounded as if Arkady had just started throwing milk pails. "Am I the only one who didn't get anything? But that wouldn't be a surprise, would it? But I'll bet all the good kids got something, didn't they? And all the bad kids didn't. That's the way the world works. That's what people call fair. I've never had anybody give me anything in my whole life. Whatever I've ever had I had to take."

It sounded as if Arkady, beside himself, was striding up and down the length of the barn. From the rows of stalls came the grunting and banging of agitated reindeer. Lars glanced up as Arkady brushed past. There was a sliver of light at the rim of the barrel. He watched as it began to creep down the inside of the cask. It was the first moon of the night, angling through the jagged gash in the roof of the barn, threatening to expose him.

"I'm not going to sit around and cry about it," Arkady said. "But I will tell you what I'm going to do. I'm going to ask you and your friends to bring me all of these toys. Let me have a look. I'll give you two days."

"Two days!"

"That's what I said. Two days. And if you can't do that . . . or if I find that somebody's holding out on me . . . I'm going right to Mr. Smorgas and telling him everything."

"You can't mean it."

"I do mean it."

"But he'll kidnap us all!"

"Now wouldn't that be pretty?" The barrel shook as Arkady whacked it with the flat of his hand.

Lars should have popped right out of the barrel like a beaver out of its dam and explained everything. But he hadn't. He'd just crouched down, covering his head, barely taking a breath until Arkady and Wink had left.

Did Arkady intend to go through with his threat? There was no way of telling. But one thing for sure, he was a jerk. Jerk or not, there had been truth in what he'd said. Lars had never thought it through, who he was going to give toys to, or why. Could he really be expected to give presents to everybody? But one thing for sure. He had his task cut out for him.

That night after his mother went to bed, Lars snuck down to the whaling ship, found a piece of wood, sat on the steps, and set to work.

All through dinner, he had struggled over what to carve, what would most appeal to Arkady, what would be most likely to diffuse his anger. What he settled on was not the most brilliant idea—if anything, it was all too obvious. He would make Arkady a gorilla, beating on its chest, since Arkady was the closest thing to a gorilla he knew.

But the wood was dry and kept splintering. Lars's back ached from sitting so long in the barrel. But, worst of all, Lars was at war with himself. He hated what he was being forced to do.

All the other carvings he'd done, once he'd gotten the hang of it, had made him proud. Giving them away had filled him with delight. But this felt as if he was working with a musket to his head and it made everything impossible.

The knife seemed to have a life of its own. It kept slipping and twice he nicked himself. His first gorilla turned out so hopelessly bad he had to throw it out and go rummaging around the ship for twenty minutes to find another suitable hunk of wood.

He worked on the second gorilla for over an hour and it went somewhat better until he got a sliver under his thumbnail.

It hurt enough to bring tears to his eyes. The pain did not go away, even after he managed to pull the sliver out. It was impossible to continue. He was undone. All hope drained out of him. He was just kidding himself—this gorilla was scarcely better than the other, and if he stayed half the night it wasn't going to make a whit of difference. There was no way Arkady was going to have his mind changed by a carving as stupid as this.

Lars pitched the gorilla across the hold and listened to it rattle in the darkness.

When he got back to the house, he tiptoed past his mother's room, slipped into bed, and, clutching his rapidly swelling thumb to his chest, fell into a deep, despairing sleep.

The next afternoon when he got home, he went down to the whaling ship, hoping that one of his gorillas might at least be worth taking another stab at. As soon as he sidestepped through the splintery hole, he saw, perched on the stairs, two carved wooden boxers, no more than nine inches tall. They were so well done it was impossible to believe that they had been created in one night. Fresh shavings littered the floor.

Brain-numbed, Lars picked up one and then the other. They'd been painted, one in blue trunks, one in red. They were fat, these boxers. The one with a snarl and a cowlick looked a lot like Arkady, and the other, with a goony smile and three missing teeth, was the spitting image of Roope.

They were the most amazing toys Lars had ever seen. In the back of each were two strings. When Lars pulled one, the boxer would throw a left jab. When he pulled the other, the boxer would throw a right uppercut. Best of all, when the punch landed, the opponent's head would wobble in a very satisfying way. They were perfect, and there was no doubt who they were intended for.

Lars set them down on the stairs. Lars's discarded gorillas lay in the far corner of the hold. Whoever had done this must still be nearby, still hidden, but watching and listening and understanding everything. It took him a moment, but he finally got up enough nerve to conduct a brief search. He found nothing except some feathery tracks in the snow drifts on the top deck, nothing more than hen scratchings or the scurry-marks of lemmings.

What was he supposed to do now? It was all too obvious what he was supposed to do now. And there was no time to spare.

He set off late that night, after his mother had gone to bed. Arkady lived in a valley parallel to the one where Miko lived, in a compound of long, low buildings set close to the face of the mountain. The good news was that there was a trampled trail running one hundred yards from the mountain to the compound. Lars unstrapped his skis, hid them in a shallow cave, and made his way on foot.

The remains of a wooden fence surrounded the compound. Two dozen huskies were chained up in the central courtyard, but the only ones who seemed to be awake were Arkady's two huge blonde dogs. They sat up, ears perked and lips curled in snarls as soon as Lars ducked under the row of yellowing walrus tusks that dangled from the main gate.

Lars pulled his packet of seal meat from his pocket. He waved a couple of strips at arm's length like a flag of truce as he made his way across the compound.

Snares and booby traps were everywhere. There were tripwires and nooses and a pint-sized catapult rigged to go off at the slightest nudge. Lars narrowly avoided a pit that had been dug in the frozen earth and covered with branches and a couple inches of snow. When he cleared the branches away with his toe, he could see a dozen sharpened stakes two feet down, glowing in the moonlight.

He shuffled toward the dogs, murmuring to them, low and soft and reassuring, shaking the strips of meat. The dogs rose and wagged their tails. When Lars tossed them the scraps, the dogs pounced on them like lions pouncing on zebras, growling and tearing at the frozen flesh.

Arkady's sled was pulled up under the eaves of the nearest house. Lars went to the door and took a couple of deep breaths to calm himself. Behind him, one of the dogs hacked away, trying to dislodge a piece of gristle from its throat.

Lars turned the knob carefully and pushed the door open three or four inches. He reached around, groping the air with his fingers. After a second, he found what he half-expected to find—a taut length of twine stretching from the inside doorknob to the frame above.

He angled his shoulder into the four-inch gap and reached up as high as he could. At first he felt only the rasp of coarse bone, but then he felt metal.

Rising on tiptoes, he was able to get hold of the hilt of the scimitar with both hands and lower it soundlessly to the floor. Lars had never seen a sword more enormous. It had a long curved blade and an ornate ivory hilt. Lars tested the razor-sharp edge with his thumb. If it had fallen on him from the door frame it would have sliced him in two.

He surveyed the house. It was much better kept than Miko's house, but equally strange. Animal traps hung from racks in the ceiling and earthenware jugs lined the shelves. A live chicken roosted atop a cupboard, and Arkady's parents snored in tandem in a massive bed.

His mother, in a tasseled nightcap, was a good-sized woman, but his father was a giant, with unruly red hair and an ugly scar that ran from one ear to his chin. On his nose was a large wart.

Arkady was curled up in a cot at the foot of the bed, his fist to his mouth. But as Lars bent over to have a closer look, he saw that Arkady was sucking his thumb. Lars could scarcely believe it. He was filled with glee. He couldn't help it. If Lars told the kids at school, imagine the fun they'd have with that!

The chicken clucked in its sleep. Arkady clutched the tattered remains of what must have once been a baby's blanket, pressing it to his cheek. Could this possibly be the same person who would wake up in the morning ready to pound people?

Lars squatted, studying him intently. This was even harder than he'd thought it would be. How was he supposed to give a present to someone who'd just tried to cut you in two with a scimitar?

Arkady was totally at his mercy. For just a second Lars was tempted to yank the thumb out of Arkady's mouth and conk him on the head with one of those earthenware jugs.

But then Arkady began to toss and turn as if he was having a nightmare. Lars rose and took a step back.

Writhing in his sleep, Arkady tossed off his quilt. "No, no!" he whispered. 'No, no!" He covered his face with his arm as if he expected to be hit.

Arkady was wearing pajamas decorated with frisky ponies. Because of his thrashing, the top of the pajamas had ridden up, and Lars could see the red welts on the small of his back.

He bent down to pull the quilt over Arkady's shoulders. His parents continued to snore, loud as steam engines. Lars scanned the room, trying to find a good hiding place for the two boxers. The last thing he wanted was for Arkady's mother and father to find the carvings first. He finally got down on one knee and shoved the boxer as far back under the cot as they would go.

He retreated cautiously. He stepped over the scimitar, slipped out the door, and closed it behind him.

The two blonde dogs strained at their chains. Their soft brown eyes seemed almost wounded. As far as they were concerned, the scraps of frozen seal meat were just appetizers, a bit of a midnight snack. They wanted more.

Lars pulled his pockets inside out to show them he didn't have any more, but when he backed away, they began to whine. Lars put a finger to his lips. One of the dogs barked. Lars broke into a trot. The dog barked more sharply, waking the other huskies. Lars began to run, dodging to avoid the snares and booby traps. By the time he ducked under the dangling walrus tusks, the barking of the dogs had risen to a howling din.

He ran down the trampled trail, stumbled, fell, and righted himself. Looking back over his shoulder, he saw people pouring out of the long, low buildings. There must have been at least thirty of them, some with muskets, some with spears and clubs, and a doddery old man carried what looked like a crossbow. Arkady was there too, standing in his doorway in his pajamas, looking bewildered.

Lars turned and ran again. There was no way he was going to be able to outrace an army of sled dogs. His only hope was to get to the cliffs and pick his way up the rugged slopes where it would be impossible for sleds to follow.

He had another sixty yards to go to make it to the base of the mountain, but his legs were beginning to cramp. A half dozen sleds were already on their way, closing the distance at an alarming rate.

Lars could hear the men shouting, see them wave their weapons over their heads. There was a sharp pop, and a second later something whizzed past his ear and sent up a spray of snow five or six feet beyond him.

Lars bolted like a rabbit flushed out of a farmer's garden. He zigged and zagged, not wanting to make himself an easy target.

It wasn't until he was a few yards from the base of the mountain that he remembered his skis, hidden away in the shallow cave. What an idiot he was! The last thing he needed was for this to be any harder than it already was, but he had no choice. If he left the skis here, someone was bound to find them and figure out whose they were.

He retrieved his skis and hoisted them on his shoulder. The first part of his climb was a scramble up a steep icy trail of loose rock that eventually wound around to an overlook. Wrestling with the skis made it twice as difficult as it should have been. His lungs felt like they were about to burst.

He squatted, trying to regain his breath, then rose. From the edge of the overlook he peered down at the roiling mass of men and sleds at the bottom of the cliff.

The men argued and pointed, and a few were unhitching their dogs. Lars couldn't figure out what they were doing until the men began to pull their dogs by their collars over to the trail of Lars's bootprints leading up the slope. Once the men set them loose, the dogs bounded up the ice and scree, eager as wolves.

Lars's heart leapt to his throat. What had he done to deserve this? All he'd done was give Arkady a present. If only he could have had a chance to explain himself. But it wouldn't have mattered. There was no difference now between the men and the dogs. They were all one pack, ready to tear him limb from limb. Whatever deep, unspoken thing had stirred them to such rage was a mystery to him.

He eyeballed the incline above him. It was almost straight up and down, and littered with boulders the size of houses. If he'd been a mountain goat, it wouldn't have been so bad, but he wasn't. He worked his way around one boulder and then a second. He edged higher, teetering on one rock and jumping to another, a ski in each hand to help him keep his balance.

The barking of dogs below him grew louder and louder. Another musket popped, the sound echoing off the rocks. He began to climb faster, taking more chances. His leaps from boulder to boulder grew longer and riskier.

A rock tower loomed above him like a fortress, but just a few feet below it was a narrow pass where it looked as if he might slip from one side of the mountain to the other, maybe even ski down and escape from all his pursuers.

Lars lurched up the final incline and picked his way through the narrow pass, his skis banging and scraping against the rocks. The dogs' barking grew higher-pitched and more bloodcurdling.

The far slope of the mountain wasn't what he had hoped. In fact, it was no slope at all, just a sheer drop-off, two hundred feet to the valley floor. It wasn't just dogs he heard now, there were men too, cursing and shouting instructions.

Lars knew he was done for. He flopped down on his back and covered his face in his hands to keep from bawling. What, he wondered, would they tell his mother when they were finished with him?

There are all kinds of snorts. There are angry snorts and milk-up-the-wrong-tube snorts and I-can't-believe-you-think-that's-funny snorts. There are also familiar snorts, the comfortable, curious family kind of snorts you've heard a million times before, and when Lars heard one, lying there on his back, skis crisscrossed on his chest, he didn't even bother to open his eyes. He was convinced that it was just his mind playing tricks on him.

But then there was another one. Lars slowly took his arm away from his face and stared up at the rock tower. On a narrow ledge, halfway up, were several sets of glittering eyes.

Lars scrambled to his feet. "Is it you?" he whispered. "Is it really you?"

The only answer was an impatient tinkling of sleigh bells.

There is no graceful way to climb an icy rock wall, particularly when you're tussling with a pair of skis, but Lars wasn't worried about grace. He lunged and scrambled, nearly fell twice, and banged a knee.

When he finally made it to the ledge, he lay on his belly for a couple of seconds, panting, eyes closed.

A rough tongue licked his cheek. Lars winced and pushed a wet nose away. Who could it be but Alfred? He glanced over his shoulder. Harnessed to the sleigh, the eight reindeer loomed above him. Reindeer are small animals, but from where Lars lay they looked as majestic as elk.

Lars rose and went around to pat each of them with a trembling hand. "Liv? Ulrike? Everyone all right?" A couple of them were skittish and seemed almost half-wild. Siegfried still sported a burn mark of his flank from the Winter Festival bonfire. But they all looked fat and sleek. The sleigh, on the other hand, was a little the worse for wear, with one of the doors bashed in.

The moonlight reflecting in their huge eyes made them look like creatures from another world. Where had they been, Lars wondered. And why would they show up now, at this very moment?

Lars gathered up his skis and hoisted himself into the sleigh. The reins were frozen stiff. He bent them backward and forward to shatter the ice, and then gave them a shake. "Antlers up!" he shouted.

The ledge was too short for a running start. The reindeer took Lars totally by surprise by stepping sideways off the ledge like swimmers stepping sideways off a diving board.

The sleigh tipped and nearly pitched Lars out on his head. "Whoa!" he shouted, clinging to the rails, but before he could utter a second word, the reindeer were in their paces, straightening out.

They rose quickly. Lars had forgotten how fast they could fly. Wind tore at his face and the sleigh rattled and groaned as if it might blow apart. The reindeer seemed stronger than ever. Lars steered them in a long, sweeping circle, his skis tucked under his feet.

When they passed over the ridge, Lars peered over the edge of the sleigh. A hundred feet below a dozen of his pursuers were gathered at the narrow mountain pass. One of them had managed to climb halfway up the rock tower and was gesturing to the others with open hands that he'd found nothing. Confused dogs swirled in and out of the knot of men, getting their ears boxed by their owners. One man was hopping up and down. Another threw his hat in the snow and then kicked it over the sheer drop-off.

Lars had seen enough, and he didn't want to risk being spotted. He gave the reins a hard shake. "Haw!" he shouted, and the reindeer banked left, leading toward home. Stars bounced overhead.

TWENTY-FOUR

he next morning Beluga Hall was in an uproar. A mob of students was gathered in the corridor while Mr. Smorgas and the teachers tried vainly to herd them into their classrooms.

Arkady was in the middle of all the pandemonium. Nearly everyone had already heard of the break-in, the wild chase, the dumbfounding escape of the intruder.

"So did you see him?" shouted one of the younger students.

"Oh, I saw him all right," Arkady said. Lars stood with the cooks all the way down the hall, his head bowed, listening.

"But weren't you frightened?" shouted one of the girls.

"Me? Frightened? He was the one who was frightened. He took off like a scared rabbit. I chased him once around the house and out the door. The heck of it was, I would have caught him, but I was in my pajamas and that snow can get awfully cold on your bare feet."

"And did he leave you anything?" The question had an edge to it. All heads turned. The questioner was Miko, standing near the door. Arkady paused for a moment, taking everything in—the bulky burlap sack sitting between her feet, the somber band of students who'd just come in, standing at her shoulder. Wink and Muleface were with them.

"Leave me anything? No, he didn't," Arkady said. "I don't see why he would. A guy like that, he's a lot more likely to slit your throat."

Mr. Smorgas had heard enough. He elbowed his way into the middle of the mob, his arms held high. "All right, everybody! I know this is all very exciting, but we're not going to stand here all day. The teachers and I have been hired to give you an education, and as daunting a task as that may be, we're going to give it a try! Everyone! Let's go!"

Arkady was a mystery. A great calm had come over him. Had he found the boxers? There was no sign of it. Could Lars have shoved the carvings too far under his cot? Could they still be there, untouched and gathering dust?

Four days passed. On the fifth day, after school let out, Lars noticed several of the younger boys acting goofier than usual, exchanging mysterious hand signals, slipping each other notes, lurking like spies in doorways. Something was up, there was no doubt.

When he walked outside, he saw three boys disappear around the corner of Beluga Hall. A fourth, much smaller than the others, hustled on short legs to catch up.

"Hey!" Lars shouted. The boy stopped and looked back at him. "What's going on?" The boy tilted his head to one side as if he hadn't heard and then began to look worried. His mouth opened, shut, and opened again.

"Come on, out with it!"

The boy winced. He couldn't have been older than eight, and to say no to a twelve-year-old took more nerve than he was capable of. He waved for Lars to just follow him.

As they went around the corner, Lars spotted a fur hat vanishing behind the open door to the meat cellar. Lars was astonished. He'd never seen the door open before. The meat cellar was located directly beneath the kitchen and had the reputation of being a foul and forbidding place.

Lars halted, not sure he wanted to go any further, but the boy beckoned him on with an impatient wag of his finger.

Lars followed him down a rickety staircase. The cellar seemed to be nearly as revolting as its reputation. Bits of discolored fat speckled the stone walls. Huge barrels of frozen blubber and intestines and fish eyes were stacked in the corners. Stained aprons hung from hooks. Embedded cleavers gleamed from scarred butcher tables like tomahawks. The floors were slippery with a meandering stream of goo.

But the jibbering cluster of boys in the middle of the cellar didn't seem to mind any of it. Whatever was at the center of the circle had them in a complete state. They elbowed and clawed at one another's shoulders to get a better look. Wink and Donald Donkey-Ears grinned madly; two other boys closer in exchanged hand slaps. Another yipped only to be shushed by his classmates.

Lars squirmed in as far as he could and stood on tiptoes. At the heart of the throng, Arkady and Roope sat on low stools, facing one another. Arkady, jaw clenched, held the boxer in the blue trunks six inches before his nose. Roope, jaw clenched just as tight, held the boxer in red trunks six inches in front of his nose.

They were staging their own little slugfest. They bobbed their fighters through the air, darted them forward to throw a quick jab and ducked them out of the way of a mighty uppercut.

It was a mismatch. Arkady worked the strings in his boxer's back like a master, landing four blows to his opponent's one. Roope was getting more and more flustered, still trying to figure out how to make the strings work. The mob of boys was delirious with joy.

Lars could scarcely believe what he was seeing. Arkady had found the two carvings, after all, and here they were, trading punches, ducking and moving. They were so fluid and quick it was almost impossible not to imagine that they were just as real, just as much flesh and blood and bone as the circle of agitated boys around them.

Arkady was spellbound. A bomb could have gone off and he wouldn't have noticed.

The boys went into a frenzy as the head of Roope's boxer spun like a whirligig. Arkady kicked his stool aside and rose to his feet.

He waved his wooden pugilist over his head and broke into a little

was no lack of abandoned buildings far out on the tundra for them to practice on. The problem was that the reindeer had no clue what he was asking of them.

The first time he tried to get them to land on a rooftop, four of them tried to do as he instructed and the other four panicked. The result was that they overshot the roof by ten feet and plowed into a snowdrift.

On their second attempt they all panicked and veered left. On Try Number Three, several of them managed to touch down briefly, but they were going too fast to stop and ended up pitching over the far edge of the roof into a pile of rocks and caribou hides, pulling Lars and the sleigh down on top of them.

As bruised and banged up as they were, it was a miracle that they were willing to come back for a second night, but they did come back. They were still like baby birds trying to fly from a nest, but they made progress on the second night and even more on the third.

All this progress came at a cost. Lars chipped a tooth, there were many scraped knees, and one of the reindeer broke off a tine of his antlers. But by the fourth night they were getting the hang of it. By the fifth, they were gliding onto the rooftops without a single tinkling of a sleigh bell and skidding to a stop on wide, soft hooves. If Lars hadn't known better, he would have thought that landing on rooftops was something they were born to do.

But they were not ready yet. The next big task was figuring out how to get down a chimney. As tricky as learning how to land on a rooftop might have been, it seemed to Lars that he had the more difficult assignment, and probably the more dangerous one.

He remembered when he was young, watching the chimney sweeps clean Lord Borland's chimneys. He had marveled at how they could disappear in a twinkling and then re-appear ten minutes later, face and clothes black with soot, holding their brooms and scrapers aloft. How fearless they had seemed and how easy they had made it look!

But they had been doing it for years, and the chimneys of Lord Borland had been things of beauty—well-built, enormous, and meticulously maintained. The chimneys Lars had to contend with were a different matter altogether. The house that Lars had to practice on hadn't been lived in for years, and some of the chimneys looked as if they might collapse with a single nudge of a finger.

He was cautious. He inspected several before he made his choice, and even after he settled on one that seemed the sturdiest, he stalled for as long as he could, tying and retying the rope around his waist (the other end of the rope was lashed tight around the chimney).

The reindeer were there with him on the roof. If they hadn't been, he might have postponed the whole thing for a few more nights. But they were there, and Lars had his pride. He had no intention of looking like a coward, not after all he'd put them through.

He swung one leg into the chimney, then the other, then tossed in the extra length of rope. He took a deep breath and lowered himself, hand over hand. Legs spread wide, he braced himself with his knees and held tight to the rope. Glancing up at the tiny square of starlit sky, he saw the head of the lead reindeer staring back down at him.

As dark as the Arctic night could be, the inside of the chimney was darker still. There was the smell of ash, and the muscles in his arms started to burn.

He felt the first twinges of panic. He shook out one leg, trying to keep it free of the loose length of rope below him. He heard a twittering and a flapping of wings. Something brushed against his face. Disgusted and spitting, he let go of the rope with one hand to wipe at his eyes and mouth, but when he did, he lurched hard to one side and slammed against the chimney wall. He heard a brick fall and smash somewhere beneath him.

He swung back and forth, holding on for dear life, but his arms were giving out. He could feel the chimney narrowing. If he got stuck, no one was ever going to find him. He would die here.

When he let go of the rope, he didn't have far to fall, no more than five or six feet. He landed hard on his side. All the wind was knocked out of him. He lay on the hearth for several minutes until his breath returned. Everything hurt, but it didn't seem as if he'd broken anything. When he rolled onto his back and stared up the chimney, he could see the antlered heads of three or four curious reindeer silhouetted against the sky.

His arms were dead things. There was no way he was going to be able to climb all the way up again. He got to his knees and picked furiously at the knot in the rope around his waist until he finally undid it.

The floor of the abandoned house was a single sheet of ice. A tattered calendar fluttered on the wall. A tall cupboard stood in the corner, door open, as if its owner had just stepped away for a minute.

Taking tiny steps across the ice, Lars made his way outside. The reindeer on the roof all had their backs to him. Lars waved. "Hey, everybody! I'm over here!"

This was not the most auspicious start, but Lars was determined not to be outdone by the reindeer. Each night for the next several nights, they returned. The ache in his muscles never went away, but Lars slowly grew stronger, and he began to overcome his fears. He tried a number of chimneys, and every night he did a little better, climbing halfway back before having to let go of the rope, then three quarters of the way, and then through sheer grit and willpower, he made it all the way up.

He scrambled out of the chimney and collapsed on the rooftop, lungs bursting. He punched one fist in the air and then the other. "All right, guys, I think we've got it! There's no stopping us now!"

Having the reindeer back changed everything. Lars was now able to deliver ten carvings a night instead of the one or two he'd been able to deliver when he was on skis. He was no longer leaving telltale tracks in the snow and was able to range miles farther out onto the tundra to leave presents at the most remote dwellings.

However, going down the chimney of a house that had people living in it was a much trickier business than going down the chimney of an abandoned house. He had no way of knowing what awaited him below—dogs or old men standing guard with muskets—and if the chimney was in use, it was usually caked with soot blisters and smelled of everything from fetid clams to bear grease. But the biggest problem was fire.

If there was a major blaze crackling in the fireplace, Lars had no choice but to turn back. But if there were just embers or a few low flames guttering over charred logs, he would descend as far as he could until he felt the soles of his mukluks getting toasty, and then cast about with his toes until he found something solid. Spreading his legs wide, he would try to put one foot on one andiron and one on the other.

He would duck silently into the dark room, undo the knotted rope around his waist, tiptoe into the bedroom of his schoolmate, and stash a carving in a spot where only he or she could find it. Then back he would go, retying the rope, and then ascending, hand over hand, keeping his eyes shut to avoid the cascading soot.

He was taking new precautions. Now that he was ranging out farther on the tundra, he had to be careful to avoid the lookout towers of Mayor Wolfpaw's deputies. Because his forays were now sometimes lasting for two or three hours, each night before he left his house he would fashion a dummy out of pillows and stuff it under his blankets so that in case his mother came to check on him it would look as if he was dead to the world.

What an education it was, seeing all those sleeping families! Some slept six to a bed. Some slept scattered in every corner. Others curled up in a circle around the stove. A mother dozed with her arm thrown over her infant. Others tossed and turned. A little boy slept in a pen with a goat. A grandfather snored in a chair with his granddaughter asleep on his lap.

To see all of them sometimes filled him with a deep sadness. Lars didn't have a family anymore, not really; it was just him and his mother. To see all these sleeping families was just a reminder of how much he missed his.

He had thought it would go on forever, the four of them, but it hadn't, and it wouldn't go on forever for these families, either. Some of these people might not make it till morning. But as long as he kept carving, as long as he kept going out night after night and leaving toys, it felt as if he was keeping all that grief at bay.

Sometimes he dreamed he was carving his father in wood, taking immense care not to nick him as he etched the lines in his face.

One morning, for the first time, he woke up and felt something very strange on his chin. He scratched and rubbed at it, wiggled it back and forth for nearly a minute, before he realized it was a hair.

Lars knew that it wouldn't be long before Mayor Wolfpaw returned and that when he did, things would get more difficult. Lars was determined to give as many presents as he could for as long as he could (the good news was that his invisible helpers had stepped up their production and were keeping pace).

The mood in Beluga Hall was radically changed. People had a new bounce in their step, and when someone was knocked down on the playing field, there were always one or two sets of hands there to help him up. The boxing matches in the meat cellar were attracting more and more spectators.

Perhaps the most miraculous change of all came when Lars began to deliver carvings to the older students. He'd held off because he figured they were a lost cause, but also because it seemed too risky. As addled as the older ones were by the skarn-liver oil, Lars wasn't sure he could trust them to keep anything secret.

But he felt worse and worse about everybody but them getting toys, and he finally threw caution to the winds. Over two nights he gave carvings to Gunnar, Inuksuk, Maja, Finn, and several others.

It did not take long for the carvings to work their magic. It was just a few days later that Maja laughed at a joke, to everyone's astonishment. One day after that, Gunnar, the least playful of the older students, wadded up pellets of bread in the lunch room and began tossing them at the backs of the necks of his schoolmates, setting off a food fight. Later that afternoon, Lars came upon two of the biggest, lunkiest boys playing hopscotch.

But the most astonishing thing of all, from Lars's point of view, occurred the very next day in Ancient History class. Mr. Ostertag was going around the room, quizzing each of the students on the week's reading.

"Okay, Inuksuk, I believe you're next. Imagine that you're Marco Polo. You've been travelling for three years. You're expected at the court of Kublai Khan by the weekend. Suddenly you're confronted by an enormous wall. It's forty feet high and stretching for miles in both directions. What would you do?"

As usual, Inuksuk, the boy without an imagination, looked stuck. He fumed. He rubbed furiously at his forehead, thinking as hard as he could. Mr. Ostertag, who always got much pleasure in pointing out just how dense Inuksuk was, took a moment and was about to move on to the next student when Inuksuk shot a finger into the air.

"I've got it!" Inuksuk said.

"What's that?" said Mr. Ostertag.

"You get a whole bunch of parrots, tie strings to their feet, and tie a rope to the strings. Then you fire a gun into the air to scare them, and when they fly over the wall and settle down on the other side, hopefully the rope gets tangled in some branches, tangled firmly enough that people can climb up the rope to the top . . ."

Mr. Ostertag was dumbfounded. "That's interesting, but I'm not so sure . . ."

Inuksuk was only getting started. "Or how about this? Maybe you could dig a tunnel. Or build a hot air balloon. Or put together a battering ram and keep smashing and smashing until the whole thing come tumbling down . . ."

It was reported over the next week that many of the older students were refusing to swallow their daily doses of skarn-liver oil. Several times Mr. Smorgas had to come in to admonish them. "What's gotten into you all? You're acting like a bunch of children!"

Which was exactly what they were doing. They were recovering something they thought they had lost forever—guffawing at stupid jokes, playing tag, and hide-and-seek, and fox and geese, and doing it all openly, without shame. All their younger schoolmates could do was look on in awe.

Most of the teachers remained oblivious. And with Bjorn Snortblossom and the deputies far off on the tundra searching for the villian behind the Winter Festival debacle, and Mayor Wolfpaw still peddling his jugs of golden oil in northern Europe, Lars could be forgiven for thinking that he was getting away with murder, for believing that no one knew.

Yet there was one who did know.

Three nights in a row Lars had spotted smoke rising from a volcano that was supposed to be extinct. Several times, on perfectly calm nights, the sleigh had begun to shake uncontrollably for ten or fifteen seconds as if in the grasp of some unseen power. Once as he was swinging his leg out of a chimney, he caught a glimpse of a towering antlered beast standing on a hillside, but when he turned to look, there was no trace of it.

Toys and skarn would seem to have little to do with one another. Skarn have multiple uses. Toys have none. The only thing a toy can do is bring joy. A skarn repulses. A skarn can breathe underwater. A toy breathes not at all. A skarn can swim. Most toys sink like a stone. Skarn devour plankton and young crustaceans, many pounds per day. Toys require no food. A bite from the fangs of a skarn can result in infection and death. The injury from a toy is most commonly a knot on the head from a wooden mallet.

But the great geniuses are able to make connections between widely different objects when others can't. And Nacht Ruprecht was, without question, a genius. For centuries he had required his minions to take skarn-liver oil for its many stellar qualities. It improved bone density, lowered blood pressure, reduced pain, improved the immune system, and prevented the build-up of plaque in the arteries. But it also had one other quality that he was quick to note: it obliterated delight.

For a century Nacht Ruprecht had a recurring nightmare. Toys floated in an ocean, some of them bobbing, some slowly sinking. Skarn, attracted by the movement, rose quickly out of the depths to snap them up as if they were flies or moths. But only moments later, the blind fish began to writhe in agony, jaws snapping, and then slide to the very bottom of the sea.

One bitterly cold night Lars's mother awoke, quite sure she'd heard a noise. She listened intently. Could it have been the front door opening and closing? Maybe Lars had gone out to get more fuel for the fire.

She waited, but the sound of someone reentering the house never came. She got up, tiptoed back to Lars's room, and peered in. What a relief it was to see him, all bundled up and sound asleep, with his blankets pulled over his head to keep him warm.

It was not the first time she'd thought she'd heard him moving around at night, but each time she checked he was always buried under his quilts and dead to the world.

Staring down at his sleeping figure, she was filled with remorse. What a terrible coward she was! She had put it off and put it off, telling him that she had decided to accept Wolfpaw's offer of marriage. She could scarcely delay any longer—the mayor was expected back in a matter of days.

She was so ashamed. She couldn't imagine that Lars would ever hold out on her the way she was holding out on him. He had always been an honest boy. It was a little different now that he was twelve, but when he was young, he would tell her everything.

She stood in the doorway of Lars's bedroom for two or three minutes. Not once did he twitch a muscle or utter a sigh.

This would not be an easy thing to explain. She knew how much Lars disliked Wolfpaw, and the truth was, more often than not, she was repelled by him herself.

But for her son to have any kind of life, a price was going to have be paid. The mayor had made her a promise: if she would be his wife, he would take her and her son away from here. He would take her anywhere, he'd said, and the only place she wanted to go was home. She wanted to live among her people again, to see the sun in the morning, to tend a garden. She wanted her son to grow up in a world where kindness and gentleness were at least a possibility.

Many times in the two months Wolfpaw had been gone she had thought, I would rather die than marry him. She shuddered at the idea of Lars having to live in the same house with Wolfpaw, of having to treat the mayor as if he was his new father. What a scandal it would be for her to walk down the cobbled street, arm in arm with this bizarre creature with his scarred face, his white fur coat, jangling medals, and stovepipe hat.

She still feared him. How would it be to sleep next to him, night after night? The story had been repeated many times of how he had killed his stepbrothers by tearing their throats out with his teeth. The rumor was that he preferred to clean himself by licking, like an animal.

The rafters groaned in the wind. "Lars?" she whispered.

He didn't move.

"Lars?" she repeated, but a little more loudly than the first time. "There's something I need to tell you."

She moved to the bed, but he never stirred. She reached down and touched his blankets, but didn't shake him. It was best to let him sleep. Certainly putting things off for one more day wasn't going to hurt. As she turned to leave the room, she saw, through his window, a shooting star, a flash of light in the sky.

TWENTY-FIVE

Whip cracking above his head, Mayor Wolfpaw led the way as four hundred dogs and fifty sleds labored up the mountain in the waning light. It was four in the afternoon before they reached the pass and descended swiftly into total darkness.

Mayor Wolfpaw's trip had been a grand success. He had sold three thousand jugs of skarn-liver oil and could have sold twice that. Many of his buyers were repeat customers—prison wardens, school superintendents, the usual black marketeers, and the overseers of the great estates who were interested in creating docile and obedient workers.

Did Mayor Wolfpaw care who they were? He had learned not to think about it, the thousands of young lives that were being stunted, all those whose horizons were sinking, bit by bit, day by day, all the children who were being dulled the way a knife that is much too sharp is dulled so that everyone could use it.

The trips south had always been a kind of holiday for the mayor. He had always taken pleasure in the jostling and noise in the great cities of northern Europe, the ever-present cutpurses and hawkers of wares, carts and carriages clattering in the streets, the drunken laughter coming from the inns until the early hours of the morning. He remembered standing outside the opera house in Copenhagen one night, listening to the music for over an hour, tears running down his cheeks as he tried to fix every note of it in his memory.

This trip was nothing like the others. Now, as he and his deputies sped from city to city on their sleds, he tried to imagine if it would be possible for him to live in any of these places.

He had every intention of making good on his promise to Helga—if she would marry him, he would take her and Lars from the land of endless darkness, never to return. They would settle wherever she chose. But how would he ever fit in? Even now he could feel people cringe as he strode past them on the streets of Oslo and Stockholm with his ruined face and his small army of deputies padding along behind him in their bulky parkas and mukluks, blowing their noses in their fingers or scratching their behinds with a bit too much intensity.

He would be a man without standing in these places. All the rooms were stuffy and hot. Even in the winter, the sunlight burned his eyes.

One afternoon he visited the Berlin Zoo and joined a crowd watching the wolves at feeding time. Cats and rabbits and tiny dogs were pitched into the enclosure. The throng howled as the small animals scrambled and screeched, trying to get away, but there was no getting away. They were pounced on, torn limb from limb, and devoured.

After the feeding was over the crowd dispersed. Wolfpaw stayed on to watch the wolves pace restlessly behind the wire mesh. After a time they became aware of him and stopped to stare at him with unblinking yellow eyes.

It was clear to the mayor that they recognized him as one of their own. He was quite sure he could read their minds. Don't do it, they were saying, don't do it, or you will end up with us.

Yet he was determined not to go back on his word. He yearned for a human touch. Helga hid her disdain for him well enough, but he knew it was there. All the same, if he gave her and her son what she so desperately wanted, surely her gratitude should make some difference.

The descent had become treacherous. They entered a series of switchbacks, and canyon walls towered above them on both sides. Glancing over his shoulder, Wolfpaw saw the line of heavy-laden sleds stretching back as far as he could see. Many of them struggled in the deep snow, and the barking of dogs and the cursing of men echoed off the sheer cliffs.

It took them another forty minutes before the canyon opened up and they could see the tundra stretching out before them. Here and there lanterns twinkled in remote dwellings. Mayor Wolfpaw leaned over the handles of his sled, trying to hold his dogs back. His destiny was down there, waiting for him, and he was in no hurry to meet it.

It was mid-afternoon by the time the caravan of sleds pulled up in front of Wolfpaw's mansion. The staff rushed out to greet him and helped the deputies unload. Bundles of firewood freshly cut from the forests of Europe were lugged to the sheds in the back, and the duffel bags of frozen hearts and livers to be delivered later to Nacht Ruprecht were stored in the tunnel beneath the house.

When they were finished, the deputies were invited in for hot grog, heartily toasted, and sent on their way. Except for one of the butlers, all the domestic staff were let go early. This was a night the mayor preferred to spend alone.

An hour later Wolfpaw stood before a long table piled high with coins in the upstairs library, stacking them neatly. This was the one part of his six-week ordeal that gave him the most pleasure. He was exhausted and had barely slept for three nights, but this was not the time to rest or wash his face or even change his clothes. His once-beautiful white coat was now filthy, the fur matted and snarled by dog spittle, and with his face spotted by frostbite and his pistol still tucked in his belt, he looked more like a pirate than a man of some standing.

The library was lined with books, books purchased from the great libraries of Berlin and Paris, though it seemed doubtful that any of the volumes had ever been opened. Several portraits of the Ratvass clan hung above the fireplace, their faces shining with duplicity and low cunning. An untouched glass of cognac sat atop a linen napkin on a side table. In the corner two sacks spewed more coins, with a variety of bank notes mixed in.

The mayor paused when he heard voices below. One of the voices was the butler's. The other, to Wolfpaw's surprise, was Snortblossom's.

The mayor's first reaction was annoyance, the second unease. Snortblossom had worked for him long enough to know that he was never to disturb him on his first night back. All Wolfpaw could imagine was that it must be something serious.

"Send him up!" the mayor shouted.

Head bowed, he waited, listening to the heavy tread on the stairs.

"Sir?"

Wolfpaw looked up. The head peering around the corner of the door was as big as a moose head. The mayor had always found it mildly astonishing. Wolfpaw waved him in.

"I hope I'm not interrupting anything, sir." Snortblossom's hands were clasped in front of him, fingers twined in the drawstrings of a large pouch. "I trust your trip was a great success?"

"Better than ever. Did you find him?"

"Find who, sir?"

"Who do you think? Whoever it was that destroyed the Winter Festival."

"I'm afraid we didn't, sir. Everyone did their best, sir, but I'm afraid we didn't find anybody out there but a couple of poachers."

"Then why are you here?"

"I'm afraid to say there have been developments."

"What kind of developments?" The mayor picked up a handful of kroners and set them on the proper stack. Snortblossom had been his most trusted aide for years. He had many virtues, including loyalty, physical bravery, and a way with dogs, but forthrightness was not one of them.

Snortblossom took a deep, steadying breath. "We've just been back a few days ourselves. But last night Mr. Smorgas showed up at my door. Apparently one of the teachers discovered some of the boys down in the meat cellar after school, playing with these . . . "

Snortblossom offered the pouch to the mayor, but Wolfpaw motioned for him to handle it himself. Snortblossom obeyed, opening the pouch, reaching in and pulling out the wooden boxer with the red trunks.

The mayor cried out and stumbled backwards as if he'd been struck.

"I'm so sorry, sir," Snortblossom said.

Wolfpaw reached behind him for the edge of the table. "What else is in there?" he said, pointing to the pouch with a shaking finger.

Snortblossom put the boxer on a chair and retrieved its twin from the leather sack. The mayor pushed away from the table, snatched the boxer in the blue trunks out of Snortblossom's hand, and shook it in Snortblossom's face. "Do you know what this is?"

"I believe I do."

"And these two, are they the end of it?"

It took all the willpower Snortblossom had to answer. "I don't think anyone knows for sure. Mr. Smorgas suspects there may be more."

The mayor held the tiny figure under a lamp, examining it with care. Everything about it was unnervingly real, from the snarl on its lips to the puffy swelling under one eye. When he pulled one of the strings its left arm flicked out quick as a lizard's tongue.

Thunderclouds of emotion rose up in him, dark and lethal. How bright his future had seemed, just an hour ago. He'd had one of his most successful trips to northern Europe, by any measure, and if Lars's mother said yes to his proposal he would be leaving this place forever with a fortune in coins in his pockets. The world was going to be open to them both. Blind rage took him. He broke the boxer in two and threw it skittering across the marble floor.

"You fool! How could you let this happen?"

"But, sir, you sent us to patrol the border. We could scarcely be in two places at the same time."

"I left you in charge! You promised me that you would see to things! Exactly who do these belong to?"

"I can't say that I know, sir."

"But surely these villians have been taken into custody."

"Not that I know of, sir."

The mayor pulled his pistol out of his belt and pointed it at Snort-blossom's head (not a small target). As he advanced, Snortblossom retreated, stumbling over a footstool, and went to his knees.

"Please, sir. Perhaps I didn't handle things perfectly, but I wanted to talk to you first. I understand how upsetting this must be for you. And, unfortunately, there's one thing more. Apparently some of the older students are refusing to swallow their skarn-liver oil . . ."

The mayor took the pistol by the barrel and hit Snortblossom across the face with the butt. Snortblossom fell straight forward, blood gushing from his nose. The mayor hit him a second time, and a third.

Everyone had just come back from lunch when one of the sweepers rushed in to announce that someone had seen lanterns out on the tundra, approaching from the east. All work ceased. The conveyor belts slowed and came to a stop. A hush fell over the factory. Wolfpaw's return was always greeted with mixed emotions. On the one hand, it meant that desperately needed firewood would be distributed, and that, with the refilling of the village coffers, the workers' wages, piti-ful though they were, would be assured for another year. On the other hand, they would once again be laboring under the bootheel of a man they all detested and feared.

But none of their emotions could match Helga's. This was the day she'd been dreading for weeks. He would be expecting her answer, and there could be no more putting it off.

As hard as it was going to be to say yes, she was going to say yes. Night after night she had tried to think it through, and she had always come to the same conclusion. Marrying Wolfpaw and leaving this place was the only way she and her son could ever have a life.

The only question was how to proceed. She could simply go home and wait for the knock at the door. If he didn't show up tonight, she would surely see him tomorrow at work.

But the last thing she wanted to do was prolong the agony. It would be better if she went to him now. She didn't need any more courtship. She was too old to play the fainting maiden. She just needed to get this over with—get it over with before she changed her mind.

The factory shut two hours early in honor of the mayor's arrival (though it was doubtful that he would have approved). Up and down the stilled conveyor belts the doomed skarn flopped, mouths working, their lives momentarily spared.

Helga had never been to the mayor's house before, but it turned out to be easy enough to find. She followed a crude map sketched out for her on a scrap of butcher paper by a coworker, and once she'd skied up a meandering river valley for a half hour, she came out onto a wide plain. There it was, a hundred yards on, dozens of lights glowing in the dark, late-afternoon sky.

As she drew nearer, the enormity of the mansion became increasingly apparent. Because of a low mist, it seemed to float like a pharaoh's barge drifting down the Nile. It was surrounded by a wall, there were turrets and towers, and lights glittered in every window like spider eyes.

She passed an unmanned guard house, took off her skis, and pushed through a rattling metal gate. She fought back the urge to turn around and go back home. To her left was a skating pond, swept clean of snow, and a small cabin. To her right a shadow flitted through a series of kennels.

She went to the door and yanked the cord on an enormous brass bell. When there was no answer she rang it twice more. After several seconds she heard the clicking of steps. Locks rattled, the door creaked open, and a butler with massive white eyebrows scowled at her.

"Yes?"

"I would like to speak with the mayor."

"And who are you?"

"Helga Claus." He showed no sign that the name meant anything to him. "I am one of the workers from the factory."

The butler remained unimpressed. "Ahh, well. I'm afraid he's upstairs meeting with Mr. Snortblossom. Perhaps this can all wait until tomorrow."

A chorus of howling dogs broke out in the darkness, followed by a string of curses. The butler stepped past Lars's mother and down the front steps. "Yes?" A reply came from the kennels, but so heavily accented, Helga couldn't make heads nor tails out of it. It did, however, make the butler furious.

"Excuse me for a moment," he said to Helga and began to walk toward the kennels. "Use your eyes, my friend!" he shouted to the unseen keeper of the hounds. "The cook put two baskets of bones out for the dogs just an hour ago."

Helga stared in at the immense hallway with its marble floor, cabinets of curios, stuffed polar bear balancing precariously on one foot. She knew that if she didn't act now, she never would. She bolted up the stairs.

On the second floor landing she was faced with a bewildering number of rooms to choose from. But then she heard, on her left, a thump and a groan.

She approached a half-opened door. Snortblossom lay on the floor, his shirt and his face bloodied. Wolfpaw stood over him, holding a pistol by the barrel.

Snortblossom shuddered and tried to crawl away. He made it as far as the table, but when he tried to use the table leg to rise, all the coins showered down on his head. The mayor chopped the butt of the pistol down on the back of Snortblossom's rather large Scandinavian head. Snortblossom went down again and lay motionless except for the twitching fingers of his right hand.

Helga cried out. Wolfpaw swung around. He showed no sign of recognizing her.

"What is going on here?" she said.

He blinked several times and set the pistol meekly down on the table. When he reached for her, she shied away. "Why are you here?" he asked.

She couldn't answer. She had come to tell him she was accepting his offer of marriage, something that was no longer possible. She rushed past him and knelt at Snortblossom's side. She gently lifted his head. His mouth hung open. She yanked the white linen napkin from the side table, wiped the blood trickling from his eye, and daubed carefully at what was surely a broken nose. He was conscious, but barely.

Heavy breathing at the door made them both turn to look. The red-faced butler stood in the entry, heaving. He was not a man used to so much exercise. "I'm so sorry, sir. I told her you were busy . . . "

"Out!" The mayor shouted.

"Please, sir, if I could explain . . . "

"Out!"

Once the butler had vanished, the mayor slammed the door shut. Lars's mother rose, the bloody napkin in her hand. Snortblossom laid his head back down on the floor and closed his eyes, looking for all the world like a man swooning into unconsciousness.

"If you will only let me explain," the mayor said. "This is not what it seems."

"No, please," she said.

"My hope is that you've come to tell me that we will be wed."

Snortblossom's left eye popped open like a quail flushed from cover. Could he possibly have heard what he thought he'd heard? His mayor? Marrying?

"My offer still holds. If you will accept my hand in marriage, I will take you away from here. Forever. You will never have to see this god-forsaken place again."

Snortblossom shut his open eye, heart racing. His mayor was going to abandon them? He willed himself to be still. He knew that to move a muscle now was to risk death.

"There is just one unfinished piece of business I need to tend to," Wolfpaw said.

Lars's mother had crossed to the far side of the room. "And what kind of business is that?"

He retrieved the two boxes, one intact, one broken and tangled in string. When he held them up, she felt a sudden chill. "These are toys," he said. "And they say there might be more."

"Could I see?" she asked.

"Of course."

She took the pair of boxes from him. If there was one thing she knew, it was carving. Some in wood, some in whalebone, these were beautifully done. And so familiar.

He took the boxes from her and set them on the table. "I have no choice now," he said. "I am going to have to gather all the deputies. We will have a house-to-house search."

"What do you hope to achieve by all this?"

He stared at her. How could he ever begin to say? "If you can only trust me," he said. "For just this one night."

Without another word, she fled. After she was gone, the mayor went to the side table and downed the glass of cognac in one swallow. His heart had turned to stone. He took a sidelong glance at the portraits of the Ratvass clan above the fireplace and wiped his hands on his filthy white fur coat.

Snortblossom stirred with the greatest caution. He squinted with one eye and then opened both. Grimacing, he propped himself up on an elbow.

"Sir?"

Wolfpaw turned. "Yes?"

"She is not good enough for you, sir."

"Maybe so, maybe not." In the corners, the spilled coins glittered. There were enough there to make any pirate proud.

"You're not thinking of leaving us, are you, sir?"

"No, Snortblossom, I'm not."

"Sir, I'd like to have a chance to redeem myself. If I'm not being too presumptuous, I'd like to volunteer to take charge of this house-to-house search tonight."

"You will not let your feelings for these people get in your way?"

Snortblossom touched his broken nose gingerly. "No, sir. I am as determined as you are to get to the bottom of this."

"You will spare no one?"

"No one. And by that I assume you mean . . . "

"Yes, including her. You may be as ruthless as the situation calls for."

TWENTY-SIX

When she topped the ridge, she saw a lantern burning in a window of her house. A wave of relief washed over her. This was all that mattered—that her son was home and safe.

When she went into the house, Lars's backpack was on the table, but he was nowhere to be found. Alarm rose up in her, caught in her throat. She checked the bedroom and called out several times. When there was no answer she went to the front door and opened it. Scanning the hillside below, she spied a glow in the belly of the whaling ship, arrows of light flickering through the planks.

She stumbled back into her skis and glided down the slope. She kicked free of the skis and made her way across the snow toward the ragged hole in the hull. She put a hand up to block the flutter of light. She heard munching.

She ducked through the gash in the side of the ship and was confronted by the strangest scene she had ever witnessed. Eight reindeer rested on beds of straw. Some were asleep, while others regarded her with huge, curious eyes. They looked quite at home. A dozen carvings perched on a railing. Lars sat hunched over on the steps to the quarterdeck, whittling manfully at a chunk of wood, so absorbed in his work he didn't even notice her.

She gave a cry, the sound of a bird strangled in the night. Lars looked up and dropped the block of wood. He stood and wiped the sawdust from his trousers.

As she moved into the hold, the reindeer scrambled to their feet. Chips and wood shavings littered the floor, and a sleigh was pushed up into the corner.

She went to the railing. There was a cat, a rat, a seagull with its wings spread, a knight carrying a lance, a milkmaid carrying buckets, a portly tuba player, a pirate, and a piglet, all lined up in a row.

She reached for the rail to keep from passing out. Of course, it had to have been him. Who else could it be? He was, after all, his father's child.

But the stupidity of what he'd done was overwhelming. She just wanted to pull his pants down and give him a good paddling.

"You made these?"

"Pretty much, yes."

"So you're the one who's been leaving toys at people's houses?"

"I guess so."

"You *guess* so? You *guess* so?" One of the reindeer was chewing on something quite crunchy, tiny brown flakes dropping from its jaws. She could have sworn it was pastry. With a swipe of her arm she sent all the carvings flying. She sat down on a barrel, buried her face in her hands, and began to sob.

Lars reached out for her. "Mom, Mom, don't . . . It's going to be all right."

She looked up at him, furious. She hated it when he said stupid things. "No, it's not going to be all right. They've found two of these . . . " She motioned in the direction of the scattered toys, though she couldn't bear to look at them. "Mayor Wolfpaw's back and he knows. There's going to be a house-to-house search."

Lars's face grew hot. "But when?"

"Tonight, Lars. What could you have been thinking?"

"I don't know." Overcome with humiliation, Lars batted the handle of the knife in his palm, again and again. "Are you sure, Mom?"

"I was there, Lars. At the mayor's house. He had these two boxers."

Lars's eyes widened in wonder. "The boxers? But how could that be?"

She pointed to the reindeer. "And where did *they* come from?"

"Nanu gave them to me."

It was her turn to be dumbfounded. "But Nanu's dead."

"I know. But I saw her. On this iceberg."

He said it so matter-of-factly she was convinced he'd gone mad. The cold, the endless dark, the grief over the deaths of his father and grandmother and his best friend had undone him.

The reindeer glowered at her, ready to defend themselves.

"You are in serious danger. Do you understand that?"

"Yes."

"We are going to have to leave this place." Lars gave her a sidelong glance but wasn't about to argue. "But how are we going to do that?" she continued. "I can't imagine . . . "

"Mom?"

"What?"

"The reindeer."

"What about them?"

"They can fly."

She was about to weep. The conversation had become preposterous. "Please stop talking like that."

"I'm serious, Mom!" He tossed the knife away. "We could leave right now. We would never have to come back here. Ever."

"Lars, it's not possible. Reindeer can't fly."

"No? Then how come you've never seen footprints? How do you think I've been feeding them? Where do you think these bales of hay came from?" She was not convinced.

He scooped the carved seagull with its wings spread and waved it at her. "How do you think I've been delivering these toys every night?"

"Every night?" Her voice went weak.

"Well, nearly."

She rose from the barrel, went to the sleigh, and shook the door. More than anything, she did not want to be here. She just wanted to be back in her house. She was having trouble breathing. The hold smelled like someone's stables. Two thoughts warred within her: how profoundly her son had deceived her and how miserably she had failed as a mother.

She was not, however, a stupid person. "Lars?"

"Yes?"

"Remember what happened at the Winter Festival?"

"Yes."

"Was that you?"

"Yes."

"Oh, Lars."

She was suddenly frightened of him. He had always been the kindest, most obedient little boy. "I can't imagine him hurting a fly," was what everyone said. What had happened to him? Could he be possessed?

"So are you a wizard?"

"No, Mom."

Whatever he was, she thought, he is not mine anymore. She pushed away from the slod. As she approached the reindeer they tossed their heads and moved away. Nowhere did she see signs of wings.

"How far can they fly?" she asked.

"As far as you need them to fly." A reindeer with a white blaze on its chest sniffed at the scattered carvings.

"Could they fly us all the way home?"

Lars rubbed his nose furiously. "I hope so."

"All right then, let's get to it."

"Do you mean it?"

"I don't see that we have much choice." He had wounded her deeply, and she had not forgiven him, but all that was going to have to be put on hold. "Can I help you get them harnessed?"

It turned out to be easier said than done. The reindeer knew the sounds of trouble, and this did not make them happy. They swung their antlers, spit out their bits, kicked and shied when their cinches were being tightened. A bratty reindeer is not a lot of fun. Lars scolded them and slapped the most unruly on the rump with a length of reins.

Everything was taking more time than it should have, and it took even longer when Siegfried tried to clatter up the stairs onto the top deck.

Attempting to cut him off, Lars was bowled off and fell down the steps. It took him and his mother another ten minutes to corral the orneriest of the reindeer in the forecastle. Breathing hard, Siegfried didn't object when they threw a rope over his neck.

His mother put a hand on Lars's sleeve. "Listen," she said.

He didn't know what she was talking about, but when he was still and concentrating, he could hear what she heard—the far-off barking of dogs.

"It's the deputies, Lars."

"It can't be, Mom. There hasn't been enough time . . . "

Siegfried stiffened and raised his head. Lars heard the barking again, growing louder. It was not one team of dogs, but several.

Without another word Lars hurried Siegfried toward the stairs and, making small clicking sounds, led him down the steps. Siegfried worked his jaws into the bridle as soon as Lars lifted it to his muzzle. It was all too amazing, his mother thought. What a skillful little herdsman my son has turned out to be!

She pointed to the reindeer already in harness. "Couldn't we just take these five?"

"No, it would never work." Lars retrieved a harness from a peg on the wall and threw it over Siegfried's back.

"Well, then," she said. "You let me handle the deputies. You stay here and get the rest of them hitched up."

"But, Mom, what if they come down here?"

"I'll stall them as best I can. You know the caves by the shore?"

"Yes."

"If I do my job, you should be able to get the reindeer and the sleigh down there without anyone seeing you. But you have to clear everything out of here."

He looked as if he thought that this was a totally cockamamie scheme, and she wasn't sure that he was wrong. "Mom?"

"Yes?"

"Do you really think this will work?"

"You just do as your mother says."

As soon as she had gone, Lars turned the wick of the lantern as far down as it would go without going out. The reindeer knew enough not to make a fuss; it took him only a few minutes to get the rest of them harnessed.

Working as fast as he could in the half-light, he collected his carvings and tools, pitched them in a gunnysack, and heaved a couple of bales of hay in the back of the sled. As he swept the floor, making sure not to leave a single telltale speck of chaff or wood shavings, he heard the dogsleds pull up in front of his house, heard the sound of men's voices and then his mother's voice, and then silence.

Lars waited several more minutes before leading the reindeer to the hole in the hull. All the lights in the house seemed to be on, and he heard something crash.

The reindeer were anxious to move. Reaching back to calm them, he heard a soft knocking coming from somewhere in the bowels of the ship. He looked quickly over his shoulder—Siegfried and Alfred turned their heads as well—but saw nothing. The century-old masts rattled in the wind.

He led the reindeer out into the moonlight. They were fifty yards below the house, and if anyone had been looking out one of the back windows, Lars and his reindeer would have been spotted easily enough. But apparently no one was looking.

Lars led the reindeer along the base of the slope. The eight animals were quiet as cats. He could hear men shouting back and forth, merry as house painters, the tinkling of broken glass, his mother's objections. A half dozen sleds were parked out in front, and the dogs, silhouetted by the moon, were still as statues.

The house slid from view. The quickest route to the shore was also the most treacherous. Twice the sled nearly capsized as the reindeer floundered and got tangled in one another's traces, but in spite of the mishaps they all made it down in one piece.

There were three or four caves within easy reach. The one Lars settled on was pitch dark. The ceiling bristled with jagged outcroppings of rock and was so low his mother would have to stoop to enter. Several of the reindeer had serious objections to their new quarters, snorting and bucking, and had to be held by their halters until they calmed down.

Lars spread hay on the slick icy floor. The cave angled back into the cliff at a sharp enough angle for the animals to be protected from the wind off the ocean, but the surrounding small caverns and crevices whistled and moaned in the gusts.

He got the reindeer bedded down and covered them with the remains of several tattered blankets he had stored in the sled. He spoke in low tones, assuring them that everything was going to be all right, warning them that above all they needed to stay put. Their eyes were huge as saucers and filled with alarm.

With every step, cold stabbed the bottom of his lungs as he labored up from the shoreline. The sky was immense and swarmed with stars. He felt such shame. How could he claim that he hadn't meant to hurt anyone? But he hadn't. What could he have been thinking? He'd thought he'd been generous and kind; all he'd really been was selfish.

As the house returned to view, he saw a number of bulky deputies standing by the gate, talking. After they'd clambered onto their dogsleds and sped over the ridge, Lars reached down, adjusted the wick on the lantern, and headed up the slope.

The silverware drawer was overturned in the middle of the floor, knives and forks and spoons scattered everywhere. The cuckoo clock was smashed into smithereens, the sofa turned sideways, and the rugs soiled by footprints of melting snow. Everything smelled faintly of whiskey and fish oil. It looked as if a rampaging bear had been locked inside for a day.

"Oh, Mom."

"I know. But it doesn't matter. We've spent our last night here." She was trying to stay composed, but it was clear that she was as shaken as he'd ever seen her. "I want you to go pack your things. As quickly as you can."

He hesitated, started for the hallway, and then stopped. "Were they terrible, Mom?"

"Terrible enough."

"And were they suspicious?"

"I don't think they were any more suspicious than they would be with anyone else. Apparently they're all out tonight, every last one of them. It sounds as if Wolfpaw has gone totally insane."

"Have they found anything yet?"

"They've found a couple things, but they're just getting started. Go on, Lars, there's no time to waste."

Lars stepped over broken glass on the way to his bedroom. It was not hard to figure out what had happened. Wolfpaw had been furious at the deputies for failing their assignment, and now, their feelings wounded, they were taking it out on everyone else with a vengeance.

His pillows had been ripped open with knives, and feathers floated like gently falling snow. He threw socks, several sweaters, three shirts, and a pair of trousers into a satchel. Freezing air poured through a cracked windowpane, but it scarcely mattered. After they were gone, the cold and the animals would reclaim the place soon enough.

When he lugged his satchel down the hall, he discovered his mother already at the front door with a pair of bags. "Maybe it would be easier if I got the reindeer and brought them up here," he said.

"Let me go with you," she said.

On their way out she stopped in the doorway and glanced back to give the house a final look.

"I hate to leave it like this."

"Mom . . ."

"Remember Nanu telling us how grand it was going to be?"

"But she really didn't know, did she?"

"No, I guess she didn't."

Together they hurried down the hill, half-running, half-walking. The magnitude of what he'd done was still dawning on him. Every house in the village was going to be torn apart just as theirs had been torn about. There were going to be babies woken from their beds, there would be crying and shouting and worse. They picked their way crabwise down the steep final descent and clambered up to the cave.

His mother entered the cave first, holding the lantern aloft. Lars was just a step behind her. They were met by a perfect silence. Shadows from the lantern slid along stone walls. The reindeer were gone.

But it wasn't just that the reindeer were gone, it was everything— sleigh, blankets, straw, the sack of carvings.

His mother swung the lantern around, her face filled with dismay. "Lars, what did you do?"

"I didn't do anything."

"Then where did they go?"

"I have no idea. They must be around here somewhere."

But when he went back to the mouth of the cave and stared out across the frozen sea, he saw nothing. He couldn't believe that the reindeer had abandoned him again.

"Is there something you haven't told me, Lars?"

Of course there was. There was so much—the freeing of the tomten, the mysterious assistance he'd received with his carving—but he wasn't fool enough to bring all that up now.

Her patience was at an end. "Okay, then," she said. "Don't bother. I've had enough of this nonsense. Flying reindeer and grandmothers coming back from the dead. Let me tell you what we're going to do. I've going to leave you at the house. I'm going to go solve this."

"But, Mom, how?"

"You'll see."

TWENTY-SEVEN

As much as he pressed her to explain, she wouldn't. After she left, he was in a state, and because it was too distressing to simply sit and wait for her return, he found himself cleaning up, pointlessly—sorting the silverware and putting it back in the silverware drawer, straightening the sofa, sweeping broken glass into a dustpan.

No boy is capable of blaming himself for everything, and so Lars found himself trying to blame some of it on his mother. If she hadn't let Nanu bully her into coming north, everything would have been totally different. If she hadn't been so clueless and wrapped up in her own worries, she might have noticed that things were getting weird and figured it all out, laid down the law, and stopped him before everything exploded.

But he could only blame his mother for so long. What if she got lost out there in the night and the cold? What if she died? She was all he had in the world.

He went down to the shore and searched for an hour, looking for some sign of the reindeer. He nursed the slimmest of hopes that they might be coming back, but he knew in his heart that they wouldn't. What cowards they had turned out to be.

The sea ice shrieked and groaned, powerful enough to swallow a ship in seconds. How amazing it was that he was the one everyone was looking for, when here he was out in plain sight. He prayed to Nanu to make the reindeer come back, just one last time, and for a moment he thought his prayer had been answered.

There was a series of low grunts, behind and above him. He

whirled and looked up at the top of the cliff. Framed in moonlight was the head of an enormous polar bear.

When he got back to the house he was dizzy with exhaustion. The house was getting rapidly colder—Lars knew of at least one window the deputies had broken, and he expected that there were more. He jammed the stove full of planks, and once he'd gotten it blazing he took the quilts from his mother's bedroom, lay down on the sofa, and was asleep within minutes.

Once the deputies were sent off to begin their search, the mayor tried to calm himself. Maybe things weren't as disastrous as they seemed. Perhaps the carvings were just a fluke, a freakish occurrence, like the comets that streak across the sky every couple of hundred years.

But in less than an hour the first report came in that a second toy had been found. Then came the reports of a third and a fourth. By one in the morning more than two dozen carvings had been found. There could be no more wishing it away: they were facing full-blown rebellion.

What was to be done? That was the question. The children who'd been the recipients of the carvings were being held in a warehouse down by the pier. The toys were collected and brought to the mansion. And though it was the middle of the night, Wolfpaw sent word that he wanted the headmaster to report to him immediately.

An hour later Mr. Smorgas came staggering in, crusty-eyed and terrified, and was ushered into the massive dining room by Snortblossom. The schoolmaster was in awe, having never been in the mansion before with its chandeliers, painted ceilings, and massive mirrors.

Afraid that the mayor was on the verge of a heart attack, his valet had insisted that Wolfpaw take a long, soaking bath to settle his nerves, so the headmaster encountered a mayor very unlike the mayor they were used to seeing. Although rosy-cheeked from the hot water, it was clear that he was a shattered man. He sprawled in a throne-like chair, fondling a massive regal mace studded with diamonds. He was, however, only partially dressed, wearing a scarlet smoking jacket and little else. One hairy leg hung over an arm of the chair, and he was barefoot. His toenails looked as if they hadn't been cut in a year. If a person was so disposed, he could have easily imagined that those toenails were claws.

"Sir," Mr. Smorgas said.

"You have heard what's happened?" Wolfpaw's hair stuck up in all directions like a wheat field after a tornado.

"Yes. I am so sorry, sir. Whatever I can do to help."

That was enough to enrage the mayor. "It's a little late for that, isn't it?"

The schoolmaster bowed his head. "That's a point, sir," he said. Snortblossom stood silently at his side, his bandaged nose looking like a white vole clinging to the middle of his face.

"I've been told that some of your older students have been refusing to take their skarn-liver oil. Is that true?"

"I'm afraid it is."

"But how could that be? Surely you have teachers supervising them."

"We do. And I've gone in twice to speak to them. In no uncertain terms. Frankly, I don't fully understand it. I'd been getting a few reports of some unusual behavior, but when you work in a school, you get used to taking these things in stride."

"What kind of behavior?"

Above them on the ceiling was an enormous mural of two parka-clad seal hunters reaching across a stretch of open water to touch the tips of their harpoons. Behind the hunters was a wilderness of icebergs and mist and a single whaling ship.

"Girls laughing in the hallway who've never laughed before. Kids playing games. Acting like six- and seven-year-olds. One of the teachers came in to tell me about a student exhibiting a bit more imagination that he'd ever thought the poor boob was capable of."

The mayor looked as if he'd just been bitten by an adder. He shot out of his chair. "Did you say *imagination*?"

"Yes."

The mayor let out a scream that sounded more animal than human. Snortblossom followed Wolfpaw with his eyes as the mayor began to circle the room. "Do you have any idea if these children have been given toys?"

"I don't, sir," the schoolmaster said.

Round the dining room table the mayor went, smoking jacket billowing, pounding the mace in the palm of his hand, toenails clicking on the marble floor. The petrified schoolmaster watched the reflections of the mayor in a dozen mirrors.

"I want you to give me a list of names of all these children," the mayor said.

"When you say all . . ." Snortblossom said.

"I mean all of them! All of those who've refused to take their skarnliver oil, all of those who are laughing without cause, all of those who are exhibiting these flights of imagination . . ."

"But you need to be careful about overreacting, sir," Mr. Smorgas said. "These are not all bad children. They may be just going through a phase."

The mayor grabbed Snortblossom by his wrist. "I want you to see that all the children on that list are rounded up and taken down to the warehouse and locked up with all the others."

Mr. Smorgas, who'd never been known for bravery, was not backing down. "Sir, I'm afraid I have to object."

"You *object*? And what might that mean? As long as I'm the mayor here, there will be no objections!"

The mayor whirled and hurled the mace with two hands. The schoolmaster and Snortblossom both ducked, but they weren't the target. The mace shattered the chandelier over the table and a thousand prisms of glass rained down on all three of them in a glittering cloudburst.

Lars heard a tinkling. It faded so quickly he thought he must have dreamed it and just rolled over and pulled the quilt over his head, trying to go to sleep, but then he heard it a second time, louder and more distinct. He opened his eyes and was amazed to find himself on the couch. The air was freezing cold on his face. The fire in the stove had burned down to almost nothing.

He threw off the quilt, hobbled to the window and squinted out. A small dark object sailed through the western sky. It darted like a bug, zigged and zagged erratically, plummeted and rose. Lars wrestled into his parka and raced outside. As the object drew closer, he saw to his great astonishment that it was the reindeer and the sleigh. The sleigh lurched from side to side as if it was about to capsize. It was coming right at him, and as far as he could see there was no one holding the reins.

He leapt out of the way just in time. As the sleigh whooshed a couple of feet above his head, he caught a glimpse of eight terrified and not-quite-human faces with owl-like eyes peering over the rails.

The sleigh regained altitude and circled back over the ocean. It vanished into the clouds, but when he spotted it again it was on its way back, speeding low over the ice. Too low. Just as it seemed it was certain to crash, it rose just enough and came bouncing up the slope toward him.

The reindeer were trying frantically to stay ahead of the runaway sleigh, their legs churning. One of them went to its knees, but recovered in time to keep from being trampled by its harness-mates.

It was not a smooth landing. There was a metallic clang, and two of the tomten somersaulted out, pitching headfirst into a snowbank. One of the runners was seriously mangled and vibrating wildly. The sleigh fishtailed to a stop halfway between the house and the whaling ship, sending up an icy spray.

Six more tomten popped out of the sleigh like popcorn, spanking their palms together. A trembling hand appeared, clutching the door of the sled. Very slowly a decrepit old man pulled himself up to a sitting position.

He waved for assistance and two of the tomten rushed to help. The flight had left the old man dazed. Even when he was on solid ground he swayed a bit, tapping at the snow with a cane. His hair was wild, tangled, and hanging down over a pair of dark glasses. He looked like a musk ox that had been banished from the herd. He wore a tattered blue servant's coat, and his teeth hung precariously from his gums.

The tomten wasted no time getting down to business. One of them trotted about, trying to calm the nerves of the distraught reindeer. The two who'd landed in the snowbank sprang up and scampered back to join their comrades as if they'd just come from a refreshing dip in the lake. Three others hopped back into the sleigh and began to toss small satchels down to the others. Still in their soiled green jackets, they couldn't have been cheerier, chattering away as if they'd just returned from the grandest party.

"Hello!" Lars shouted.

They all stopped working and raised their misshapen little heads. The trembly old man raised a hand in greeting. "Hello!" he called out. The tomten began to whisper warily to one another.

"And who would you be?" Lars said.

"My name is Marius. Marius the Zookeeper, they called me. I was the tomtens' caretaker, many years ago. Before you were even born."

Lars shuffled down the slope, went to the reindeer, scratched them behind the ears, and patted their flanks.

"And you are Lars, is that right?"

"Yes," Lars said. He could see now, from the way Marius held his head, that he was blind. "I appreciate your bringing the reindeer back." Several of the tomten beamed at him, their razor-sharp little teeth glittery as the teeth of baby crocodiles. "Can I get you anything? Something to drink, maybe? Something to eat?"

"No, we're fine," Marius said. The reindeer were getting impatient, pawing at the snow, sleigh bells ringing. "The first thing we should do is make sure this sleigh is useable."

The sleigh seemed to be a mess. Not only had one of the runners torn loose from the body, but it was listing badly, and one of the doors was nearly caved in.

"Why don't we take it down to the whaling ship?" Lars said. "It will be easier to work on it down there."

Lars took Siegfried's halter and gave it a yank. He led the reindeer down the slope, the sleigh quivering along behind them like a wounded bird. Marius followed, and after Marius came the tomten, waddling like ducklings, their satchels flung over their shoulders.

Once they were inside the whaling ship, Lars lit several lanterns and helped the tomten unharness the reindeer. The examination of the sleigh took a good twenty minutes. Lars tugged at the damaged runner and when he let it go it twanged like a bowstring. Once they turned the sled over they could see that a dozen bolts had been ripped from the wooden frame.

The tomten were not discouraged. They pointed and peered and consulted with Marius from time to time in that strange language of theirs. They seemed to understand much of Lars's Swedish, but made no attempt to speak it.

"I think it would be best if we left the repairs to them," Marius said. "They're awfully good at this kind of thing."

Lars and Marius sat together on the top step of the stairs while below them the tomten undid their satchels and laid out all their tools—wrenches and mallets, saws and knives no bigger than slivers of toenails. They went to work straightening the mangled runner, dimpling it with a thousand hammer blows, accompanied the whole time by the furious chiming of sleigh bells. The reindeer huddled in the far corner, pained by the din.

The tale Marius had to tell—and was determined to tell—took an hour. He had been working for the Ratvass family when the young wolf-boy was brought in by the hunters. Marius told Lars every detail of that remarkable time—of how cruelly the wild creature had been treated and how close Marius had grown to him. He talked about the tiny schooner that was the first and last thing to fill the boy with joy, and the horrific night the toy boat was discovered, and the night when Marius stood on a hillside with Mayor Wolfpaw on a leash beside him, watching as the boy's beloved tutor was hanged.

"And could you have stopped it?" Lars asked.

"Every day of my life I ask that question. God knows what they would have done to me. I was just a servant. But at least I could have tried. I was a coward. And that's why we're all sitting here tonight."

Marius's major responsibility had been the tending of the tomten, visiting them beneath the factory to see that they were meeting their responsibilities in a timely fashion. He'd learned to speak their language and developed a certain fondness for them, despite their melancholy nature. They all loathed the work they were doing, and complained constantly, telling him nearly everything. But the one thing they kept to themselves was their extraordinary gifts as carvers.

Whatever glimmers of innocence Mayor Wolfpaw may have exhibited as a child quickly disappeared as he grew to manhood. He murdered his two stepbrothers and became a tyrant, ruthless and capricious. Marius, who had once been the boy's most steadfast protector, was dismissed and retreated to the farthest reaches of the tundra, where he led a hermit's existence. When Lars freed the tom-ten from the bowels of the factory, they were at a loss for where to go, how to live. It took them more than a week before they stumbled upon Marius's hovel in the middle of a howling blizzard, delirious and half-starved.

It was a grand reunion. So much time had passed. Marius was not the man he had once been. He was nearly blind now and could only walk a few yards at a time. He lived on next to nothing but was happy to share what he had.

They could not have been more grateful. After years of being caged up in the dark with the troughs of thrashing skarn, all that mattered to the tomten was that they were free, that there was a lantern flick-ering above them as they slept beneath a single ragged blanket, and that there was once again a kindly presence to watch over them.

At night they would sometimes venture out and roam, hunting for food, lemmings and voles and small birds. It was on one of these rambles that two of them came upon Lars in the hold of the ship, carv-ing. They were flabbergasted. Here was this boy, doing what they had been forbidden to do so many years ago, although, to be honest, he was doing it remarkably badly.

They alerted their fellow tomten and for a week they spied on Lars, hanging silently from the riggings on the deck like bats. When Lars began to give the carvings away, they were beside themselves. This was craziness, sheer idiocy.

One night they were all going on about this when Marius, who'd been out gathering more smoked char from the drying racks, poked his head in.

"Now what is this? You're all picking on this poor boy."

"But the whole thing is suicide. The kid can't carve. He's a rank beginner . . ."

"Well, my goodness. And this is something you know about?"

The tomten all looked at one another. "I think we do."

And so it all came out—all the carvings they had done so long ago, when the village was young, the terror they'd felt when they'd been hunted down and locked away beneath the skarn-liver-oil factory.

"Has it ever occurred to you that you might help this boy? Rank beginner though he may be. He was the one who set you free."

They talked for an hour before it was decided that they would come to Lars's aid. Early every morning before Lars awoke, they would sneak into the whaling ship with their tools and make improvements to his carvings. Eventually they would create new ones and leave them on the railing for Lars to discover.

Once they began to carve, all their fears went away and a kind of crazed elation took its place. They had rediscovered their true calling. Marius had never seen them so happy. When they returned to the hovel in the mornings, the tomtens' hair and eyebrows would be powdered with sawdust. They were finally making up for the decades they'd been playing for the wrong team.

Lars's feelings were a little wounded over being called a rank beginner, but he did his best not to show it. "Can I ask a question?" Lars said.

"Of course."

"Why did they run off with the reindeer and the sleigh?"

"Because they were here, hiding in the riggings when you and your mother were talking. They realized things had taken a terrible turn."

Progress had been made on the sleigh. The mangled runner had been straightened and rebolted and seemed ready to take to the skies. The reindeer, on the other hand, looked as if they didn't want to have any part of any of it. They'd yet to be fed, had been hidden away in a dismal cavern, flown hither and yon, and crash-landed in a snowbank. They looked very dubious about whatever they were going to be asked to do next.

Marius rolled his cane back and forth in his hands. "And there was one other thing."

"Yes."

"After you took the reindeer down to the cave, they all went up to your house, curious creatures that they were. They peered in the window and watched the deputies tear room after room apart. When they were finished, the deputies came outside to meet with one from another crew. The tomten all dived for cover behind the pile of whale bones and furs and listened in.

"It seems that several of the other teams of deputies had already found children who'd been hiding toys, and they'd been taken away. And word from the mayor had come down that if none of the children who'd been given carvings stepped forward and confessed who had given them these toys, they would never be heard from again."

Lars looked over at Marius, incredulous. "But none of those kids know anything."

"I understand." The tomten had all stopped their tinkering. "When our friends here came to me, they were distraught," Marius said. "They were convinced that everything that had happened was their fault, and they didn't know what to do."

"But you did know?"

"I had an idea."

"And what was that?"

He gestured for a tomte with a wispy white beard, who retrieved one of the satchels from the back of the sleigh. "I put them to work, and I think they've done an awfully good job."

The tomte handed the satchel to Marius, who undid it and pulled out a small, three-masted schooner, perfect in every detail. It was all there, jib and mizzenmast, foresail and mainsail, windlass and anchor. There was even a small cannon. It was perfectly balanced, with a long sleek prow, and the wood had been sanded until it was as smooth to the touch as butter.

"What is this?" Lars aksed.

"This is the boat Mayor Wolfpaw loved as much as anything when he was a child. The one that cost his tutor his life."

"Why are you showing this to me?"

"Because I want you to deliver it."

"To Wolfpaw?"

"Who else?"

"No! Not in a million years! If you want to do this, do it yourself!"

"That's impossible. You've seen what happens when this bunch tries to drive a sleigh."

"You think giving Wolfpaw this is going to change anything? That's just nuts. He's the worst person who ever lived."

"Oh, you think you know him, Lars? I don't think you do. I knew him when he was a boy, no different from you. When he wanted to do nothing but to play with this thing for hours on end . . . " He ran his palm along the sleek prow of the schooner. "People get old, Lars, they get all twisted and crusted-over and disappointed, but that doesn't mean there still isn't a spark in there, a spark that hasn't quite gone out. And that's what we always have to trust."

"But how can I leave?" Lars said. "My mother's going to come back any time."

"This will not take long."

Lars was still not convinced. He glanced over at the reindeer. Jonas looked more timid than ever, and even the vain Canute, his magnificent antlers held high, seemed uncertain. They all knew that their fate rested in Lars's hands.

"Do they know which children have been taken?" he asked.

Marius spoke with the tomten in their sing-song language for a moment and then turned to Lars. "They don't. But they remember one of the deputies saying something about a couple of rough boys and some sassy dark-haired girl with a ballerina."

Lars's eyes stung with tears. There was no question now what he needed to do.

"Okay, then," he said. "You win."

"We've made you a map." Marius pulled a wrinkled piece of paper from inside his tattered jacket and handed it to Lars. Lars folded it and stuffed it in his pocket.

"And if my mother gets back before I do . . . "

"We will explain."

Once the reindeer were harnessed Lars grabbed the rail and heaved himself up. Marius handed the schooner to him.

"It's beautiful, isn't it? I know this is hard. But if you take this carving to Wolfpaw, these eight promise that they will do your bidding for as long as you live. They will carve you millions of toys, enough toys for every child on earth."

That didn't seem like much of a reward to Lars. He said nothing, wrapping the schooner in blankets and slipping it under the front seat. The tomten led the reindeer out through the hole in the hull, Lars ducking low to keep from hitting his head. When he shook the reins, the reindeer set off at a brisk trot, and then began to lope. As the sleigh rose in the air, he glanced down at the wisp of smoke twining from the chimney of their house. He circled back over the whaling ship, heading toward Mayor Wolfpaw's. Far below, eight tiny creatures waved madly. Marius stood apart from the others, looking worried.

TWENTY-EIGHT

She had set off with her paltry savings in a pouch and a fierce determination that she was going to find a way out of this place. If there was no one able to guide them through the mountains, she would buy a team of dogs whatever the price, and she and Lars would try to navigate those fearsome passes by themselves. She was aware that it was not much of a plan.

Among the many things she hadn't thought through was just what a terrible night this was for everyone. The first four houses she stopped at had already been searched by the deputies and had a child marched off to the warehouse. She was greeted by wailing and hysterics, men vowing retribution.

No one was in any mood to discuss dogs.

One old man nearly bent double with a twisted spine waved a polished stick at her. "Have you gone mad? Do you have any idea what's going on out there tonight? Leave us be! Did you hear me? Leave us be!"

Twice, as she made her way through the dark and cold, she passed teams of deputies pulling stumbling children through the mist, bound by ropes as if they were calves on their way to market.

After an hour she knew that time was running short. The thought that came to her was a cold one. If she was going to have dogs, she would have to steal them.

In her right mind, she wouldn't have ever considered such a thing. But she wasn't in her right mind. She feared for her son's life.

She had been raised to be upright. She'd never told a lie or peeked at a classmate's paper during a test or picked up a kroner that someone had dropped on the cobblestones. Yet here she was, running down a list of those who might be easiest to steal from. The only name that seemed halfway possible was Ilya Popov.

Ilya was a block of a man who worked at the skarn-liver-oil factory, stacking crates. In his youth he was reputed to be a crack seal hunter, but after he fractured his hip when his sleigh overturned, he'd been relegated to menial labor.

Nearly deaf and half-blind, he lived just north of Woolly Mammoth Glacier, his hovel sitting amidst a number of sheds and dog hutches.

The mist had cleared by the time she arrived at the north end of the glacier. A lantern still burned inside Ilya's ramshackle hut. She gave the hut a wide berth, making her way around to the back where everything was still, the dogs all asleep in their hutches. She found a sled stored in a shallow cellar and slid it out onto the snow.

She moved from hutch to hutch, waking the dogs with whispers and the gentlest of pats. There were a couple of startled yips and a few low woofs, but she managed to get them out and buckled without a chorus of howls. She left her packet of kroners wrapped around a nail in one of the hutches. Through the lighted window of Ilya's hovel she could see him snoring in his chair, and felt a terrible pang of remorse. Only God was going to be able to forgive her for this.

The dogs could only contain themselves for so long. When she pushed off, clicking her tongue, they began to bark. They were a hundred yards out before she heard Ilya shouting behind her, heard the boom of the blunderbuss, the spatter of buckshot on the snow around her.

It was a miracle that she found her way home. The dogs didn't know her, and she didn't know them. Which was supposed to be the lead dog, which the swing dogs, or the wheel dogs, she had no idea; she just buckled them in. They were testy and sensed her lack of confidence. Twice they got their harnesses tangled, and when she had to stop to untangle them they began to snarl and fight. Once she was sure she was lost, plunging through heavy drifts, but eventually she found a hard-packed trail that took them all the way to the familiar cliffs.

She could see a lantern burning in the window as she pulled the dogs to a stop in front of the house. But when she opened the door and called out, there was no answer.

She turned and looked back down the hill. A spot of light winked on and off from somewhere inside the ruined hull of the ship. There was singing as well—high-pitched, reedy, strange, incomprehensible. All the dogs' ears were up.

She hurried down the slope. She ducked through the hole in the hull and was stopped dead in her tracks by the strangest sight she had ever seen—seven grotesque little creatures gathered around an eighth who was strumming on a mandolin no larger than a boot.

They were crooning in high falsetto voices, in a language Helga had never heard before. The tallest of them was perhaps three feet tall. They had fur on their ears, huge eyes, blue lips, and a dank reptilian air. They looked a little like turtles who had managed to exchange their shells for soiled green jackets.

Their audience of one was a decrepit old man sitting on the steps, tapping his feet to the music.

"Where is my son?"

The singing stopped. Scaly eyelids blinked. The creatures began jabbering to one another. Leaning on his cane, the old man swayed to his feet.

"You must be Lars's mother."

"Yes."

"My name is Marius. And these are dear friends of your son's. The tomten. They are the ones who've been helping him with his carvings."

"I was not aware that anyone was helping my son."

"Please, do not be alarmed. We expect him back any minute."

"But where has he gone?"

The tomten all turned somber. The blind man grimaced and rubbed dry lips with a knuckle. "Please allow me to explain."

It was a long and tangled story, explaining who they were and how they'd gotten there. Much of it she had trouble following, though to be fair, as distracted as she was by the bizarre appearance of the tomten, she would have had trouble following a nursery rhyme.

What she did understand was that the reindeer had come back and that the tomten had carved a beautiful toy for Mayor Wolfpaw that would somehow melt his heart and cause him to spare the lives of the children he was on the verge of snatching. Fine enough. The only catch was that they had managed to convince Lars to deliver this toy.

She was outraged. Here she was trying to save her son from Wolfpaw, and here they were, these repulsive creatures who claimed to be Lars's friends, delivering him to the mayor like a roast pig on a silver platter.

She turned and darted through the jagged hole in the hull. The tomten scampered after her, but on their short legs in the deep snow they were no match for her, falling farther and farther behind as she ran up the slope.

As she slammed into the house she looked over her shoulder. The blind old man was struggling up the slope as well, but was a good twenty yards behind the others.

She threw open the hall closet and began tossing things onto the floor. It had been months since Taya Kerensky had presented her with a flintlock to protect her and her son from hungry polar bears.

She remembered quite clearly storing it in the closet, but where exactly? It wasn't on the upper shelf, and it wasn't in any of the baskets hanging on hooks. Could she have moved it and forgotten? Could the mayor's deputies have found it and taken it without telling her? She was on the verge of panic when she finally found it, tucked in a cracked leather boot in the far corner, and, behind it, buried under a pile of woolen sweaters, were the horn of gunpowder and the half-dozen small iron balls.

She stuffed them all into the pockets of her parka, but as she rushed out the door she ran into the eight tomten rushing in. The blind man had fallen halfway up the slope.

Two of the tomten tried to tackle her by the ankles. Two clung to her sleeves. One hugged her around the waist and hung on for dear life. One by one she threw them all off.

She ran to the sled and leapt on the runners. The dogs were going crazy, hurtling themselves against their traces, and the tomten were afraid of getting too close. She sicced the dogs up, shaking the reins, and they were off, charging through the mob of tiny creatures, scattering them like tenpins.

It was a spectacularly clear night, moon-drenched, and the dogs were running well, lines taut. Helga leaned into the turns, standing on a single runner. How much like a pack of wolves they seemed. And now they were taking her to one of their own.

By now Ilya had probably alerted the deputies. No doubt they were on her trail somewhere back there. Even if Lars had somehow delivered the tomten's toy and slipped out of the mayor's mansion undetected, it wouldn't matter. After the uproar Helga had created, there was no doubt where all the fingers were going to be pointing.

The runners rumbled on the hard-packed snow. The sled whipped back and forth like the tail of an enraged snake. She felt the flintlock heavy in her pocket.

Was she capable of using it? The thought of her son being in danger had made her crazed. She no longer knew who or what she was anymore.

Mayor Wolfpaw was a tyrant, merciless and arbitrary, threatening to kidnap children for the most innocent of offenses. She had seen him pistol-whip Bjorn Snortblossom.

Yet she had seen another side of him. She had seen how alone and desperate and full of yearning he could be. He had offered to give up his entire kingdom for her. He had offered her and Lars a way out, and she had walked away.

She felt as if she had never quite understood anything. How could she have ever ended up in this place of endless night? More than anything she wanted to see the morning sun again, shining on her garden! And why had that bizarre half-man, half-wolf never left her alone? She had no answer. It was just one mystery opening into another.

The clouds came up quickly and it began to blow. Snowflakes fell huge and wet, and suddenly they were in the midst of a squall. The dogs disappeared into a rushing billow of white. One of the runners slipped off the hard-packed trail into a deep, soft drift and the sled overturned.

Helga lost her hold on the handlebars and she was thrown backwards. She landed with such force all the air was knocked out of her.

She grabbed for the catch-rope as it slithered past and missed, but the snow hook, swinging free, pierced one of her mukluks. She covered her face with her hands as she was dragged by her foot through the drifts, rolling over and over again like a piece of trolled bait. She gasped and gasped again, struggling to breathe. She could feel her hood and parka filling up with snow.

The dogs never stopped. It was impossible to tell if she was dragged one hundred yards or two, but the sleigh finally hit something. There was the sound of shattering wood and the snow hook pulled loose, ripping the mukluk to shreds.

She was free, but battered and alone. The barking of the dogs faded in the wind. She sat, slumped over, and spit blood into the snow. She took one of her mittens and with trembling fingers tried to stuff it into her torn mukluk, but did a bad job of it. She shook out her parka, but she could still feel the ice-crystals trickling down her neck, down her belly. The flintlock was still in her pocket.

She tried to push herself up, but her hand slipped and she fell. It would be wiser, she thought, not to struggle anymore. When she laid her bare cheek on the snow, it burned like fire.

TWENTY-NINE

he night was electric. Great washes of green and blue rolled across the mountains and tundra beneath him. The reindeer had not had an easy day, but they did their best, fighting a crosswind that battered the sleigh and rattled the three-masted schooner under Lars's feet.

It was a half hour before he spotted the pale cone of light shining above the walls of Mayor Wolfpaw's mansion. Lars pulled the sleigh into a wide arc so he had time to scrutinize the tomten's map. It was sketchily drawn, and he was flying high enough that it was difficult to make out many of the features of the landscape below, but when he came to the circle of giant stone slabs fifty yards beyond the walls of Wolfpaw's estate, they were impossible to miss.

Lars leaned forward and slapped the reins across the reindeer's flanks. "Tundra!" he whispered. "Tundra!"

The reindeer skimmed to a perfect stop just outside the ring of pillars.

Lars tied the reins to a rusted iron gate and made his way to the center of the circle of stones. Some were twenty-five feet high, and some had equally gigantic granite slabs balanced on top of them, as if a race of giants had been building something, got distracted, and ran off never to return and finish the job.

Lars moved from one towering pillar to the next, scrutinizing them. On most of them there was writing etched on their inner faces (writing that vaguely resembled the hen scratching of the tomten). But what he was searching for was the likeness of the coiled snake, a match for the drawing on his map.

He'd made an entire circuit of the pillars before he found it, six feet up, on the tallest of the stones. For several seconds he was confused about what to do next. He edged around the mammoth slab, patting it up and down as if it might magically open for him. Then he tripped.

"Ouch!" he cried. He hopped on one foot, looking back resentfully at the spot where he'd stubbed his toe. A corner of planking glistened in the snow. Lars got on his hands and knees and brushed away the icy crystals until he had exposed an entire door.

It was frozen shut, but after a dozen stabs at the icy edges with his knife and a dozen hard yanks, he was able to pry it open.

He stared down at a flight of broken stairs that led into pitch-darkness.

He went back to the sleigh, retrieved his lantern, and eased the schooner out from under the front seat as if it were a sleeping infant.

The reindeer were uneasy, looking back over their haunches, trying to figure out what he was up to. Lars trudged back to the tunnel, lantern in one hand, schooner in the other. The moon cast long shadows on the gleaming drifts.

Lars stood for a moment above the open door. The pillars stared down at him like mute, ancient gods.

He took one deep breath, bent low, and made his way into darkness. A second flight of stairs brought him to the brick floor of the tunnel. Lars lifted the lantern high to check out his surroundings.

The ceiling was reinforced with netting, the walls lined with huge jugs of a slimy yellow liquid. There was the faint smell of sea water.

As Lars crept down the tunnel he came upon more racks. Some were stuffed with bales of fur, others lined with row after row of fine wines. He passed an arsenal of pistols and muskets.

The shaft narrowed for a stretch, and Lars had to turn sideways to wriggle his way through, holding the schooner on his shoulder with both hands. When the shaft opened up again, he was suddenly surrounded by piles of burlap gunnysacks, some streaked with frozen blood. One had been ripped open, its contents scattered across the passageway. He wanted desperately to believe that the dozen objects he was staring at were something acceptable, bowling balls, say, or large loaves of bread, but he knew better: they were frozen organs, the hearts and livers of sizeable creatures.

Lars hurried on. Beyond the sacks the brick walkway led upwards. Lars could make out a glimmer of light ahead.

It took no more than a couple of minutes to reach the end of the tunnel. Overhead was a latticed grating. Peering through the tiny squares, Lars could make out what seemed to be a cheerful, brightly lit kitchen.

He set the lantern and the carving down on the icy bricks. The grating was too far up for him to reach, but after a brief search, he was able to find a pair of sturdy wooden crates.

He stacked one on top of the other and climbed up. It was an unstable perch, and Lars rose carefully out of his crouch, arms spread wide to keep his balance.

His first effort at pushing open the grating rewarded him with a shower of grit. He spat, left and right, wiped his eyes and mouth clean, and tried again. As he pushed against it, the grate lifted inch by inch. The kitchen was the size of Lord Borland's stables, with a half dozen roaring fireplaces, a half dozen ovens, and enough pots and pans hanging on the walls to feed a czar's army.

Directly over Lars's head was a sturdy butcher's table. He laid the grating down on the tiles and ducked back into the tunnel. He retrieved the schooner, clambered up the stacked crates, and slid the carving onto the kitchen floor. He blew into his hands. This was turning into a lot of work.

Leaving his lantern behind, Lars grabbed hold of one of the table-legs and pulled himself into the bright kitchen. He huddled under the table, surveying the room. Several freshly strangled Arctic swans hung next to one of the fireplaces, and a dozen small and beautifully iced French pastries dotted a row of trays on the counter.

The house was perfectly silent. Lars set the grating back in place, pushed to his feet, and picked up the schooner. He made his way on tiptoe to the kitchen door and peered out.

In the front hallway, a corpulent man in a chef's hat slept in a chair, his hands folded across his lap and a dab of chocolate frosting on his chin. Lars passed a massive dining room where three deputies, also dead to the world, sprawled across long tables like seals dozing on the ice.

He tiptoed up a marble staircase and entered a second massive hall. Everything, just as in the kitchen, seemed outsized. The carved wooden chairs were large as thrones, and the tapestries hanging on the walls, decorated with scenes of bear-baiting and the harpooning of whales, were over twenty-five feet long. At the top of the vaulted ceiling was the skylight, and beyond it, stars twinkling in the endless darkness.

Off the great hall was a series of doors. Lars made his way down the near corridor, inspecting each room. The first two were lavishly furnished but empty. In the third was a white lynx pacing silently in a cage.

The last door was a different matter. Pushing it open, Lars stared in at Mayor Wolfpaw, asleep in a large, canopied bed, one arm thrown over his eyes. The bed was piled high with embroidered quilts and some very slippery-looking satin pillows.

A fire crackled and popped in a brick fireplace, making the room much too warm. On one wall was a painting of Mayor Wolfpaw, dressed in a general's uniform, standing in the prow of a small rowboat with his hand tucked inside the flap of his coat, looking remarkably resolute while a miserable-looking crew strained over their oars, trying to navigate their way through a maze of towering icebergs. A dozen stovepipe hats, each a different color, were lined up on a shelf.

Lars glided silently across the room. Mayor Wolfpaw moaned and muttered in his sleep. As Lars sat the schooner down just inches from Wolfpaw's head, the mayor gave a snort in his sleep. How yellow his teeth are, Lars thought, how foul his breath.

It occurred to Lars that this might well be the last present he ever gave. But was this carving going to have any effect on Mayor Wolfpaw at all? Lars had his doubts.

Something clattered on the roof. He stared upwards, open mouthed. The clattering sounded again—the clattering of hooves. Lars was furious. How could his reindeer be so dumb? Did they think they were rescuing him? The last thing he needed was their acting like heroes.

Somewhere above him, a door creaked open. Flames guttered in the fireplace. The clattering drew closer, as if descending a staircase with a heavy tread. They may have been hooves, but they weren't the hooves of reindeer.

Lars did a quick survey of the room, looking for a place to hide himself. He yanked open the door of one closet and then another, but they were both jammed tight with clothes. A long shadow fell across the doorway. Lars could hear a low, bestial breathing.

There was no place to go but under Mayor Wolfpaw's bed. Lars dropped to all fours and lifted the corner of one of the drooping quilts. To his dismay, the underside of the bed turned out to be littered with boots and socks. He began to toss the boots aside to make room for himself.

"It is too late, my friend." The voice sounded as if it was coming from the center of the earth.

Lars glanced over his shoulder. The creature filling the doorframe was so huge that all Lars could see of it was an immense torso of straw and eight deer legs chattering like castanets on the marble floor.

Lars was too petrified to speak. The creature bent over and entered the room. Its antlers—there were at least six of them, tangled together—brushed the chandelier and sent it tinkling.

It had to be at least ten feet tall, and at first it seemed to be featureless, but as he swung around, Lars caught a glimpse of something resembling an eye behind the curtain of straw, something small and dark as a cinder. Its hands, protruding from wrists of straw, were gloved in gray leather.

"Stand up, my boy," it said. Lars did as he was told. His mind was racing; whoever or whatever this was, it was much too big to be a butler.

"Who are you?' Lars asked.

"You don't know who I am?"

"No."

"I am Nacht Ruprecht."

"And what are you doing here?"

As the creature moved past an enormous mirror, Lars saw that it had no reflection. "I have come to take Mayor Wolfpaw away."

"And where are you taking him?"

"To the bottom of the volcano. To a pool of molten lava where he will suffer for all of eternity."

"That sounds bad."

"It's very bad." Wolfpaw snorted again and rolled over on his side. A wind had come up suddenly, rattling the windows. "And your name is?"

"Lars."

"How old are you?'

"Twelve."

"I see you've brought the mayor something. Could I have a look?" Lars slipped his hands under the schooner and carried it to him. Nacht Ruprecht took it from him and scrutinized the wooden boat with his burnt-out eye. "Did you carve this?"

"No."

"It was my tomten, right? It looks like their work. Are they the ones who've been doing all the carving?"

Lars could have lied. For whatever reason, he chose not to. "No, I did most of it. But they helped."

"Ahh." Nacht Ruprecht rustled like a cornfield in the wind as he moved across the room. He set the schooner back down on the bed. "And who taught you to carve?"

"My father."

"And what did you carve with?"

"I have his knife."

"Can I see it?" Nacht Ruprecht extended a gloved hand. A trickle of sweat rolled down the back on Lars's neck. Nacht Ruprecht's hand did not move. Lars fumbled about inside his parka, found his knife, and gave it to Nacht Ruprecht. The demon tested the blade on a gloved finger.

Mayor Wolfpaw's snoring had softened to a gentle sputtering. Lars was so confused. All along he had been so sure that the mayor was the tyrant who'd been keeping them under his thumb, but now it seemed as if he was nothing but a lowly go-between.

"I take it you're the one who's been delivering all these toys?"

"Yes."

As Nacht Ruprecht set Lars's knife on the mantel of the fireplace, a single sprig of straw corkscrewed to the floor. "And what did you think you were going to accomplish by all this?"

"I guess I thought it would make people happy."

Nacht Ruprecht's laugh sounded like the croak of a frog. "But didn't you know that toys were banned here? Weren't you warned? Weren't you required to sing that song?"

"The song just seemed so stupid."

"Stupid? And you don't think that trying to make people happy with these miserable toys is stupid?" Irate now that he was not being treated with proper respect, Nacht Ruprecht moved across the room, his eight legs flickering like fingers across a piano keyboard. He scooped the schooner off the bed, clasped it in both hands, and with one quick twist snapped it in two.

"No!" Lars shouted.

Nacht Ruprecht flung the schooner into the fireplace. Sparks flew and smoke billowed. The splintered masts glanced off one of the andirons and slithered down between burning logs. He shook the remains in a gloved hand.

"Do you know what this does to me? Just the thought of it . . . "

Nacht Ruprecht hurled the rest of the schooner ino the flames. Sparks flew and smoke billowed. Lars gave a small, stifled cry. When the smoke cleared, the fire was roaring with new life, reflecting off the walls of the room.

Nacht Ruprecht watched the fire for a couple of minutes without speaking. He held a gloved fist to the straw where a mouth should have been, clenching and unclenching his fingers. The sight of the flames devouring the carving seemed to calm him.

"What I want to know, son, is who is behind this."

"There's nobody. It's just me."

"Oh, come now. There have to be others. You must have your lieutenants."

"There was my grandmother. She's the one who gave me the knife." He made a quick decision not to mention the reindeer. "But she's dead. And my friend Pytor. But he's dead, too."

"Then who freed the tomten?"

"I did. And Pytor."

"And the Winter Festival?"

"That was me, too."

"Are you telling me you're just a troublemaker?"

"I didn't mean to be."

"So it was all an accident? I don't buy that for a minute. But accident or not, it sounds as if I do away with you, all my problems go away too." Nacht Ruprecht took a poker from its stand and stirred the fire, sending up a fresh flurry of sparks. "But look what I'll be stuck with." He nodded at Mayor Wolfpaw, rolling over in his bed and sputtering. He slipped the poker back in its stand.

"What a buffoon! I'm very disappointed in him. I had no idea how dense he was. Imagine, being outsmarted by a twelve-year-old."

As Nacht Ruprecht moved across the floor, the shadows of his antlers on the ceiling looked like writhing snakes. He ran a gloved hand across the mantel. For the first time Lars could see that his arms were held together by twine.

"But even if I get rid of him, who am I going to get to run things? I can't see that there is anyone in this godforsaken place who inspires confidence. Really, young and dewy-eyed as you are, you do show some promise." Nacht Ruprecht paced before the fire. "You're clever. You have gumption. And a certain talent for mayhem. The problem, Lars, is that you're a little misguided. And a little too good to be true. I never believed that creatures like you existed, but apparently they do. You came all this way to give a present to a man you loathe? That's really twisted, Lars."

Lars thought of mentioning that it hadn't been his idea, giving Wolfpaw the schooner, but decided against it. Snow pelted the windows. The wind had turned into a full-blown squall. Lars pitied anyone who might have gotten caught out in it.

"You think the world is a gentle place? Or that anyone is going to be changed by your being generous or kind? If you do, you're living in la-la land. The world is ruled by fear and cruelty and intimidation. And it's always been that way. Oh, I know you think you know better, but you're twelve years old, and you know nothing. I've been around for hundreds of years and I've watched you people, and you're all the same. Even you, Lars. You think you're some saint? But you're no different. You hate this man. Come on. Admit it."

"That's not true."

"Oh, come on, Lars! Wake up! He's a ridiculous human being! He wanted to run off with your mother. He was willing to snatch your classmates away forever, and he wouldn't have thought twice about it." He grasped Lars by the jaw and spun him around. "Look at me! Look at me!" The single coal winked behind the curtain of straw. "Doesn't it bother you, just a little? Doesn't it keep you awake at night?" Lars tried to turn away, but Nacht Ruprecht's grip was too powerful.

"That's only natural, son. And there is one thing that would make you feel better. Killing him. Oh, I know it sounds terrible, but it's not nearly as hard as you think. The man is totally at your mercy. It wouldn't take more than a second. No one would blame you. You'd be a hero to everyone. And then you can have my entire kingdom."

Nacht Ruprecht grabbed Lars's knife from the mantel and thrust it in Lars's hand. "Go on."

"I can't."

"What do you mean, you can't? It's time for you to grow up, son."

Lars glanced over his shoulder at Mayor Wolfpaw. He was curled up, clutching his pillow, his hair sticking up in every direction. Lars raised the knife. He was trembling. He tried to turn away. Nacht Ruprecht clamped a gloved hand on Lars's wrist. "Come on, Lars, let me help you."

Nacht Ruprecht gently steered the knife to Mayor Wolfpaw's throat. "One firm stroke, my boy, one firm stroke, and all our troubles are over."

Lars's mind darted like a wasp trapped between two panes of glass. Nacht Ruprecht hovered above Lars like a puppeteer. His gloved hand squeezed tighter, and Lars could feel prickly dried stalks pressing into his back. It was as if he was sinking into a haymow.

But then the mayor sneezed. Still sleeping, he wiped his nose on his pajama sleeve. It was such a small thing, but it reminded him of Sniffles at school. Would he ever have cut Sniffles's throat? Never. Never ever.

Lars tore free of Nacht Ruprecht's grasp and tossed the knife on the bed. "Uh-uh," he said.

"Uh-uh? You surprise me, Lars. I never took you for a coward."

"But what if I am?"

Nacht Ruprecht leaned over the bed and retrieved the knife. "Do you know what I do with cowards, Lars? I cut out their hearts and make them watch while I eat."

Lars broke to his left, trying to get to the door, but Nacht Ruprecht was too quick for him, blocking the way. Nacht Ruprecht lunged at him with the knife, but Lars sprang back. The blade grazed the front of his parka. He ducked under a second lunge, and a third, but then stumbled and fell.

Lars retreated on his hands and knees as Nacht Ruprecht lurched forward. He was cornered. He could feel the heat from the fire on his trousers and the soles of his mukluks.

Lars glanced over his shoulder at the fireplace. A slender stick of kindling had slipped through the bars of the grating to the bricks below. Tiny tongues of fire licked up and down half of it, the other half still untouched by the blaze.

Lars snatched the stick by the unlit end and scrambled to his feet. Nacht Ruprecht swung at him with the knife, but Lars parried the blow with the slender slat of kindling. Sparks flew. Nacht Ruprecht tried to grab him with his free hand, but Lars spun out of reach.

Back and forth across the room they went like dueling sword-fighters. Nacht Ruprecht flailed away, knife-blade slicing the air. Lars blocked some of the wild swings and ducked others.

It was scarcely a fair fight. Nacht Ruprecht towered over him. Lars had no more chance than a mouse battling a bear. He kept throwing things between them to slow Nacht Ruprecht down, but that only seemed to enrage him more.

Mayor Wolfpaw slept through it all like a baby, making little whistling sounds. Embers smoldered on the rug.

Lars kept retreating, bobbing and weaving. He swung around a bedpost and leapt up on a stool. Nacht Ruprecht lunged at Lars's knees. Lars parried the blow and felt the stick of kindling splinter in his hand.

Lars lost his balance, stumbled backwards, and fell into the curtains. He was sure he was done for, but when he untangled himself he saw that Nacht Ruprecht had dropped the knife and was batting at his chest.

For a moment Lars was confused, but then he saw a dozen points of light twinkling like fireflies in Nacht Ruprecht's chest and belly. Nacht Ruprecht pawed frantically, trying to put out the tiny sparks, but the more he pawed, the more they caught on his hands and hopped to his arms.

Lars moved quickly to the fireplace. He grabbed a set of tongs, clamped them onto a blazing log, and hurled the log at Nacht Ruprecht like a fisherman hurling a net into the sea. The log hit Nacht Ruprecht squarely in the back, and he exploded into flames.

The cry that came out of him was like the cry of a raven. Mayor Wolfpaw sat bolt upright in bed, blinking. Nacht Ruprecht careened around the room, tearing great clumps of blazing straw out of his back.

Mayor Wolfpaw was stupefied. Nacht Ruprecht began to dance, swatting at himself as if he'd been attacked by bees. Smoke enveloped him as a set of antlers tumbled to the floor.

Mayor Wolfpaw jumped out of bed, dragging one of the quilts with him, and tried to wrap Nacht Ruprecht in it. Nacht Ruprecht tried to fight him, but there was not much left of Nacht Ruprecht to fight. The two of them tumbled together. All around them on the carpet, tufts of straw burned like candles.

"No! No!" Mayor Wolfpaw wailed. Weeping, he wrapped and rewrapped the quilt, trying to smother the flames, but it was a hopeless task. With each squeeze, a little puff of smoke rose from the quilt, as if Mayor Wolfpaw was sending Indian smoke signals.

Lars retrieved his father's knife, sprinted out the door and down the corridor. He could hear deputies shouting below him on the marble staircase. He darted behind a stone column, pressed himself flat, and waited until they had all rushed past. Lars ran again, tripping down the stairs.

Shrieking echoed in the upper corridors. Turning back to look, he saw eight deer legs bounding down the staircase, graceful as gazelles. They sped past him. Two smashed through a window and the others followed, leaping into the darkness.

Lars made his way to the kitchen. He opened the grating under the table and lowered himself into the tunnel. The good news was that his lantern was still burning.

He stumbled down the winding tunnel—past the sacks of frozen organs, the bales of fur, the stacks of wine bottles, the arsenal of weapons, the jugs of greasy yellow liquid.

When he finally crawled out of the tunnel, he collapsed onto his back. The snow was still coming hard.

A grunt made him twist around onto his stomach. The sight of the reindeer still tethered in the circle of great stone pillars nearly made him weep. They shook their bridles and pawed the ground, ready to go home.

Lars climbed into the sleigh and shook out the frozen reins. Up into the sky they went. Flames rose from Mayor Wolfpaw's mansion, and there was a far-off sound of screaming. All that mattered now was finding his mother and getting her away from this terrible place.

His expedition had taken much longer than he'd bargained for. His mother most likely was back by now, and if she was, she would be worried sick.

He should have never taken Marius's word for anything. His trip had been a fool's errand. The mayor's heart was not going to be changed. The classmates who'd been taken away were not going to be spared. All he'd accomplished was setting fire to a mansion and coming within an inch of slitting Wolfpaw's throat.

The only one to be changed was Lars. He may have slain the monster, but the monster had left its mark in return.

The squall had passed, and there were only a few drifting flakes in the air. Lars was a little more than halfway home when he spotted, far below, a team of dogs dragging an overturned sled.

Alarmed now, Lars scanned the tundra. A quarter of a mile further on, he saw a figure lying face down in the snow. Eight smaller figures stood around it, waving furiously.

His first thought was that the downed figure was a dead animal, or possibly Marius; that he and the tomten had set off on one of their cockamamie adventures and come to a bad end.

Lars was still angry enough at them that he thought seriously of passing them by, but in the end found that impossible to do.

He angled the reindeer around in a wide loop. "Tundra!" he shouted. "Tundra!" They landed in a bank of newly fallen snow and disappeared momentarily in a billowing cloud of white.

The tomten all came running. They jabbered and pulled at his sleeves as he dismounted. Lars pushed them off and made his way toward the downed figure he was convinced was Marius, but then he saw the long blonde braid protruding from the collar of the parka.

The cry he made was a terrible thing. He stumbled forward and slid on his knees. One of his mother's arms was raised and her head was turned to the side as if she was listening to something deep beneath the snow. Her eyes were closed.

Her fingers were like ice. He began to weep. He had lost everything—his father, Nanu, Pytor, and now his mother. The reindeer and the tomten all gathered round, watching, downcast. Canute shook his magnificent antlers, nearly overcome with sorrow, and the painfully shy Jonas turned his head away. A million stars shone in the endless sky. It could have been a manger scene from some ancient story, except that all the animals could fly and all the magi were wizened gnomes in soiled green jackets.

But as he worked one hand under her shoulders, intending to lift her, he felt her shudder. He lay her back down again and pressed his cheek to her chest and heard the slow, muffled thud of her heart.

"Mom? Mom?" She stirred. Her eyes flickered and opened. She stared blankly as if she had no idea where she was.

"Mom, it's me. Lars."

He touched her face. She tried to speak, but no words came. A wavering sheet of green and blue light fled across the sky. She lurched up on one elbow and fell back again. "Mom, don't. Let me."

He managed to wrestle her to her feet, but was unable to move her any further until the tomten came to his aid. They maneuvered her to the sleigh, and when they boosted her into the front seat something heavy fell out of her pocket.

Lars looked down and saw a flintlock, handle up, half-buried in the snow. Lars retrieved it and fingered the icy barrel. He held it up for his mother to see.

"'Did they put you up to this?" he asked. She was in no shape to answer, but he could see from the look in her eye that the tomten had nothing to do with it.

He heaved the pistol far out into the darkness and climbed into the driver's seat. The tomten had no intention of being left behind, so they quickly scrambled in behind him.

Lars yanked a blanket from under his seat and bundled his mother as warmly as he could. With two clicks of his tongue they were off.

The reindeer floundered at first in the soft, newly fallen snow, but once they were in the air, a brisk wind out of the east took them higher and higher. Lars's mother opened her eyes briefly, long enough to see the ground falling away beneath the sleigh, the eight reindeer bobbing before it like kites.

But where to go, that was the question. If there was a doctor, Lars would have taken his mother there, but he didn't know any doctor. If he could have taken her over the towering mountains, he would have, but he could see massive dark storm clouds building to the south, and he was afraid to chance it.

They were high enough that he could see the frozen sea to his left, and then, as they turned, he could see the mansion still burning, a tiny flickering jewel in the darkness,

It all came back to him, that morning that he and his mother and Nanu had set out in Farmer Thornberg's wagon, scarcely knowing where they were headed or what awaited them when they got there. How naked to the world he had felt. But at least they'd had a map. And he'd had his mother and Nanu. Now he had to figure it out on his own.

He felt a tap on his shoulder. The tomte with the wispy beard was pointing north. One by one, the others did the same. It was hard to believe they knew anything, but they did seem convinced.

So north they went.

THIRTY

ayor Wolfpaw dreamed that his den was filling with smoke. He dreamed that the hunters, somewhere above him, were pitching smoldering rags into the burrow, trying to flush him out. He cowered among gnarled roots in the far corner, choking and hacking on fumes. Every few seconds he caught a glimpse of a human, alien and terrifying, peering into the packed, frozen entrance and jabbing at him with a long pole. The hunters were all cursing and shouting, and in the distance was the howling of dogs.

He woke sitting upright in bed, gasping for air in the smoke-filled room. Nacht Ruprecht, on fire, danced across the floor, tearing at clumps of blazing straw.

Flames leapt from window to window and raced along the eaves. Mayor Wolfpaw's mansion filled with white smoke, then with black. The dogs howled in their pens, fifty yards away. One of the footmen made the mistake of rushing back to open one of the doors, and the fire exploded, showering embers everywhere. The upper floor groaned and then collapsed.

Miraculously, all of the staff had been wakened in time to make it out alive. They stood shivering, groggy and amazed, while Mayor Wolfpaw dashed about in nightshirt and mukluks, shouting orders, until one of his footmen chased him down and threw a fur coat over him.

Four of the groomsmen raced down to the equipment shed by the pond and emerged a moment later with the two fire engines.

The engines were the invention of Mayor Wolfpaw, inspired by something he'd seen on his trips to Europe. They were the size of a small stage coach, painted red, weighed several hundred pounds, and had handsome metal handles.

The four grooms staggered under the load, but never faltered, and once they made it back up the hill they quickly attached hoses to the cistern next to the guard house.

They worked valiantly, taking their turns manning the hand pump, sending two columns of water forty feet in the air. But in the end their efforts were no match for what had turned into a raging inferno.

In less than an hour the great mansion of Mayor Wolfpaw was no more. In its place stood a glittering ice palace created by the spray of water that had frozen instantly in the fierce cold.

Some of the staff comforted one another. Others gaped open-mouthed. A soot-covered butler who'd barely made it out alive giggled hysterically. No one felt the need to stop him.

Mayor Wolfpaw stood apart from the others. One waxed tip of his handlebar mustache had burned off, and his eyebrows were singed. When others came up to console him, he waved them away.

He was still not exactly sure what had happened. He remembered waking, seeing Nacht Ruprecht on fire and reeling around the room. He remembered wrestling him to the floor and trying to smother the flames with a quilt.

As he moved toward the smoldering ruins, the tallest of the footmen tried to intercept him. Mayor Wolfpaw swore at him and jabbed an angry finger, warning him to keep back.

He stumbled through the smoking debris, stepping over charred beams. A half dozen small fires still burned, impossible to put out. Here and there he spotted the remains of his writing desk, a pair of skates, the mounted head of a musk ox. A row of his stovepipe hats had been reduced to heaps of powdery ash.

He slipped and slid on the icy rubble. Further on, where his billiards room once stood, he spied one of Nacht Ruprecht's antlers. Glancing back over his shoulder, he spied another. The prong of a third poked out from under a scorched Turkish rug.

His first thought was that without Nacht Ruprecht he was nothing. It was Nacht Ruprecht's power that had made him what he was. He had been able to rule with an iron hand, but only because Nacht Ruprecht had ruled over him. Without Nacht Ruprecht's protection, he was lost, an old man tottering around the rubble in his nightshirt. Once the word spread of just how pathetic he was, once people saw they had nothing to fear, his life wasn't going to be worth two cents.

The burned-out shell of what had once been his home rose about him. What was the nursery rhyme they all used to sing? Ashes, ashes, all fall down . . . The north and the south towers, made of brick, had survived, as well as the two chimneys.

In the valleys of the collapsing roof, long columns of ice hung down nearly to the ground, and charred spires, coated by ice, rose out of the debris. All of it sparkled in the moonlight. It was as if he was stumbling about in a magical forest.

Wolfpaw spied, across a field of rubble, the cook tiptoeing into the remains of the kitchen, retrieving his pots and pans. The cook was a man who loved his utensils more than he loved his wife, yet what he was doing was supremely foolhardy.

The kitchen ceiling had collapsed, exposing the underside of the massive marble staircase. The staircase loomed above the stoves and serving tables like a jutting cliff. Whatever beams had once supported it had burned away. One false move on the part of the cook and he would be crushed by a ton of falling stone.

"Get away from there!" the mayor shouted. "You're going to get yourself killed!"

He slipped on the icy debris and fell hard on his side. One of the cooks came bustling over to help him, but he put up a hand to stop her. Sticking up out of the rubble, no more than ten feet away, was what looked like a tiny shark's fin, glistening in the moonlight.

He rose to his feet, wincing. He had seriously bruised his hip. He hobbled over to conduct an inspection. He saw now that what he thought was a shark's fin was made of wood. He kicked some of the smoldering debris away and bent over as best he was able.

He retrieved the wooden scrap from the blackened wreckage. He still couldn't make heads or tails out of it. At one end it narrowed to a point. The other end was badly charred and looked as if it had been broken off. The surface of the rest was smooth as butter.

Only when he raised it to the moonlight did he see that it was a carving, and what he had imagined was the fin of a shark was actually a rendering of a rippled sail and mast.

It wasn't an exact replica of the schooner his tutor had made for him, but it was close. A good two-thirds of it had been consumed by the fire. All that remained were a mast, a sail, the prow, and one of the cannons.

He scraped off a bit of the charred wood with a thumbnail. This was not possible. Wolfpaw had seen it smashed underfoot half a century before. There was no one living in the village who even knew of its existence.

He struggled for some way to understand. He was not a man who believed in miracles, and none of the more rational explanations made much sense. All he knew for sure was that of all the humiliations he had suffered—the freeing of the tomten, the assault on the Winter Festival, the clandestine giving of gifts—this was the one that cut the deepest.

His staff and and a group of newly arrived deputies stood huddled by the front gate. There was not one of them he could trust. It was no different from the way it had always been. He was still the wolf-boy, the one to be put on display in the village square, the one to be mocked and jeered at.

The mayor turned on the lot of them and held the schooner aloft. "Which one of you is responsible for this?" There wasn't a peep out of anyone. "Come on, out with it!"

He went around to each of them, made them all examine the ruined boat, and peppered them with questions. Some were too terrified to speak. None had ever seen a toy before, and to most of them what they were looking at was nothing but a piece of charred debris.

But as the mayor made his way around the circle, he became aware that a little girl had emerged from the darkness and was following him. Wide-eyed and pig-tailed, she was perhaps five years old, the daughter of the gamekeeper. The mayor had seen her maybe a half-dozen times before, but couldn't remember her name.

Unable to contain her curiosity, she finally plucked at the sleeve of the mayor's nightshirt. "What's that?" she asked.

"This?" the mayor said. "Oh, this is a boat. Would you like to see it?"

She nodded that she would, but when the mayor gave it to her, she was at a loss about what to do with it. Her father, the gamekeeper, stepped forward, alarmed, as if Wolfpaw had just handed his daughter a loaded gun.

"Here, let me show you," the mayor said. He took the boat back, got down on his knees, and patted the snow. "Let's say this is the ocean. And once you get your boat out of port and get the wind in your sail, it can take you anywhere in the world."

He moved the schooner softly across the surface of the snow and then offered it to her again. Curls of smoke rose here and there in the rubble like small campfires.

"You want to try?" he asked.

She murmured yes. She got down on her knees next to him. With his hand over hers, they began to make long figure eights in the snow with the boat. As they did, he began to tell stories, soft-voiced, about the schooner's adventures, of battles with pirates and terrible storms and ferocious sea dragons. These were stories he had told before, when he was not much older than she was.

They played together for perhaps ten minutes, lost in their own world, while on the far side of a cluster of icy spires, a fire flared, guttered, and finally died away, issuing fresh billows of black smoke.

The mayor's staff was awestruck. None of them had ever seen a toy in their entire lives, much less imagined they would ever see Wolfpaw playing with one.

The deputies were another matter. They were in no mood to be forgiving. They and their colleagues had been hard-pressed, belittled, found wanting time and again. They'd spent the night searching houses. They were out for blood. They did not find it charming, the mayor entertaining a small child with a charred bit of wood.

One of the deputies finally stepped forward. He was the most formidable of the lot, with a scarred face, tufts of curly black hair sticking out of his nostrils, and almost no neck.

"Sir?"

Wolfpaw looked up, tears in his eyes.

"No offense, sir, but we await your orders." Painted a bright red, the fire engines looked as stout as hogs.

"Orders? Why do you need orders?"

"Well, sir, if we're going to catch the dirty bastards who are responsible for all this, every minute counts."

It had somehow slipped the mayor's mind until now—the boy slipping out of his bedroom door. A boy he knew.

"I do have an order," the mayor said.

"And what is that?"

"All the children you arrested last night. I want you to free them."

"Free them?"

"Yes."

"I don't think you're going to be able to get the other men to go along with that."

The little girl looked up at the mayor, schooner in hand, not understanding why they'd stopped. He reached across to stroke her hair.

"That would be a shame, but I certainly understand. It looks as if I may have to do it myself. But that wouldn't be the worst, would it?" The mayor said this with a smile on his face, and the deputy wasn't sure if he was joking or not. But when the mayor rose, brushed the snow from his knees, and surveyed the waiting deputies, his face turned hard. "But what I will ask of you then, is to tell your men here that their services will no longer be needed."

THIRTY-ONE

I t had been eighteen months since her husband had died, and Lady Borland still did not sleep well, so it was not unusual that she found herself awake at three in the morning. What was unusual was that as she tossed and turned she thought she heard sleigh bells high above the house.

Because that was quite impossible, she dismissed it as part of a dream. It was only a few minutes later that she thought she heard the sound of chopping, but by that point blessed sleep was sweeping her away.

She was finishing her breakfast of croissants and stewed prunes the next morning when Snell the overseer rushed in, white-faced, clomping in muddy boots.

"Ma'am, I'm so sorry to interrupt you, but I think you need to see something."

She wiped a dab of jam from her lip. "And what would that be?"

"It would take too long to explain. Please . . . "

She got her coat and they hurried out to the servants' graveyard. It was the middle of December, and three inches of snow had fallen during the night. A mourning dove cooed deep in a stand of birches. The sky was the color of lead.

The plot of headstones in the glade of trees was untended. A number of the stones had fallen and were, as usual, overgrown by briars. But what had caused the overseer's alarm was immediately apparent.

Newly planted in the snow atop Lars's father's grave was a line of carvings – a piglet, a portly tuba player, a tilted pirate, a seagull with its wings spread, a milkmaid carrying two buckets. Together they looked like a drunken parade. One more snow would bury them all, if the animals at night didn't carry them off first.

Just beyond the grave where a small fir tree had once stood was a small stump. Fresh wood chips and green needles encircled it.

"What is this?" Lady Borland demanded.

"I don't know," said Snell. "But look."

He pointed to the bootholes leading from the gravesite to the far edge of the glade where a narrow pair of grooves ran for perhaps a dozen feet in the snow. Within the grooves were a trample of hoof-prints. They sat pristine, with no trail leading to or from them, as if a giant, many-footed bird had landed and then taken off again.

Much had changed in the village. The children had been set free, but not without strife. Some of the deputies wanted to obey the mayor's order and others did not. Violence had broken out. A number of harpooners and trappers had picked up weapons and joined the fray. When the smoke cleared, the mayor had fled for parts unknown, and most of the deputies were gone as well.

The village was now essentially ungoverned, with a handful of the most deluded deputies pretending to still have some smidgen of authority. No more toys were discovered, which made further house-to-house searches unnecessary. There was no more singing of the anthem at school, and no more mandatory doses of skarn-liver oil for those over thirteen, or anyone else for that matter. During the uprising the factory had been destroyed, and the tanks of skarn poured out onto the snow where the blind, translucent fish were quickly killed by the cold.

Yet life was not without trials. The population of wildlife had been steadily dwindling, which meant that the desperate predators had become more and more daring. There had been several polar bear attacks on trappers' cabins, and packs of wolves had been spotted on the outskirts of the village.

Were people better off or worse? It was hard to say. They were less oppressed, certainly, yet in other ways, they were more afraid. There was a feeling, hard to define, that something still hung over them, that matters had not yet been completely resolved.

Early one December morning an old woman came out of her house to shovel out the snow that was blocking her windows and was stopped short by the sight of a small fir tree standing in the middle of the village square.

She stared, dumbfounded, for half a minute. She had never seen a tree before. She had never seen anything so brilliantly green. She approached it warily, as if there might be something hiding inside it, waiting to spring out and strangle her.

She touched the needles and recoiled when they pricked her finger. She sniffed at the branches and found the smell pleasing.

The sound of scraping made her turn. She was not alone. An old man stood on a roof with his shovel. A pair of tinkers sat on the steps of the jail, sharing a bottle. All three were as transfixed as she was.

"So what is it?" shouted one of the tinkers.

"I don't know."

It was that time of the morning when the villagers began to stir. And as people emerged from their hovels—students heading off for school, hunters packing up their harpoons, a hump-backed old woman throwing a bucket of slop to her dogs—they were all immediately thunderstruck by the sight of the tree.

A crowd slowly gathered. Those who were brave enough came up to stroke the branches of the little fir. The blacksmith wiggled it back and forth, establishing that it hadn't taken root. His brother got down on his back to see if anything was concealed underneath. Mr.

Ostertag, schoolbooks under his arms, examined the needles skeptically over the top of his glasses.

"Any idea?" asked one of the tinkers.

"I believe it's a tree," Mr. Ostertag said. "I've seen pictures of them in an old book."

Sonja, the oldest woman in the village, teetered out of her house, aided by one of her great-great-grandsons. Her arms were full. A path was cleared for her. The years had done their work; her face looked like a dried fruit.

She had brought candles, and one of the tinkers helped her secure them on the branches of the tree with scraps of wire. A harpoonist set his weapon down, took out a match, and lit each of the candles.

People began to murmur, their faces shining in the flickering light. A dog barked. A window slammed. Eight skiers glided in from nowhere.

Most people didn't do anything but stare, open-mouthed, but others ran back to their houses and returned a minute later, carrying makeshift decorations.

Nelly Chinchilla tied a fork and a knife to a low bough. Someone strung up a dried cod. Someone dug a small carved rooster out of her pocket that Wolfpaw's search parties had somehow overlooked. With a length of cord it was hung just above the spoon and fork. The dozen candles perched like slender white birds, twelve tiny yellow flames glowing in the darkness.

A cheer went up as two burly men lifted Annuchka on their shoulders. Someone handed her a jade necklace and she threw it as high as she could, looping it over the very top of the tree.

"What the hell is going on here?" The voice rang out in the chill air. Everyone turned to gape at the two deputies standing next to the trading post.

They were the last two survivors of the Wolfpaw regime. One was tall and stooped and nervous as a cat, with a musket under his arm.

The other was as broad as he was wide, gap-toothed, neatly mustached. Both were seriously aggrieved, hopeless diehards. Whether they were in charge or not, they certainly continued to believe they were.

"Which one of you put this up?"

No one said a word. The two burly men let Annuchka slide to the ground. The sturdily built deputy strode forward, grabbed the tree two feet from the top, and hurled it onto the snow. Ornaments flew. Candles were immediately snuffed out.

People cried out in dismay. One of the burly men lunged forward as if he was about to attack the deputy and had to be restrained by several of the villagers.

The taller of the two deputies looked as if he had no idea what to do, but the shorter had no doubts at all.

"All right, everyone!" he announced. "Let's stand back here!" Some of the villagers were weeping. He grabbed the upended tree by the stump and began to drag it across the square.

Annuchka bent low to retrieve the jade necklace from the snow. As she raised her head, she spotted a pack of wolves massed in an alleyway on the far side of the square. She reached for her father's hand.

Several of the animals rested on their bellies, panting softly. Others stood erect, ears perked. A strange creature crouched in their midst, two legged and covered in a mass of dangling pelts. Its open-jawed wolf head was wrenched skyward as if silently baying.

With a click of its tongue, the creature released the pack and they raced across the snow. The villagers scattered, screaming. A mother scooped up her child, fell, regathered herself, and ran.

But the wolves had no interest in the villagers. They streaked past them, heading for the two deputies. The deputy with the musket barely had time to raise it to his shoulder before he was struck in the chest by a leaping wolf. The musket boomed, and grapeshot rattled off a nearby roof. The deputy was knocked to the ground.

His partner fared no better. He tried to run, dragging the tree behind him, but quickly gave that up when two of the younger wolves sprang on his back. They were little more than cubs, but determined, and not to be shaken off as the deputy twirled and bucked and swatted awkwardly over his shoulders.

In less than a minute, both men were down. Wolves swarmed over them, tearing at their sleeves and trousers, ripping off mukluks. Fangs sank into an exposed wrist. The deputies curled up as best they could, covering their faces with their arms and screaming for mercy.

Mercy was what they got. The strange creature had loped down from the alleyway, following the pack. He waded into the melee, shouting like a ringmaster, tossing one snarling animal aside after another. By the time all the pack had been pulled off, the two deputies had been reduced to a jibbering heap of torn parkas and bloody appendages, but miraculously neither of them had their throats torn out or Achilles shredded.

It took them a moment to summon up enough nerve to lift their arms from their faces and peek up at the strange creature standing over them. The lanky deputy, winking back a thin trickle of blood from the corner of his eye, was too afraid to move. The other had no intention of missing what might be their only opportunity to escape. He nudged his petrified partner and then nudged him again, harder. They finally managed to stand, then lurched off, one clutching his mangled wrist to his chest, the other hopping, his bare foot aloft.

The youngest of the wolves licked the strange creature's hand. Two others rubbed up against him like house cats. The villagers, stunned by this morning of astonishments, were now scattered about the farthest margins of the square.

Now that the creature was fully erect, it was evident that it was a man. He pushed the fawning wolves away, walked back to the tree, and pulled it back to its original location. As he wrestled to right the fir, his wolf head fell away, revealing the head of a hollow-eyed man with a long, uncut beard.

Sniffles was the first to recognize him. "Mayor Wolfpaw!" he cried.

No one believed him, not at first. The idea was preposterous. The man before them was at least fifty pounds lighter than their mayor, his bony legs and arms criss-crossed with scars, his long hair greasy and unkempt. They all remembered their mayor as being a bit of a fop.

One of the factory's former janitors rushed up to him, fell on his knees, and threw his arms around the man's legs. "Welcome home, sir, welcome home."

Any doubts about who this stranger was were erased by Wolfpaw's familiar roll of the eyes.

"We have missed you so much, sir," the janitor said. Most of the crowd would not have agreed with him.

The mayor seemed indifferent to what they thought. He stepped out of the janitor's clutches and stabbed at the hole in the snow with the stump of the fir. The villagers and wolves watched as he got down on his knees. With one hand he began to pack snow around the base of the tree while trying to keep the fir upright with the other.

It was not a one-person job. Several men and women stepped out of the crowd to come to his aid. The wolves gave way, and the crowd moved forward to take their place.

The number of people willing to pitch in grew from four to eight to twelve. The candles that weren't broken were set back on the low boughs and relit. Ornaments were retrieved and hung.

An old man on a cane began to sing. An old woman joined him. The mayor had never heard such a song. Who could have taught it to them? He had thought he'd been in control of everything, but there were so many things he didn't know.

Others began to link arms, adding their voices to the voices of the two old people. Because most of them didn't know the words, all they could do was go la-la-la. As a circle formed, several people glanced back at the mayor and not all the glances were warm. He may have saved the tree, but they were still not willing to forgive him for what he'd done to them over a lifetime.

But Miss Bord was different. Her eyes were kind as she gestured for him to come join them. He backed away, shaking his head no. Two or three others began to gesture as well.

The mayor retrieved his wolf head, ducked into it, and secured it with a tug. His eyes glistened with tears through the open jaws. When he turned and ran, the wolf head wobbled, and he had to reach up and hold it in place, like a knight trying to hold on an ill-fitting helmet. The pack streamed after him, disappearing down a crooked lane.

THIRTY-TWO

ventually summer returned to the village. Because it is so far north, the season is short, but glorious. At the summer's height, the sun is in the sky for twenty-two hours of the day, and every creature great and small is trying to fatten itself up for the long winter ahead. Tens of thousands of birds roost in the high cliffs and plunge like arrows into the sea for fish; the tundra is carpeted with a million bright flowers, and wolves and foxes trot the edges of the ponds, looking for unwary rabbits and voles.

In time, the people of the village recovered. Roope did very well for himself, floating barges of freshly cut ice south every summer to sell to the Danes. Annuchka created quite a stir when she ran off with some seal-hunter from Heggenhougen, but when she returned she was welcomed back by everyone. The twins she gave birth to several months later grew into the finest whale-ball players the coast had ever seen. Mr. Smorgas, after many years, married Miss Bord, the math teacher, and they had a half dozen little Smorgas-Bords.

A few scraggly trees finally took root on the tundra. Each Christmas Sniffles and Muleface go out, cut down the finest-looking one they can find, and haul it back to the village.

Once it is properly set up in the square, everyone takes part in its decoration. A week later, they all gather around the tree to exchange presents and sing. Over the weeks that the tree remains up, it is not uncommon to see, during the night, a wolf slipping into the village to stand guard over it.

Miko taught the History of Snow at the village school for nearly a decade, until one morning someone spied her speeding north along the Walrus Cliffs on a dogsled. She was never seen again. According to her old friend Annuchka, she had gone off to find Lars and marry him.

As the years passed, people ceased to talk about the terrible events that transpired that night when the mayor's mansion was burned to the ground. When the young asked questions, they were told gentle, evasive lies. As for the old, they'd suffered enough. No one needed to be reminded of what they and their families had gone through.

The legend of Lars Claus quickly spread across the globe, though it isn't Lars Claus any more, but Santa Claus to everyone but the increasingly small number of people who knew him when he was a boy.

The reason for his fame, of course, is that every Christmas Lars (or Santa, if you prefer) delivers presents to boys and girls around the world. No one has ever been able to figure out how that is possible, and there are a million theories. No one has ever laid eyes on him. Though there are occasional claims of flying reindeer spottings, these nearly always prove to be of dubious origin.

Santa Claus became so celebrated that during the winter holidays, nearly every street corner in every major city on earth has a Santa Claus ringing a bell, asking for donations. All the finest stores, from London to Paris to Saint Petersburg, hire a Santa so children can line up and wait for hours to have a chance to sit on his lap and whisper what they want for Christmas into his ear. There are endless songs about him, plays and pageants. His likeness appears on piggy-banks, beer steins, tapestries, salt shakers, stained glass windows, and ornaments of every kind.

On the other hand, there are a growing number of people who find all this to be rubbish, who insist that Santa Claus doesn't exist. For them, he is just a fairy tale, a charming but useless bit of hokum. How could any child not understand that it was really their parents who went out and bought them those presents?

This kind of talk made Arkady furious. Lars's old nemesis had left the village in his early twenties and moved to a small Norwegian city on the coast where he made his living as a boatbuilder.

When the subject of Santa Claus arose, Arkady would wax eloquent for hours about their shared youth. His children and, in turn, his grandchildren, were held rapt by these stories when they were small, but as they got older they grew weary of them.

His neighbors, on the other hand, were merciless. They didn't buy these improbable tales for a minute. A monster that lived under a volcano? A mayor that had been raised by wolves? They all viewed Arkady as a bit of a nutcase. What was one to make of a man who swore he'd once beaten up Santa Claus?

By his late seventies, Arkady was too frail to make the difficult trip back to the village and track down any remaining schoolmates who might have been able to corroborate his stories. He guessed they must have all been dead by now—Roope and Snic and Snee, the whole lot of them.

By the time he turned eighty, the only one who believed his stories was his youngest granddaughter, six-year-old Sofie, but even that was not destined to last. Two days before Christmas, Sofie came home from school in tears. One of her classmates had told her that there was no Santa Claus and laughed at her when she insisted that there was.

Arkady, as hard as he tried, couldn't console her. When he tried to hold her, she pushed him away, incensed at him for lying to her for all those years. That night, after she went to bed, he sat at the kitchen table for more than an hour, listening to her sob.

Arkady had been wounded before, but never as deeply as this. He had tried, on a number of occasions, to stay awake long enough on Christmas Eve to catch his older schoolmate coming down the chimney. But each time he'd dozed off, and on Christmas morning his family would find him sprawled asleep in his chair.

This time, he vowed, it was going to be different.

On Christmas Eve, Arkady downed a couple of mugs of strong coffee, bundled himself up in his warmest clothes, and trudged out to the woodshed.

He pulled a blanket over his head and crouched on a pile of logs next to the small window where he could keep a keen eye on the night sky. Hours passed. When he got sleepy he fortified himself with an occasional swig from a jug of rum. His rump began to ache. He stomped his feet and clapped his arms around his chest to stay warm. Once he saw a shooting star. Once he saw a brilliantly red fox creeping across the snow.

Then, just as he was about to nod off, he saw a bright dot skim along the horizon. His first thought was that it was just another shooting star, but it was moving too slowly. It glittered like a diamond, dimmed, and began to change course. Arkady's heart pounded. Whatever it was, it was coming right at him.

Arkady crouched low, pulling the blanket tightly around his head, leaving the narrowest slit to peer through. Peeking out the dirty window, he could make out for the first time the prongs of reindeer antlers and a sleigh rising and falling behind them.

The sleigh circled the house twice, scouting everything out (Arkady's hunch had been correct), and then landed on the roof without a sound. A stranger got out of the sleigh. He was a very old man, portly and stooped, dressed in red, with a magnificent white beard, black boots, and a red hat topped with a white tassel.

The stranger removed a ladder from the back of the sleigh, lowered it over the side of the roof, and shook it to and fro until he was sure it was lodged securely in the snow. He got a huge gunnysack from the front seat, heaved it over his shoulder, and made his way carefully down the ladder.

Arkady strained to see. If only his eyes were better! There was something vaguely familiar about the red-suited figure, but it wasn't enough to say for sure who it was.

The stranger eased the front door open and disappeared inside. Arkady waited, trying to calm himself, then tossed the blanket aside and rose to his feet. He crept out of the woodshed and made his way to the house.

Inch by inch he opened the front door and stepped inside. The stranger was on his knees, putting presents under the tree, his back to Arkady.

"Lars?" Arkady said. The figure froze. "Lars, is that you? It's your old pal, Arkady." The stranger pulled the drawstrings on the gunnysack tight. "It's okay," Arkady said. "I'm not going to wake anyone."

The stranger rose, wary as a wild animal, and swung his sack over his shoulder. Smiling, Arkady stepped forward and offered a hand in greeting. That was all it took to send the stranger bolting for the side door.

But Arkady was too quick for him, cutting him off and spreading his arms wide. The stranger spun around and scuttled for the front door with Arkady in pursuit.

They were not gazelles. They were two gimpy old men, but Arkady was a step faster. Just short of the door Arkady tackled the stranger, who went down with a thump. The gunnysack slid across the floor, emitting a cacophony of moos and baas and tinkling.

From one of the dark bedrooms came an alarmed voice. "Arkady? Arkady, what are you doing?"

Arkady, sprawled on top of his old classmate, put a hand over Lars's mouth. "Oh, nothing, dear," he shouted. "I was just wrapping a few last presents."

Neither man moved for several minutes. When they finally heard a soft snoring, Arkady slid off and rose to his knees. "Are you all right?" he whispered.

"I think I may have broken a rib." It was not the first time Lars been tackled by Arkady.

"I'm sorry. Can I get you anything?"

Lars sat up, wincing. "No."

Arkady still could not get over Lars's beard. It was immense, glistening and soft as an ermine pelt, but behind it he could still make out the eyes of a boy. "A glass of water, maybe?"

"That might be good."

Arkady lurched to his feet, got a glass from the cupboard, and filled it at the water bucket. When he brought it back to Lars, Lars drank thirstily, scanning the room.

The house was a humble affair. There was a spinning wheel in one corner and a freshly cut Christmas tree in the other, decorated with gingerbread men and tinsel. A calf with a worrisome cough that they'd brought in from the barn lay asleep in a box of straw by the stove. The room smelled of pine.

"Thanks," Lars said, handing the glass back.

"Could we talk for a minute?"

"I'm a little busy tonight, actually."

"I understand," Arkady said. "But you never know if we'll ever have another chance."

Lars arched his back, wincing in pain. Arkady was the last person in the world he should have been doing favors for, but there was something so urgent in his old classmate's voice it was hard to ignore.

"Where would you like to talk?" Lars said.

"It would be best if we went outside."

Arkady let Lars and his sack of toys go first and then let the front door close silently behind him. He considered where they might be out of earshot of the house.

"How about over here?" he said, pulling his shawl around his shoulders. He pointed to a dilapidated wagon just beyond the corn crib. Two enormous pigs and a shaggy pony stared up at the reindeer on the roof of the house.

The two men hobbled across the snow and hoisted themselves onto the back of the wagon. The sky shone with a million stars, and across the fjord Christmas tree lights twinkled in a half dozen houses.

"Looks like you've been eating well," Arkady said.

"Looks like we both have," Lars said.

"You and Miko ever have children?"

"No," Lars said. "But we stay busy the way it is."

Arkady jabbed a finger in the direction of the reindeer. "How long you figure you're going to be able to keep this up?"

"Long as I'm able, I guess."

Arkady's legs dangled off fhe edge of the wagon. "You're a huge deal now, you must know that. Huge. I would have never guessed it. A puny little kid like you."

The tinkling of sleigh bells made them turn. Canute was restless, shaking his magnificent antlers and pawing at the roof.

"I'm sorry, Arkady, but I'm afraid I don't have a whole lot of time."

Arkady blew into his cold hands. Now that the moment had arrived, he found it almost impossible to speak. He had no choice but to blurt it out like a child. "You know what it is? Let me tell you. Knowing you has kind of screwed me up."

"And how is that?"

"Think about everything we went through together. All those terrible teachers. The Winter Festival and that whole business with the toys. I could have gotten kidnapped and worse, thanks to you. But people just laugh at me when I try to tell them."

"So why even try?"

"Because it's important. Because you changed everything. And I'm the only one left who knows that whole story."

"Maybe you should just try to write it all down."

The floorboards of the wagon creaked as Arkady shifted his weight. "I was thinking you could send us a sign."

"And what kind of sign would that be?"

"I don't know. If you could just show yourself."

"That would ruin everything." A series of soft grunts followed by a squeal made Lars look up. Siegfried was butting the rump of the reindeer in front of him, creating a stir. "I'm sorry," Lars said. "I really need to go."

He hopped to the ground and brushed off the back of his trousers. Arkady didn't let him get far. He slid off the wagon and grabbed Lars's wrist. " Please, I have to tell you something, It will only take a minute.

"My granddaughter, Sofie, she's just six years old. She came home two days ago. She was all to pieces. One of her classmates had told her that there was no Santa Claus. You've never seen so many tears! She was furious. She accused me of lying to her. And that night, listening to her weeping, I started to wonder if she was right. Maybe I had invented the whole thing."

Lars twisted free of Arkady's grip. It seemed to him that there was something quite wrong with this man.

"And what would you like me to do?"

"I want her to see you."

"No."

"Please. Please." The shaggy pony crossed the barnyard, banged at the ice in the trough with its nose, and broke enough of it that it could dip down and guzzle.

Lars hated Arkady for being so pathetic, but even more he hated hearing himself be so uncharitable, on this night of all nights. Plus he hated the idea of being tackled again.

"All right," he said. "But just for a minute."

The two old men tiptoed down the hallway, past the sound of hearty snoring, past the linen closet, to the bedroom of Arkady's granddaughter at the end of the corridor.

They entered the pitch-black room. Arkady eased the door shut and put a match to a lantern. The light swelled. An apple-cheeked girl with dark bangs lay in a tangle of sheets, clutching a stuffed giraffe.

Standing outside on the stoop, Arkady had filled Lars in on the barest outlines of the story. Arkady's son and his wife worked for a wealthy ship builder who had dispatched them to London for the year to tend to the renovation of his estate there. The six-year-old Sofie was left behind in the care of her grandparents.

It was clear that Arkady had been an indulgent grandfather. The room was filled with toys—a shelf jammed with dolls, a rocking horse, a tower of blocks in the middle of the floor.

Arkady and Lars crept around the sleeping child like two bears. Arkady straightened her sheets and pulled a quilt up to her chin. She flopped an arm free, but didn't wake.

Arkady watched her for several seconds and then glanced at Lars, who set his sack on a chair and nodded that he was ready. Arkady touched his granddaughter's shoulder. "Sofie? Sofie? There's someone here I want you to meet."

She stirred and opened her eyes for just a moment, wincing in the glare of the lantern, then rolled over on her side, trying to bury her head under the quilt.

Arkady gave her shoulder a soft shake. "Sofie? Someone wants to say hello to you."

She rolled onto her back and shielded her eyes with a hand. She was too groggy to make out anything at first, but then Lars moved forward into the light.

Sofie's eyes went wide with alarm. Who was this man? Had her grandfather been drinking with one of the neighbors?

Slowly she began to put all the pieces together—the beard, the vast belly, the red cap with the fluffy tassel, the kindly face with ruddy cheeks chapped by cold and wind.

Her mouth dropped open, inch by inch. Her grandfather crouched next to the bed, holding the lantern high, grinning like a mad goblin.

Lars took another step forward. She was a little afraid. She reached up and touched the beard. "Did my grandfather really beat you up?"

"Many times," Lars said. "You won't tell anyone about my speaking to you, will you?"

"No."

"You promise?"

"Yes."

"Good."

As he leaned over he could feel a stab of pain from his injured rib. He kissed her on the forehead and patted her arm. Arkady stepped back to give them room and knocked over the tower of blocks. He lost his balance, reeled across the room, banged off the wall, and sent all the dolls tumbling off their shelf.

"Arkady?" The voice from the other bedroom sounded unforgiving. "What are you doing?"

"Everything is fine, dear."

"I want you to come here. Right now!"

"Yes, dear." He looked back at the distressed faces of Lars and Sofie, then put his hands out as if to reassure them that he had everything under control. "I'll be right back," he whispered.

Trying to pull the wool over the eyes of his wife was no mean feat. She had put up with his nonsense for too many years. It took a good while to quell her suspicions, but after he went to fetch her favorite chocolate wafers and sat by the side of the bed while she munched them, she finally went back to sleep. But it all took too long. When he hurried back to Sofie's room, there was no sign of Santa Claus, and his granddaughter was dead to the world. The only clue to what might have happened was the cold air pouring in through the open bedroom window.

Arkady cursed softly, scanning the room, at a loss for what he might do until he heard the clatter of hooves above him. He ran to the window and craned his neck. The reindeer swooped off the roof. The only glimpse he got of his old classmate was the white tassel of his hat, bobbing in the wind like a fleeing rabbit.

The reindeer rose above the fjord, weaving their way across the sky, heading toward Oslo. Arkady stood for a moment, watching the sleigh get smaller and smaller.

He finally closed the window and made his way back to the living room. The calf raised its head for a second and then lowered it, closing its sleepy eyes.

Arkady was much too worked up to think of going to bed. Whatever happened to him, it didn't matter now. There would still be one person in the world who knew that Santa Claus existed. And it would be his granddaughter.

He had so many memories buzzing around in his head, like bees in a stirred-up hive. Knocking Lars down in the whale-ball games. Stuffing Pytor in the trash can. Glossy bits of blubber floating in his soup. His two huge blonde dogs. Those had been some great times. How could it be that nearly seventy years had passed?

He glanced over at the tree. There seemed to be so many more presents than there had been before. How many could Lars have left?

Curious, Arkady tiptoed across the room. He tried to count on his fingers how many gifts there were, but he kept losing track. Some of the presents were large, some were small. Some were hidden under others, some looked so much alike he was not sure if he was counting them twice or not. He picked up one and then another, checking the tags.

No matter how young or old you are, once you get started with this sort of thing, there's no stopping. It didn't take long for Arkady to find not one present addressed to him from Santa, but two, tucked away in the back.

The two presents were the same size. Both were wrapped in blue paper. Arkady gave one a shake and then the other, trying to guess what was inside. He gave each a squeeze. They were both about a foot long and hard. Could Santa Claus really have given him saltshakers? Candlesticks?

The ceiling creaked, and then everything fell silent. Arkady couldn't help himself. He took a quick glance at the sleeping calf and then unknotted the red ribbon on one of the presents. He broke the sealing wax with a fingernail and carefully unfolded the wrapping paper.

"Oof!" He sounded as if Snic had just butted him in the stomach. There in his huge, callused boat-builder's hands was a wooden boxer in blue trunks. It was nine inches tall, with a snarl and a cowlick and two strings in the back, a perfect replica of the boxer Lars had given Arkady nearly seventy years before.

He didn't bother being careful with the second present, ripping it open in a single motion, like a bear ripping open a log. The boxer in the red trunks looked as goony as the original, with a lopsided grin and three missing teeth.

Arkady pulled one of the strings. The boxer in the blue trunks threw a left jab. When he pulled another, the boxer in the red trunks unleashed an uppercut that sent his opponent's head wobbling. It was a miracle. Arkady had watched them both burn, seen them crumble into ashes, and now here they were again, ready to mix it up.

Arkady lurched to his feet, a boxer clutched in each hand. He went to the window and rubbed the glass so he could peer out. He figured that Lars was long gone by now. He didn't expect to see anything, and at first he didn't. The sky was empty of everything except stars, but when he squinted, he thought he saw the tiniest dot drifting across the moon.

But he was old, and his eyes were so bad there was no way to be sure he wasn't imagining the whole thing. But it was Christmas morning, and his heart was full. What need, really, was there to be sure?

ABOUT THE AUTHOR

The author of nine books, including *Famous Writers I Have Known*, James Magnuson lives in Austin, Texas, with his wife Hester. A member of the Texas Institute of Letters, he is also a playwright, screenwriter, and for twenty-three years was the director of the Michener Center for Writers. He once spent Christmas in an igloo in the Arctic when the temperature was thirty-five degrees below zero.

www.ingramcontent.com/pod-product-compliance
Lightning Source LLC
Chambersburg PA
CBHW031153050726
47495CB00019B/1661